MADE
for
MERCY

MADE for MERCY

LAUREN SMYTH

AMBASSADOR INTERNATIONAL
GREENVILLE, SOUTH CAROLINA & BELFAST, NORTHERN IRELAND

www.ambassador-international.com

Made for Mercy

ISBN: 978-1-93230-750-4
eISBN: 978-1-62020-742-0
Library of Congress Control Number: 2020935489

Cover Design and Page Layout by Hannah Nichols
eBook Conversion by Anna Riebe Raats

This is a work of fiction. Names, characters, and incidents are all products of the author's imagination or are used for fictional purposes. Any resemblance to actual events or persons, living or dead, is entirely coincidental. Any mentioned brand names, places, and trademarks remain the property of their respective owners, bear no association with the author or the publisher, and are used for fictional purposes only.

AMBASSADOR INTERNATIONAL
Emerald House
411 University Ridge, Suite B14
Greenville, SC 29601, USA
www.ambassador-international.com

AMBASSADOR BOOKS
The Mount
2 Woodstock Link
Belfast, BT6 8DD, Northern Ireland, UK
www.ambassadormedia.co.uk

The colophon is a trademark of Ambassador, a Christian publishing company.

DEFINITION OF ABBREVIATIONS

CAUS - Central Agency of United Scientists

KASU - Kalideyes Armory Scientists United

SAS - Social Adjustment and Strengthening

ADPA - Anti-Depressant Personality Adjustment

PROLOGUE

Tomorrow is where it all begins. Tomorrow I'm going to lose my identity and become a completely different person. I won't be allowed to keep anything, not even the simplest characteristic that makes me—me.

What kind of beginning is that? It's more like an ending.

I'm starting to think that coming here was a bad idea. I thought it would fulfill my need to do something that will outlast me, but apparently, I was wrong. I don't feel any different. I still feel useless and worthless and any other "less" words I can think of.

So where is it? Where is the first real change?

I wish I knew.

PART I

CHAPTER 1

"New names!"

Makise stood at attention, arms pinned to her side, eyes staring straight ahead at nothing. The sergeant paced back and forth before the line, back and forth endlessly, until with a click of her polished heels she finally came to an abrupt halt in front of the first recruit.

"Ayano," the sergeant said loudly and clearly. "Ayano. Repeat it."

"Ayano," said the recruit mechanically.

"Now don't forget." The sergeant moved to the next recruit. "Makise."

The real Makise shuddered. "My name . . . ?" she whispered. "They gave my name to somebody else?"

"Repeat it!" The sergeant's voice broke in on her thoughts.

"Makise," said a lifeless voice.

I'm not myself anymore. The real Makise shuddered with something between excitement and fear. *I'm . . . I'm . . .*

"Maru." The sergeant stood face-to-face with Makise, who jumped in surprise. "Maru. Repeat it."

"M-Maru," she stammered uncertainly. Then clearer: "Maru."

Without acknowledgement, the sergeant moved on down the line and Maru sighed in relief. There was something unnerving about staring into the bright blue eyes of somebody who could take something as personal as your name and give it away at will.

"Maru, Maru," she whispered to herself. "That's me. I'm Maru."

As her tension dissipated and the sergeant moved further down the line, she allowed her rigid gaze to relax. Scanning the faces around her, she saw a multitude of expressions: fear and excitement, like her own, mixed with a few happy and a few tearful faces. And there was one face that registered absolutely no expression at all.

Makise—now Maru—found her eyes fastened to this face. Its owner, a tall, muscular man with intensely black and messy hair, was standing in the line across from her. His eyes seemed to jump out of his face. Maru expected them to be at least a darker shade of blue, but they were a weird electric blue which shone brightly even out from under his wild black mane. As Maru watched, they shifted and locked fiercely with her own. She blushed, embarrassed to have been caught staring, and looked away.

"Rin," said the sergeant's voice. "Rin. Repeat it."

Maru looked back with interest. The dark-haired recruit now re-named Rin stared at the sergeant without a word.

"Repeat it!" insisted the sergeant.

Rin said nothing.

Somebody whispered in the sergeant's ear, and she laughed. "All right, silent black-hair," she said graciously. "If you don't want to talk, you don't have to. Just don't forget your name. It won't be my fault if it gets you killed one day."

Maru shivered. It was one thing to simulate fights in training, and another to hear death mentioned so casually, as if it was something that didn't matter.

The sergeant moved on, and Maru noticed Rin close his eyes for a split second. His face still showed nothing, but Maru could guess that he was trying to bottle the annoyance he could not show—whether out of respect for the higher-ranking officer or his apparent inability to speak. A second later those eyes opened again, fastened onto Maru.

"Team matching," came the sergeant's voice, much to Maru's relief. "Two teams of five, as usual. I'll read the lists. Remember your new names. Rest!"

Maru sighed, relaxed her tense muscles, and listened carefully.

"Team One," read the sergeant. "Yuri, Shinae, Kala, Makise—"

For a moment Maru stiffened, then remembered: she was no longer Makise.

"—and your leader is Shuji."

One of the recruits stepped forward from the other line, saluted, and returned to his original position.

"Team Two," continued the sergeant. "Naito, Maru—"

I've done it! Maru inadvertently smiled.

Rin's eyes were still fixed on her from across the parade ground.

"—Rin—"

A general sigh went up from the recruits, into which Maru did not join. She looked around in surprise. *They must know something about him.* She stole another glance at him. His eyes were closed again in evident disgust. *He looks nice. I wonder . . . ?*

"—and Kita. Your leader will be Saito."

A recruit at the far end of the opposite line stepped briefly forward, saluted, and stepped back. Maru could not see his face; it was too heavily shadowed.

"Team One: Yuri, Ayano, Kala, Makise, and Shuji. Team Two: Naito, Maru, Rin, Kita, and Saito. Got it? If you weren't assigned to a team, don't worry. Your turn will come eventually." The sergeant shut her notebook with a final snap. "For those of you who weren't assigned, the day is over. Usual penalty for breaking curfew, so don't try it. Go back to your dorms and don't linger on the way. The ten of you who were assigned, follow me at once."

Nobody moved an inch, and the sergeant crossed her arms with irritation. "Rest!" she yelled loudly.

The recently-christened Maru put a hand to her forehead. Everything had been happening too fast lately. It was apparently an abbreviated step from recruitment to team assignments—unless her skills had been—

"Hey!" A loud voice in her ear startled her. "I'm Naito. Looks like we're on the same team."

Maru looked the newcomer up and down curiously. He was small, slenderly built, and obviously full of vibrant energy. His blond hair was neatly slicked back and made a little wave above his forehead. Right behind him was a girl whom Maru recognized as Kita. She had already made a name for herself as a lover of all things soft and effeminate and was the last person Maru would have expected to see recruited into Rigel. Maybe there were unexplored depths to her personality. In any case, she and Kita would be spending plenty of time together.

"Earth to Maaaru, earth to Maaaru," said Naito, waving his finger in her face. "You look sleepy or something! I thought we weren't allowed to be sleepy!"

"True," Maru replied without thinking. "Where's—where are Saito and Rin?" Bad grammar was a Sign she did not want to display. In these days, even suspicion was enough to condemn.

"Probably gone inside already," replied Naito, completely careless of Signs. "Heartless, both of them. Not wanting to talk to the only rookie on the team."

"Rin never talks," Kita reminded him.

"These code names are super confusing," continued Naito without a pause for breath. "Last mission, Rin's name was Ellie something-or-other—"

"Elsaku," interrupted Kita.

"Elsaku, and nobody could ever remember it. Which was lucky, because we all know he won't open his mouth to defend himself."

"Defend himself?" asked Maru curiously.

"Who wants to be called Elsaku?" laughed Naito. "By the way, what's your real name? Let me guess—Marasy? It must be similar to Maru somehow."

"I was told not to mention it to anybody," said Maru a little anxiously.

"Stop asking questions, Naito. Let's go inside." Kita took his hand and pulled him away.

"Why are girls always in a hurry?" Naito complained, a humorous smile on his face. "Let's go then. I'm sure there'll be some food to make up for these boring meetings."

"How do you have room to eat anything else?" Kita asked. "You sit on your rear end all day working, and then you go off and eat whatever you want. It's not fair. I wish I could do that!"

"You could, chérie," replied Naito. "All you need is an iron constitution like mine."

"Coming, Maru?" asked Kita, turning around to Maru.

"Sure," she said, blinking. "I'm not sure where I'm going. I'll follow you."

The building indicated by the sergeant was one of many old brick apartments that looked almost ready for demolition—at least on the outside. The insides were different, with shining white walls kept clean at the expense of many hours of punitive labor and bright overhead lights designed to save energy and mimic the outdoors. There were healthy renewing plants scattered here and there and sanitizing stations every few feet. Nobody was expected to get sick, and if they did, it was blamed not on whoever gave them the illness but on their own stupidity. The buildings were almost ferociously healthy both in intent and atmosphere.

Maru could never go inside without a mounting sense of awe. If they were sterile, they were also very beautiful and bright. The sense of openness Maru felt was almost equal to the effect of a wide open prairie on a cloudless day. And yet, it was somehow oppressive, too, in a way she could not quite define. There was nothing wrong with it, in fact everything was right—it simply wasn't natural.

She followed Naito and Kita hesitantly past the plants, past countless sanitization stations, past a few darkened offices. Naito and Kita laughed and talked the whole way, and Maru shut out their voices. She already had too much to think about, and regret played a big part in her thoughts. What right had she to go up against the Kalideyes?

"Where are you going?" asked Naito, obvious laughter in his voice. "You're literally walking right past the office. Good luck being the last person to come in!" And he skipped inside a wide-open door without waiting for her to reply.

Slowly Maru turned around and stood in the doorway, faced by nine pairs of inquisitive blue eyes. There was a moment of motionless silence which felt like a century to Maru, broken only by Rin seating himself in a squeaky corner chair.

Maru's eyes darted toward the noise, and Rin smiled encouragingly—at least, smiled for someone as habitually expressionless as Rin seemed to be.

"Have a seat," said the sergeant, appearing from nowhere behind Maru. "What are you all gawking at? Freaks. You should at least make her welcome."

Maru knew perfectly well what everyone had been staring at, but she kept her mouth closed. Explanations at this point were not required.

"We'll divide into teams now," continued the sergeant. "Team Two, you're in here with me. Team One, I'd like you to go exactly two doors down the hall. Quick march."

Five of the assembled recruits came suddenly to attention and marched in a row out the door. Rin watched them go, leaning back in his chair, not bothering to brush away the thick hair that shadowed his face.

"Let's start with introductions." The sergeant's manner had become much friendlier. "Rin, you go first."

There was a long silence.

"Sorry," said the sergeant, flipping through her papers. "This is Rin . . . member of Team Two." She paused and searched vainly for anything else to say. "I guess that's it. Naito?"

He stood up in the corner and waved. "I'm Naito, expert hacker and proud boyfriend to Kita!" He smiled so widely that his eyes almost closed, as if he were very proud of the information he had bestowed. Maru couldn't help laughing with the rest of the group.

"Naito's a character," began the sergeant, but was interrupted by an annoyed Kita.

"You have no right to say that! We haven't discussed this!"

"All the world knows it," said Naito placidly. "You know it, too, chérie Kita!"

"You—"

"Not now, please!" cried the sergeant. "Saito, interrupt them before they keep arguing about this."

Saito had seated himself in a reclining desk chair across from Rin. He stood up as his name was called and bowed his head slightly. His regal manner, which might have seemed artificial on anyone else, fit perfectly with his tall, slender figure and bright blue eyes—which, Maru noticed, were still not even close to the startling color of Rin's.

He rested his hand on the chair, his pose resembling a vintage coronation painting, and said quietly, "My name to you is Saito. I am the leader of Team Two, experienced on five previous teams against the Kalideyes. I should get this straight now: I make the final decisions. If you have questions, ask; otherwise, stay quiet." With which he sat down in his chair and turned away from the group, fixing his eyes on the window where the sun was slowly setting.

"Kita?"

Kita huffed and put her hands on her hips. Maru noticed suddenly that she looked very much like a kitten and nearly choked on her laughter. Rin watched with an amused smile in his eyes, arms tightly crossed as if to protect his chest.

"I'm *not* Naito's girlfriend," Kita prefaced stubbornly.

"The lady doth protest too much, methinks," interrupted Naito, laughing.

"Stick to the topic at hand!" pleaded the harassed sergeant.

"I'm the nurse and resident psychologist," continued Kita, tilting her sharp nose up in the air. "I dispense the bandages and sew you up when you're dying. So, you should appreciate me and not tease me like Naito always does."

Slow, sarcastic applause sounded from Rin's corner. Maru glanced at him in surprise, and found Naito looking mischievously over the back of his chair. Rin leaned away from him and rolled his chair further into the dark corner.

"Excellent, Cherie!" cried Naito, continuing his applause at a faster tempo. "Congratulations on your successful debut into—"

"Stop," said Saito wearily. All noise ceased in an instant.

"Thank you." The sergeant put her clipboard and papers on the desk. "Experience, now? Saito, you've told us about yourself. Good. You're the only one who made a complete introduction. Please lead us—nobody wants to hear me talk. I'm not their leader."

Saito stood up again and pushed his chair under the table. "You heard the sergeant. Please discuss your level of experience." He stared aggressively at Rin, who stared back but did not answer.

"He's been on six missions before," said the sergeant hastily. "All against the Kalideyes. He's a registered assassin and completed his training with re-cord marks."

Rin did not take his eyes off Saito, and Maru thought she saw a gleam of satisfaction enter his eyes at the sergeant's last words.

"You should learn to speak for yourself," said Saito harshly before turning away. "Naito?"

"I've been on only one mission, but it was the best experience of my life." Naito inflated his chest and put one hand theatrically over his heart. "I met Kita there."

"Stop it, you—!"

"Kita," said Saito quietly. "Tell us your experience."

She fumed but did not dare disobey. "One mission, like Naito."

"Rookie?"

It took Maru a moment to realize that Saito was talking to her. Immediately she dropped her eyes, "I haven't been on any missions."

She wondered why Saito had bothered asking. Clearly he knew, because he had called her by the unflattering name of *Rookie*.

"Let's clear something up right away," said the sergeant, taking up an ag-gressive stance at the head of the central table and waving her clipboard for added emphasis. "Maru's eyes are blue. Got it, everyone? They may have a grayish tint, but they are undoubtedly *blue*."

"Of course." Naito and Kita laughed in unison.

Saito locked eyes with her for a moment, then, turning away, agreed, "Blue."

Rin said nothing, but Maru felt sure she would have known if he disapproved. A weight fell instantly from her shoulders. Her hazy gray eyes were always the reason she was mocked and shunned by everyone who did not know her very well. And they were the reason why she was so terrified of displaying Signs.

"Saito's in charge now," said the sergeant, retreating. "If you ever feel like arguing, remember why we're here. Blue eyes should be allies." With this unfortunate rhyme she shut the door behind her and left the room in oppressive silence.

CHAPTER 2

"Well? What do you think of Saito? And Naito?" asked Kita excitedly, as she was walking with Maru to the dorm room they were now expected to share.

"Their names are confusingly similar," said Maru absently.

"Oh, but I mean, do you like them? Saito is a little scary."

"Saito . . . the leader. Right." Maru shrugged. "I don't know him very well yet. When he talks, people listen, so I guess that's a good thing."

"And then there's Naito! He has got a terrible sense of humor, but he is pretty funny—"

Maru did not bother trying to decipher this.

"—and we have lots of fun together, even on missions. He can't stand the sight of blood, though. Don't know why. I've asked him but he never says anything about it. Someday maybe he'll tell me, don't you think? Especially if he continues with that boyfriend nonse—"

"Rin."

"What?" Kita paused her flow, surprised.

"Rin," repeated Maru. "What do you know about Rin?"

"Does anybody know anything about Rin?" Kita laughed. "And he can't talk about it, even if he wanted to. But I don't think he does want to. He's probably some deep, dark, romantic hero with a scarred heart left in shadows from—"

"Is the problem that he can't talk, or won't?"

"I don't know! But who cares?" Kita scrunched her face into a cute, childish smile. "Oh, don't tell me you're interested in Rin? But no, that can't be. Nobody likes guys like him who never respond to what you say. When I talk, I want somebody to answer me."

"You won't like me much then," muttered Maru, who was already slightly overwhelmed by Kita's friendliness. "I'd rather room with a recluse like Rin."

Suddenly she jumped back to avoid the heavy metal door that Kita swung carelessly open. "This is our new home!" she twittered, bouncing from wall to wall in search of the light switch. "Our—new—home!"

Maru felt to the left of the door and flicked the switch. Kita stopped moving as soon as the lights came on and folded her hands demurely in front of her.

"Upstairs!" she continued, unabashed. "You'll like my room. It's nice and soft and comfortable."

Maru sighed. It had been a long day, and the last thing she needed was an overly affectionate roommate who forced her to stay up all night and talk about what she considered "ridiculous feminine subjects."

"Ta-da!" said Kita, swinging her door open. "How do you like it?"

"It's beautiful," admitted Maru, somewhat dazzled by all the sparkling objects. "I didn't know you were allowed to redecorate this much—whoa—"

Kita pulled her to the center of the room. "I can do whatever I want," she boasted, touching a little child's chandelier with the tip of her finger. "As long as I work hard and do my job well, nobody minds. And I do!" With a suddenly fierce expression she turned to Maru, and an uncharacteristically serious smile crossed her face. "I always do!"

Maru stopped in surprise, but Kita was already whirling away to display her collection of graphic novels and small painted figurines.

"Graphic novels are the best!" she gushed, handing one to Maru. "Look, aren't the pictures pretty?"

Maru flipped through it. The pages were covered in black-and-white drawings of the characters, with the dialogue written in small boxes next to them. It was not Maru's style at all, but she was tired of textbooks and decided that they might be fun to read. She tucked the book under her arm and followed Kita.

"Is there anything to eat?" she interrupted practically after what felt like hours of patient observation. "Rations, at least?"

"No *standard* rations here!" said Kita, and Maru believed her. Nothing about this girl was normal. "Noodles, lasagna, chicken, sweets—anything you want!" She threw open all the cabinet doors—in one huge swoop, it seemed to Maru—and displayed dazzling treasures of snacks. It was like Aladdin's cave. Maru's mouth watered as she surveyed all her delicious favorites which she had not been allowed to touch for months. Apparently there were perks to living with the enigmatic Kita after all.

"And I have a microwave, too!" said Kita, pointing to what Maru had assumed was a pink box for the storing of childish treasures. "Enjoy yourself!" She twirled off to the bathroom and slammed the heavily decorated door behind her.

Maru took a deep breath and leaned against the counter. "Whoa," was the only expressive word which came to her mind. "She's . . . she's . . . adorably crazy."

Deciding that there could not possibly be anything else to discover about her extroverted roommate, she turned her attention to the cabinets. "These are the best . . . " She extracted her dinner of choice, which was probably much higher in sugar than any doctor would have approved, and spread the materials on the counter. "Where does Kita get all this?" she asked herself, filling her mouth with cookie. "Mmm . . . should have moved in here sooner." She unwrapped the next package and started in.

When Kita came out of the bathroom, dressed in a white plush robe with cat-shaped slippers on her feet, Maru had curled up on the sofa with a bag of chocolate and one of Kita's books. "Tell me if there's anything else you need," laughed Kita. "I'm going to bed."

So she wasn't planning to keep me awake. Maru watched as she disappeared into her room. *It's only eight!*

She flipped a few more pages of the book.

"This is pretty good," she sighed to herself, dropping the now-empty bag of chocolates into the pink trash can. "I need to be more careful, though. Looks like Rin and I will be training together. Wouldn't want to lose to—"

She shook herself.

"—a boy."

*****   *****   *****

"Up, down! Up, down! Up, people!"

Is it possible for one bag of chocolate and—how many cookies?—to make a person as slow as me?

"Up!"

The command had to be obeyed, and Maru launched herself in the air for an effort she was positive would be her last, either because of her speedy and merciful death or an equally relieving faint. Much to her surprise, the instructor called break.

"Decent work," he said grudgingly, sipping from a bottle of water that hung at his waist. "If you're thirsty, get water. Otherwise, don't move. And don't you dare sit down!"

Maru staggered to the bleachers and searched for her water bottle. Like those of the others, it was regulation steel, the healthiest and most resilient material choice, but it had her name on it. Usually Maru had no trouble finding hers, but this time it seemed to be missing.

"Maaaru!" came a familiar voice. Maru spun around and faced Naito. "I put all our bottles over here so we could find them easily," he said, gesturing to the field of canteens that covered the bleachers. "Wouldn't want to get mixed up in that. Who knows, somebody might share your name!"

"You know nobody shares names here," corrected Kita, taking a delicate sip from a jewel-encrusted plastic bottle. "You should be more like me and bring your own bottle."

"If only we had the same privileges as you," teased Naito. "You're so cute, everybody likes you. Please, kitten, show me how to be cute, too!" He put his hands up to his face like paws and assumed a ghastly smile. Maru choked on her water.

"Not like that!" Kita frowned. "You're not a kitten—you're just a big, mean cat with no sense of grace at all. Go back to training!"

Maru was a little surprised at the insult, but it did not seem to bother Naito at all. "I still get the better of you here!" he announced. "C'mon! Let's do this again!"

"Let's not," muttered Maru, jogging back to the field.

This time, as she took her place in line, the recruits had all switched places according to a prearranged plan to confuse the instructor. Maru found herself sandwiched between a remarkably similar girl of her own height and an unruffled, silent Rin.

Maru jumped when she glanced in his direction, then slapped herself on the cheek for being so silly. This action did not go unnoticed by the instructor, who yelled at her for her unnecessary violence.

"I'm standing next to an assassin, and *I'm* too violent?" panted Maru, taking care that the words did not travel too far. Rin heard and looked down at her with an annoyed expression in his sharp blue eyes.

"Up!" shouted the instructor suddenly. "Up, down! Up, down! I'll keep you at this until I see some improvement."

The sky darkened for an instant above Maru, and she looked up to see the bottoms of Rin's regulation tennis shoes sailing high over her head. In her astonishment she missed the next beat, and the instructor came running to make his lecture a bit more personal.

"You lazy rookie!" he shouted, and Maru wondered if that was the derogatory term of choice at Rigel. "Pushups, one hundred, now!"

Maru dropped gratefully to her knees and breathed while the instructor continued down the line, screaming as he went.

"Up, down!" She timed her lethargic pushups to the instructor's directions. "Up, down!"

"All right, break!" shouted the instructor. A general relieved sigh went up and all motion ceased. Maru struggled to her feet.

"I didn't say *you* were done!" cried the instructor, pointing at her. "How many have you done?"

"Twenty-five," said Maru weakly.

"What's that again?"

Maru could not resist the temptation. "Twenty-five!" she screamed at a horrifying pitch which rivaled the instructor's.

Rin stepped back, closed his eyes irritably, and put his hands over his ears.

"Whoa, okay," said the instructor, looking between Maru and Rin. "That was . . . loud. You can stop for now, then."

After a brief pause, the instructor gathered himself together and shouted, "Now for a brief run!"

"No," said Maru to herself. "No, no, no."

Something shiny appeared at the bottom of her peripheral vision. Her eyes travelled downward and focused on her water bottle, suspended in mid-air by a pale, muscular forearm.

"Rin!" she cried in surprise. He looked away immediately and sipped from his own bottle.

"Thanks," she said hesitantly, opening and drinking without taking her eyes off him. "How did you get over there that fast?"

Rin did not answer, but instead held out his hand to take her bottle back.

"S'okay," she said. "I'll go myself."

Rin shook his head slightly and glanced toward the instructor, who was already leading the recruits in a brief two-mile run.

"I see," she said. "You don't want me to end up in the back. Well, thanks, Rin!" With a friendly wave she took off running, leaving Rin to trot quickly back to the bleachers, swinging the bottles around his fingers and moving his lips soundlessly.

Maru muttered to herself. It was an excellent way of distracting her mind from the torment that awaited. "Rin can hear, why can't he talk? Is it because he prefers not to? Or is there some medical reason?"

She ran a few steps forward, ignoring the instructor's loud pleas for speed.

"Not that it matters. Although it will be hard, having one completely silent team member. And those creepy eyes!" she added as an afterthought. She had never seen that exact color before, especially not framed by such dark hair. Obviously, Rin's identity as a human had never been in question; his eyes ruled out suspicion entirely. Maru sighed enviously. "I wish I could wear contacts so people wouldn't question me."

"You won't get to lunch that way!" shrieked the instructor. "Speed up, now! Only a mile to go!"

Maru wondered dismally where the first mile had gone, and deeply suspected the instructor of illicitly shortening the course. She inhaled desperately and tried to ignore her painful legs.

Somebody shot past her at a ridiculous speed. Maru gazed in dull surprise at the back of Naito's straw-colored head. He was laughing and encouraging the other runners, occasionally even running backwards to hurl remarks at somebody in the back. Maru could understand only about half of them; slowly it dawned on her that Naito was speaking in several different languages at once, none of which she could recognize.

"He needs a harder challenge!" shouted the recruit next to her.

Someone else sailed into the lead, easily passing Naito. He kept his eyes fixed on the road in front of him and did not seem to notice that he was leaving the group behind. Maru gazed skeptically at the back of his head. It was black and ruffled and looked remarkably like Rin.

"Hey, you! No passing!" shouted Naito.

Rin—if it was him—did not seem to hear and kept running, leaving the group further and further behind with every huge step.

"That's it!" cried the almost tearful instructor. "Why can't you all do that?"

"We're not Rin!" cried Naito and burst past the flag at the end of the course. "Hey! Didn't he see the flag?"

The entire group stopped and gazed at the rapidly disappearing back of Rin, who did not seem to notice that everyone else had stopped.

"If he wants to run more, he can," said the instructor. "I've never seen anything like it!" He turned back to the recruits with an unnervingly determined expression on his face. "We're all going to beat him someday. We'll train extra hard. We'll run four miles instead of two. We'll—"

The lunch bell cut his speech mercifully short. "All right, we'll resume tomorrow. Attention!" he added. The recruits, exhausted and panting as they were, shot immediately to their positions in a neat formation. Only Rin's place was empty. The instructor glared disapprovingly at the imperfection and sighed. "Rest. Lunch."

Maru staggered slowly toward the bleachers. Rin had placed her bottle next to Naito's and Kita's, and she wrapped her hands gratefully around the chilled metal. It heated up almost immediately.

"Want to sit with us?" said a voice behind her. Maru turned around and saw Naito, who was lying on his back in the grass and looking up at her. "We usually stay outside, but it's way too hot today."

"Sure," replied Maru. She took a last drink from her bottle and replaced the lid. "Let's go!"

Naito rolled to his feet and started toward the building, singing an extremely off-key and unrecognizable song. Maru followed more slowly, wondering—as she always did after training—exactly what had prompted her to join Rigel in the first place. The humans probably did not need her help, and what could somebody as inefficient as her do against a force as powerful and undefinable as the Kalideyes?

As she was thinking bitterly over her life choices since middle school, she glanced to her left and saw Rin rounding the corner of the track. He had certainly slowed down, but he did not look tired and his breathing was as regular as usual. His face had not lost its abstracted look, and Maru wondered what he was thinking about.

Something sad. Maybe he wishes he could talk about it with somebody.

"Coming?" asked a high-pitched female voice. Kita appeared out of nowhere and seized her arm. "The other recruits will get all the lunch!"

"'Course I'm coming," said Maru, not wanting to admit that she was almost too tired to walk to the cafeteria. She took a deep, reassuring breath and started after Kita. "Is there a place for me to refill my bottle?"

"Inside the cafeteria," replied Kita, skipping playfully ahead without a sign of exhaustion. "Hurry up!"

Maru shook her head and forced herself to a painful trot.

"There you are!" cried Naito, once they were finally inside the cafeteria. Maru panted and scanned the tables for a water cooler.

"Right over there." Kita pointed. "Make sure you wash your hands first."

Sanitation—sterilization. Always the words of the day.

Maru filled her bottle and returned to her friends. "I thought you were just blushing!" said Kita, poking her cheek. Maru stepped inadvertently back and tried to cover with a nervous laugh. She was used to more respect of her personal space. "But you were really just overheating! Too bad."

"Why should she be blushing?" asked Naito curiously.

"Ooh, I'm not sure yet." Kita put a thoughtful hand to her chin. "Who is it, Maru?"

"I've been here for only a month." Maru drank from her bottle to cover her embarrassment. If she hadn't been blushing before, she certainly was now. "So, it's nobody—of course."

"I'll keep an eye on you, then," replied Kita, laughing brightly. "Especially since we're roommates!"

"You're crazy, Ki—!" began Naito; but she interrupted him.

"Hey! Naito, invite Saito to sit with us."

"My almost-twin," said Naito. "That naming thing is going to get confusing real quick. But doesn't he usually like to sit by himself?"

"He's on a team now. He has to sit with us," Kita insisted. "Go get him!"

"Fine, fine. Anything for the little kitten." Naito stood up. "Do you see him anywhere?"

"Over by the window."

Naito pushed through the other recruits until Maru could see only his glowing blond head. Saito was sitting alone in the corner, reading something on his watch display. He glanced up when Naito appeared suddenly beside him, and even from that distance Maru could see him jump.

"He's nervous already!" mocked Kita. "And we don't even have a mission yet. Besides, nobody knows we're Rigel agents. You're especially useful, Maru, because of your eyes."

"Oh—my eyes?" Maru tried not to express her annoyance.

"Of course!" Kita did not notice. "All of us have blue eyes, so it's obvious what side we're on. But your eyes are more grayish-bluey and they won't be sure about you!"

Maru had never thought about the problem that way before. "Interesting. Maybe that's how it works."

"Some of the Kalideyes are gray, too," continued Kita. "You could be a top-secret-super-special agent who poses as a Kalideyes official!"

"Umm . . . no," said Maru abruptly. "No, no . . . no. I'm not that valuable."

"Don't underestimate yourself." Maru could tell Kita was about to launch into a long and cliché explanation on self-confidence, but Naito had returned.

"Saito said he'd be over in a minute," he explained, collapsing in his chair. "Whew! It's hot in here, too."

"What was Saito reading on his display?" Kita inquired.

"How should I know? Unlike you, I try not to pry into other people's business. Besides, he turned it off as soon as he saw me coming."

"Which wasn't until you were right in his face. If you're really so delicate, maybe you should try staying a few feet away from him. You know he hates people in general."

"Doesn't matter now." Naito leaned back comfortably in his seat. "Here he comes."

Maru resisted the urge to stand up and salute as the regal Saito sauntered toward the table, pulled up a chair, and reclined. "G'morning," he said briefly. Then he activated his watch display and started reading, ignoring further conversation.

"Good!" said Naito, once the pause had become awkward. "Where's . . . where's Rin? Then we'd have the whole team here."

"Still running, right?" suggested Saito, without taking his eyes off his watch display.

"I saw him near the bleachers," said Maru. "He looked like he was planning to stop."

"Then he should be in here somewhere." Naito stood up and scanned the recruits. "Saito, you haven't seen him?"

"No."

"Right there!" Kita pointed to the outdoor patio. Maru could just make out a dark figure leaning against one of the poles. "That's him, right?"

"Looks like it. I might as well go get him . . . the more the merrier!" With his customarily cheerful laugh, Naito stood up and bounced toward the door.

"Unnecessarily energetic," observed Saito, still without looking up from his display. "We'll have to work on that."

"You know all non-combatant personnel are specially trained to be happy all the time!" said Kita with a childish giggle. "It's to cheer you up!"

Saito raised one eyebrow and did not reply.

"Besides," continued the irrepressible Kita, "it's to make up for all you introverts. Rin, you, Maru—you're all so quiet."

Again, she did not receive a reply, which Maru felt uncomfortably confirmed her point.

"I've brought him back!" declared Naito, appearing suddenly behind Maru. "Rin the Silent. That could be his Norse nickname."

"Not very informative," said Kita. "What we'd all really like to know is exactly why he's silent." She looked at Rin as she spoke, evidently expecting him to explain the mystery on the spot, but he did not seem to hear her. Instead he seated himself in the chair next to Maru and leaned back to read Saito's watch display.

Saito turned it off in annoyance. "Show your clearance number if you want to read this."

Rin activated his display and beamed it toward Saito. "Top secret clearance?" cried Naito. "I work in computer systems, and I don't have one of those."

"Some of the assassins have them for mission intelligence purposes," said Saito. "Read whatever you want, Rin, but do it on your own display. That's what they make them for." He turned away.

"Don't we have a meeting later this afternoon?" asked Naito, obviously trying to change the subject. "What's it about?"

"Mission assignment and strategy," said Saito. "And valid certifications for all team members." He swung suddenly around to face Maru and looked her up and down, finishing his observation with a long stare straight into her gray eyes. "You and Rin will be working together on marksmanship, stamina training, and whatever else goes along with being an assassin. Kita, you'll be training with the other medical staff, and Naito, you'll be in the computer room."

"Making myself blind as usual." Naito sighed. "I'm going to have my eyes fixed again before we go on a mission, or I won't be able to see anything."

"You'll have to pass a vision and color genetics test."

"At the moment, there's no way I could pass the vision test." Naito made binoculars from his hands and peered at Kita. "Hey, this is helpful!"

"Of course, it isn't," said Kita haughtily. "You're just being ridiculous as usual."

"Knock it off, both of you," said Saito roughly. "If you're not done with lunch, eat—don't talk. If you are done, clean it up."

Kita's eyes widened in surprise, but she said nothing and turned her attention back to her tray.

Maru glanced to her left and saw Rin staring quietly at Saito. If looks were his only form of communication, they were effective, because Saito almost immediately turned around to return his level gaze.

"What do you want?"

There was a long silence where the two seemed to talk with their eyes. Maru watched curiously.

At last Saito scowled and said, "Rin, if you don't want to be on this team, take it up with the sergeant. Otherwise, you'll listen to my orders."

Rin's face darkened, but Saito was clearly done arguing. He stood up, shoved his chair under the table with a loud crash, and stalked out of the cafeteria, accompanied by a brief but universal gasp.

"Take it easy," said Naito quietly to Rin. "The whole world knows you two don't get along, but don't get yourself in trouble by defending us. After all, Saito is our leader, and by all the laws we have to respect him."

Rin did not bother looking toward him. Instead he, too, stood up and, taking his tray, left the group to sit alone.

"What . . . just happened?" asked Maru curiously.

"Saito and Rin don't really work well together." Naito shrugged, turning his attention back to his sandwich. Between mouthfuls he added, "They're too similar, in my opinion."

"There goes the psychologist!" Kita shouted with laughter. "You have no idea what you're talking about!"

"Well, neither do you, pretty girl!"

"Hey!"

Maru sensed the beginning of another pointless argument and did not want to be involved. She pulled up her watch display, scrolled aimlessly through the daily news, and tried to find something worth reading on the library application.

Rigel placed strict controls on what the recruits were allowed to see—"stricter than Mom," as Maru had said more than once before. The books in the digital library were almost without exception biographies, textbooks, and how-to guides, none of which interested Maru. The night before, when Kita had shared her library, had been a great relief. Maru missed the comfortable nights she had spent with her parents, when they all huddled together in front of the artificial fireplace and read real paper books, pretending to be just like families in the old days. It was idyllic, and Maru wished she could go back to the days before she had been scouted by Rigel.

"What now?" she asked herself dismally. It hadn't quite hit home to her that she was training at Rigel for one purpose: to become a lethal assassin. How would that change her? If the sight of death had caused Rin enough pain to silence him forever, how could Maru hope to hold her own?

She shook her head stiffly. Rin had probably always been quiet.

"Why are you jerking your neck around like that?" inquired Kita. "It looks a little weird."

Maru opened her eyes suddenly. "Sorry—sorry," she stammered. "I was just thinking."

"You're not supposed to start thinking until after you've assassinated somebody," said Naito. "It's a general rule around here."

"And Rin?" Maru could barely say his name.

"What about him?" Naito glanced into the corner where Rin had hidden himself, his face obscured behind his watch display. "Oh, you mean—is he thinking? Well, I guess so. How many missions did the sergeant lady say he's been on? Five?"

"Six," said Kita.

"Right. And I'm sure he had plenty of work to do on every one of them."

"You mean . . . he's assassinated at least six people—I mean, Kalideyes?" Maru corrected herself.

"Probably something like that." Naito regarded her quizzically. "You're overthinking this, Maru. Don't. It's not worth your time."

"This is something that has to be done," added Kita. "None of us are exactly sure why, but it's normal and you just have to believe that. And remember, the Kalideyes aren't people."

"I guess not," said Maru doubtfully. Suddenly realizing that she was displaying a Sign, she blushed. "I know."

"You'll get used to it," said Naito with a nonchalant yawn. "Death is a part of life."

"What kind of crazy paradox is that?" The moment Maru said the bitter words, she wished she hadn't.

Both Kita and Naito stared at her in surprise, as if her eyes had suddenly turned orange. "We all have to die, right?" said Naito after an uncertain pause.

"But what is death? Oh, I don't know what I'm thinking." Maru sighed. "We tried to extend human life and look how well it worked out. We ended up with the Kalideyes. But death is just as bad as life like that—at least, I think so."

"I dunno," said Kita doubtfully. "The Kalideyes are evil."

"Only because the government took control of them." Naito lowered his voice, and his face, which had been so light and cheerful only a moment before, stiffened. "The Kalideyes aren't evil on their own. But after a hundred and twenty years of life, they no longer control themselves."

"How do you know all this?" murmured Kita, her huge blue eyes wide and frightened.

Naito immediately relaxed and chuckled. "I occasionally read things I'm not supposed to. Don't we all?"

"I didn't understand," said Maru. "What was that about a hundred and twenty years?"

"Long, long story," said Naito. "I will tell you about it another time, or you can go do your own espionage. File number seven-seven-seven—easy to remember."

"You don't have a clearance, and the Seven files are all—"

"Well, no need to announce it to the world," said Naito calmly, standing up. "We all have questions we want answered. I'm sure you're no exception."

"A hundred and twenty years," Maru mused. "Isn't that what scientists used to say was the upper limit of the human lifespan?"

"Connection? I think so." Naito picked up his tray and winked mischievously. "You can figure the rest out. I don't want to get in any more trouble."

"Then shut your mouth and leave now, before I report you myself," said a stern voice from behind Maru.

"Yes sir, Saito!" Naito skipped away, his cheerful laughter trailing behind him.

Saito crossed his arms and looked down at Maru. She had not realized how ridiculously tall he was until she found herself staring at the middle of his chest. She jerked her gray-blue eyes upwards and met his icy blue ones, which seemed to challenge her to disobey his authority. Her gaze met those eyes fearlessly, and for an instant they held a tug-of-war.

"Class in Studio C, fifteen minutes." Saito turned on his heel and walked away.

Impossible—it had to be. And yet, Maru was sure. She had won the battle of wills, but just barely.

"He's a little scary," commented Kita unnecessarily. "Let's hurry—we don't want to be late with him on the prowl."

"For real," muttered Maru as she put her tray with the others on the cleaning belt. She watched it disappear slowly into the washer, thinking hard. There were already too many mysteries, but something specific was troubling her. She could not quite pinpoint what it was, but as she watched the trays sail forward, one after another, the question came to her.

Why was everyone so similar?

Naito and Kita were a perfect example. Maru thought they were adorable together, but until now she hadn't analyzed exactly how or why. She realized suddenly that they were like twins. They laughed at exactly the same pitch, smiled at exactly the same times, and thought almost in the same words. It was completely unnatural. Maru wondered if they were related, but as if to disprove this theory, another comparison immediately came to her: Saito and Rin. Both were taciturn, strong, and demanding. Neither ever smiled nor laughed. With their flat faces and thin, pinched lips, they demanded respect and implicit obedience. Somehow, though Saito was abrasive, and Rin was merely quiet, they were still almost horrifyingly alike.

Maru blinked sharply to clear her head. With a tiny smile she half-heartedly mocked herself for thinking something so silly and childish.

"I'm turning into Kita now," she scolded herself, and, ruffling her hair, scurried down the hallway toward Studio C.

CHAPTER 3

"Nice to see you're all here," said Saito with deep sarcastic intonation. He stood in front of a large electronic whiteboard, flourishing a black stylus in his left hand. Each team member's name, with the exception of Saito's own, had already been written at the top of the board and given a neatly divided section. Saito stepped to the left side of the board and pointed to Maru's name.

"No previous training," he began; then, as Maru was about to protest, "which means you'll need a physical and color genetics test as soon as possible. Tomorrow, preferably."

"I've had them both already," interrupted Maru. "Sir."

"Well, you're going to have them again." Saito's voice had lost its weariness and become quiet, commanding, and businesslike. "It's a requirement for all new recruits joining active teams, and neither headquarters nor I care if you've done it before. I'll schedule it for tomorrow at eight o'clock sharp, and if you're late, you'll have to get another appointment yourself."

Maru subsided.

"What is your record in marksmanship?"

"Ninety," she said, shifting in her chair.

"Not bad," commented Saito drily. "Nine times out of ten, you manage to hit the target. Let's all hope that the tenth time isn't during your first mission." He turned to the whiteboard and scribbled a few words under Maru's name. "There's your class schedule. Copy it onto your watch right now, and as I said before, don't be late."

Maru pulled up her display and quickly typed in a copy of Saito's neatly arranged program. Marksmanship, martial arts—chemistry? She almost raised her hand to ask why this seemingly unrelated topic was included in her classes but decided against interrupting Saito again.

"Kita," he was saying, "is your child and adult CPR certification still valid?"

"Until next year," replied Kita.

"Good. That will save you some time. I expect you to attend at least one martial arts class per week—which day would you prefer?"

"Umm . . . Monday? I don't have a preference, really."

"Then I'll schedule you for Tuesday, since that's when most of the openings are. Enjoy training with Rin. The rest of your schedule will be assigned by the head of medicine."

"What about me?" asked Naito.

"I'll get to you." Maru noticed that Naito's name was next on the list, but Saito skipped him. "Rin, you'll have combat training and martial arts twice every day except the weekends. You'll also continue running special missions, to be assigned by the departmental head. Don't you dare mess this up." He took two threatening steps forward until he stood directly in front of Rin, staring down from his full height. "Don't get yourself killed over some idiotically chivalrous action. Rigel has better plans for you."

Rin did not reply.

"Naito," continued Saito, returning to his original position next to the board, "your schedule is entirely under the head of technology's control. Ask them for more details." He replaced his stylus on the shelf under the board and crossed his arms. "We'll meet as a team once a week, on this day and at this time, to discuss schedules and potential missions. I'd like to have a full team when the time comes for mission assignment, so don't get yourself killed in the meantime. That goes especially for you, Rin. Think before you act. And remember that your blue eyes are your biggest liability because they prove your identity."

Rin closed his eyes as if to disprove Saito's last statement. With an obviously irritated sigh Saito pressed a button, and the whiteboard retracted into a slot on the ceiling. "That's all for now," he said. "Maru, Rin, you'll observe that marksmanship class starts in ten minutes."

Maru had a less than perfect sense of direction, and she always worried about arriving on time. Standing in the doorway, she looked left and right in some concern. On which side of the building was the shooting range?

A hand pushed past her and gestured left. She glanced back and saw Rin's expressionless face and pale forearm.

"Left!" said Saito. "Rin, use words."

Whether Rin could or not, he did not bother trying, but instead squeezed his way out the door, past Saito and Maru, and down the hallway.

"Rude," muttered Saito. "Follow him. He'll get you where you need to be."

Maru hurried down the hallway after Rin's rapidly disappearing figure. He stopped at the front door and held it politely open to her. Taking a page from Saito's book, she tried to thank him with her eyes, but his were fixed on the floor and would not meet hers.

She paused outside the door, and Rin again took the lead. He walked rapidly around the side of the building, turned several confusing corners, and somehow finished in the middle of a wide grass field. Maru looked around in confusion. She had no idea where they were or how they got there, but she recognized the coach standing at the far end of the field.

"There you are!" he cried in exasperation. "Line up!"

Maru picked up a rifle from the barrel at the front of the range and took her position in front of the target. Marksmanship was obviously her best skill. Very few recruits in Rigel had as flattering a record as her own, and she was proud of it. The rifle felt cool in her hands as she peered through the sight and adjusted her grip. She was at home here.

A few younger recruits lined up beside her. She glanced shyly to her left. So far, there was nobody there. Rin was standing beside the coach, evidently listening quietly to his instructions. Maru shook herself. She wanted him to take the target beside her—she wanted somebody to compete with. She was sure she could win easily, but at the same time there was a lurking sense of doubt in measuring her abilities against Rin. After all, he was a trained assassin who offered his gruesome services in exchange for shelter and enough food to keep him alive. The thought made her blink in surprise, and she turned for one more glance at the apparently mild, silent man.

"Assassin," she whispered, and a cold shiver spread over her as she realized that the word applied to her as well. She had never killed anyone, never seen anyone die, but all these years she had spent training and strengthening herself were all leading up to that moment.

"Maru!" a voice shouted.

The shiver was replaced with sweat. "Yes sir!" She came abruptly to attention.

"Change of plans. You and Rin are going to SAS training right now."

"SAS?" Maru was confused, unfamiliar with the acronym.

"Societal Adjustment and Strengthening," said the coach, stabbing the air with his finger as if the words were written in front of him. "You'll have to watch some videos and read some exercises. Not bad at all. Not much work. Nothing to worry about."

Maru looked past him at Rin, who was standing with his eyes fixed resolutely on the ground. She could swear he had shuddered at the word "videos," and his movement had caught her attention.

"Videos . . . ?" As she said it, she realized suddenly that she was not in a position to question the coach. "Yes, sir."

"Follow Rin. He'll take you where you need to be."

Reluctantly she put her rifle back in the barrel and trailed off after Rin. He never looked at her, but walked slowly back toward the building, every step seeming heavy as lead. Maru watched him curiously, wondering what was going through his head.

Stress from training? She laughed uncertainly.

Suddenly Rin turned around with a strange expression on his face. He locked eyes with Maru and seized her shoulders, squeezing tightly.

She gasped in pain and tried to wriggle out of his grasp, but he held her firmly. Still looking straight at her, he shook his head violently, as if he were trying to express with motion what he could not with words. His lips moved but made absolutely no sound. Maru stared up at him, her alarm diminishing as she realized that he was trying painfully to speak.

If he was really trying this hard, he must have something important to say, but somehow nothing happened. Maru tried her best to understand his blue eyes, which had somehow dimmed—maybe because of the shade—but she could not.

"Rin . . . ?" she began.

He jumped back violently, shaking from head to foot, covering his ears with his hands as if she had yelled at him.

"I'm sorry!" she cried, confused but realizing above everything else that she had hurt him in the worst possible way. "What—are you okay?"

Slowly he took his hands from his ears and straightened himself up. His hands still trembled slightly as he pulled his gaze from the ground back up at her, but there was apology written all over his face. Clearly, he had no idea what he had been doing, and Maru suddenly felt intense pity for him.

What could possibly have happened to make him like this?

His lips moved again, and Maru tried to read them. Before she could make any sense out of his message, he turned suddenly away from her and started walking rapidly in his original direction.

What was wrong with him? Why did he cover his ears like that? It wasn't as if she was loud.

She nearly tripped over a rock as she struggled to keep up without running like a schoolgirl after an older brother. Rin was paying no attention to her now, obviously lost in his own thoughts, and he seemed not to even care whether or not she was still behind him. His indifference annoyed her.

Suddenly brave, she ran up to him and tapped him on the shoulder. "Rin?"

The effect was spectacular. Exactly as he had done before, only this time even more desperately, he jumped away from her and squeezed his hands over his ears. His knees shook until he fell, still covering his ears and now bending as if something heavy was sitting on top of him. He was gasping for breath, shivering, trying desperately to talk and strangling his words at the same time.

Maru's eyes widened. "What did I do? What did I say?" she cried, kneeling down beside Rin. "Can I—?"

He hit her hand roughly away, never raising his head. Somehow, without looking, he had known exactly where she was.

The painful slap of his hand on her arm irritated Maru. She stood up coldly and said, "Are you going to take me to training or not? At this rate we'll never get there."

There was a long pause, during which she wondered if he had heard her. Then he stood up, looked at her with a rather sad expression, and headed slowly toward the building.

*****   *****   *****

"What in the world are you doing here?" The instructor looked at Rin in derision. "You're in no shape for SAS training, you idiot. Look at you. I'd swear you had another attack on the way over here. Am I right?"

Rin did not answer.

"I am right." The instructor turned to Maru, looked her up and down, and said, "You can't do this by yourself, either. You'll have to wait for Rin to get better. Come back and see me tomorrow."

Rin seized the instructor by the shoulder and led him off into a corner, where he then moved his arms and lips in a desperate but futile effort to convey his thoughts. The instructor stared at him for a moment, then laughed.

"Don't overdo things," he said. "This is not something you can over-come—it's something you have to learn to live with. And please, just give in already and take the drugs. They'll help you, and they're neither dangerous nor addictive."

Rin shook his head silently, evidently giving up on communication.

"Your funeral, quite literally," said the instructor flippantly. "Anyway, we've wasted plenty of time. Lunch is in ten minutes."

CHAPTER 4

"Post . . . traumatic . . . stress . . . disorder. PTSD," said Kita precisely. "Most of the assassins have it. Then again, most of them take medicines to control their reactions to triggers. Rin would be the one to refuse." She sipped her drink, as if the words she had just said so casually meant nothing to her.

"Are you saying that Rin has . . . PTSD?" Maru's fork stopped halfway to her mouth. "But why?"

"You're an assassin, right? You'll find out eventually!" Naito squeezed his eyes shut and smiled comically.

"But . . . isn't that kind of serious?" Maru was confused by their levity. "Shouldn't Rin be retired?"

Kita laughed. "Of course not," she said. "If everybody around here with PTSD got retired, there'd be nobody left."

"What exactly caused it?"

"What's *it*? Rin's symptoms?" Naito irreverently pointed at Kita with his fork. "She's the psychologist. Ask her."

"I dunno." Kita shrugged. "Could be anything. Could be the people he's killed—"

"Tell me about that," Maru interrupted.

"Why are you so curious?" Naito tapped the table thoughtfully. "Could it be already . . . ?"

"Don't be silly!" Kita smacked him playfully on the top of his head. "Maru isn't that kind."

"What?"

"Nothing!" insisted Naito and Kita together.

"About his assassinations," continued Kita, "I believe he's done six so far. He's a good shot and never misses, so it was all over quickly and there isn't really a good story to go with it."

"No story?" murmured Maru. "Somebody dies, but there's just no story?"

"What did you say?"

"Umm . . . nothing. Go on."

"I just told you, there isn't anything else to say." Kita started to giggle. But suddenly, as she looked at Maru's downcast eyes, her face straightened, and the corners of her ever-smiling lips drooped. "Maru," she said quietly, "are you afraid?"

"What?" Maru looked up. "Afraid of what?"

"Be honest. I'm a psychologist, so I'll know if you're not. You're asking me all this because you don't want to become like Rin, right?"

"Maybe. I don't know." Maru dropped her eyes again and played thoughtfully with her utensils. "I wish I could help him."

"I'm here to tell you that you can't possibly do that." Kita's face was still serious. "You accidentally found one of his triggers today. He hates being touched and called by name at the same time. I don't know for sure why this is, but I recommend that you never do it again. If you're going to address him by name, absolutely do not touch him. Don't hold his hand, tap his shoulder—anything. He won't know what he's doing, and he'll hurt you."

"Did you say he had an attack on the way to SAS training?" inquired Naito. Maru nodded.

"Understandable. SAS training takes a toll on everybody." Kita nodded and returned to her lunch.

"What in the world is it, anyway?"

"You seriously do not know?" Maru wondered if Naito's face was really turning pale or if it was just a trick of the shadows. "I am not going to tell you, then."

"Somebody should prepare her." Kita sighed.

"Not volunteering." Naito glumly put his fork down and hid behind his napkin.

"What's so scary about it?" asked Maru curiously.

Kita and Naito both flinched. "It's not," Kita said quickly. "Not once you get used to it."

"Stop asking," said Saito quietly, appearing suddenly at the end of the table. "Rin will be fine tomorrow, and you'll go with him then. I apologize for his behavior today."

"It's okay." Maru wondered why Saito felt responsible. "Are there any other things I should know about that might make him have another episode?"

"Loud noises, including all gunshots except sniper rifles," said Saito. "I don't know how he knows the difference, but he does. A pistol and an ordinary rifle will both trigger his anxiety. I guess SAS trained him out of . . ." He paused.

"Certain kinds of music have the same effect," he continued after an awkwardly long pause. "Country music, specifically."

"I don't listen to that," said Maru absently.

"What, are you planning to share your music with him, too?" Maru was jerked out of her thoughts and looked up to see Saito scowling at her. "Stay away from Rin. He can be a jerk, as you saw today. Whatever is behind his mental disorder is no excuse for his conduct toward you. I'll have a talk with the Panel about it."

"Wait, don't!" cried Maru. "He had no idea what he was doing! It's not his fault!"

"Really, Maru? And what if it had ended differently? If you're right and he really didn't know what he was doing, he might have hurt you. And if he did know, why did he treat you like that?"

"He's never hurt anybody yet, has he?" demanded Maru, looking to Kita and Naito for support. "Has he?"

Naito and Kita avoided her eyes.

"Wrong again." Saito smiled bitterly and rolled up his sleeve. "This happened a month ago."

Maru followed his glance down and stared at a long, deep, painful scar across Saito's forearm.

"He accused me of being a traitor to Rigel," continued Saito, "and tried to kill me with his knife."

"Wait, he actually said something to you?" Kita was wide-eyed.

"No. I only found out because he started filling out indictment forms. Fortunately for all of us he came to his senses in time and dropped the charges. But that should be enough to prove to you, Maru, that he's not worth worrying about. Stay away from him and keep yourself safe. I'll take care of the rest." Without waiting for her to reply, Saito picked up the tray he had set on the end of the table and stalked away.

"He's bitter," remarked Kita.

"Sherlock," replied Naito scornfully.

For a moment there was silence. Maru watched Naito and Kita and observed that they were both looking around the room.

"He's not here," sighed Kita at last.

"You can't find him either?"

"Who are you looking for?" asked Maru.

"Rin, of course. Who else?"

"I can see him from here."

Naito and Kita both turned around. "Where?"

"In the corner by the window."

Rin was sitting alone, plate and tray in front of him, book balanced precariously against them. He was pretending to read, but Maru, who had been watching him, saw his head drift occasionally to the window and around the cafeteria. His face was flat as usual, and Maru was too far away to see any expression in his eyes.

"He looks so creepy." Kita made her hands into binoculars like a child and stared at him. "Always frowning."

"Well you know, whenever I think about what must be going on inside your head, that smile of yours looks pretty creepy, too." Naito's tone was cheery, but his face had not recovered its cheerfulness.

"Was that an insult?"

"It was an observation."

Kita laughed hollowly. "Maru has no idea what's going on," she said stiffly, lowering her hands. "She probably wouldn't care if she did know. Let's talk about something else."

"No time," said Naito. "We should be in training."

"Already? Maru, what are you doing next?"

"No idea." She had completely forgotten to keep track of time, and her mind was still elsewhere.

"You can do after-lunch marksmanship," suggested Naito. "Saito should have given you the schedule, but he seems ridiculously out of it today."

"He's just busy insulting—" Kita stopped herself. "Help me put my tray away, Naito."

"Hey! I'm not your servant!"

"Today you are!" Kita tugged playfully at his sleeve. "Let's go!"

She dragged Naito after her, leaving Maru feeling somewhat confused and deeply curious.

"They might as well speak Greek," Maru muttered to herself disgustedly. "What's going on? And where am I supposed to go?" She doubted she could find her way back to the combat field by herself, but at the same time she was reluctant to ask for help. She pulled up her watch display and gazed at it, wondering what the combat field's proper name was.

A finger came between her and the display, indicating a specific dark patch on the map. Maru hadn't heard anybody approach, but since the movement was not accompanied with any actual words, she could easily guess it was Rin.

"Right here?" she asked, fighting off a sudden temptation to blast country music or otherwise test his various triggers. She reproved herself for being so unkind and turned her attention back to the map. "The combat field?"

Rin nodded and started for the door. Maru trotted after him like an obedient student.

*****   *****   *****

"You're back," observed the instructor unnecessarily. "It's only you two this afternoon. I expect to see some good shooting, because competition should motivate you. Although . . . " He sidled up to Maru and whispered dramatically in her ear. "You'll have a hard time beating Rin. He's a cold-blooded killer."

Maru shivered and looked at Rin, who was quietly cleaning his rifle.

"Nervous, are you?" The instructor laughed. "Don't be. You've got a pretty good record, too. We'll see how you do together."

Maru stepped up to the target feeling anything but sure of herself. What if Rin decided to use his weapon to—? But that was ridiculous. Whatever Saito said, Rin was not violent or cruel, and so far, he seemed nice enough.

Putting her fears resolutely to the back of her mind, Maru shouldered her rifle.

"Stop!" The instructor hurried up to her. "Why are you shooting with that piece of junk? Take this." He took away her traditional rifle and replaced it with a sleek black sniper rifle. "This is what you'll be using anyway."

Maru was deeply confused until she suddenly remembered Saito's words: *A pistol and a rifle will both trigger Rin's anxiety.* She took the new weapon and aimed.

"You both know what you're doing?" The lackadaisical instructor smiled gleefully. "This means I get a break, right?"

Maru looked at Rin. Then they both looked wordlessly back at the instructor.

"Ooh, scary," he said, involuntarily taking a few steps back. "I'll stay and . . . watch."

Maru raised the rifle to her shoulder and aimed again. Her rifle and Rin's fired at the same moment, aimed at the same target. They looked at each other in surprise, then smiled. The huge holes their bullets had torn in the target melded into one, right at the center.

"Prodigies," murmured the instructor, lackadaisical no longer. "This is amazing. You should shoot competitively."

"I once did," said Maru.

"Really? That's great! You'll be a perfect addition to our snipers, then."

Maru flinched at the word, then laughed wonderingly at herself. Things were changing too fast.

"I've never seen such good first shots," continued the instructor. "Rin's always good. I didn't think anybody could challenge him."

From the corner of her eye, Maru noticed that Rin was smiling brightly at her.

"Rin should really be your teacher." He rambled on. "Six assassinations . . . plenty of experience . . . plus you two seem to get along well!"

Rin's smile faded as the instructor mentioned his assassinations and disappeared completely at the word "experience." He turned quickly away and reloaded his rifle.

"Shoot as long as you want," said the instructor comfortably. "Compete. I want to see it."

Maru looked shyly for Rin's approval. He nodded slightly and pointed two fingers at different targets.

"He means to say," Maru translated for the instructor, "that we should shoot at different targets, and whoever gets closest to the center wins. Am I right?"

Rin nodded.

"Let's go then!" The excited instructor was almost jumping up and down. "I want to see!"

Maru cursed his excitement under her breath and glanced at Rin. The gunshot did not seem to bother him, nor was there any sign that he remembered the events of earlier.

"Rin first!"

He raised his rifle casually to his shoulder, took a split second to aim, and fired.

"Ce-e-enter! You'll have a hard time beating that, Miss . . . ?"

"Maru," she informed him briefly. To herself she whispered, "I can do better—I can do better." She raised her gun, took brief aim, and fired. Her shot was as close to the center as Rin's had been.

"Why did they bother sending you to me?" mumbled the instructor. "On second thought, though, your records are going to make me look good. And I could use some support. You don't mind if I take credit for this, do you?"

"What are you talking about?" Maru suddenly felt that her boundaries were being violated by this extremely outgoing but lazy instructor.

"It's going to look like you're doing this because of me," he explained. "Like I taught you all this stuff. And since my record isn't very good right now, I could use some star students."

Maru stared at him. Was she really talented because she knew how to shoot? After all, a person was just supposed to look through the sight and pull the trigger.

"Ooh, I shouldn't be explaining this to you. I should have kept it a secret!" The instructor laughed until he nearly fell out of his chair, and Maru wondered if he was drunk. "Star . . . students . . ."

Rin approached him with an unusually mild look on his face and shook him hard by the shoulders.

"I'm recovering," gasped the instructor, his face suddenly becoming serious. He sat very still for a moment, staring past Rin, then laughed shakily. "What did I just say?"

Rin's face twisted into a sideways smile.

"Sorry." The instructor blushed like a girl. "I don't . . . I don't know why that happened. Please just keep shooting."

Maru stared back and forth between him and Rin, completely at a loss. Rin shook his head and ran his finger across his lips. Maru understood him to mean that she should avoid asking questions, so, stifling her curiosity, she reloaded her gun.

*****   *****   *****

"See you in the morning," said Kita, drawing out her vowels ridiculously. "I'm shleepy."

"Me too," Maru lied.

Kita reached for the door keypad, but her hand stopped in mid-air. "Hey . . . there's a note," she said. "Why can't they put a light out here?" She pulled the paper free and squinted at the tiny handwriting.

"I think it has your name on it," she said at last, handing the crumpled paper to Maru. "Ooh, is there something I should know?"

"I don't think so." This final bizarre incident seemed to put the cap on an already stressful day. "I mean . . . I don't have any idea who this could be from."

"Oh well," Kita sighed. "I was hoping for a story. First dibs on the shower!"

Maru blinked as the door swung open and revealed Kita's sparkling residence.

"Don't worry, I won't make you read it to me," said Kita as she threw her bags down and danced around the room. "Gooooooood night!"

"Apparently she's not sleepy after all," muttered Maru, seating herself on the white sofa and unfolding the letter. Her name was written on the outside in extremely neat, tiny cursive lettering that she did not recognize, and the paper was probably torn from an ordinary notebook. At first, glancing over it, she thought the paper was otherwise blank. Then she saw an even smaller message written in the bottom right corner:

"Apply for SAS exemption."

There was no signature, and no more words.

SAS . . . ? It took Maru a moment to place the acronym. *Social . . . Adjustment . . . and Strengthening. That's it. But why should I apply for an exemption? And who wrote this note? If it was Saito, then I should definitely do what he says. But wouldn't he have signed it? And why wouldn't he just tell me at lunch or something?*

Maru sighed and buried her head in the soft fur pillows. *SAS training is tomorrow. I'll never get an exemption by then, so I might as well give up already.*

Maybe one of the other recruits is just trying to give me a hard time. Maybe this is a Kita prank or something.

"Hey!"

Maru jumped.

"What did it say?" Dripping wet and wrapped in a soft pink bath towel, Kita was staring at her from around the bathroom door, eyes wide and not at all tired.

"I thought you said you weren't going to make me read it!"

"Oh, come on!" Kita pleaded. "I finished my very last book yesterday. I need a good story!"

"There's not really much to see," said Maru stiffly. "It only said 'Apply for an SAS exemption.'"

Kita's face froze. "An exemption . . . ? I didn't even know you could do that."

"It wasn't signed, so I think it's just a prank."

"I would do what they say."

"What?" Maru looked up in surprise. Kita's voice had suddenly gone flat.

"I said you should apply for the exemption. You won't regret it, trust me."

"But the first class is tomorrow. I can't get anything done by then."

"You can give the papers to Saito tonight. I'll tell you where his dorm is." Kita's fingers tapped the doorframe nervously. "It's worth trying. Please trust me on this."

"I don't think I can wander around campus alone at night." Maru shrank from the idea of leaving the warm, comfortable apartment again.

Kita burst into high-pitched, artificial laughter. "You're an assassin, right?" she gulped. "You should be fine . . . but . . . I'll go with you if you won't go alone."

No getting out of it. Aloud she said, "That's fine, thanks."

"Give me just a minute." Kita ducked back into the bathroom.

Maru put her favorite sweatshirt over her uniform and stuffed her hands gloomily in her pockets. Paperwork late at night was worse than nightmares.

Kita reappeared a few minutes later, gaudily dressed in a soft pink bathrobe and a wet towel turban. "Ready!" she announced, putting on her outdoor slippers.

"Are you sure?" Maru looked her up and down uncertainly.

"Nothing's going to happen! Let's get this over with. I want to go to bed."

Maru shrugged and opened the door.

The chilly night air rushed inside with a vengeance, and Maru shivered. She would much rather stay inside . . . why was she being childish enough to act on instructions probably delivered as a prank? She had the note in her pocket, and, pausing in the middle of the sidewalk, stopped to re-read it. There was little to see. She thought back to Saito's handwriting on the whiteboard, trying to remember exactly what it had looked like. With a clear picture in her mind, she snapped her eyes open and looked at the note. The writing was not even remotely similar.

"Kita," she said aloud, "I really don't think this is a good idea."

Kita did not answer, but, pulling her bathrobe tighter, trudged past her.

"Kita!" cried Maru.

"I'm going if you're not," Kita's muffled voice drifted back. "I don't want you to end up like me."

"Why won't you just explain what you think is going on? You seem to have a much better idea." Maru ran to catch up with her.

"I don't want to."

"Is there something I should know that I'm missing? I'm new, you know, and I—"

"Shut up already!" cried Kita. "You don't know what you're talking about. You don't understand what I'm trying to do for you. If you did, you'd thank me from the bottom of your heart for days on end and you'd never stop bowing. But you don't, so stop arguing and do what I say."

Maru paused, completely amazed by this uncharacteristically violent speech.

"Can you please tell me one thing?" she asked after a long pause. "Can you tell me who wrote the note?"

"Let me see it." Kita held her hand, and Maru gave her the paper.

She examined it and handed it back. "I don't know."

"Saito?"

"No."

"Naito?"

"No, definitely not."

"Well then . . . Rin?"

"I just said I don't know, so you might as well stop bothering me!"

Maru squeezed the note tightly in her hand, wondering bitterly what had suddenly happened to the mild, happy-go-lucky Kita.

"That's Saito's dorm." Kita lowered her head and pointed. "Go talk to him."

"You're sure he won't be asl . . . " The words died in Maru's mouth. Kita was right; there was no reason to argue. She hurried up the steps and knocked nervously at the door.

After several minutes of uncomfortable waiting, it opened to reveal Saito, still dressed in his uniform. He looked her up and down, taking his time, and then said simply, "Yes?"

"I—I—" Maru realized suddenly that she had not decided how to explain herself. On an impulse she handed Saito the crumpled note. "I found this taped to my door keypad. It suggested I apply for an SAS exemption, and when I showed it to Kita, she told me I should talk to you." Any guilt Maru might have felt in blaming this nocturnal expedition on Kita was immediately overcome by a comfortable relief.

"An SAS exemption?" Saito laughed bitterly. "I know you're a girl, but please don't pull that excuse on me. I think you can handle it, and if you can't, you have no right to be here. Good night."

"Wait!" cried Kita, appearing behind Maru. "This isn't her fault. She doesn't even know what SAS is. I told her to do it. Look at the note, please, Saito."

He held out his hand coldly. "Give it to me."

Maru handed it to him with undisguised reluctance.

"So, Rin is up to his usual tricks." Saito crumpled the note into a tiny ball and put it in his pocket. "I should have known after what happened today."

"How do you know Rin wrote that?" asked Maru.

"Nobody else could write in such small characters." Saito smiled at her, but it was a scornful, humorless smile. "Why do you care who wrote it? Didn't you just assume it was a prank?"

He leaned close to her face, and his smile disappeared. "Don't ever ask me for an SAS exemption again. It's part of your training, and I won't let you shirk. Now get some sleep. And if you ever see this handwriting again, bring the note to me." Without further explanation, he stepped back and slammed his door. Maru heard the lock click back into place, and everything was suddenly silent.

Kita exploded. "That hard-hearted—ugh! I knew he'd say no. And he just does it out of spite."

"I'd really like to know a little more about what's going on," said Maru soothingly. "Could you please explain to me—?"

"You'll know tomorrow," interrupted Kita. "I won't tell you anything before then. When you come back, we can talk about it if you want."

"Okay. But wait, Kita. I just want to know one thing. Why is everybody so afraid of SAS training?"

There was a long pause.

"The point of SAS training is not to be afraid of it," murmured Kita. "But that's not its real effect. It doesn't destroy your emotions; it only takes away your ability to act based on them. The feelings—good, bad, horrific—are all still there."

"I don't know what that means!"

"You will." Suddenly Kita's face resumed its habitual childish smile, and she giggled. "I must look ridiculous in this bathrobe. I didn't mean for Saito to see it, but oh well. Everybody knows I like soft things. When I first came here the room inspector told me . . . "

Maru looked back at Saito's dorm. She could see a light on in his window, and as she watched, a dim silhouette took shape against the blind. It was Saito, standing perfectly still and watching them.

CHAPTER 5

"Rin," murmured Maru to herself. "If he wrote that note, then he'll want to know I acted on it. I have to find him and explain why I couldn't do anything."

She hid behind the tray return station as Kita and Naito passed, laughing and chatting like best friends. Then she looked around the cafeteria, but there was no sign of Rin. His usual window seat was vacant, and when Maru checked the sign-in sheet, his name was missing.

She was just about to give up and join Naito and Kita when she felt a strong hand on her shoulder. With a jump she turned around and found herself face-to-face with Saito, who was balancing a tray on his other hand. She noticed that it contained two meals instead of one.

"Come with me," he ordered shortly, and turned away without waiting to see if she followed his directions.

After a second's hesitation she followed him across the cafeteria to a quiet table in the far corner, kept private by a row of short palm trees. With his back to her, he put the tray on the table and arranged the plates across from each other. Then he sat down and turned to Maru.

"Sit," he ordered, pointing to the chair opposite him.

She obeyed nervously.

"I hope you understand that what happened last night is not to be repeated. I do not grant exemptions based on anonymous penciled notes," he said, looking suspiciously at her over a forkful of scrambled eggs.

Maru looked down at the plate in front of her. "Of course."

"Good. Then we won't discuss that further. You'll continue to SAS training today with Rin as scheduled, but before you do so, I'd like to ask you what you know about Rin."

"What I know about . . . ?" Maru was completely caught off guard. "Not much."

"Specifics." His lips smiled, but his eyes did not. "And you don't have to be nervous. I didn't poison your breakfast."

Maru took the hint and picked up her fork, starting on the scrambled eggs while she collected her thoughts. "I don't know much about him," she said slowly. "All I know is that he has some sort of anxiety disorder that causes him to . . . to . . . shake whenever I touch him and say his name. And when he hears loud noises and certain kinds of music. I don't even know his real name."

"Well done," said Saito drily. "Now I'll tell you what you don't know, or maybe haven't thought about. Rin is a killer—a murderer of sorts. Think about it this way: he betrays and kills people to earn just enough food and shelter to keep him miserably alive. And yet, you never see it bother him, do you? His emotions are dead. He's inert from exposure to violence and brutality, and he's becoming what he sees. Yesterday when he attacked you—do you remember how frightened you were?"

Maru shivered, wondering how Saito knew. Had he been watching? Before she could ask, he continued.

"Rin excuses himself by blaming it on his mental illness. If he really had such minimal control over himself, Rigel would have discharged him a long time ago. Whatever he may say—or not say—his actions are deliberate. Every day you have a new example of his cruelty, although he tries to hide it behind his flat-faced, blue-eyed mask. Because you don't know him, allow me to give you a warning." Saito leaned across the table and locked eyes with the terrified Maru. "Do not become like him. And do not become friends with him."

He leaned back and crossed his arms, examining Maru up and down in his habitually slow way. "We're on a team together, so we're stuck with each other for now. I can't change that. But it doesn't mean you should do what he says, or ever let yourself be left alone with him. He's a killer, Maru. I know he won't hesitate to kill you, too."

Maru's eyes widened, and she could feel the blood draining from her face. Saito's speech had been in horrific sincerity, despite the slight smile on his lips. He clearly meant every word he had said. Somehow Maru's mental picture of Rin, which had been so kind and generous before, darkened to almost a solid black. She could no longer see his face, only his huge and icy blue eyes. She read hatred in them—hatred for her, Saito, Rigel, and for their mission.

"I see you believe me," said Saito quietly.

"Somehow—I—" Maru stopped herself, took a deep breath, and continued. "If Rin is really so violent, why hasn't Rigel discharged him?"

"Because death is unfortunately a part of life," replied Saito cryptically. "Rigel has to kill, and they need people to do it."

"Oh." Maru could think of nothing else to say.

"You're about to be exposed to horror beyond what you ever imagined or dreamed of," continued Saito, taking a drink from his coffee cup. "You'll have a chance to break. Don't. But don't bottle everything up either. Talk to Kita if you need to, or . . . me." Maru felt a question in his glance but did not understand it.

"Talk to me. That's what I'm here for." Saito closed his eyes and bowed his head. "Don't forget, I've been through it all, too."

Maru shivered. "What is everybody talking about? You're so secretive. I can't figure this out on my own!"

Saito did not open his eyes. "Unfortunately, you are alone right now."

"But I thought you just said—"

"Once you've experienced this, you'll join those whose innocence has been cruelly shattered. You'll bond by common experience. And I hope—" here he did open his steely blue eyes—"I hope you'll take advantage of that."

Maru felt uncomfortable, but she did not know exactly why.

"SAS begins in ten minutes." Saito stood up and looked coldly down at her, his eyes empty and his face expressionless. "Find Rin and go. You're together for this first round." In one swoop he had all the plates on the tray and was turning to leave.

"Saito . . ."

He stopped and looked over his shoulder. "What?"

"Why did you tell me all that?"

There was a long pause, during which the noise of the cafeteria outside seemed to diminish.

Saito turned all the way around, brushed a stray wisp of streaked brown hair off his face with his free hand, and smiled coldly. "Because I think you're worth it." Then he disappeared abruptly behind the palm trees.

Can somebody just please say what they mean for once? She sighed. "Ten minutes to be at SAS training—ten minutes until I'm apparently going to be exposed to all the horrors of the ages. Great fun."

She stood up slowly, stretched, and rounded the corner of the palm tree wall. Her next mission was to find Rin, which turned out to be easy after all. He was leaning against the wall by the entrance, staring with an abstracted expression through the skylights.

"Are you ready?" asked Maru timidly.

He looked down at her and tried his best to smile. His lips twitched, and he turned away.

What's wrong with him? Maru looked curiously up and down his strong, broad back, wondering if Saito's description was really true. Rin was certainly not emotionless. He was human, just like she was.

She trailed him outside, down the sidewalk, and to a small, shabby building on the left side of the road. Rin held the door open for her. She tried to meet his eyes to thank him for the small favor, but they were covered by his long hair.

The building was extremely small inside, most of its area being taken up by a dark room in the back. As Maru and Rin stood quietly waiting, the door squeaked further open and a tiny man appeared around the corner. Maru shivered in dread. He was wrinkled and twisted almost beyond recognition as human. His eyes were void of feeling or thought, and the skin on his face hung loosely around muscles that refused to smile or show any other emotion. If ever Maru had stared death in the face, it was now. This shriveled creature was like a walking skeleton, unfeeling, ready to die because there was no more joy to be had in life.

"Rin," he slurred, barely moving his lips. "And who are you, little girl?"

Maru took an involuntary step closer to Rin's side. "Maru," she said faintly. Feeling something warm touching her fingers, she squeezed it instinctively. It was Rin's strong hand, and she let go as soon as she realized it, embarrassed for her timidity.

"I've got everything set up," continued the man. "Come on in."

Maru had never felt such reluctance to enter a room, but she had no choice. Rin was waiting for her, and she refused to show her weakness. She found herself in a dark, dome room with two seats in the center, surrounded by a huge projection screen. There was a quiet and barely noticeable humming noise in the background, which only made the room even more eerie.

"Sit down," commanded the old man.

Maru took the left seat and looked at Rin for reassurance. His lips were squeezed tightly shut, and his hands gripped the side of the chair so tightly that his knuckles were bloodless white.

"The show will start in a moment," said the old man with a hoarse, inhuman cackle. "Enjoy!" He slammed the door behind him, and Rin and Maru were left alone.

The projection screen illuminated, and the room began to glow slightly.

Maru leaned back in her chair, trying to get comfortable, and felt something tap her arm. Rin was looking at her, extending his hand as if asking her to take it. She stared at him uncomprehendingly for a moment, and then suddenly the movie began to play.

Less than a minute in Maru seized his hand in sheer horror and held onto it for dear life. She wanted to scream, to express her emotion rather than keep it suppressed inside, but when she opened her lips nothing happened no matter how hard she tried. Her mouth was dry, and her breathing was shallow and rapid. Her eyes widened and burned, but she could not blink.

The movie became louder. The hum of the projector seemed to increase with the volume, and it nearly drove Maru crazy. She tried to close her eyes, but they were glued to the screen where all hell played out in the most extreme violence and inhuman brutality. She was dimly conscious of Rin's grip getting tighter and tighter until her fingers went numb. She felt moisture on her face, but she did not recognize its source. All her energy was concentrated on the screen and the attractive horror it presented to her. She drank in the evil and it nearly broke her.

The film lasted for only ten minutes, but for Maru it was much too long. When it was over there were tears streaming down her face, and her skin was cold as ice. Her sobs choked her, and no matter how hard she tried, she could not hold them in. She buried her face in her hands and cried, shoulders shaking heavily with every strangled breath.

After a few minutes she recovered herself, senses painfully numbed and mind almost blank. She glanced at Rin, vaguely wondering whether he had actually seen the film and what his reaction had been.

He sat frozen in his seat, hand still entwined with Maru's, staring expressionlessly at the blank screen. His face was flat as usual, but his eyes were pools of deep despair. Maru almost let go of his hand, but when she saw those painful blue eyes she shuddered and squeezed it tighter. Rin, she realized with sudden horror, was suicidal. And it was no wonder. Death and forgetfulness were certainly better than the things they had just seen.

"Don't do it," she whispered. "Don't, please, Rin, don't!"

Whether he understood her or not, he did not look at her.

The door squeaked open and the old man came inside, cackling softly. "How did you enjoy the experience?" he asked, shining a flashlight in their faces. Satisfied with the result, he curled his lips into a cruel, thin smile. "Always the same reaction," he said. "Rin is priceless with that blank stare. You'd think nothing ever affected him but get past that scary mask of his and you'll see for sure. In fact, watch this." He put his hand on Rin's shoulder, leaned close to his face, and said, "Rin?"

The reaction was immediate and spectacular. Rin shot up from his seat and slammed the old man violently against the wall, twisting his wrists painfully around in an apparent attempt to defend himself. He obviously had no idea what he was doing. A few seconds later he let go, backed up with a confused expression, and sank back into his chair, shaking in every limb.

"Why did you do that?" cried Maru to the old man. "Why did you hurt him like that?"

"It's funny, isn't it?" laughed the twisted creature. "Struggling against the pain. He'll never win. And neither will you!"

Rin seized her arm and pulled her toward the door. The old man did not try to stop them, but called, "Come back and I'll have some more fun with you!"

The bright sunlight outside seemed to wash away Maru's memory of that horrible theatre. When she closed her eyes, a series of images from the movie flashed across her vision, and she immediately opened them again. Her breathing evened out, and her hands stopped trembling. It was over. There was still beauty somewhere in the world. Death had not won everything yet. She took a few deep breaths to calm herself, and then remembered—Rin.

She spun around in a confused circle, looking in every direction. He had completely vanished.

Vaguely remembering her apprehensions in the theatre, she nearly panicked. "Rin!" she cried. "Rin, please, answer me!"

"Can I help you?" said a quiet voice behind her.

She froze suddenly. "S-Saito," she stammered.

He walked casually around in front of her. "Don't worry about Rin," he said drily. "I've had multiple people tell me that he's suicidal, and nothing has ever happened. He'll be fine."

Maru wondered how he had known the cause of her fear.

"How was the experience?"

The word brought back a vivid memory of the old man, the dark theatre, Rin's hand, the faint hum of the projector. She buried her head in her hands as the best alternative to showing Saito her tears.

"I thought so," he said calmly. "It's the same for all of us. At least you didn't have to do it alone."

"Does anyone—ever do it alone?" asked Maru, trying to keep her voice steady.

"I did," replied Saito. "And so did Rin. Multiple times."

He sat down on a nearby bench and crossed his arms, resting his chin on his chest. "We all wish we could kill ourselves, but at the same time, we're too scared. What's the point in dying if death doesn't bring rest? So we live in uncertainty. And you will, too, for the rest of your life."

"Don't!" cried Maru desperately. "No more!"

"Try not to think," advised Saito, looking at her from the corners of his eyes. "Thinking only makes it worse. Don't ask questions. Accept things as they are. They're never going to get better, and if you take it too much to heart, you'll end up like Rin. Suicidal."

"He's—he's not going to kill himself, is he?" sniffled Maru.

"No." Saito stood up. "I'll go look for him."

"Don't leave me alone!" The words came out before Maru could think.

"Come with me then." Maru thought she could detect a very sad but sincere smile on his face. "I told you that you can always talk to me. In fact, I'd like that."

"You said not to think. I don't want to say anything about it. I'll remember everything if I do."

"True."

They walked along in silence for a while until Maru grew desperate. "Where are we going?" she asked as casually as she could.

"To the bridge," was Saito's short answer.

"What bridge?"

Saito pointed ahead, and Maru sighed in relief. She had been imagining a huge bridge where Rin could easily jump and kill himself, but this was a small stone bridge over a pond. Sure enough, Rin was leaning against the edge, looking down at the fish.

"Why don't you talk to him?" suggested Saito. "You seem to get along well. Just bring him back to the cafeteria and he'll be fine like he always is."

"What—what am I going to say?"

"Whatever comes into your head. I need to finish some paperwork before noon. I'll see you later." Saito turned away abruptly and left Maru standing near the edge of the bridge. She took one step toward him to call him back, then looked hesitantly at Rin.

"So inconsistent!" she muttered. "Just yesterday he said not to be alone with him . . . " She looked back sharply. There were plenty of places Saito could be watching from. Then she laughed nervously at herself and stepped onto the bridge.

Rin did not look up as she approached, so she continued until she was standing right next to him. She leaned against the wall and looked up at him, trying to break his fixed gaze.

"Saito—asked me to talk to you," she said after a long pause. "I don't know exactly what's going on, but I saw the look on your face when—" The images rushed back into her head and she shuddered. "Please don't!" she cried. "Don't kill yourself, Rin! I need your help with this!"

Rin turned his head to look at her.

Maru cursed herself for her weakness, but she could not stop her tears. She buried her head in her hands and tried not to let her shoulders shake. She felt a hand on her shoulder, and in surprise she looked up to Rin. He was smiling gloomily at her, the words of comfort that refused to come out of his mouth written on his face.

"You won't do it," said Maru mechanically. "Please tell me you won't kill yourself and make me go through this by myself."

Rin nodded and squeezed her shoulder.

"Thank you." Maru blushed suddenly. Why on earth was she asking this man she had never met until two days ago—? "I'm sorry," she said. "I'm such a wimp. Let's just go back to the cafeteria."

She turned to leave, but Rin's grip on her shoulder tightened and she turned back around. He held her there for a minute, his smile gone, his face expressionless, then released her. He bowed his head in apology, then motioned toward the cafeteria.

*****   *****   *****

"Are you okay?" asked Kita at lunch. "You look pretty pale."

"You would be, too." Maru avoided her eyes.

"SAS training?" asked Naito. "Don't worry. You'll get used to it."

"What in heaven's name are they doing it for?" asked Maru sullenly. "I wouldn't blame Rin if he did commit suicide. Those images will never go away."

"If you're thinking like that, you need to ask for antidepressants," said Kita quietly. "The point of SAS training is to make sure you're ready to handle extreme violence if necessary. Also, studies have shown that recruits with SAS training make better assassins than those without it. It is important and necessary, but you certainly shouldn't be talking about suicide just because of a video."

"How can you say that when you've seen it yourself?" asked Maru.

"The videos they show you are different," said Naito. "Sounds like mine were comparatively mild."

"Mine were mostly psychological or medical," said Kita. "Murder mysteries, procedures, stuff like that."

"Mine weren't," said Maru. "They were—they were—" The images blurred in her mind, and she could not sort them out. "I don't know. I don't want to know."

"Let's talk about something else," Kita began, but Maru interrupted her. "What's the point in talking about something else? We're going to come back to this subject eventually. All this does is help us avoid it for a little while. I need answers. I need an explanation."

"An explanation—?"

"Don't ask." Maru subsided, suddenly ashamed.

"Excuse me," Saito looked up from his watch display. "One of you needs to go sit with Rin."

"What for?" asked Naito. "Why doesn't he come over here?"

"Because he's an introvert. Who's it going to be?"

"I'll go," said Maru, happy to escape the group.

"Thank you."

She gathered her plates and put them on a tray, then looked around the cafeteria. Rin was sitting alone at a table near the window, as usual, and Maru hurried to join him.

What do I say? She stared at the top of his dark head. *How can I help him reply?*

He glanced up at her and smiled, moving his plates out of the way so she could sit across from him.

Maru said aloud, "I need to explain about the note."

He nodded.

"You wrote it, didn't you?"

He nodded again.

"I'm sorry I couldn't do it," she said. "I understand now what you wanted and why. Last night Kita took me to talk with Saito, and he said that he wouldn't grant any exemptions."

Rin's eyes darkened. He reached in his pocket and pulled out a notebook. In it he wrote: "Where is the note? And what did he say?" and passed it to Maru.

"He took the note and crumpled it up," she explained. "And he told me never to ask for something like that again."

"Did he know I wrote the note?" scribbled Rin.

"He recognized your handwriting," replied Maru aloud.

Rin's finger tapped the notebook as if he were considering writing something else, but instead he put the pen down and nodded.

"Rin . . ." asked Maru. "What's your relationship with Saito? Do you guys know each other?"

Rin raised one eyebrow and picked up the pen. "Why do you ask?" he wrote.

"I don't know. Saito seems to have a grudge against you for some reason. I'm probably overthinking this, and I'm just curious, so you don't have to answer. I'm sorry. I'm meddling."

Rin shook his head, picked up the pen, and chewed thoughtfully on the tip. Finally, he wrote, "I've known him for a while."

"Oh." Maru could think of nothing else to say.

Rin continued writing. "We don't get along very well, but I don't think he hates me."

"Oh . . . good then," said Maru a little desperately.

Rin smiled and wrote, "Why are you curious about me?"

"I don't know—I mean, I'm not—that is, I am, but it's not creepy or anything." Maru shut her lips tightly, deciding that it was better to say nothing than to make the confusion worse.

"Tell me about you," wrote Rin.

"I . . . I'm Maru," she began idiotically.

Rin's smile widened, and he rested his chin on his hand.

"I came to Rigel because I wanted to fight the Kalideyes." Maru cursed herself for this lie. "Actually, it was really because I was scared. I don't like how you can't tell who they are. I thought it would be safer here and that I could at least do something to help. Now I don't think I'm very useful. I'm not made for this. I hate violence. I'm easily scared. I don't want to kill—people or not-people. I hate this. All of it. I—" She paused in horror at how much she had said. "I . . . talk too much," she finished with a weak laugh.

Rin shook his head. His face was serious but not expressionless as usual.

Maru understood that he wanted her to keep going, but she was too embarrassed. "I've made an idiot out of myself all day," she said aloud. "I apologize. I know you don't like hearing people talk."

Rin reached for the pen. "That's not true."

"What about you? Is there anything you want to say?" Maru searched desperately for a way to change the subject. "Why don't you ever talk? Is it because you can't? Or—oh, my mouth. Please, you don't have to answer that!"

Rin scribbled a single word and handed her the paper. "Weakness."

Maru looked up at him in amazement. He was staring levelly at her, smiling, but there was nothing happy in his expression. He twitched the notebook from her hands and continued writing. "I'm sorry if I hurt you yesterday. I don't remember what happened at all. I only know because Saito said something about it."

"It's okay," stammered Maru. "It's my fault. I . . . I called you by name and touched your shoulder. Saito said you don't like that. I'm sorry."

"It's my fault if I can't control myself," he wrote, pressing the pen hard into the paper.

"Kita mentioned there were some medicines you could take," suggested Maru shyly. Rin shook his head and made no attempt to elaborate.

"What training do we have this afternoon?" asked Maru brightly. "Let me see . . . " She pulled up her watch display. "Shooting again. Are you going to be there?"

Rin nodded.

"Good . . . " Maru could think of nothing else to say.

Rin picked up the paper and pen. "The best friend is the one you don't have to worry about entertaining." He handed it back to her with a smile.

"Are you saying that I don't have to talk so much?" Maru laughed in spite of herself. "Let's just coexist peacefully then, as friends."

Rin smiled and put the notebook back in his pocket.

Maru continued eating her lunch, deeply regretting how much she had been talking. "I always say the wrong thing," she whispered to herself. "Keep your mouth shut. It's the only way to make friends. Keep your mouth shut."

The notebook appeared under her nose. "What are you saying?" Rin had written.

Maru blushed. "I'm—just—talking to myself," she said lamely, avoiding eye contact.

Rin took the notebook back and began scribbling. In a few moments he handed it back to Maru.

Messily written under his previous note was: "You know that people like it when you ask them questions. It gives them the opportunity to open up if they want to. If they don't want to, they won't answer and if they get mad it won't be your fault."

"Would you get mad?" asked Maru curiously.

Rin shook his head. "No," his lips mouthed silently.

"Thanks," said Maru shyly. "But I really should learn to control my mouth more. I talk too much . . . make too much noise . . . you name it."

"Don't silence yourself," wrote Rin briefly; then, without further explanation, he picked up his tray and went to the sanitization station. Maru was left staring at him wide-eyed, wondering what he meant.

CHAPTER 6

"Stamina!" cried the instructor. "The art of working hard without stopping for the longest amount of time possible. It's obviously important for your kind of work. Today we're going to warm up with a one-mile run, then try some combat training."

"Warm up with a one-mile run," Maru repeated to herself with a sigh. "What a novelty." It was the first class of the day, and she was not quite awake yet.

"Did I hear you say something?" inquired the instructor menacingly.

Maru snapped to attention. "No, sir!"

"You may begin with fifty pushups—twenty-five for mouthing off, and twenty-five for telling a lie. The rest of you, follow me!" He trotted onto the track.

Rin winked as he passed, and Maru felt instantly better.

When the instructor had reached the opposite end of the track, she allowed herself to fall onto her stomach and relax her tense muscles. She closed her eyes and buried her fingers deep in the soft grass, trying to get the most out of her brief respite. Something sounded in her ears, something she could not immediately place. She hummed the rhythm quietly to herself, repeating it over and over until suddenly the words occurred to her: "Don't silence yourself. Don't silence yourself." And the voice in her head that spoke them was deep and rough and masculine—Rin's.

Am I dreaming? She snapped her eyes open. *Rin doesn't talk. Rin has never talked. I've never heard his voice . . . he probably doesn't even have one anymore.*

Don't silence yourself.

"What does that mean?" cried Maru, pinning her hands over her ears. "Why should I listen to that?"

Don't silence yourse—

"What are you doing?" an aggressive voice shouted. Maru instinctively leapt to her feet. "Laying there like a princess in her garden day-dreaming away! Get your rear end up here and get moving!"

Maru obeyed the instructor without hesitation, and the mysterious ragged voice slowly faded away.

It was when the training was finally over, and Maru dropped exhaustedly on the bench, that it recurred.

Don't silence yourself, it insisted repetitively, with exactly the same intonation every time. *Don't silence yourself.*

"I won't, okay?" said Maru aloud. "I have no idea what that means, but I won't. I won't silence myse—" She cut herself off abruptly as Rin approached.

His pale skin was moist with sweat, but his breathing was regular and steady. Maru wondered enviously how he could be so immune to the rough training. Casually, thinking about this, she put the voice to the back of her mind.

"Rin!" she called, running up to him. "How come you don't look tired at all?"

He had just buried his head in a towel, and only his eyes looked out at her in mild confusion.

"Ah—sorry." Maru backed away. "Didn't mean to interrupt."

He removed the towel and smiled, the closest he could ever come to a laugh. Playfully he swatted at her with it, waving it around his head like a lasso.

Maru chuckled. "Aren't you tired at all?"

Rin nodded and put the towel on the bench. He fished around in his pocket, produced a small plastic tube, and opened it at one end. A small tablet fell out into his hand, and he presented it to Maru.

"Umm . . . " she said. "What's this?"

He handed her the plastic tube and pointed to the label.

"Enhancing minerals," she read aloud. "You put this in your water?"

Rin nodded.

"And it makes you not tired?"

He shrugged uncertainly and smiled.

"Do you mean for me to try it?" asked Maru. Privately she wondered who in their right mind would give someone a tablet to put in their drink and expect them to use it.

Rin nodded again.

"Okay . . . thanks," she said, smothering a laugh. "I'll take it with me." She put it in her pocket.

Rin seemed satisfied and buried his face back in his towel.

The instructor approached, and Rin threw the towel over his shoulder. "You're both good," said the instructor abruptly, looking back and forth between Maru and Rin. "Don't get carried away. This is not a compliment—it's the standard around here. I think if you work extremely hard, you might be able to do better than the others. No guarantees, of course, and it's up to you. But I'd like to see you try." He turned on his heel and left them staring after him.

Rin looked questioningly at Maru. "I dunno," she said. "What exactly does he want from us?"

Rin shrugged and picked up his water bottle. His expression clearly interrogated Maru.

"I'm ready," she said hastily in reply. "What's next?"

She loaded her watch display and read the schedule. "SAS . . . ?" Her mouth went dry. "We have it again today?"

Rin looked calmly over her shoulder and nodded.

"I don't want to go back!" she cried, looking at Rin as if she expected him to have an answer. "They'll break me. I swear they will!"

Rin put a hand on each of her shoulders and squeezed—gently, soothingly. It was his only way of reassuring her, and it worked. Maru's breath slowed and she took a deep breath, swallowing the tears that had almost shamed her. "I'm sorry," she said. "I've said that so many times today. It just goes to show that I shouldn't be here."

She shook Rin's hands off and turned to face him. "Who do I ask about resigning?"

Rin's face was impassive.

"Who, Rin? Tell me!"

Rin mouthed something incomprehensible and turned away.

"You can't get away that easily!" cried Maru. "Tell me!"

Rin's back registered nothing, and he continued walking away from her.

"I'll stop you if I have to!" Maru ran after him. "Rin—ahh!" She paused in astonishment.

Rin had turned around suddenly and wrapped his arms around her in a giant bear hug. She was so startled that she froze; he squeezed her so tightly that she could barely breathe. For several seconds they stood there, perfectly still, Maru a little frightened, Rin doing his best to convey what he could never say aloud. Then he let her go and smiled down at her.

"What—was that?" gasped Maru, taking several steps back and gasping for breath.

Rin closed his eyes and smiled even wider, although he never opened his lips. Maru was caught off guard by how genuinely and angelically sweet he looked. Then the smile faded, and his intense eyes opened, and he was once more the assassin Saito had warned her against learning to admire.

He motioned for her to follow, and together, silently, they set out for the SAS building.

What—why? Why in the world did he do that? Does he even know what happened? I didn't touch him when I called his name, so he wasn't having an episode of—PTSD or whatever he has.

She absently felt her shoulders where Rin had squeezed them. It had felt good. And she had liked it . . . just a little

Suddenly she realized that Rin was no longer in front of her. She turned abruptly and found him holding the SAS door open, looking rather puzzled.

"Oh . . ." she stammered.

As she approached the door, she felt her skin shiver and freeze. Her eyes widened, her breathing quickened, her hands shook. One ten-minute session had been enough to curse her with this involuntary horror, and she wasn't even inside.

She forced herself to walk forward and enter the theatre. Mechanically she sat down in the chair on the left and closed her eyes. This time, she swore to herself, she wouldn't look. She would close her ears and eyes and keep them closed no matter what. Nothing could tempt her to look at the screen. Nothing—nothing.

Then the film began.

The projector hummed, the horrible sounds echoed, and she could hear them despite her attempts to block everything out. She opened her mouth and found herself screaming in despair. Something touched and enveloped her hand, warming it and comforting it, but somehow the touch felt to her like ice. She jerked her hand away and accidentally opened her eyes. Once they were open, she knew she could never close them again.

Death was all she saw. It was the death of everything in millions of grue-somely creative ways. Those who lived died a more horrible death than the real corpses, because they had to go on living after what they had seen. They killed themselves and each other in an attempt to deaden the pain. Despair only survived. They tried to blind themselves, and it only made the visions more real. They tried to die, and only lived on in pain. Nothing worked. There was no cure for hell like this. It was endless and lurid and completely out of their control. They compensated by cursing horribly, inviting and sheltering evil of the darkest description, making bonds they could not keep in the hope that something would change. It only got worse. Maru was sick. The last face appeared on the screen, twisted, alive but half-dead, laughing and smiling in a demonic frenzy of evil joy. At last Maru was able to wrench her eyes away and stop her ears with her fingers. And then the film ended.

She looked up cautiously, panting and trying desperately to focus her eyes. Rin was still next to her, face buried in his hands, tears glittering brightly in the half-light, dripping from his fingertips. He shook uncontrollably.

Maru suddenly felt an intense pity for him. With it came a deep hatred for those who had broken Rin to the point where he could no longer hide his deeply buried pain. These two emotions—sympathy and hatred—temporarily blotted out her fear, and she thought only of what she could do to rescue Rin. In the film there was only death and despair. But this was humanity, and here there was life and hope. There had to be.

One phrase came to her mind, and she repeated it over and over. "Don't silence yourself. Don't silence yourself! Rin, listen to me! Don't silence yourself!" She had no idea what she was trying to say, but inside she knew those were the only words that would help her friend.

Rin let his hair fall over his face and conceal his eyes. Immediately she pushed it away and repeated herself: "Don't silence yourself."

Her hands fell from Rin's face, and she burst out crying. She backed away, trembling.

When at last she controlled herself, she saw Rin on his knees in front of her, calmly drying his own tears with the corner of his shirt. When he looked up at her, he smiled. It was horribly artificial, but it meant that he had not yet given up trying.

He stood up and playfully tugged her ponytail. Ordinarily Maru would have laughed, but at the pull she had a horrible mental vision of one of those ruined people trying to drag her down to the pit of their misery and gruesome death. Instinctively she stepped away and slapped him as hard as she could.

Rin put a thoughtful hand to his red cheek and sighed. He mouthed an apology, but Maru did not care. "Get away from me!" she yelled shrilly. "You devil—you twisted, sick thing—get away from me!"

Rin retired quickly to the door and bowed his head, hiding his eyes again. This time they were perfectly dry, but they were far sadder than they had been before. They were perfect pools of despair, the kind that is not dead but alive and deadly in its effects. There was absolutely no hope in them. Looking into Rin's eyes was like looking through a window into the deepest parts of hell, completely Godless and endless. He opened the door and slipped out like a shadow.

After a few minutes of tense silence, Maru looked up and blinked. "Rin?" The room was empty except for herself. "Rin?"

A confused memory of what she had said to him filtered into her mind, and she was horrified. She looked at her hand, wondering if she had really dared to hit him. Overwhelmed with guilt, she stumbled toward the door and stepped outside.

I hurt him.

Instinct told Maru that Rin had entirely lost control of himself and his emotions, and it was easy to deduce what he would try to do. She had to stop him, because this was her fault. She hurt him. Where had he gone? She looked right and left in despairing confusion.

"Where would I go if I wanted to . . . ?" Her gaze snapped to the rooftop gardens above the cafeteria. The building was several stories high, and access to the roof was permitted at all times. Rin would be alone up there. Rin would be—

"Stop!" she screamed and took off running.

The few recruits she passed stared at her in astonishment, wondering if she had gone suddenly crazy. She did not notice them. Her whole attention was focused on that building, slowly growing larger and larger in her field of vision. Rin would be on the back side, of course. The front was too public. The back—there was a large water reservoir which would hide all traces. She shuddered and ran faster.

She darted up the stairs two at a time, ignoring the security guard who wanted to see her pass. There was no time. She prayed desperately to no one that Rin would really be up there and that she would find him before it was too late.

Once on top, she stared around in dismay. The chairs, the plants, the statue—what statue?

Poised atop the wall on the back side of the building was a perfectly still figure, which Maru had assumed was some sort of iron statue. It was not. It was Rin. He was perfectly still except for his long hair, which blew around his face in the gentle summer breeze. The toes of his shoes were exactly aligned with the edge of the wall, and he swayed without fighting to keep his balance.

"Rin! No!" Before Maru had thought, she was up on the wall beside him. "Stop it, Rin! I need you here! Your team needs you! And you can't do this to us!"

He did not seem to hear her.

In desperation she grabbed his wrist and tried to pull him to safety. He was anchored like a rock, and nothing she could do seemed to rouse him at all. He still stared vacantly at the horizon, swaying dangerously, asking with wide-open eyes for Death to remove his memory. She reached up as high as she dared and pulled his hair sharply. Still he did not move.

"I don't want to do this to you," she screamed, hoping he would hear her. "But I don't want you to die!" She jumped down from the wall, grabbed his wrist, and yelled at the top of her lungs, "Rin!"

All her pulling and speeches had effected nothing, but this one shout did more than she could have imagined. Rin stumbled backwards, thankfully, missing the wall and falling toward her. Everything seemed suddenly slow. She reached up to catch him, foolishly hoping she could somehow stay upright herself. His weight pushed her into the ground and knocked the breath out of her, and for a moment she was convinced she was going to die immediately. After several seconds of breathless panting she crawled out from under him, rolling him off her like a log. She shook herself off, took yet another deep, calming breath, and looked back at him.

There was blood on the ground, and Maru saw a large wet spot in his hair. He had hit his head hard on the pavement when he fell and was unconscious, sleeping peacefully on the ground, completely forgetful of the pain a few moments ago. His face looked so momentarily happy that Maru hated to try waking him. It would be then he would remember what he had just tried to do.

She pulled up her watch display and was about to call for medical help when she saw his eyes lazily blink open. He raised himself slowly, first to his elbows, then to his hands, and finally he stood up. He was unsteady, and he did not seem to see Maru.

"Rin?" she whispered nervously.

He looked back at her in uncomprehending astonishment.

"Are you okay?" Maru was still whispering. "Do you remember . . . what you just did?"

Rin rubbed his head, and his hand came away bloody. He glanced at it for a second, then sighed deeply. Obviously, he remembered.

"I don't want you to leave." Maru stepped toward him and met his eyes, holding them locked to her own. "I need you here. Your whole team needs you here. Don't die, please, Rin."

He ducked his head and brushed past her. She heard his feet clattering down the stairs to the cafeteria.

"Rin," she whispered, sliding down the wall to a sitting position. "Please don't hate me. I did the best I could."

She raised her head to the sky and squinted in the strong light. "What does all this mean?" she asked nobody in particular. "Why does violence like that have to exist? Why does pain like this have to exist? And if Rin had killed himself . . . would that have made him forget?"

Maru had tried to convince herself that death was sleep, but the comparison made no sense because she did not know what sleep was. She usually defined it as "lack of consciousness," but without consciousness, what was there? If you didn't know what was going on around you, did it matter if you forgot what happened before? Was death the beginning of a new life, or was it simply the end? She shivered. There was a horrible finality to that thought.

The rooftop door swung open, and Naito appeared, closely followed by his shadow Kita. They were carrying heavy trays, laughing, talking, pretending that evil didn't exist. They caught sight of her sitting against the wall and stopped abruptly.

"Maru? Are you okay?" Kita asked, running lightly up to her and touching her shoulder. "Why are you up here?"

"Rin was up here, too, a few minutes ago," commented Naito. "What were you two doing?"

Maru winced at the direct question. "We were—we were—having an argument," she lied.

"No," said Kita firmly. "You couldn't possibly have argued with somebody who can't speak. Did Rin hurt you?"

Maru did not reply, and Kita walked past her. "There's blood on the ground," she observed. "Yours or Rin's?"

"Rin's."

"Did you try to murder him?" asked Naito with wide eyes.

Maru shook her head silently.

"Be honest," said Kita after a thorough inspection. "Rin came up here to kill himself, didn't he? And you tried to stop him?"

"What?" asked Naito. "Why do you think that?"

"Rin and Maru had SAS training this afternoon," said Kita. "As I'm a psychologist, I've known for a while that Rin is suicidal. Finding him and Maru on a rooftop eight stories from the ground doesn't surprise me at all."

"You're right," interrupted Maru. "But don't tell him I told you. When we were in SAS training, I . . . I called him some awful names and slapped him. I didn't realize what I was doing, but when I figured it out, he had run away. I was scared about what he might do, so I came up here, and he was standing on the back wall above the reservoir."

"He would," muttered Kita.

"He was swaying, and he almost fell. I managed to get him back, but he hit his head and knocked himself out. That's where the blood came from."

"I see," said Kita, staring hard at Maru with none of her usual flippancy. "You're not thinking of killing yourself, too, are you?"

"I don't see why not," said Maru seriously. "But I don't see why either."

"You need to be prescribed antidepressants, now," said Kita. "I'll take you to the infirmary."

"Are you just going to leave Naito here?" asked Maru drily.

"I'll wait for you." He waved cheerfully, but his face was anxious.

Maru followed Kita automatically down the stairs, out the cafeteria door, and down the sidewalk to the hospital. Kita exchanged some mysterious dialogue with a white-clad pharmacist behind a sterile counter, and then shoved a plastic bottle of pills into Maru's hand.

"Take one of these, every six hours," she said. "Make sure you do it regularly. And . . . " She paused.

"What?" asked Maru.

"They're addictive, so make sure you don't increase the dosage without asking."

"What are you trying to do, turn me into a drug addict?" Maru put the bottle back on the counter. "Give me something else. I don't want this."

"We don't have anything else that works for the specific stress caused by SAS training," explained the pharmacist, leaning out over the desk. "It's highly unlikely that you'll get addicted to them, and even if you do, it's not that difficult to break it. Trust me, these are safe to take."

Maru looked at the bottle in disgust. "No."

"I'll have you removed from the team on the grounds of instability if you don't," threatened Kita. "One member trying to kill himself is enough."

"Why don't you force him to take the drugs, too?"

"He's tried them before and he claims they don't work," said Kita. "I'm done arguing with him. But I can save your life, and I mean to do it."

Maru was long past caring. She shook one pill out of the bottle and swallowed it obligingly.

"Good. Keep doing that." Kita was satisfied. "Now let's go eat lunch."

"No offense, Kita." Maru chose her words carefully. "I think I'd rather not go back with you. I need to talk to Rin. I need to apologize."

"Fine by me." Kita smiled and squeezed her eyes shut. Suddenly, as Maru was turning to leave, she snapped them open again. "Maru! Wait!" she cried, running after her. "There's something you should know."

"What?" Maru stopped.

"Rin . . ." Kita stared at her speechlessly.

"What is it? What about him?"

Kita smiled slyly. "Never mind," she chirped. "You'll find out eventually."

"That's not nice."

"I think it's best. You should listen to your psychologist!" Kita waltzed past her and out the door.

Maru shook her head in disgust and slowly followed her. She had no idea where to look for Rin if he wasn't in the cafeteria, and she had no idea where else he liked to be. She walked slowly down the sidewalk, thinking, and suddenly found herself face-to-face with him.

He handed her his notebook. "I'm so sorry," was written in large, scrawled letters.

"Be honest with me," said Maru. "Were you trying to kill yourself?"

Rin slowly took the notebook back and started writing. A moment later he scribbled out what he had written and started over, writing rapidly and messily. Then he gave it back to her.

"I wasn't, I was just—" had all been written and then violently scribbled over. The note itself said, "You're right, I was. Thank you for saving me. I owe you more than I can ever repay, besides an apology for how I treated you. I didn't mean for you to ever find me."

He dropped to his knees and touched his forehead to the sidewalk in deep, sincere apology.

"Stop!" cried Maru. She knelt beside him. "Get up, you idiot. This is all my fault for the horrible things I said to you. I'm so stupid and thoughtless, I don't know what I was doing. I told you I let my mouth run away with me. Please forgive me, Rin!" She also touched her head to the pavement, and then they sat up and looked at each other, embarrassed.

Rin's mouth broke into a slight smile. He stood up and offered his hand to Maru, pulling her firmly to her feet. Then he put his hand on the back of his head, displayed the blood dripping from it, and pointed to the hospital.

"Why on earth did you stop and talk to me?" demanded Maru. "You're bleeding all over the place."

Rin shrugged and smiled like a mischievous child.

"I'll come with you," said Maru, but Rin shook his head and pointed to her watch. "The schedule?" She pulled up her display and read it. "I have an eye color test?"

Rin nodded.

"Ugh, no lunch break?"

Rin pointed left with his thumb.

"After the test, you mean. I guess that's okay." She looked up at him. "Rin, are you okay?"

He nodded.

"Don't bother asking," said a stiff voice from behind them. Maru jumped in surprise, but Rin only closed his eyes and did not bother to look. "How many times have you tried to kill yourself, Rin? Is it five now?"

"S-Saito!" stammered Maru.

"He always backs down at the last minute. I've stopped worrying about it now."

Rin's eyes darkened, and he swung at Saito's nose.

The team leader ducked and smiled bitterly. "I should have you put under house arrest, Rin," he said. "But in consideration of what you did for me, I will not."

Rin deliberately turned his back on Saito and walked toward the hospital.

"I'm sorry you have to be involved in this," said Saito coldly to Maru. "Will you walk with me to your eye color test?"

Maru had a vivid image of Saito covered with icicles, and she nearly choked on her smothered laughter. "Yes—yes," she said, unable to think of another answer. But suddenly she felt her hand seized from behind.

She glanced uncertainly over her shoulder and saw Rin, still bleeding, glaring angrily at Saito from his eerily blue eyes. His hand that touched hers was smeared with blood, and she tried to pull it away. But Rin would not let go. He spoke to Saito with his eyes, and Saito understood perfectly.

"Hurt her and I'll kill you," said Saito quietly, then turned and walked quickly away.

Rin stood perfectly still for a moment, still holding Maru's hand. Then, with a sigh and head bowed in apology, he let go.

Maru was irritated. "There's blood all over me!" she complained, holding up her red hand. "What was that for?"

Rin, of course, did not answer, but bowed again humbly.

"I'll wash my hands in the hospital, I guess," she said, with extra annoyance in her voice. "But I'm going to be late for my eye test."

Rin motioned for her to hurry and follow him. Reluctantly she obeyed, and he led her into the hospital and down the long white hallway to a bathroom on the left.

She scrubbed the blood from her hand, puzzling over what Rin had intended to communicate to Saito. Those two, she had noticed, obviously disliked each other, but they talked often and there was mutual understanding between them. Why did she have to be involved?

Absently she wrapped a paper towel around her hand, looking dispiritedly at herself in the mirror. She was very pretty, with light brown hair and very dark features, but she was exhausted, and it showed on her face. She rubbed at the dark circles under her eyes, willing them to disappear, but they only stood out blacker against her pale skin and gave her raccoon eyes. Irritably she threw the paper towel into the trash can and walked out into the hallway.

Rin was lying at full length on the floor, and she nearly stepped on him. "Gahh!" she shouted, jumping back. "Rin? What are you—?" Then she realized that he had fainted.

"Somebody! Help!" she cried, and two nurses came running. Between the three of them they managed to convey Rin to the nearest room and stretch him out on the table. A few seconds after they did, he revived, blinked, and immediately passed out again.

"He has a head wound," explained Maru. When the nurses asked her why, she lied shamelessly: "He got hurt in training. I think he fell and hit his head on something, but I didn't really see it happen."

Now that Rin was taken care of, she finally set out for her eye appointment. By this time, she was very late, and the doctor was not pleased to see her. "Please don't repeat this behavior," he said severely. "I'm going to do my best to fit you in today, but don't expect too much."

Maru sat in the waiting room for an hour before the doctor managed to find time to take her blood. It was another half hour before the results came back: Maru's eyes, despite their gray appearance, were genetically blue, which proved her identity as pure human. She was allowed to go after a few more reprimands from the doctor and his whole staff, and she scurried out of the room with a feeling of deep relief.

"Maaa-ru!" shouted a cheerful voice. Maru's heart sank. It was Kita. "I thought you'd be in there forever! I've been waiting and waiting and waiting to take you to dinner with me and Naito. I—"

"Don't you want to go on a date with Naito or something? Something by yourself?" asked Maru sharply. Instantly she regretted it and tried to think of something mild and apologetic to add, but nothing came to mind.

But Kita, whether with childish innocence or great tact, simply laughed. "I thought you'd feel left out if we did that," she said. "Of course, I'd like to have dinner alone with Naito—not that he's my boyfriend or anything, but we've known each other for a while. Sure you won't mind?"

"Not at all," said Maru, relieved. She could spend the evening alone, perhaps reading one of Kita's books or stealing cookies from her cabinets. "You two have fun. I don't want to be a third wheel."

"Okay then!" Kita laughed and waved. "See you later!"

Maru felt that it was distinctly unfair to be rude or sarcastic around Kita, since she seemed completely oblivious to any intended insult. But for some reason, she was feeling rather malicious and she could not resist shouting after her, "I hope you get all your talking done with him!"

Then she fled.

*****   *****   *****

Maru made herself a box of food gathered from the cafeteria and took it to her dorm room, intending to eat it alone and quietly. The bookshelf awaited her, and she had been eyeing a box of French biscuits on Kita's top shelf. It would be a quiet evening, and Maru felt desperately in need of some rest.

She let herself into the apartment and switched on the lights. Her desk, at the far left corner of the room, was covered with papers, computers, and books from her training and research projects. She put her food on the counter and sighed, not wanting to move it all. Then she glanced at Kita's desk. It was surprisingly neat and Spartan, devoid of figurines and other knickknacks. In fact, there were only three things on its clean white surface; a leather book, a pen, and a pill bottle.

Maru swept them to the side and replaced them with her dinner. Leisurely she selected a book from the pink shelf, curled her legs under her in Kita's furry desk chair, and slowly started eating.

About half an hour later she looked up, resting her eyes from the dim light and small letters. Immediately the pill bottle caught her attention, and she realized that she had forgotten to take her second dose of medicine. It was about time. She fished the bottle out of her pocket and swallowed one of the little tabs, accidentally letting it melt in her mouth and wincing at the bitter taste. She put the bottle on her desk and absently returned to Kita's.

Why was Kita on medications? She was always so cheerful; surely she never struggled with depression. Maybe she had periodic stomachaches. Maru laughed at herself for her ridiculous ideas and picked up the bottle to read the label.

"Don't touch that!" A hand came between her and the bottle and jerked it away. Kita stood trembling, clutching the bottle tightly in her right hand, hugging it to her chest as if it was some priceless treasure. "This is who I am now," she said, shivering. "This is the real me!"

"I'm sorry!" Maru backed away. "I was just curious to know if you were taking the same med—"

"And who told you to mess with the things on my desk?" Kita's normally gentle, smiling face was twisted into an angry snarl. "Did you read the book? Did you read it? Answer me!"

"No!" cried Maru. "Of course not!"

Kita's hold on the pill bottle relaxed slightly, and she dropped her hands to her side. "I'm sorry, too," she said breathlessly. "Someday I'll explain, but not—right—now." She sat down weakly in a chair and laughed. "That makes an interesting end of the evening."

"I really should apologize," said Maru. "I didn't mean to mess with anything."

"It's okay. If I didn't want you to see it, I shouldn't have left it out." Kita wrapped herself in a blanket and rested her chin on her knees. "But let's talk about something else."

"How . . . how was dinner with Naito?" asked Maru conversationally.

"It was fun." Kita laughed nervously. "You might be surprised to know that we talked about you and Rin most of the time."

"Why do you say that like it's one word? Youandrin?" asked Maru suspiciously.

Kita affected surprise. "Well, it's going to be, isn't it?"

"The day Naito becomes your boyfriend is the day you can say our names together."

"Fine then!" Kita crossed her arms and sat up straight. "We were talking about Rin's attempted suicides and your intervention. I really think if you hadn't been there, he would have pulled it off this time."

"Saito mentioned that he's tried this before."

"Four times previously," said Kita. "The first time he tried to drown himself in the reservoir, but somebody fished him out. The second and third times he jumped off things, but succeeded in only breaking a few ribs. The fourth time he tried to overdose on antidepressants and ended up sick for a week." Kita shook her head. "I lied to you earlier when I said that Rin claims the medicines don't work. The truth is, we're too afraid to give them to him, because we're afraid he'll try to overdose again. He doesn't have much to like about life, but you—" Kita examined her thoughtfully. "You might be helping him with that."

"How?" Maru was surprised. "I'm struggling with the same questions, and I have the same stupid, meaningless answers. And I was so rude to him earlier. I'd think if anything, I'm making things worse."

"Shows how quiet Rin really is," said Kita cryptically. "You'll figure out how it works eventually. For now, just be his friend. I think you need him as much as he needs you."

"Probably."

There was a short silence, then Kita jumped up. "I'm going to bed," she said brightly. "Don't stay up all night reading my graphic novels. And don't get cookie crumbs between the pages. See you tomorrow!"

Maru waved good night, her head busily occupied with other things.

"Rin," she said to herself, leaning back on the sofa and marking her place in the book. "Why does he want to die so much?"

Even as she asked herself the question, she knew the answer. It was because of the images, the memories, and the guilt that came with them. Rin had not only watched the SAS training videos: he had been a killer himself. If he could not forgive himself, nobody else could do the job for him. He had to live with his self-hatred, cursing every new day and praying to no one that somehow the guilt would be erased. Maru wondered if it could ever really disappear. And if it couldn't, maybe it was truly better to turn amnesiac or simply fall into the void of eternal, unconscious sleep called Death.

"If death is sleep," Maru said aloud, "why does nobody ever wake up?"

With that thought she tucked herself under Kita's vacated blanket and closed her eyes, burying her face in the comfort and safety of the warm sofa pillows. She was too tired to get up and get to her bed. Almost as soon as her eyes closed, she was sound asleep.

CHAPTER 7

"Da-dee-deedle-ee, da-dee-deedle-ee-dee-dee-dee!" Maru was roughly awakened to Kita's whistle. "Time to get up!" she sang to the tune of Reveille. "It's time to get up, it's time to get up, you're already very late, and I'm not responsi-ble."

"I'm late?" Maru looked questioningly at the clock. "It's only six-thirty."

"Yes, but it's a Saturday," said Kita. "And on Saturdays, we start an hour early—at seven—but we have only a half day of training."

"Oh." It was Maru's first full week with her team, but she felt silly for not knowing the routine. "'Kay. I'll be up in a minute."

"I won't wait for you if you decide to shower!" said Kita. "Hurry up!"

Maru shook her head to clear her thoughts and threw off the blanket. Immediately as she stood up a heavy depression settled over her. Her thoughts spiraled from beauty to darkness to complete nothingness, and all she could see when she opened her eyes was Rin standing on the edge of the wall, ready to jump to death. Though she had not seen his face during the actual event, she could see it now—joyless, suffering, ashamed of the tears he had accidentally shown her.

Almost gasping with the physical heaviness of the depression, she reached drunkenly toward her desk and seized her pill bottle. She shook out two, then put one back. One was enough, and Kita had said it was dangerous to increase the dosage.

"Kalid-eyes class today!" sang Kita, who was apparently never depressed. "Lesson plan includes the three states of humanity, their various pros and cons, and—what's wrong with you?"

Maru paid no attention to Kita, lost as she was in her own painful thoughts.

"Hey! Over here!" Kita tapped her shoulder. "You look terrible. We can be a little late—come with me."

She whisked Maru into the bathroom before she had time to complain and seated her in a chair in front of the mirror. "You're going to look so cute!" she tittered, slamming a huge box onto the counter.

Maru jumped, the sound bringing her back to life. "Hey!" she cried. "What are you do—?"

Kita silenced her with a slap from a makeup wipe. "Here we go. And don't you move, or this will take longer."

"But we shouldn't be doing this at all!" protested Maru. "You just said we're going to be late, and it doesn't matter how I look."

"Yes, it does," said Kita inexorably. "We're going to do this. Shut up and let me work."

Maru sighed and gave up.

For a few minutes Kita labored in silence, applying foundation, concealer, blush, and several other unfamiliar products to Maru's face. Then she rubbed some gel into her hands and brushed it gently into Maru's long hair, replacing it when she was done into a neat ponytail. In fifteen minutes, the transformation was complete, and she stepped back with a laugh of satisfaction.

"Look!" She handed Maru a mirror.

"Oh . . . my." Maru shuddered. "I look ridiculous. We have to take this off."

"No, you don't," said Kita. "You're leaving it just like that the whole day. And I'll do it again for you tomorrow."

"Absolutely not!" Maru put the mirror on the counter and fled. "No more of this, please!"

She hurried outside, down the sidewalk, and into the cafeteria two buildings down. Naito and Rin were already sitting at the team's usual table with trays of food. Naito seemed completely oblivious to the fact that Rin was not listening to him and talked without stopping for breath.

Maru approached self-consciously, hoping they would notice no changes in her appearance. It was not to be. Naito's mouth opened wide when he saw her, and he actually stopped in the middle of his sentence to say, "Hey, Maru!"

She raised her head shyly. "It's not my fault," she mumbled. "Kita made me do it."

Rin turned around to look at her, caught her eyes, and smiled slowly. He expressed his approval with a nod, but seemed rather startled by her appearance.

"Look at Rin staring," chattered Naito. Rin immediately ducked his head. "I like it, Maru. You should do that more often."

"Never," said Maru shortly. She seated herself across from Rin and tried to pretend that she was fully absorbed in her breakfast.

A few moments later she looked up. Rin immediately looked down, but it was too late to conceal that he had been watching her a moment before. He proceeded to choke down his eggs and buried his face in his elbow, coughing silently.

"Time for training," said Naito suddenly, piling his trash on his tray and standing up. "You two ready?"

Maru gulped the last of her oatmeal and nodded. "Sure."

"Class is in the back of this building—same meeting room we used on the first day. See you there in a few minutes."

"You're not coming with us?"

"No, I'm going to check on Kita. She seems a little depressed this morning."

Maru shook her head violently. "Nope. Not at all."

Naito laughed. "Well, maybe you don't know her as well as I do. Or maybe you're not taking ADPA's."

"What's—?"

But Naito turned his back on her and walked away, whistling.

"Oh well," said Maru to herself, then added aloud, "Ready, Rin?"

He nodded and stood up, handing her his notebook.

"Your hair and makeup. I like it. You're very pretty."

Maru blushed and turned away. "Thanks," she muttered softly, then hurried to the shelter of the sanitization station.

What kind of stupid comment was that? I look ridiculous. She dropped her spoon into the box with unnecessary clatter. *I don't look pretty at all. And I don't care, either.*

Nevertheless, she felt her spirits rising at the unexpected compliment. This had begun as a horrible day, but things could only get better, and she felt that they had already done so. Now for class—Kalideyes class. That would certainly be interesting, and she would have a chance to see the other recruits whom she had been friends with before her team assignment. She smiled and set out for the classrooms.

"Hey! Mak—Maru!" she heard a voice behind her. "Wait up! Are you going to Kalideyes class?"

Maru turned around. "Ayano!" she cried. "It's so nice to see you again!"

"You, too!" Ayano hugged her. "Seriously, I've been missing you. I hate how they keep the teams isolated from each other. Tell me everything. Tell me about your team, your teammates, your leader—everything."

"How much time do we have?" Maru laughed ruefully. "It's a lot of information."

"Twenty minutes, I think." Ayano looked at her watch. "Want to sit outside?"

"Sure," said Maru. "I am glad to have somebody to talk to. I need to process all this. Although . . . " she looked around. "Naito just said it was time for training."

"Naito, your teammate? He must have been wrong."

"Oh, well," sighed Maru. "He probably just wanted to get rid of Rin and me. Anyway, about all this Rigel stuff—"

"It's a lot," interrupted Ayano. "But I'm glad I came. Let's take the bench right outside before somebody else does."

Together they went back down the hall, through the wide glass front doors, and out to the nearest bench. Ayano seated herself comfortably at one end, leaned back, and sighed loudly.

"Do you ever really feel like yourself here?" she asked without preface. "Everybody follows such a stereotype. The assassins are all quiet and unfriendly. The medics are all cheerful and doing their best to make you feel better. The computer coders are nerdy. I wonder why?"

"If I'm quiet and unfriendly, it's because of—" Maru cut herself off abruptly.

"SAS training. I know." Ayano's face grew serious. "It's enough to break anyone."

"It almost broke Rin—my teammate Rin. He tried to kill himself yesterday."

"I'm not surprised," said Ayano. "If I thought it would do any good, I'd try it myself. But I don't think it would help. After all, if death is anything like sleep, it must get boring after a while."

"I'm glad I'm not the only one who thinks like that." Maru sighed. "Most of the time I think I'm really weird for thinking that death might be better than this. I don't have anybody to talk to who understands what SAS training is like. Kita and Naito are weirdly cheerful all the time, and nothing seems to get them down. Rin can't talk, and everything he says is either done with looks or written in his notebook. And Saito—"

"What about him?" asked Ayano. "He's really weird. Almost mechanical sometimes, I guess you could say. But he comes across as really rude."

"I'm not sure." Maru paused. "Do you think he's close with Rin?"

"How should I know?" Ayano looked amused.

"Sometimes you know things," said Maru absently. "Anyway, it's funny. He and Rin hate each other so much, but even though Rin can't talk, Saito always understands him. It's like they've been communicating for years."

"Maybe they've been friends for a long time. Or enemies."

"Could be."

"But I'd like to hear more about what you think of Saito. Is he a good leader?" asked Ayano.

"I'm not really sure." Maru shrugged. "I don't see him very often, and most of the time when he does talk, he's bad-mouthing Rin. But he keeps every-thing very well organized, and I think he's dependable. I guess I'll have to wait until we have a real mission."

"I wonder what missions are like," said Ayano dreamily. "I hope they're as adventurous as I imagine."

"I don't think blood and death are as adventurous in that sense as any-thing we ever imagined," said Maru bitterly.

"SAS training goes to show it. But heroism—surely that still exists."

"I'm not sure."

"Sacrifice."

"It's all right if you're not the one who still has to live."

"What?" Ayano looked startled.

"If you survive, you almost have it worse than whoever died to save you." Maru laughed nervously. "I don't know. I'm still thinking this through."

"You'd better hurry up and get to the answer," said Ayano, looking at her with obvious anxiety. "You're suicidal, Maru."

"I don't think so."

"If Rin had died, would you have killed yourself?"

"No," said Maru, simultaneously wondering what the true answer was.

"Yes, you would have." Ayano crossed her arms and looked away. "You'd have thought that there are plenty of recruits who could replace you and do better than you, and you would have been right. You'd have thought that everybody would forget about you eventually, and you would have been right. Maybe you would also have thought that your best friend died with Rin—am I right?" She smiled slyly.

"Huh?" Maru blinked. "What do you mean?"

"I've seen you and Rin sitting together at lunch," said Ayano mischievously. "Are you good friends?"

"Yes, we're good friends. Don't be ridiculous, Ayano. Rin can't even talk!"

"That obviously doesn't stop you from communicating with him. Look, here he comes now."

"That's not Rin," said Maru. "That's Saito."

"Maru, Ayano, why aren't you inside getting ready for training?" asked Saito severely.

"Apologies, sir!" said Ayano, jumping up. "We were just going in."

"Go, now, while I'm watching."

Maru and Ayano silently walked inside, closely followed by Saito. He left them at the entrance without another word, and Ayano laughed.

"Good luck with him," she said. "Shuji is a lot nicer."

"I bet," said Maru ruefully. "Let's not make things worse. Let's get to class."

The classroom was already almost full by the time they arrived. Rin was sitting in the corner, as usual, half hidden by a potted palm tree. Naito and Kita were in the front row, whispering, laughing, and chatting with the other recruits. Maru turned away from them.

"Let's sit in the back," she whispered to Ayano.

"With Rin, right?"

Maru glared at her.

"Sorry, sorry! It's just so much fun to tease you!" She laughed.

"You sound like Kita," said Maru in mock disgust. "Too cheerful for your own good."

"You have to hide the pain somehow," said Ayano, shrugging. "There are two seats left. And look, they're right next to Rin."

"Let's sit on the other side." Maru pulled her away.

The instructor dimmed the lights, and Ayano pushed Maru into the seat next to Rin. "Good luck!" she whispered and sat down beside her.

Maru prayed desperately to no one that the instructor would start talking soon, and fortunately for her, he did.

"Here is a brief recap on what you should already know," he began, wiping the whiteboard clean. "Humanity is divided into three classes—pure human, modified human, and Kalideyes. The definition of a pure human should be obvious—those people who retain all the characteristics they showed at birth, such as organic minds, natural skin, and ordinary bones. They are more delicate than modified humans, of course, but they can never become Kalideyes.

"Modified humans are those who accepted the theories of Shinya Kado and allowed their bodies to be artificially modified. The first transformation occurred about one hundred years ago, and the test subject was a forty-five-year-old man who suffered from no special illness or deformity. His bones, skin, brains, and, in fact, nearly everything about him was artificially produced in laboratories, and his memories were copied to his new man-made body. His eyes, which were blue before the experiment, shifted to a dark brown color because the genetic material that creates blue eyes cannot be copied to a modified human. That was one failure of the experiment, but the other was much more serious.

"The original goal was to make this man live forever, immune to accidents, disease, and dementia. The experiment was so successful that two thousand other people were also modified, and none of them ever became sick or hurt. However, every single one of them died at the age of one hundred and twenty, without exception. Science is unable to offer an explanation, although some people believe it has something to do with a limit set by God. That, of course, is an untestable hypothesis, so we won't waste time talking about it here. The point is, the experiment was successful up to a point. But what happened to the modified bodies when the human souls inhabiting them died? That is where the Kalideyes come from.

"We know that Kalideyes are the artificial bodies of modified humans who have died, and that they are controlled using complex artificial intelligence. Because they look, sound, and act like pure or modified humans, they can go everywhere and do everything we can. But they are not human, and they are not under their own control, because they have no minds and wills of their own. We have proven that they are being remotely controlled from an unknown location by an equally unknown organization created specifically for this purpose, and that their mission, though we don't know exactly what it is, definitely was not designed for the good of humanity. How do we know? Last year, twenty political assassinations were performed in this country alone. The killer was one lone Kalideye. And those are just the killings we know about. We believe they also target those who are close to the truth, those who are likely to have connections with the dead people, and anyone who happens to get in their way. A rough estimate tells us that we can attribute nearly eighty percent of all the murders in the last ten years to only fifty of the nearly two thousand Kalideyes.

"You all know why you're here: to kill not only the Kalideyes but all remaining modified humans. Already the five scientists who knew the secret of creating modifiable human bodies are dead. Rin, you were part of that mission, I believe."

Maru glanced at him from the corner of her eye. His lips were pinched shut, and his blue eyes tightly closed.

"They're out of the way, and once these modified humans are dead, nobody can recreate them. As I've said before, the Kalideyes are not human—they are only machines, and to destroy them is just like destroying an ordinary computer. I understand that killing the modified humans is different, and that you really are taking a probably innocent life. But it must be done. We know they will become Kalideyes once they die, and even leaving a few of them free is dangerous. Look what only fifty of them have done to the world you live in now. Mothers are afraid to send their children out at night. Families don't know if their loved ones will return. That alone is proof that the Kalideyes are pure evil. Or at least, enough to know they are controlled by a source of evil."

"Why in heaven's name can't we let these people live and destroy their bodies after they die?" asked a strained voice from the corner.

"Because the government has ruled that all artificial bodies should be preserved. After the deaths of those five scientists, the secret to making them was completely lost. If they want to reproduce them, they must study them. We can't let that happen. We can't let anyone figure out how to do this."

"How many modified humans are left?" asked another voice.

Saito stood up. "Exactly ninety-eight," he said briefly, then sat back down.

"Those ninety-eight must die by the end of the year," said the instructor. "Once they become Kalideyes, we can't identify them. Of course, we know it's impossible for them to have blue eyes, but otherwise they look perfectly human. And besides destroying them, we have to figure out who's making and controlling them."

"We're going to kill ninety-eight innocent people?" One of the recruits at the back of the room stood up. "No. I won't be part of that."

"You can resign if you want," said the instructor, shrugging. "You can resign, but the work will go on without you, because for the good of humanity it has to be done."

"If it's for the good of humanity, why doesn't the government sanction Rigel? Why do we have to operate in secret?" insisted the recruit.

"You're going to depend on the government to tell you what's right and wrong?"

"There should be a standard for that."

"There is. It's called your conscience," said the instructor ironically. "It might not be exactly the same for everybody, but—"

Rin stood up and made his way to the front of the room. He picked up a marker and started writing on the board in his neat, small print. Everybody watched him in curious silence.

"It's wrong. But it's necessary," read the instructor. Rin stepped back, bowed his head, and returned to his seat. "And I agree with that, except that if it's necessary, how can it be wrong?"

"Is there no other way?" asked the recruit in a subdued voice. "Is there no way to do this without killing the modified humans?"

"No other way," said the instructor firmly. There were a few murmurs from the class, but after that nobody asked any more questions.

"Now for what you don't know," continued the instructor after a brief pause. He erased Rin's writing. "The organization controlling the Kalideyes has a name. We believe it is called KASU, but we're unsure of what the abbreviation stands for. We believe that its purpose behind the scenes is to program and control Kalideyes.

"You're probably wondering what they plan to do with the Kalideyes, and we're not entirely sure of the answer to that question. But since the Kalideyes are almost indestructible and use extremely advanced AI, we think they want to build an army from them. If they can concentrate the Kalideyes in one location, then attack unexpectedly, they stand an excellent chance of winning any battle they start. Kalideyes cannot be destroyed with nuclear or chemical weapons. You can shoot them, but their bodies are much less delicate than ordinary human ones and they don't bleed or feel pain. And they don't know fear."

"A fearless army," murmured Maru. "A fearless, painless, bloodless army."

"That's why we have to first destroy the modified humans that are left, then destroy the Kalideyes themselves, and finally attack the organization that controls them."

"What if a modified human wanted to work for Rigel?" asked Ayano. Her clear voice carried all the way to the front.

"They couldn't, of course," said the instructor. "We'd have to kill them first."

"Is death always your answer to everything?" somebody screamed horribly. Maru winced as if he had hit her. "What about life? What about beauty? Where is the humanity in all this?"

"Sit down," said the instructor sternly. "If you didn't know that was going to be your job, you shouldn't have come. There's no place for cowards here. There's—"

Rin stood up again and walked slowly down the aisle to the board. The instructor did not try to stop him as he wrote quickly. Then he stepped aside and looked directly at the recruit who had been speaking.

"The humanity is saving humanity."

"That makes no sense!" cried the recruit. The sound of heavy, uncontrollable sobs drifted forward from the back left corner. Rin's eyes softened, and he began writing again.

"The life is human lives."

"Circular reasoning!"

"And the beauty is in the sacrifice we make." Rin returned the marker to its place and went back to his seat.

"We're sacrificing them, not ourselves!" the recruit managed to say between sobs.

"Leave, now!" the instructor thundered, pointing to the door. "You can give your resignation tomorrow."

"No!"

"Yes! Now get out!"

The recruit stumbled to the door, let himself out, and slammed it violently behind him.

There was a moment of shocked and fearful silence.

"Let that be a lesson. Don't be like him." The instructor again erased Rin's writing. "Let's finish this lesson so you can have your half day."

***** ***** *****

"Yuri was one of my teammates," said Ayano quietly as the classroom began emptying.

"I'm sorry." Maru could think of nothing else to say.

"I noticed he was acting weirdly after SAS training the other day, but I didn't realize that he'd completely lost it. I feel bad now. I should have said more to him, only I didn't know what to say. There's no answer to this question. It's horrible however you look at it."

"Necessity," said Maru, then repeated for emphasis: "Necessity."

"That's nonsense and we both know it."

"It's not nonsense. If humanity is going to survive, we have to destroy the Kalideyes."

"This isn't a question of humanity surviving. It's only a question of our country surviving. The government doesn't matter, does it?" Ayano turned to her in sudden anger. "It's about the people."

"And the people are going to die if the Kalideyes attack."

"They're going to die anyway." Ayano dropped her eyes.

"It's ninety-eight versus several thousand. I think this is the right choice."

"But those ninety-eight are completely innocent," said Ayano softly.

"I know."

Maru felt a soft tap on her shoulder and realized that Rin was trying to get past her. "Sorry," she said, stepping aside. He started to walk by, then paused.

"I'm fine," said Maru in answer to his quizzical look. "Ayano and I are just talking about the lecture." She turned to Ayano. "This is Rin, my teammate."

"Pleasure. I'm Ayano," she said, holding out her hand for him to shake.

He took it and bowed his head politely but silently. Then he looked back at Maru.

"I'll meet you outside in a few minutes," she said, but he shook his head and produced the notebook from his pocket.

"Don't bother meeting me. I don't want to interrupt, but I'm still not sure you're okay," he wrote.

"I really am fine," she shook her head irritably. "Ayano and I are going to talk some more. I'll see you later."

He nodded and left the room.

"Dear me, don't be so abrupt with him. He's going to think you hate him," teased Ayano, recovering her good spirits.

"No, he won't," said Maru. "I saved his life yesterday."

"Look how casually she says that," crowed Ayano. "It just so happened that while I was walking by the cafeteria building, I noticed a man about to jump off the roof. It occurred to me that he might need help, so with my super-power-glue-tape hands, I scaled the wall and—"

"Stop being ridiculous," said Maru, laughing in spite of herself. "Want to go back outside? We're free now, right?"

"I want to meet your other teammates," said Ayano.

"Will you introduce me to yours?"

"Another day," said Ayano. "I'd rather leave them alone for now—after what just happened."

"Are you sure you want to stay with me? I understand if you'd rather be alone."

Ayano shook her head vigorously. "Absolutely I don't want to be alone. I'd think too much, and I need somebody to distract me. Let's go."

"If you're sure." Maru looked toward the front. "Kita? Naito?"

"A-a-a-at your service!" Kita popped up magically from behind the desk. "I was spying on you. I wanted to make sure you were all right."

"That's not in your job description!" Naito appeared beside her. "You were just being sneaky and using your title as psychologist to your advantage."

"Well, maybe," she said, laughing. "But it worked! I heard the whole conversation!"

"You're not supposed to admit it!" protested Naito.

"You're no fun," said Kita. Then she stood up. "I'm Kita," she said, stretching out her hand to Ayano. "I'm a psychologist."

"And I'm Naito. I'm a computer programmer and engineer."

"Nice to meet you both," said Ayano, clearly doing her best not to laugh. "You sort of startled me."

"Sorry!" Kita put on her most innocent smile. "We were just . . . you know . . . waiting around in case either of you decided to go be like Rin. Speaking of which, we should probably keep an eye on him, too. Where did he go?"

"Don't know," said Maru shortly.

"You make the psychologist do all the work. Well, I'll go look for him. Come with me, Naito!"

"Nowhere I'd rather be," he said, with a sly wink at Maru. "Isn't it already time for lunch?"

"You're always hungry." Kita's voice faded as she went out the door and continued down the hallway.

Naito ran after her. "Wait up!"

Ayano and Maru looked at each other and burst out laughing.

"They're so ridiculous," gasped Ayano. "Ugh. I wonder if you have to have a special personality trait to become like that."

"What are you talking about?" asked Maru. "That is their personality, isn't it?"

"Have you not heard about the ADPA?"

"ADPA? What's that?"

"You should ask Kita or Naito," suggested Ayano. "They're taking them, so they should know."

"I saw a pill bottle on Kita's desk last night, but she got mad when I tried to read the label," said Maru. "I'm not going to ask her anything. She might go crazy and hit me over the head with one of her graphic novels."

"Kita likes graphic novels?" Ayano was temporarily distracted. "I haven't gotten to read one of those in a very long time. Does she have any of the popular series?"

"You want it, she's got it. I think she has more graphic novels than the bookstore. But seriously, tell me about this ADPA thing."

"Let's go outside first," said Ayano. "It's dark and boring in here."

"Back to the bench?"

"Sure."

The outdoor air was crisp and fresh in comparison to the stuffy classroom. Maru breathed it in, savoring the crispness and the warm sun on her skin, wishing the weather would stay this way forever. Ayano walked straight to the bench and sat down, never seeming to notice how nice it was. She put her elbows on her knees and head in her hands and stared at the sidewalk as she spoke.

"ADPA stands for Anti-Depressant Personality Adjustment," she said, "similar to SAS—Social Adjustment and Strengthening. The support system—meaning the engineers, psychologists, nurses, and doctors—are all supposed to be cheerful and happy even in the worst situations so they can help the assassins do their job. These medications help them do that by slightly altering their personalities to make them naturally silly, outgoing, and cheerful all the time. Kita probably has little to no control over what comes out of her mouth. She can't help being happy. She probably hates being happy and wishes she could be sad and feel pain, but she can't. The medicines block all that out for her."

"How can they do that?" cried Maru. "You're saying that when Kita and Naito are acting so happy, it's really just because they're on drugs? That, in reality, they're suffering more than I am?"

"That's exactly what I'm saying." Ayano looked up at her. "Remember that whenever Kita annoys you."

"But her smile—her laughter—her love for everything soft and girly—none of that is real?"

"I don't know," said Ayano. "Maybe some of it is. You probably need to have a certain personality in the first place for the drugs to even work properly. But it's not all real. Look at the impression SAS has left on us. It hurt you and it nearly killed Rin. But somehow it doesn't seem to bother them at all. They still laugh and smile and play with each other like children. It's unnatural. All of this is unnatural. Humans weren't made to kill each other and still be happy."

"Who is she then?" asked Maru in a daze.

"Who is Kita?"

Maru nodded.

"You should try asking her sometime and see if she still remembers."

"How can a person change like that just because of a little white pill every six hours?" Maru insisted. "Surely she hasn't really changed much. It probably just helps her overcome any SAS-related depression."

"Maybe," agreed Ayano uncertainly. "But I remember when my friend Makise started taking them—not you, Maru, but the other Makise. She used to be quiet and a little introverted, but not anymore. She acts just like Kita. In fact, she could be an exact copy."

"That's creepy," said Maru. "Rigel shouldn't be able to control something as personal as that. They can't just alter us into the humans they want us to be. They're modifying us more than those five scientists ever did."

"I know," said Ayano, "but we agreed to this. We have to go through with it now. And it's just as your friend Rin said—the beauty is in the sacrifice we're making. I shouldn't have let myself forget that."

"It's easy to lose sight of anything beautiful here." Maru sighed. "I had started to really admire how childish and sweet Kita is. Now it just seems horrible. And twisted. It wasn't meant to be."

"I'm not sure what you mean by that," said Ayano. "'Meant to be?' Who puts the meaning into this?"

"It's just an expression."

"I know. I am sorry. But I just hate people who even reference God in times like this. It is stupid, really. There is no meaning to life like this. There can't be."

"The meaning of life is to do the best we can with the time we have so that whoever comes after us can do the same," said Maru. "It's not good enough for me, but it's what we have. I try not to think about it. It's too much to take in all at once." Realizing suddenly how much she was talking, she snapped her mouth shut and dropped her eyes.

"That's right," agreed Ayano.

There was a long pause.

"Hey, Rin's coming," said Ayano, pulling Maru's sleeve. "Sit up straight and show that pretty face of yours. Your hair and makeup, by the way, are gorgeous. You did a good job."

"It's not my fault!" protested Maru, trying to free her sleeve. "Let go of me! Kita did this!"

"You're so violent," said Ayano blandly. "Sit right here and just act normal. Let's talk about graphic novels, something nice and relaxing. Rin won't have any idea we set him up for this. He'll—"

"We? We set him up for this?" Maru was enraged. "This is all your idea! Besides, I don't care what Rin thinks. He's seen me at my absolute worst, which is just fine. I'm not going to make up some crazy charade every day just to look my best in front of him. I don't even like him!"

"That's harsh. You don't like him at all? Even as a friend? Come to think of it, you were pretty short earlier." Ayano put a thoughtful hand to her chin, but she was laughing.

"He's coming this way!" hissed Maru desperately.

"The graphic novels." Ayano managed to straighten her face, but her lips puckered suspiciously. "You said Kita has a good collection. What genres?"

"She's low on fantasy and supernatural, but you can find pretty much everything else." Maru glanced at Rin from the corner of her eye. He was walking quickly, head down, eyes covered by his long hair. He did not seem to see them.

"Does she have that new series? I think it's called . . . *Guilty* something."

"*Innocent*. It's called *Innocent Memories*."

"Exactly. Does she have that?"

"Up to volume seven."

"Ooh, do you think she'll mind if I borrow it? I've been wanting to read it for a while. I think Alena is the best graphic novel author and I've read everything else she's written. I was really excited about this new series, too. *Innocent Memories*—very odd title. What could it be about?"

"I dunno. Bacteria?" Maru answered vaguely.

"You're no good at this!" whispered Ayano. Then aloud she said, "Have you read it?"

"I read the first volume last night. It's pretty good."

"You read an entire volume in one evening? Control yourself, girl. This isn't the *Academic* series. There are only nine volumes in total. You won't get to enjoy them if you read them too quickly."

"Why are graphic novels so entertaining?" murmured Maru. He was getting closer, but she could not see his face.

"I don't know. The combination of pictures with words is nice, but you can still enjoy having a real book in your hands. That's what I like. The first graphic novel I ever read was *A Noisy Voice*, and I was immediately addicted. It was a bit like watching a movie."

"I've read that."

Rin was passing the bench without looking up. He still seemed oblivious of their presence and was buried in his own thoughts, barely watching where he was going. Maru wished she could talk to him, but with Ayano nearby, that was obviously impossible.

"Hello, Rin!" cried Ayano.

He did not look up or slow down.

"Wow, he's unfriendly," commented Ayano. "He reminds me of the character Eight from *Peace*."

"Sure."

"Does Rin ever read graphic novels?"

"I don't know," said Maru, "but if he did, they'd be violent and disturbing."

"Something along the lines of *Boom*, right?"

"Rin doesn't read graphic novels, silly. Only girls do that. Besides, he has way too much to think about."

"That's the only reason to read them. They distract you. They let you go to a completely different world where you don't have to worry about saving people's lives. The main character does that for you, or he dies, and you get to sympathize with whoever he leaves behind. It's a much more perfect world than the one we live in."

"I thought you just mentioned *Boom*. You know it doesn't work out well for the main character when he gets absorbed into the story."

"True." Ayano laughed. "I hadn't thought about it that way."

"How many more days of training do we have?" asked Maru, changing the subject. "How long is it until we get our first mission?"

"What, are you excited or something?"

"I don't know. A change is always a good thing, right?"

"Maybe." Ayano raised a finger. "Thirty-one days. Just like the movie."

"Would you stop making obscure references and give me a real answer?"

"Okay, okay." Ayano grew serious again. "We will probably get our assignments very soon—likely within the next week or so. You never know. It depends on how urgently they need something done and how well we do in training."

"What are you going to do now that your team—?" Maru stopped herself.

"Yuri?" Ayano sighed. "We're all going to miss him. I hope that if he really does leave Rigel, he can get his life back and maybe forget about some of this. But the team won't let him get in the way of what we need to be doing. We'll find somebody to take his place and train them as quickly as we can. That's the best answer I have right now."

"I'm so sorry. For you and for him."

"It's probably best that this happened here and not while we're out on a mission. That's the only good thing I can see about it. Now can we talk about something else?"

"Please let it not be graphic novels or Rin," said Maru.

"Nothing sad either."

"That rules out a lot."

"Hey, too morbid! This is our day off. We should be enjoying it."

"Uh-oh," said Maru. "Here comes Saito."

"Disperse!" cried Ayano merrily, seizing Maru's wrist. "I know we're off duty, but I don't want to talk to him anymore today. He's so dark and cold and mean. Let's go somewhere else."

"Too late," said Maru, shaking herself free. "He's coming this way. We're obligated to at least see if he talks to us."

"Oh man," said Ayano, scooching to the end of the bench. "Hey, maybe after this we can go explore Kita's novel collection. I'm sure she's out doing something—shadowing Rin, probably."

"Sure, I guess she won't mind. If one goes missing, she'll just assume I've taken it. But seriously, can we talk about something other than graphic novels? I love them, but you already heard me say I read an entire volume last night. It was too much, honestly."

"Sure. What else do you want to talk ab . . . " Ayano's words trailed off as Saito approached.

"There's a meeting in fifteen minutes," he said shortly, stopping in front of their bench. "Maru, you need to be there. Ayano, you're free for the rest of the day as far as I know, but check with Shuji if you decide to leave the base."

"Yes, sir!" said Ayano, leaning back against the bench and crossing her arms.

"Where is the meeting?" asked Maru.

"In the same room the lecture was a few minutes ago. Please make sure you're on time." He turned and started walking away, then looked back with an expressionless face. "Maru, will you come with me now?"

"Oh . . . sure," she said reluctantly. "Sorry, Ayano. Maybe we can continue this talk later."

"Fine by me," Ayano said, nodding.

Saito put his hands behind his back and stood waiting.

"Okay. Um—well, see you later then. Meet me at Kita's room. Do you know where that is?"

"Sure, I can find it." Ayano smiled and waved.

Maru trailed Saito back into the cafeteria, wondering why he had asked her to come with him. He never looked at her or said anything, just continued rapidly in a straight line to the classroom. It was empty when they arrived.

"Front row," said Saito briefly, and Maru obediently sat down and watched him clean the whiteboard, read over some papers, and pace up and down in front of the window.

"Can I help you with anything?" she said at last.

"No," he said and continued pacing.

She waited in uncomfortable silence for a few minutes longer, hoping that her teammates would show up soon. It was with great relief that she heard Kita's loud laughter preceding her up the hallway and Naito's cheerful voice saying, "You're no fun to tease, Rin. You just stand there and take it with a mysterious smile, and you never say anything about it."

"It's because he can't talk!" cried Kita. "You should know that by now. What's this meeting for, anyway? I thought we were supposed to have a half day."

Rin slipped in the door and seated himself unobtrusively next to Maru. They smiled at each other, and Rin nodded politely to Saito, who did not return the greeting.

"Eek!" said Kita. "You're already here, Maru? We looked everywhere for you!"

"Kita thought you and Ayano might try to steal her books," added Naito.

"Why would I do that?" asked Maru innocently. She pretended to laugh, but her attention was focused on Kita's face and actions. There was nothing remotely artificial about them. Had Ayano really been right about the medications she was forced to take? Did they really change her personality, or had she always been like this?

"The sergeant will be here momentarily," said Saito from the window.

"Ooh, the sergeant's coming," whispered Kita. "And we're all sitting in the front row, so it must just be us. A special meeting with the sergeant. What did we do? Did anybody break any rules?"

"I'm blaming it on Kita, whatever it was," said Naito, poking her hair. "It was definitely something you did."

"Not fair!"

"Is too!"

"No!"

"None of you did anything wrong," said Saito quietly. "On the contrary, I think you did something right."

"That's the biggest compliment ever coming from Saito!" bubbled Kita excitedly. "Something good must be happening!"

Saito did not smile.

"What could it be?" asked Naito. "It had better be something good. We're giving up part of our half day to hear it."

"Freedom to leave the base whenever we want?" suggested Kita.

"Nah, they won't let us do that no matter how well we do in training."

"Hopefully they don't just assign us more training. That would be kind of—"

"Shut up and let me think, please," said Saito.

"—boring," continued Kita in a whisper.

Maru tapped her shoulder. "Here comes the sergeant," she said. "We should be ready to listen."

CHAPTER 8

The sergeant was the same whom Maru had met on the first day of her team assignment. She was a small woman with great charisma and leadership ability. Ordinarily her face was either furiously angry or glowingly happy, but today it registered only anxiety, and her eyes looked tired. She was holding a thick white binder, which her fingers tapped nervously.

"I've been up all night figuring out the details of this, so forgive me if I don't explain things very well. Ask questions if you need to," she said, putting the binder on the podium and moving the microphone out of her way. "I'm sure you're all wondering why we called you in here on your half day for a meeting in a dark, stuffy room. I'll give you the brief answer first, and then I'll elaborate. This is about your first mission together as a team."

Maru stiffened.

"Today you heard about KASU, most of you probably for the first time. You heard that we don't know exactly who they are, but we're doing our best to figure it out. We're investigating various organizations who are connected in any way with the modified humans or the Kalideyes, and we think we may have come close to finding the source of the evil."

She picked up a marker and wrote on the blackboard. "Central Agency of United Scientists—CAUS," she read it aloud. "This was the organization who created the first modified humans. Everyone who knew the secret of how they did it has already been assassinated, but CAUS still exists and is run by other state-educated scientists. KASU is a subordinate organization designed to figure out how the modified human bodies were made. They're funded by the government, even though they are technically a private organization, and they've been difficult to infiltrate or even get close to."

"The reason we're trying now," interrupted Saito quietly, "is because we've noticed some unusual activity at their nearest lab. They're not investigating the biological materials needed to make the modified human bodies; they're experimenting with microchips, explosives, and artificial intelligence. These are exactly the things we would expect if they were really managing the Kalideyes."

"It's interesting," commented the sergeant, "because this new activity just started within the last few weeks. We had only one spy inside the organization, and he told us everything we know about it. Unfortunately, he went missing yesterday. And by 'went missing,' I mean . . . "

"He was shot," said Saito coolly. "The police labeled it robbery. We think it might be because he was onto something at CAUS."

"All of this is to say that your team is assigned the mission of figuring out what CAUS is really doing." The sergeant wiped the whiteboard clean. "We hope that Naito can find employment with them as a computer scientist. Kita will be supporting him, acting as his clingy but wonderfully innocent girlfriend who hangs around all the time and asks the most ridiculous and nonsensical questions."

"Sounds like her," interrupted Naito. Kita slapped him.

"Rin and Maru, you'll be on hold in case you're ordered to perform an assassination, but until then, you'll apply for jobs at CAUS as trainees or unskilled workers." The sergeant paused for breath. "Saito will be managing things from here."

"Will we still be living here?" asked Kita.

"No, once you leave the base on a mission, you can't come back. We'll find each of you an apartment downtown. Most likely, Kita and Naito will be somewhere close to each other—that makes sense since they're supposed to be in a relationship. I'd like to spread Rin and Maru out a bit to make the fact that they know Kita and Naito a little less obvious. That way, if one team gets caught, the other can keep working. Any questions?"

They shook their heads.

"All right then. You will have funds set up for rent, utilities, and food. Maru, Rin, and Naito, I'll have your job applications by this evening. Fill them out and get them to me in the morning."

"When do we leave?" asked Kita.

"Whenever we hear about your jobs," replied the sergeant. "In any case, you should be ready."

"Eeh! This is so exciting!" Kita clapped her hands together and smiled.

"It's dangerous too," said Saito. "Don't forget—if our hypothesis is right, Shindo has already given his life for this. I'd rather not see it happen again. Be watchful."

"My best defense is my innocent face," said Kita proudly.

"It's cute, too," observed Naito.

"You can't say that!"

"No more of this," interrupted Saito. "Take the rest of the day off, except for filling out the forms. I've already printed them out. I want them back by this evening, not tomorrow morning. And I have only one extra copy in case you make a mistake. We don't have the equipment to reproduce the electronic marker in the paper."

Maru took hers and silently read it over. Experience? Training? She raised her hand.

"You're going to ask about the experience and training sections," nodded the sergeant. "Well, for experience, put Star Communications, since that's our public name. For training, put team building and whatever you learned in college."

"The irony!" laughed Kita. "This is going to be fun!"

"One more thing," added Saito. "Don't mention this to anyone, not even your friends here."

"As soon as word gets out, you're all in very real danger," said the sergeant. "We can't let them know what we're doing. So please be very careful."

"Shh," said Naito, putting a finger to his lips.

"You're dismissed," said the sergeant. "Papers to Saito by this evening."

"These are short applications," said Naito. "I'll just stay in here and fill mine out."

"Me, too," agreed Maru.

Rin nodded.

"And I'm going to enjoy the warm sunshine!" cried Kita, jumping up. "See you later, hard-working adults!" She danced out the door with a parting wave.

"Are you sure the ADPA is affecting her positively?" asked Saito drily. Nobody answered him.

"Here are some pens," said the sergeant. "Take your time and do the best you can. We'd like you to all be accepted if possible."

Maru bit the tip of her pen, deep in thought. She was young and had very little life experience outside of Rigel. Her "Experience" section looked rather bleak with just "Star Communications" and the few internships she had done in college, and there was nothing else she could add. Still, she was evidently applying for an unimportant and unskilled position. There shouldn't be too many requirements, and she hoped she wouldn't even need to interview.

"Done!" said Naito suddenly, slamming his pen triumphantly on the table. "Whew, that was easy."

Maru glanced over his shoulder at the application. The whole paper was covered in tiny, neat handwriting, continued in the margins when the writer ran out of space. Naito had apparently found time for plenty of internships and student work outside of college, and his "Experience" section overflowed to the back of the page.

"Nice work," said the sergeant. "You're free to go."

Rin glanced at Maru, who was busily filling in her answers to the last two questions. He waited patiently until she was done, then handed his paper to the sergeant right after her.

"Thanks." The sergeant stacked the papers neatly and put them into an envelope. "I'll let you know as soon as we hear back from them. Meanwhile, you can go."

Rin slipped out the door past Maru, but she stopped him before he could leave. "Can I talk to you for a minute?"

He nodded.

"Outside, I mean," she insisted, pulling him out the door. "I just want to ask you something."

Rin followed her obediently down the hallway, out the doors, and to a little shaded bench behind the building.

"Sit down," she ordered, and he did, looking up at her expectantly.

"Do you have your notebook so you can answer me?" she asked.

He nodded.

"Then tell me, Rin. Why did you try to kill yourself yesterday? And are you going to do it again?"

He shrugged and made no effort to find his notebook.

"Answer me!" cried Maru. "I can't do my work properly if I'm worried about you committing suicide when I'm not looking. Promise me you won't."

He did not move.

"Promise me!"

This time he reached for his notebook, and then he started writing. Maru waited impatiently for him to finish, twisting her fingers together nervously. Finally, he handed it to her, but to her disappointment, the message was short.

"I tried to kill myself because I have nothing worth living for. Other people can take my place and do better than me."

Maru shivered. Ayano had said exactly the same thing earlier that day.

"Please promise me you won't do it again," she pleaded. "For the team. You must stay alive for the team. For this mission. For the people we're going to save."

"And then?" he mouthed silently.

"I don't know," she said truthfully. "Until the end of this mission. Promise me, please. No more suicide attempts. Just until the end of this mission. Give life a chance."

Suddenly he smiled and nodded.

"You promise?"

He nodded again and wrote in his notebook. "Thank you."

"I won't talk about it anymore—unless you want to, of course, except—" Maru stopped suddenly, then added slowly, "I do want to ask you a question."

He did not move, but he was still smiling.

"You tried this four times before, right? But it never worked."

His smile faded.

"Why not?"

He picked up his notebook and flipped back a few pages. He had already written what he wanted to say. A single word was scrawled across an entire page: "Weakness."

"But you're not weak!" cried Maru. "You're stronger than I ever could be. You're so strong that you're about to break yourself. Please don't, Rin. I need to be able to talk to somebody like this. Stay with me."

Rin's hands shook slightly as he closed his notebook and put it back in his pocket.

Maru took a deep breath. "How's your head?" she asked to change the subject.

Rin put a thoughtful hand to his wound, then nodded and smiled slightly. His face immediately became serious again, and he looked away from her.

"I'm sorry to be so dark all the time." Maru sighed. "We should talk about something happy. I guess we really aren't obligated to be serious forever."

Rin pulled out his notebook. "Graphic novels?"

Maru eyed him suspiciously. "You heard that?"

He nodded, laughing with his eyes.

"That's so not fair," she said. "Eavesdropper!"

"Blame Ayano," he wrote.

"I try, but it doesn't seem to bother her much. Can we please not talk about any kind of book right now?"

Rin wrote in his notebook, and Maru watched over his shoulder. "What did you like to do in your free time before you came here?"

"Oh," she said, surprised. "I . . . I liked to read, of course. And sometimes I tried writing stories. I listened to a lot of music."

Rin immediately picked up his pen. "What kind?"

"Hmm. I never found a kind I liked especially," she said. "I listened to electronica, EDM, hip hop—that sort of thing. But I think I really like quieter, sadder music."

Rin pulled a pair of earbuds from his pocket and attached them to his watch. Then he scrolled through a few menus, made a selection, and handed the earbuds to Maru.

She put them in tentatively, hoping that Rin had the volume turned down. He did, so low that she could barely hear the music at first. Then the sound seemed to grow. Maru's eyes widened. The music was horribly sad, and yet beautiful at the same time. It was a voice crying but strong, notes deep but soft, lyrics melancholy but sweet. The song was about sacrifice. The singer painted such a clear picture of pain followed by hope and suffering followed by happiness that Maru almost found herself in tears. Lovelier even than the voice was the music that matched it, swaying up and down with always a slight focus on the lower notes. The song began with death and ended with life. It was absolutely the most beautiful, pure thing that Maru had ever heard.

"You like it?" wrote Rin. "The lyrics are in Icelandic. It's a beautiful language."

Maru blinked. She had been so entranced in its beauty that she had not realized the lyrics were completely incomprehensible.

"That's music," she said, staring wide-eyed at Rin. "That's what I've been looking for. It's amazing. Every sound is perfect, and I love it."

His whole face lit up with delight. "Want to hear another?" he wrote rapidly.

"Please!" Maru sat down on the bench beside him. "Don't you want to listen, too?"

He took one of the earbuds from her and selected another song. It was as beautiful, sad, and strong as the other had been. This time there were no lyrics, only a piano lead accompanied by violin and occasional electronica. It was quiet and delicate, but at the same time it expressed such strength and hope that Maru found herself wishing she could be as powerful as the music itself. She glanced over at Rin. He was entranced, his face serious and his eyes unblinkingly fixed on the sky.

At the end of the song neither of them moved for several moments. Then Rin removed his earbud and held out his hand for Maru's. She gave it to him rather reluctantly. "They're so beautiful," she said. "What are they called?"

"I don't know," he wrote.

"Can you send them to me?"

He nodded and handed her the notebook.

She wrote down her watch address and handed it back to Rin. "You can message me, too, if you ever want to talk."

He paused with the pen and notebook midway to his pocket and looked at her.

Maru had no idea why he was staring. "Rin?"

He put them beside him on the bench and typed her address into his watch. A few moments later a message appeared on Maru's device: "It's Rin."

"Heyoooo," she typed back. Rin smiled. "Maybe it's easier for me to type like this than to write on the notebook," he said, positioning the holographic keyboard on his lap and expanding it to standard desktop size. "It's a little faster."

"And I can still talk aloud like we usually do."

Rin nodded, then looked thoughtfully at his keyboard. Finally, he pecked at one of the keys, and a smiling cat face appeared on Maru's screen.

She laughed hysterically. "You're amazing, Rin," she said between gasps. "A cat? Really?"

He dropped his head slightly and allowed his hair to cover his eyes, but his mouth was still curved into a small smile.

"This was a good talk," he typed. "Thanks."

"Anytime," replied Maru. "I needed it, too." She paused. "I should probably go meet Ayano now, but . . . this was nice. Thank you for sharing your music with me."

"You're welcome. I'll send it to you in a few minutes," he typed.

"Awesome." She hesitated. "Rin . . . "

He waited expectantly.

"I'm sorry for being such a wet blanket. I feel like every time I'm around you, I'm worrying or thinking about something sad. Something that hurts us. I don't mean to be that way. I'm really sorry, and if you ever want me to leave, just say something."

Rin shook his head and typed vigorously. "I like hearing you talk about things like this. It just means that you're human and that you have a wonderfully human heart that can still be broken. It is a good thing, and it is you. Don't silence yourself."

Maru read the last sentence several times over. *What does that mean?*

Aloud she said, "Okay, then. I'll still try not to be too weird. I'm going to go find Ayano, but I'll see you later. Tomorrow for sure."

He began typing again. Maru waited, but suddenly he stopped, and his finger hovered over the backspace key. Finally, he shook his head and waved at her.

She waved back and set off down the sidewalk back toward the front of the building. Then she hesitated again and looked back. Rin was still sitting on the bench exactly where she had left him, his arm draped over the back and his head tilted up to the sky. Maru suddenly wished that she didn't have to leave him in such obvious pain, but he probably preferred to be alone. He didn't need her company or her advice or her chattering voice.

Suddenly she saw him look down. A moment later a message appeared on her watch: "I'd like to talk more. Meet tonight in the cafeteria?"

She smiled involuntarily and typed back: "Six o'clock." Then she looked at him, sitting lonely on the bench, reading his watch. Even from her distance, she could see him clench his fist tightly and lean forward, but she could not interpret the meaning of this movement. Her watch vibrated again. "Okay. Thanks."

*****   *****   *****

"I've been waiting for you forever!" cried Ayano, jumping up as Maru approached. "I'm pretty sure I've made a dent in these steps from just sitting here with nothing to do. What were you up to?"

"Talking," said Maru vaguely, unlocking the door.

"With whom?" Ayano followed her inside. "Saito? Kita? Naito?"

"Rin."

"Yes!" Ayano shouted. "Okay. Sorry. It's none of my business."

"You're really weird," said Maru. "I've known you since grade school, and I actually thought you were weird even then. Now that you're an adult you've definitely gone stark raving mad. Pick out your book."

"Whoa," said Ayano admiringly. "This is a pink room."

"Sherlock," scoffed Maru. "Want some cookies? We can raid Kita's stash."

"I didn't know we were allowed to have this stuff." Ayano touched one of the crystals hanging from the chandelier. "Wow. Just wow."

"We're not," said Maru, opening all the cabinets one by one and inspecting. "But Kita is allowed to break some of the rules. No idea why. Maybe it's just because she's so adorable. Saying no to her would be like saying no to a baby."

"True, true," said Ayano absently. She had already found the shelf of graphic novels and figurines. "Can I just stay here for a little while and read through some of these? I'll get out before Kita gets back."

"Sure," said Maru. "Here are some caramels."

"You have the good life rooming with her." Ayano, picked a caramel from the tin and unwrapped it noisily. "Looks like you've been taking advantage of it, too. You're the only person I know who dog-ears graphic novels like this. Sacrilege!"

"Don't tell Kita," said Maru hastily, smoothing the damaged corner. "She'll get mad."

"Rightly so."

"I don't need a lecture from either of you." Maru sat down on the sofa with the tin of caramels and leaned back against the pillows. "Here's the one we were talking about earlier."

"Ooooh!" Ayano took it and plumped down beside her. "I think I will start with this. Wake me if I get too absorbed in this deep and mysterious world."

"Sure."

Ayano started reading, and Maru went to the window. She could see a few recruits strolling on the sidewalks below, some birds, and one or two instructors sitting and reading on the benches. The grass looked greener than ever in the bright sunlight, and Maru wished she could spend the day outside rather than holed up in her dorm room. She turned back to Ayano.

"I'm going to go outside for a while," she said. "Maybe I'll walk around or something. Text me if you need me. You have my watch number, right?"

"Mhmm," said Ayano without looking up. "Bye."

"Bye." Maru shut the door quietly behind her and took a deep breath of the fresh, clean air.

The sun immediately felt intensely warm on her skin, and she almost laughed with the sheer pleasure of it. The warmth seeped through her and seemed to tickle her internally. There was still beauty in life after all, and today she had experienced two completely different kinds—the soft, caressing sunlight and Rin's incredible music. The thought gave her hope. Maybe the world was bright and beautiful after all.

Immediately after this thought came the darker ones. Rin's attempted suicide and his blood staining the hospital floor. Kita's drugs. SAS training. The mission.

Maru could not decide whether the mission was one of the good or bad thoughts. She was excited and nervous, hopeful and fearful, interested but passively so. She wanted to see the story without being a part of it, but at the same time she despised herself for her fear.

"I have to get over this," she told herself. "I can't talk about it with anyone else. I don't want to make them more miserable. I have to process this alone. But I have to get over it."

"Don't talk to yourself," said a voice behind her. Maru started violently and turned around. "And don't act so frightened."

Saito crossed his arms and looked down at her, an inexplicable smile playing on his lips. "You're such a child."

"What?" stammered Maru. She had no idea how to interpret that remark.

Saito stood silently for a moment, scanning her up and down and paying no attention to her question. Finally, he said, "There's nothing wrong, Miss Maru."

Her surprise deepened. Never before had Saito used an honorific with her name, and since he was higher-ranking than her, it was doubly unusual.

"What are you doing for the rest of the day?" he asked.

"I—" She suddenly felt a great reluctance to tell him that she had planned to meet Rin in the cafeteria. "I—nothing."

"Meet me in the cafeteria at six then," said Saito, his smile twisting weirdly to the right side of his face. "There are a few things we need to talk about."

"But—"

"You'll have the whole day to talk with Ayano tomorrow," interrupted Saito. "See you tonight." He turned and walked away without giving Maru a chance to respond.

She stood frozen for a moment, undecided. Then she gathered her courage and ran after him.

"Saito!" she cried, and he stopped without turning around. "I already told Rin I'd meet him at six."

"All right then," he said coolly, still without turning to face her. "We'll talk now." He spun around suddenly, and with one giant step, he was next to her. He took her hand and wrapped it in his sweaty one, looking down at her with a vacant expression in his bright blue eyes. "Come with me."

Maru tried instinctively to pull her hand away, but Saito did not let go or even seem to notice her movement. He only continued walking forward, pulling her after him and squeezing her wrist painfully.

Maru was completely unable to interpret what was happening. Where was Saito taking her, and why? What did he want to talk to her about? Why did they have to be alone?

Suddenly her mind cleared, and she scowled. Saito could talk to her here if he had anything to say, or at least he could tell her where they were going.

She stopped, twisted her hand out of Saito's, and took a step back. "Where are we going?"

He smiled slowly. "Are you afraid?" he asked. "We're going someplace quiet where nobody can hear us. If you don't trust me, we can go to the gardens. As long as nobody overhears, I really don't mind. The information I plan to share with you is highly classified."

Maru felt at once deeply suspicious and ashamed of her fears. Saito was her leader. Saito was stronger than she was. He was trustworthy. He refused to explain himself. Conflicting evidence poured through her mind, but in the end caution won. She took another step away and shook her head. "I'm sorry, Saito. I'm not comfortable with this. You could ask the sergeant to come, too, but—"

"All right then. I understand." He nodded. "I'll give the mission to Rin instead."

"A mission . . . ?"

Saito held up his hand and turned away. "I can't say anything about it. I apologize for any confusion, Maru. I really didn't mean to frighten you."

"It's okay," she said, still puzzled. "Can I help you at all?"

"No. I'll be done with Rin by the time you arranged to meet him."

Maru watched him go, desperately trying to sort out her confused emotions. "Did I make a mistake?" she muttered, then remembered Saito's comment for her to stop talking to herself. "I don't care what he says about that. I'll talk to myself if I can't talk to anyone else." She sighed and started back to her dorm room.

Ayano burst out the door, startling Maru. "I thought I was going to have to rescue you!" she cried. "What just happened?"

"Saito wanted to tell me something classified," said Maru coldly, "and he needed to take me someplace private to do it. Don't make a big deal out of nothing. I thought you were reading."

"I was," said Ayano, becoming serious, "but something told me to look out the window and I saw Saito grab you by the wrist."

"I guess he was just in a hurry." Maru sat down on the sofa. "But I can find out all about it tonight. He said something about offering a mission to Rin instead of me, because I wouldn't go with him, so if Rin says anything about it—"

"There's something I don't understand." Ayano sat on her knees and looked up mischievously at Maru. "There's an interesting combination of words here—'Rin' and 'this evening.' Don't tell me you agreed to go on a date with him?"

"We've known each other for only a week, so that's not very likely," said Maru placidly. "He just wants to talk to me. What I was saying is that if Rin mentions a new mission tonight, I can know for sure that Saito was telling the truth. And then I'll feel like an idiot."

"Guess so." Ayano shook her head. "I'm disappointed though."

"Why?" Maru's voice was frigid.

"You really don't get it? Girl, if you like Rin, you should ask him to make this a date!"

"Who said I like him? As a friend, yes. As anything else, absolutely not. You're a hopeless romantic, Ayano. Go back to your books and get your fill of grown-up nonsense there. I won't have anything to do with you." She stood up and went to the kitchen.

"I am sorry!" laughed Ayano. "I really am just teasing you. It's fun. But honestly, I think I am done reading for the day. Do you mind if I borrow just one volume?"

"You should really ask Kita," said Maru. "But I'll cover for you if she finds it missing."

"Hey, thanks!" Ayano put the book in her pocket. "You're the best. See you tomorrow!"

"Not if you keep talking about Rin this way!" Maru shouted after her, but Ayano just laughed and let the door slam loudly behind her.

Maru immediately went back to the sofa and sat cross-legged on a blanket. She felt rather weak and discovered that her hands were shaking slightly. She felt as if she had just been on the edge of a cliff, but something inside laughed at her and mocked her fears. It was ridiculous. She had acted with caution just in case, and she had probably been wrong about everything. Nothing was going to happen. And yet there was a new image etched with fire into her mind, and it was the expression on Saito's face when he grabbed her wrist and met her eyes.

"I'm so stupid," she moaned, and lay back on the pillows. As she did so, her watch vibrated, and she lifted her wrist before her eyes. It was a message from Rin and contained two audio files.

Maru smiled and jumped up. She went to her desk and rummaged among the papers until she found her earbuds, which she connected to her watch and fitted carefully into her ears. Then she lay down on the sofa, closed her eyes, and let Rin's music lull her softly to sleep.

CHAPTER 9

Maru drifted awake a few hours later and blinked twice in quick succession. The room was dark. She sat up and looked around in confusion, then glanced at her watch. It was six-thirty.

"I'm the worst!" she cried, jumping up from the sofa and running to her bedroom. "This is ridiculous. I'm late, and Rin probably gave up on me already."

She glanced at herself in the mirror. Her hair was ruffled and framed around her face, and her makeup from the morning was untouched. She sighed in frustration. "I look ridiculous," she muttered, trying to flatten her hair. "But it doesn't matter. I told Ayano this morning that it doesn't matter. And I need to hurry."

She put on her shoes, tying the laces messily and rapidly, and ran out the door without bothering to leave her earbuds behind. As she ran, she wound them carefully into a ball and put them in her pocket. She paused before the cafeteria door and took a deep breath, trying to even her breathing.

"I can do this," she muttered, and swung the door open with an overdramatic push.

Threading her way through tables, she glanced from wall to wall looking for Rin. At last she found him in the corner farthest from the door, one elbow on the table, resting his chin on his hand and staring idly out the window. He did not seem to notice her approach as she came timidly toward him.

"Rin," she said softly.

He looked up and blinked, then smiled.

"Sorry I'm late," continued Maru with a little more confidence. "I fell asleep listening to your music."

His smile widened and he positioned his holographic keyboard on the table in front of him. "That's great," he typed. "Here, watch this."

He pressed a few buttons on his watch, and a blue translucent display screen appeared before his eyes. He used two fingers to push it toward Maru and expand it slightly so she could read the text. Then he typed on his keyboard, and his words appeared in front of her. "Neat, isn't it?"

"This is handy!" Gingerly she moved it slightly down and directly in front of her eyes. "This is a big upgrade from that notebook."

Rin chuckled silently and typed out a smiley face.

"Do you mind if I grab a sandwich, and then we can talk?" asked Maru.

He shook his head.

"I'll be right back," she said, and hurried to join the line forming around the food counter.

As she waited, fingers drumming her tray, she wondered how to ask Rin whether or not Saito had actually offered him a mission. Probably he was forbidden to talk about it, but she knew that she would never feel comfortable around Saito again unless she got an answer. Surely Rin trusted her. She blushed involuntarily and directed her thoughts to other channels.

She paid for her sandwich and went back to Rin's table. He was playing with the holographic screen, moving it up and down and resizing it with the curiosity of a child. Maru laughed despite herself and sat down across from him. He pushed it in her direction, and she positioned it where she could easily read it.

"I have a question for you," she said slowly. "I'm sorry to ask, and if you don't want to answer, just say so."

"Go ahead," he typed.

"Did Saito talk to you this afternoon?"

He nodded.

"Did he talk to you about a mission?"

After a moment of hesitation, he nodded.

Maru was relieved. "Are you going to do it?"

Rin started typing. "Did something happen between you?"

"No . . . not really." Maru did not know how to answer. "He was going to offer the mission to me, but . . . something . . . I'm not sure."

"You can tell me."

"It's really nothing," said Maru, dropping her eyes. "I just wasn't comfortable going off alone with him to hear the details. It's probably stupid, but you know . . . actually you don't know, because you're a really strong giant, but . . ."

Rin typed a long series of smiley faces. "A really strong giant?" he repeated, his fingers moving like lightning on the table. "Interesting." He paused for a moment, then added, "Don't go anywhere alone with Saito, please."

Maru laughed wildly. "He said the same thing about you."

"He'd never hurt you. I just don't want—" Rin stopped typing and shrugged.

"How do you know he won't?" asked Maru quickly. "For all we know, he might be a convicted felon. He could even work for CAUS. You don't know that for sure." She laughed at her own exaggeration.

Rin's fingers moved very slowly. "Because—I've—known him for a long time."

"Oh." Maru dared not ask for more details.

"It's okay," he wrote. "I'm looking forward to this mission."

"What are you going to do?" she asked.

Rin put a very dramatic finger to his lips. "Steal apples from the Queen's garden."

"In other words, you can't tell me."

"It's nothing very special. I'm—" he paused. "I'm going to pretend to be a plastics manufacturer and ask for a tour of CAUS."

"Plastics manufacturer?"

"Biologically safe plastic. Or something like that. Something they can use in their research."

"Interesting!" Maru's eyes brightened. "I wish I could come with you. That actually sounds like a lot of fun."

Rin shook his head slowly. His fingers hovered over the keyboard, but he did not start typing.

"What is it?" asked Maru curiously.

He shook his head. "Nothing," he typed quickly, followed by yet another smiley face.

"These emojis," laughed Maru. "They're so out of character for you."

"Naito suggested I try them," wrote Rin. "I thought they might make up for the fact that I never show anything on my face."

"Why don't you?" she asked. "If you don't mind me asking."

"It's okay," he typed. "I don't know how."

"You don't know how to show your feelings?"

"I've forgotten."

"You've—" Maru suddenly realized the implications of this simple, pathetic statement. "That means you once knew how."

Rin's face turned a shade paler. "Bad things happened to me when I shared my feelings," he typed slowly. "So I taught myself to hide them, and now I've forgotten everything else."

"You know you can share them with me, right?" said Maru quietly. "You can't keep living like this. You've barely made it this far."

He nodded vigorously. "My confidante used to be Saito," he wrote. "Now it's you. And you can talk to me anytime, too."

"Wait!" Maru was confused. "Your confidante used to be Saito? How—what happened?"

"Funny, right?" was all he wrote.

"Something changed a lot." Maru stared at him in amazement. "Rin, did everything change for you? Did you—did you used to be able to speak?"

They both sat in petrified silence for a moment until Maru dropped her eyes nervously. "Don't answer," she whispered. But Rin started typing.

"I don't remember what my voice sounds like," he wrote. "It was that long ago." He paused. "The last thing I remember saying was . . . " He paused again and bit his lip. "I said 'I hate you' to my father. I haven't said a word since."

"Why . . . why not?"

A single word appeared on her screen. "Weakness."

"I'm so sorry, Rin," said Maru. "I . . . I'm sorry."

"It's okay," he typed yet again, and Maru wondered if after all his years of pain and suffering that phrase had become his mantra. "Ask whatever you want. I might not answer, but that's my own fault."

"Okay." As soon as the permission was given, Maru could immediately think of nothing else to say.

"Can I ask you a question?" appeared on her screen.

Her mouth was full of sandwich, so she nodded.

"You once said that you think the best way to make friends is to be quiet. Why do you think that?"

Maru was taken aback. "I don't—I mean, I don't know if I think that. I guess I do, but why do you ask?"

"Don't know."

"I guess it's because I always say the wrong thing." Maru put her sandwich on the tray and then rested her elbows on the table. "You heard me just now. I asked you all those personal questions without batting an eyelash. I regretted it afterwards, but I tend to speak before I think. People used to get mad at me for that."

"Don't silence yourself."

Maru scowled internally. She was tired of hearing that meaningless sentence over and over again.

"Why not? Why shouldn't I? If people don't like listening to me talk, then I have to stop if I want friends. It's as simple as that. I can handle it. I can keep my mouth shut."

Rin actually smiled. "No, you can't," he wrote. "Not like me anyway."

"If I had a medical problem like you, then I would be able to."

Rin shook his head and typed, "Psychosomatic."

"I have no idea what that means."

Rin thought for a moment. "It's a medical illness caused by something external."

"Like a bacteria? Virus? Germ of some sort?"

"No, trauma."

"A medical illness caused by—?"

He nodded.

"And that's what you have?"

He nodded again, smiling and looking at her sideways through the thick shelter of his hair.

"Psychosa—psychose—" She looked at her screen. "Psychosomatic. I've never heard of that before."

"It's uncommon."

"Thankfully," she said. "I won't make you talk about this anymore. I know it hurts you, and you must hate being around me. I'm always so dark."

"You give me a chance to question myself," he wrote. "I need that. Thank you. And I don't hate being around you. I—" He deleted his final pronoun and took his hands off the keyboard.

"Thanks, but you don't have to lie." Maru stood up. "I should go now. I've made you miserable enough already."

Rin jumped from his seat and stood across from her, then hesitated. He reached for her screen and dragged it through the air with two fingers, placing it in front of her, then did the same with his keyboard.

"How do I convince you that I want you to stay?" he wrote, then looked at her shyly through the translucent blue screen that hovered between them.

"I'll stay." Maru slid back into her chair. "You could have just said that, you know."

"I thought I did," he wrote. "I'm sorry. I've sort of forgotten what it's like to talk with people. I didn't even use my notebook for a long time. I just never said anything." He paused. "In fact, the first time I used my notebook since I lost the ability to speak was when I met you."

"Really? How long has it been since you . . . ?"

"Five years."

"Rin!" cried Maru. "You haven't spoken to anyone but me since then?"

"No," he mouthed, then typed, "Although Saito understands me most of the time."

"He's not your friend, you idiot! You're talking about not silencing yourself and living like a complete hermit for five whole years. You can't even take your own advice, so why should I listen to you?" Maru looked at him with a mixture of irritation and pity. "Stop holding it in. You're pretty strong, Rin, but you're not strong enough to do that. Nobody is. Talk to me, please. Make up for the five years you lost being all alone. I want to help you, but I can't do anything if you won't let me."

For a moment his face registered absolutely nothing, then he managed a shaky smile. "I'll prove to you that I am," he wrote, but his fingers slowed, and Maru could tell that was not what he was thinking about.

"You're only proving to me that you're not." Maru reached for his hand across the table and touched it, then drew hers back suddenly, hoping that nobody had seen her involuntary movement prompted by pity and sympathy. "There's still hope somewhere, Rin. There has to be. Between the two of us, we can find it."

Rin raised his eyes from the table. They were inexpressibly sad as they met hers and seemed to examine her heart, searching desperately for the friendship that he missed. Maru could never tell whether or not he found it, because he dropped his gaze almost immediately with a short sigh.

"When are you leaving for your mission?" Maru changed the subject in a slight panic.

"Tomorrow," he wrote. "I'll be gone for three days."

Suddenly he stood up, his head bowed. His eyes did not meet Maru's, but he reached over the table and gently dragged the screen away from her. He pressed some buttons on his watch, and both the screen and his keyboard disappeared with a click. Then he walked toward her chair, head still drooped, and put his hand on her head. She sat petrified. Slowly he raised his eyes and shook the hair from his face, allowing her to see them clearly. They were stunning and beautiful and blue. Maru read pain and regret and countless hundreds of other emotions in them. The only one she did not see was fear. She waited breathlessly for him to move, but he did not. He stood perfectly still, his eyes fixed on hers as if he was hoping to find life and hope in them. She tried to give him what he asked for, but even as she did, she realized that it was impossible.

Rin opened his lips slightly, then closed them again and exhaled bitterly. Slowly, painfully, he smiled, then patted her head twice in quick succession. It was a friendly farewell. Immediately he turned away and hurried out the cafeteria door.

"Come back," whispered Maru.

She felt tears start in her eyes and drip onto her tightly clenched hands. The despair she had been feeling was far worse now, because this pain was not only hers. It was Rin's also. She felt as if his hand was still resting delicately on her head, trying to comfort her and simultaneously deny the self-hatred that she knew was steadily taking possession of him. He could not avoid it. Neither could Maru. Touch was powerful, and Rin had accidentally transferred his emotions far too accurately. Yet something else had come with the ones that Maru could recognize. She could not quite define the feeling. It was curiously nondescript: painful but beautiful, sad but hopeful, negative but not entirely so. She decided that she liked it, and she blessed Rin for giving her the ability to feel it.

Is there ever a time when fire feels good while it's burning you? She twisted her fingers together. *Because that's right now. That's me. That's how Rin left me.*

She wondered how and why she assigned this new feeling to Rin's intervention. Something deep within stopped her from questioning it. It was just the way things were.

Slowly, very slowly, she got to her feet and looked around. The cafeteria was nearly empty. She and Rin had been talking for a long time. Somebody was laughing—a support recruit, certainly. Somebody was yelling—definitely an assassin, or possibly a team leader whose will had been broken under the cruel, heartless pressure to which they were exposed every day. It happened. Maru shuddered. She knew, now that she had met Rin, how terrifyingly real this mental pain was and what it could drive a person to do.

"I hate you," she whispered. She was not completely sure who she was talking to, other than perhaps the entirety of Rigel. No, that was too small. Rigel caused the pain but did not create it. To evil. No, evil did not create itself. To God then, for letting this happen.

"I hate you!" she shouted, looking up at the ceiling. "I hate you for hurting Rin! I hate you for hurting me! Whoever you are, wherever you are, if you even exist, I hate you!"

CHAPTER 10

Maru woke up deeply ashamed of her outburst the night before. She hoped nobody had heard her screaming at the ceiling. There was only the sky beyond the ceiling, and the sky was impersonal. Beyond that there were the stars which could not hear her. Beyond that—nothing. She had been ridiculous, cowardly. She did not need to talk to anybody but Rin. Together they could solve this unsolvable riddle.

"What are you doing?" asked Kita, removing her toothbrush from her mouth and grinning at herself in the mirror. "Are you actually leaving? This is our only day off. We should enjoy it inside."

"I'm leaving," said Maru without explanation. The truth was that she desperately wanted to see Rin before he left on his mission. Two pats on the head was not an adequate goodbye. She wanted to talk to him, to tell him to be safe, to remind him again of his promise not to consider silencing himself forever.

With her hand on the door she paused suddenly. She knew that she wanted to talk to Rin, but did he really want to talk to her? She doubted that anybody would want to be around her. There was a tangible aura of darkness surrounding her. At least, she thought so. Maybe it didn't come across that way. She sighed, and her self-confidence flew to the winds. She backed away from the door, dropped onto the sofa, buried her head in the pillows, and wept bitterly.

"What—?" Kita emerged from the bathroom and stared down at her. "What brought this on? What happened to you last night? You came crashing in here

like a tornado and wouldn't say a word to me. And now you're crying. There's
something going on. Are you really that sad about the fact that Rin is leaving
for three days? He'll be back, you know."

"Why does everybody keep teasing me about that?" moaned Maru, burying her face deeper into the soft comfort of Kita's furry pillows. "I don't care
about it! I wish you'd leave me alone, Kita!"

"I want to help you," she said, sitting down beside Maru and putting a
comforting hand on Maru's shoulder. "I can help you. Is this about Rin or
something else?"

"I don't know!"

"That's not very helpful. I'm going to guess it's a combination, then. Did
you see Rin last night?"

"Dinner." Maru sniffled.

"Oh, you had dinner together. That explains a lot. Well, I'm going to guess
that you talked about some dark subjects, right? Suicide, drug abuse, childhood trauma perhaps?"

"Why do you know all this stuff?"

"I'm a psychologist. It's my job." Kita rocked back and forth. "You need to
take your antidepressants."

"I did." Maru sighed and sat up, drying her eyes. "They don't help."

"Second," continued Kita, "you need to go say goodbye to Rin before he
leaves."

Maru started violently.

"Yes, I know that's where you were going." Kita stood up. "Hurry, please!"

"Where—where am I going?"

"He's probably getting breakfast from the cafeteria. Go, now!" Kita pulled
her up from the sofa. "I won't even come with you, although I'd really like to
hear what you say to each other."

"Don't spy on me." Maru rubbed her eyes and sat back down. "This is a
bad idea."

"No! I'm not letting you chicken out of this!" Kita was surprisingly strong. She pulled Maru back to her feet and shoved her toward the door. "You're going, and you're going right now!"

Maru suddenly found herself outside, travelling down the stairs, down the sidewalk, all at an even tempo she could barely control. She was floating, but she came back to earth rapidly. Where was she going? What was she doing? She looked irresolutely back at the safety of her apartment. No, there was no shelter there. Kita would verbally annihilate her if she came back and admitted that she had not spoken to Rin. Reluctantly she continued toward the cafeteria.

She opened the door almost shyly and looked inside. Somebody shoved past her and she almost lost her balance. A pale hand shot out to steady her. Her gaze traveled up the arm, past the muscular shoulder, up to the face.

Saito.

"Be careful," he cautioned drily, putting his hands in his pockets. "Are you looking for Rin?"

She nodded speechlessly.

"He left at four this morning."

Maru found herself still waiting for him to answer. Then his words developed meaning, and she felt an odd combination of regret and relief.

"Okay. Thanks for telling me."

She started walking back toward the door, but a quiet voice behind her arrested her immediately and she paused mid-step. "Maru."

"What?"

"I should tell you. Rin is going to—" Saito broke off abruptly.

"Is going to what?"

He stared at her for a moment, then, instead of answering, turned and almost ran away.

"What's going to happen to Rin?" she called after him. But he did not hear her.

"These people really won't let go of their secrets." She looked around the cafeteria, then realized that she was looking for Rin who had already left. "What am I doing?" she questioned herself bitterly. "My medications. I need my antidepressants." She reached in her pocket and pulled out the bottle, shook one pill out onto her hand, and swallowed it without any water. She looked longingly at the bottle, wishing she could take a second, but put it reluctantly back in her pocket. "Kita said it was dangerous."

Instead of feeling better, she somehow felt more depressed.

"Too late!" cried a voice behind her. "I was hoping you'd show up sooner. I was going to come get you, but Rin left before I could do anything. I'm sorry, Maru." It was Naito.

"It's fine," she said. "I just thought I'd say something before he left, but that's okay. He'll be back soon, and we can talk as much as we want then."

"What did Saito tell you?" he asked, following her outside.

"Not much. He started to say something but cut himself off." Maru hoped her short answers would discourage Naito from following her further, but he did not seem to notice.

"I was hoping he told you where Rin went. I'm supposed to be surveilling him, but Rin turned off all his communication devices and I can't find him anywhere. If I had a general idea of his location—"

"CAUS."

"What? Seriously? How do you know that? Are you sure?"

"Rin told me last night. But don't tell anyone else, and don't say that I told you. Rin went to investigate CAUS."

"I can find him based off that, I think," said Naito, cracking his knuckles and pulling up his holographic keyboard. He positioned it under his fingers, and it moved with him as he walked. "Yes! There he is. Hey, thanks, Maru. Your secret is safe with me."

"What exactly are you doing?" she asked, trying to see his watch. "What can you see?"

"I can't see anything," said Naito, expanding his screen so she could look over his shoulder. "It does give me information about his location and vital signs, though. Good to keep an eye on those."

"Vital signs?"

"I get the data from his watch," said Naito. "Even if he turns it off, I can still access them real-time. It's probably best that he doesn't know that, or he might take it off, so don't tell him."

"Okay." Maru looked at the charts. "His heart rate is seriously going up. What's with that?"

"Don't know. Maybe he's exercising." They watched the slender white line on the graph rise steadily and finally slow to a halt near the top. "It would take some hard exercise to get it up to a hundred and twenty. Could he be running? But why?"

"His blood pressure is high, too." Maru pointed. "Are you sure these are accurate?"

"I don't see why they wouldn't be." Naito pressed a few keys and stared anxiously at the screen. "Besides, the blood pressure and heart rate should move together, which they are. That indicates that the sensors are functioning properly."

"Hmm." Maru could think of no other explanation.

"Kinda odd," said Naito. "But who knows exactly what he's doing. I'm sure it's fine, unless we see them drop suddenly. Look, they're already going down, but slowly. That's normal."

"Well, as long as you're monitoring it, I guess it should be fine." Maru started to walk away, but Naito called her back suddenly. "Maru! Look!"

The white lines on the graphs took a sudden downward plunge into the dangerously low regions. Maru and Naito watched in horror as they kept descending. The heart rate line passed eighty, seventy, sixty, fifty, and finally stopped around forty-five. Blood pressure followed. Naito clicked his keys frantically, but they held steady and did not rise. Finally, without a word to Maru, he left his holograms hovering in the air and ran toward the hospital.

"Naito!" she screamed. "Where are you going? What's happening?"

He did not answer, and she ran after him. "Naito!"

She caught the hospital door before it shut and followed him inside, panting. As she paused for breath, she could hear the echo of his voice: "Something's happening to Rin! I need help!"

Two nurses appeared out of nowhere and stopped him. "Tell us what happened."

Naito took a deep breath. "Rin's blood pressure and heart rate just dropped suddenly," he said. "They're dangerously low."

"Do you know where he is?"

"I can get you there."

"Then we'll send somebody to look for him. Stay calm. Don't worry about your friend." The nurses had a hurried consultation in whispers before one of them took off running down the hall. The other turned to Naito. "Get us the GPS information. Is he moving at all?"

"No . . . no, he's staying in exactly the same place."

The nurse swore under her breath. "All right. Come with us."

"What about me?" asked Maru. She regretted the words as soon as she said them, because they revealed her shaking voice. She straightened her face as much as she could and added steadily, "I want to come with you."

"There's not enough room," said the nurse shortly, turning away.

"She's Rin's teammate," explained Naito. "I think she should come."

"It's not a matter of should or shouldn't. She can't come." The nurse was already halfway down the hall, and with an apologetic glance at Maru, Naito followed her.

Maru stood shivering with anxiety and fear and irritation. Where could she go? What could she do? It was the first emergency she had seen since joining Rigel, and she was absolutely useless. She crossed her arms and forced herself to stop shaking. She dropped her head for a moment, willing her face to be as inexpressive as Rin's or Saito's and reveal none of her feelings. When she looked up it was ice cold. She did not bother trying to reassure herself that nothing was wrong, because she knew deep inside that something really was happening. Somehow, she controlled herself violently from the inside, nearing the breaking point of her strength but never crossing it. In the moment she half wondered at herself, but that thought was quickly replaced by nothingness. It was almost a relief.

A nurse passed her, then turned back and said, "What are you doing here?"

"Reporting some information," said Maru briefly and icily. "I will be going now."

She let herself out the front door and stood on the sidewalk, unable to move. She felt that if she did, her self-control would fly to the winds. What was wrong with showing her emotions? They made her weak. What was wrong with weakness? It was the opposite of strength. Her reasoning was circular, but she did not bother trying to unravel it. Circles were the most perfect shapes, and after all there could be no real end to anything.

Dimly, from the corner of her eyes, she saw a long black car slide from the hospital garage and make its way rapidly out of sight. A pale hand waved at her from the window, and she wondered if it was Naito's. There was no way to tell for sure, but maybe that car was going to save Rin. A ridiculous thought, since Rin didn't want to be saved. He wanted to die, and Maru wondered suddenly if the reason he had hesitated in killing himself was because he felt it was cowardice. If he was going to die, it had to be while doing something useful. And what was the definition of useful? Maru's questions overwhelmed her, and she fled, with no idea where she was going.

"Wait up!" cried a shrill voice behind her.

Maru recognized the voice as Kita's, but she did not stop. In fact, she sped up, the long, hard hours of painful training lending her wings. She wanted to run from her questions. She never wanted to stop running. She would have welcomed anything, absolutely anything, that might take her mind off where she was and what she was doing. Mixed with these emotions was an intense pity for Rin. Her hands were clean compared to his, and she could not imagine the ocean of guilt he must be feeling. Bloodstained, dripping, his hands appeared blindingly in front of her, reaching for hers. She covered her eyes and screamed involuntarily, trying to get away. The wet hands held her fast.

"What's wrong with you?" asked a dim voice. Maru could barely hear it at first, but it became clearer as the speaker continued calmly. "Maru? Can you hear me? Why are you trying to fight me?"

Maru blinked. The bloody hands were gone and there was only Kita, her hands damp with sweat. She twined her fingers reassuringly around Maru's. "It's a side effect of the medication," she said. "Nothing to worry about. This will go away with time."

"You—you—" Swearing was strictly forbidden at Rigel. "You don't know anything! Let me go!"

"I won't," said Kita. "What were you running from, anyway? What did you see?"

"I saw . . ." Maru suddenly struggled to remember the hallucination. She tilted her head up to the sky and closed her eyes against its brightness, wondering what had just happened. "Hands . . .? Rin's hands."

"Rin? Why are you thinking about him?"

"You don't know?" Maru's voice was expressionless. "Naito noticed a drop in his vital signs. They're going to look for him now."

"What? Something happened to Rin?" Kita was startled. "Why didn't you just say something instead of running around like a maniac? It's not like that's going to help. But I can give you medicines that should make you feel better. I can—"

"Idiot!" Maru had found a suitable expletive at last. "What's wrong with you? I can't live my entire life relying on medicines! It's not real! It doesn't help! It only makes me forget for a little while, and then when I remember again, everything seems worse. You take these medicines yourself, don't you? How can you possibly not know that?"

"The relief from pain is real," said Kita quietly. "And it does help. More than you know. I know you're worried about the addiction, but I'm telling you that they're perfectly safe."

"I'm not taking them," insisted Maru. "I'm not. Leave me alone. Don't talk to me."

"It's my job as team psychologist to make sure you don't hurt yourself," replied Kita. "Therefore, I'm going to talk to you, and I'm not going to leave you alone. You don't have to be strong all the time, you know. It's okay to cry."

"But how does it help?" pleaded Maru desperately. "I don't understand how this is supposed to work."

"Well, if it's any comfort at all, neither do I. And neither does Rin, and neither does anybody." Kita released Maru's hands. "It's not meant for us to figure it out. We just have to do the best we can with the time we have."

"That seems pointless."

"It's not. People's lives aren't pointless."

"But you just said—"

"Stop trying to pick holes in my logic. I'm a psychologist, not a philosopher. That's too confusing anyway!" Kita giggled, reverting suddenly to her usual personality. "Stop worrying about this. Face the fact that you're giving up your life so other people can avoid this suffering. That's the right thing to do."

"Why should I care what they feel?" asked Maru drily. "They don't care about me. Nobody ever did. I don't see the point in this cheesy self-sacrifice line you're pitching. Why do I want to sacrifice myself? I'd rather live happy for once. I can't stand this. Nobody can. It's hell. In fact, I wish there was a hell that I could just go to right now. At least then I'd know for sure there was nowhere else to go, and I could just give up."

"Why don't you give up now?" asked Kita quietly. "It makes things a lot easier, you know."

"I can't. I don't know why. I think I'd go crazy if I stopped believing there was some end to this, but at the same time I know there isn't. This is forever.

This is eternity." She turned away from Kita to hide her white face. "I want to forget all of this. I want to die."

"So do I." Kita approached her again and put a hand on her shoulder, squeezing it gently. "But we can't. We agreed to do this, and we can't give up now. I don't know why any more than you do, but it's written into my nature to give up what I can't keep anyway just so I can make other people happy. I'm going to die. I look forward to that more than you could ever imagine, Maru. If you think you've been to hell, then I've been there and back more than once. But I have this life for now, so I'm going to do something useful with it. Don't ask me to define useful. It's vague and shadowy and I don't really understand it. This is just something I know I have to do. It's not worth questioning. It's just something I know."

"Those are just words," said Maru. "They sound beautiful. They sound convincing. But in the end, they're only sounds."

"Stop saying that!" cried Kita. Maru felt a sharp pain in her cheek and blinked in surprise. Kita's hand was raised as if she was ready to slap her again, and there was an unusually fiery light in her eyes. For once they were not empty and childish. They were more horrifyingly grown-up than Maru had ever seen. "Write your own lie and believe in it! But don't bother trying to destroy mine!"

"What are you saying?" Maru whispered, completely taken aback.

"I mean that I know these are lies! Why shouldn't they be? Why should that stop me from believing in them when there's nothing else?" Kita lowered her hand and stood quietly for a moment. "I broke character," she said at last. "Now you know who I really am."

"I don't." Maru's hands were shaking. "I've never seen you like this. But I don't understand you. Who . . . Kita, who are you?"

"My mother called me an angel," said Kita bitterly. "My heart tells me that I'm just the opposite. And somewhere in between I know I'm just a girl with a heart that's still half-human, which hasn't quite completed the transition to stone yet. Thank God or whoever for that."

"God?" Maru was dimly puzzled. "Who?"

"It's a figure of speech." Kita sat down on the edge of a nearby planter and crossed her ankles. "But I have a real motto. It's pretty simple, just one phrase. Self-sufficiency. I repeated that to myself hundreds and hundreds of times when I first started taking the ADPA. Every time I wanted to cry, I said that word. Aloud. It helped a little bit, somehow. It made me feel stronger than I really was—am." She laughed bitterly. "If you ever went into my room and read my journal, you'd probably laugh because you'd expect to find a bunch of silly school-girl nonsense. But you wouldn't. You'd see only the phrase 'self-sufficiency' written over and over and over again. I can't let go of it. I live on that phrase now. I forced myself to write it every time I was scared or doubted myself. I'm strong enough. I swear I will be strong enough for myself and for anyone who depends on me. Like you. And Rin. And—Naito. All of you—you're all I have to care about. You're the only reasons I still tell myself that I can do this."

"So you're not—you're not—"

"The shallow, self-centered brat you thought I had to be?" Kita shook her head. "No. I don't think anybody who really knows me could possibly call me that."

"Why do you do it?"

"I just told you." Kita stood up impatiently. "I do it for you. And for everybody else. If you're asking why I think the sacrifice matters, I can't answer that. Nobody can and nobody ever will. So, let's stop thinking about it. Remember that phrase—self-sufficiency. It's important." She stretched like a kitten, bending in ways that Maru had never thought possible and cracking at all her joints. "That car is back."

Maru glanced toward the hospital garage. Sure enough, the black car which had pulled out only a few minutes before had returned as silently as it had gone. Maru's attention was immediately fixated on it, and she started running without thinking. In a few seconds she had jumped over the planter and reached the hospital doors, tearing them open with brutal force. They swung widely open after her, and she disappeared inside.

*****   *****   *****

"You can't come in." It was the same nurse who had forbidden Maru to accompany them on the mission to find Rin. "Yes, we found him, and yes, he's injured. You're only going to be in the way, so unless you want to be responsible for your friend's death, you'd better get out of here. Now."

"Death?" It was the only word Maru had understood.

"Oh, you little—!" Apparently, the nurse had almost forgotten about the restriction on swearing. "Get out of my way!"

Maru stepped blindly aside, and the nurse left her standing in the hallway. She had never felt more alone in her life. She wanted to protest, to ask more questions, to find the information her heart desperately craved. But she could not bring herself to stop any of the nurses who passed her.

"Maru."

She blinked.

"Maru!"

She blinked again, and Naito's features emerged from the haze around her.

His face was anxious, and his usual smile was missing. Hesitantly he put a hand to his damp forehead, avoided her eyes, and sighed. "We found him."

"I know."

"He's in pretty bad shape."

"I know that, too."

"Were you in the room?" Naito controlled himself. "Do you know that he's going to die?"

"No, I didn't." Maru's flat answers were delivered expressionlessly, but inside she was conscious of a strange feeling. Although it was impossible, somehow it felt almost like relief. If Rin died, she had a reason to give up. And then they would both be happy.

"That's what the doctors are saying." Naito turned his back on her but continued talking. "Apparently he was shot in the chest. We don't know how or why—we only know that he's in critical condition. Even if he survives, he'll probably always have trouble breathing."

"I see."

"Do you not ever feel anything?" Naito exploded suddenly, turning back to face her, his face twisted with anger. "What are you, a statue? Do you even have emotions?"

"I'm not really sure." Maru's strength left her suddenly, and in that moment, she became herself again. She slid down the wall and buried her face in her hands to hide her honest tears. Her shoulders shook bitterly, and she could not relax them. "I tried," she gasped between sobs. "I tried to stay strong, but I can't. Just leave me alone and let me cry like the baby I am. You must all hate me for this."

"I'm—sorry—sorry," said Naito, his words jerky and disjointed. "I didn't mean it that way. Of course, we don't hate you. I just don't understand you."

"I don't understand you either."

"I don't want you to. If you did, you really would hate me." Naito clenched his fists. "Kita is the only person I've ever known who saw what I'm really like and still wanted to be my friend. There couldn't be anybody else like her."

"No, there couldn't." Maru sniffed. "I talked to her earlier."

"Where is she?"

"I think she might be right outside, unless she followed me in. Tell her I'm sorry for what I said. I'm sorry for forcing her to talk. I'm sorry for being so pathetic. I'm sorry for—"

"Stop!" Naito shook her. "You can't keep doing this."

"I think I can, at least until somebody gives me a reason to stop."

"I'm giving it to you now. You have nothing to be sorry for. You're destroying yourself with this."

"I know." She stood up and smiled painfully. "Thank you, Naito. I appreciate what you said. And thank you for telling me about Rin, too."

"That mean old lady nurse is gone," said Naito, looking stealthily up and down the hall. "You could get in there now if you wanted to."

"I'll try." Maru dried her eyes, and the very freedom to move was a relief. "But I don't want to be in the way."

"You won't be. Just stay in the corner. Kita and I will be back to check on you if you're gone for too long."

"Saito?"

Naito's face darkened perceptibly. "I guess we'll have to tell him what happened if he doesn't know already."

"How could he know?"

"News travels fast around here." Naito paused. "Maru, you should hurry if—if you want to see Rin alive."

"It's that bad? Is he awake?"

Naito shook his head. "No. But you should still be there for him."

"Why should he care?" mumbled Maru under her breath as Naito turned to leave.

"How can you ask that?" Naito's voice drifted faintly back to her.

Rather mystified, Maru walked slowly down the hallway toward Rin's room, which she recognized by the number of nurses and doctors hurrying in and out. She slipped past them and buried herself in a corner, hardly daring to look up. Beeping machines echoed in her ears, dully monotonous. Maru felt almost bored by them. Then she looked up, and her eyes were drawn immediately to Rin.

She half-stood, trying to see his face. It was deathly pale, and he was unconscious. Maru had expected him to be enjoying this forced rest. She thought his face would be calm, almost happy. But it was not. All she could see when she looked at him was pain and despair written in every feature. Physical, mental, emotional pain—all were there, and they left a pathetic mark visible even under the clear oxygen mask he wore.

"Who are you?" asked a voice. "Girl? Answer me!"

"I'm sorry," Maru backed further into the corner. "I'm Rin's teammate. My name is Maru."

"You know you're in the way, right?" The doctor sighed and removed his breathing mask. "It's okay. This is probably the last chance you'll have to see him anyway."

"You can't be serious about that." Maru searched his eyes. "Do you really mean that Rin is going to die? What happened to him?"

"You're more likely to know than me," replied the doctor, glancing over his shoulder at Rin's still figure. "All I know is that his injury is to the lungs and that it was obviously caused by a bullet. Apparently, there was a gun in his hand with bullets that match the one in his chest, but I doubt it was a suicide. If it had been, he would have shot himself in the head and died instantly and painlessly. Now—" He shrugged expressively. Rin's face for once was easy to read.

"I see," said Maru quietly. "How long does he have to live?"

The doctor hesitated. "I didn't want to tell you this," he began, "because I don't want you to believe it until I know it's true. But it's too late now, so I might as well say it. There's a chance he might not die. But even if he doesn't, he's always going to have trouble breathing. And he probably can't continue to work here at Rigel. He'll never be able to perform any physical activity without risking reopening his wound. Are you sure you want him to live like that?"

"Don't kill him," whispered Maru. "Don't kill Rin."

"What are you? Lovebirds?" the doctor mocked.

Maru turned her face away from him.

"I'm sorry," he said quickly. "I didn't mean anything by that, you know. But why would you think I'm going to kill him? We're all doing our best here."

"When will we know?" asked Maru without answering his question.

"In a few hours. If he wakes up, he'll probably live. If he doesn't, then it's too late."

"Can I stay here?"

"In this room? I guess you can if you want to."

"I want to stay." Maru pulled a nearby chair into her corner and sat firmly down, gripping the arms tightly. "I want to be here when he wakes up."

"If—" The doctor stopped himself abruptly. "When. You'll be the first person he sees when he wakes up." A slow, kind smile spread across his face. "I want to apologize again for what I said earlier. It was completely uncalled for. I'm stressed about this, too."

"It's fine," said Maru flatly.

The doctor nodded. "My name is Mikhail if you need anything. Just ask."

"Thanks."

He nodded again and left her sitting quietly in the corner, legs pressed to her chest, head resting on her knees like a child. She wrapped her arms around her legs and hugged herself tightly, taking pleasure in the tightness and pain of her self-inflicted squeeze. Every once in a while, between nurses, she caught a glimpse of Rin. His breathing was even, regular, and artificial, and his skin was an unhealthy, moist white. Once she thought she saw his lips part slightly, as if he were trying to say something. She wished she could help him, but nobody could save his life now. Maru wondered idly how the universe decided whether Rin should live or die.

She thought back to their last conversation before Rin left on his mission. "Saito . . . Saito . . . " she whispered. Suddenly she froze in horror. *Saito was going to give me this mission. That's what he wanted to talk about, but I was too much of a coward to go with him. I should have gone.* She tried to reconstruct the event in her mind. *I should have gone with Saito. I should have known that he wouldn't hurt me. Maybe if I had done that, Rin wouldn't have gotten hurt.*

Deeply buried in her misery, it took a while before she noticed the nurses had all left the room. She was alone with Rin, surrounded by only tangible beeps and hums and squeaks from the machines that were barely keeping him alive. Instinctively she was not afraid to cry, and she tried her best. But the tears would not come. Now that she was alone and could cry freely, she had no emotions left to feel. A deep emptiness replaced them, and she felt lonely but stable at last. If this was despair, she had experienced worse things.

She was wrong. It was not despair—it was the beginning of hope appearing from nowhere. Deep down inside, she did not believe Rin was going to die. She did not believe he could die because his mission was not yet over. His mission was his life, and he had not fulfilled his purpose. What that was or how he could discover it, she had no idea. But it was there, it was his goal, and he had to reach it. He simply could not die yet.

She fixed her eyes on his face. His lips were twitching, and suddenly he opened his eyes. They were wide, startled, questioning. He looked first at the ceiling, then left, then right, and finally toward her corner. His eyes fixed on her for what seemed like forever to both of them, and then his face relaxed. His lips did not smile, but the pain faded from them and he looked infinitely happier.

"I'm so happy you're awake," cried Maru.

This time he did smile. Then his eyes closed, and he was immediately asleep.

CHAPTER 11

"You should have died." Naito's cheerful remark brought a wry smile to Rin's bland face. "It's Maru's fault you didn't. She wouldn't let the doctors leave you since you got here two days ago."

Maru blushed and shrank into her corner.

Kita nodded and clapped. "What a perfect story!" she crowed. "So adorable! I want to see how it ends."

"It ends with death," said Saito coolly. "Rin got lucky this time. Don't follow his example or you'll end up in a worse situation."

"What exactly happened?" asked Naito curiously.

Rin looked at Maru.

"What do you want me to do?" she asked helplessly. "I don't know either."

He looked at his wrist.

"Oh, they took your watch off. I know where it is." She stood up, and with as few steps as possible, picked it up from the table at the end of Rin's bed and handed it to him.

"What are you doing?" asked Saito, narrowing his eyes.

"Rin likes to write on the screen," explained Maru briefly, sitting back down.

Rin enlarged his screen with the tips of his fingers, covering his face with it and positioning the keyboard under his hands. Then he began typing.

"I was going toward the target building," he said vaguely, "and there was an ambush. They expected me. Saito."

Saito jumped to his feet. "What are you trying to say?"

Rin's fingers did not move.

"S-Saito?" asked Kita with an adorable stutter. "What's going on?"

He went to the window and looked out, clearly trying to control himself. "I don't appreciate the hints, Rin," he said irritably. "Why did you type my name at the end of your message?"

Rin did not touch his keyboard.

Saito took an angry step forward and raised his hand threateningly. "Answer me, you—"

"Saito!" Naito's voice was suddenly stern. He reached up and seized Saito's wrist, pulling it forcibly away from Rin. "Stop."

Saito stood frozen in midair. Naito let go of his wrist and buried his hands in his pockets, smiling affably. "That was entertaining but unnecessary," he remarked, sitting back down.

Saito recovered himself and left the room without another word, his coat swishing against the doorframe.

"That's a relief," said Kita. "He's such a jerk. What's his problem?"

Rin's fingers moved rapidly across his keyboard. "It's not his fault."

"How do you know?" asked Naito. "What's the deal with you two?"

Rin paused, then wrote, "I've known him for a long time."

"Yeah, yeah. That's what you always say. Can't you give a real answer for once?"

Rin raised his eyebrows. "That is a real answer. It's the truth."

"Are you related?"

Rin started violently. "Why do you think that?"

"I don't know." Naito rested his chin on his hand and looked sideways at Rin. "You're pretty similar. You look alike, too."

Rin's hands shook as he typed. "He's my . . ." There was a long and suggestive pause. "Cousin."

"Oh! Now we're getting somewhere!" cried Naito, clapping his hands gleefully. "Your cousin! Tell us about it! Did you see each other often when you were little? Did you go to school together? Did you ever have a crush on the same girl? Is that why you don't like each other?"

"Before you ask him for more details, I should say something." Kita folded her hands demurely in her lap and winked at Rin. "That statement—saying that Saito is Rin's cousin—was a lie."

Rin nodded.

"This is so disappointing," moaned Naito. "Kita, couldn't you have just let me believe it?"

Maru winced at the familiar words.

"No," she said with a smile, "I couldn't. It was so obvious that I just had to point it out."

"No fair," he said. "Not at all. I was expecting a good story."

"Let Rin keep his secrets," said Kita with a yawn. "We're probably boring him anyway. Want us to leave you alone for a while, Rin? I have some stuff I should be doing anyway."

"Sure you do," interrupted Maru. "I saw a box on your front porch today."

Kita smiled, squeezing her eyes shut. "My latest library addition!" she said ecstatically. "Books, books, more books!"

"You're an addict," typed Rin.

"Even you can't say that you don't like them. Besides, I don't care what you think." Kita bounced up with a cheerful laugh. "You're welcome to borrow books from my library anytime you want."

Rin chuckled silently and typed. "Action? Adventure?"

"Lots!"

"I could bring you a few volumes if you want them," suggested Maru.

He shook his head and typed, "It's okay. But thank you."

"You're going to be bored," said Naito.

"No. I want to think."

"You're not allowed to do that!" cried Kita. "I'll cram books down your throat before I let you waste time like that. You need something to do."

He shook his head.

"Can you draw?"

He shook his head again.

"Can you write?"

"No." His lips silently formed the word.

"Can you do anything?"

He half smiled. "Not really."

"Can you watch movies?"

He shook his head violently. "No!"

"SAS," explained Maru.

"Should have seen that coming," muttered Kita to herself. "I made a mistake. Well, is there anybody you want to call on the phone? Anybody you want to talk to? Seriously, you can't just sit here. I appreciate the fact that not everybody likes books as much as I do, but still."

His fingers hovered above his keyboard, but he sighed and let them fall through it to his lap. His lips mouthed something incomprehensible.

Maru leaned closer. "What?"

He looked up at her with a half-smile and put his fingers in his ears.

"Music!" she cried. "You want your earbuds so you can listen to music. I'll go find them for you. Do you know where you left them?"

"In my room somewhere," he typed.

"What's your number? And code?"

"The number is 20, the code is 5560."

"I can remember that. I'll be right back with them." Maru jumped up, glad to have something to do.

In a few seconds she was out the door, running down the sidewalk toward Rin's dorm. By now she knew her way around, and she easily found the second building. Rin's dorm was on the bottom floor. She typed the code in the door and let herself in, looking around nervously as if she was afraid of trespassing. It was a single room with barely enough space for a bed and tiny bathroom. The room was starkly neat. The bed was made with military regularity, the bathroom was sparkling clean, and the floor was spotless. All of Rin's personal possessions were out of sight, hidden possibly under his bed or in the shelf above it.

"Where would he keep his earbuds?" Maru asked herself aloud.

Somebody laughed softly, and she twitched and stumbled back against the bed in surprise. Then she steadied herself. "Who's there?"

"You don't have to worry," said a sleepy voice. "It's me, Saito." He had pushed the front door open while she had her back to it and stood leaning against the frame, head drooped on his chest, looking at her slyly from the corner of his eyes. "What are you doing?"

"Rin asked me to find something for him," said Maru stiffly.

"Oh? Rin never tells anyone his passcode." Saito smiled suggestively. "Are you sure that's what you're doing? Looking for something—to give to him?"

Maru was annoyed. "I don't know what you're trying to say, but Rin and the others are waiting for me. Please get out of my way."

"That's a very rude way to speak to your superior." Saito did not move from the doorway. "Don't worry, Maru. I know you well and I'm sure you have nothing to hide. But you don't seem to be paying much attention to my advice about not becoming friends with Rin. Why? Do you trust him more than me?"

Maru hesitated for a split second, then pinched her lips firmly together and remained silent. She had already gone too far, and anything else she said would only make things worse.

"That's unfortunate. What did I do to lose your trust?" He stood up suddenly and towered over her, an unreadable expression in his bright blue eyes. "Tell me so I can make it up to you. I want you to trust me again."

"That's not the problem," said Maru, trying to duck past him. "Besides, getting in my way like this isn't helping your case."

He stepped in front of her and crossed his arms. "Be honest, Maru. You hate me. Why?"

"Get out of my way, Saito," she said briefly, all her nervousness fading suddenly into irritation. "If you don't know, then I can't help you."

"I'm asking because I want to be friends with you," said Saito, dropping his eyes for a split second. "Don't you understand, Maru? I'm doing my best. I'm sorry that I can't be happy all the time, and I'm sorry that I can't appeal to your emotions like Rin. But that's not why everybody dislikes me. There's something else, and I want to know what it is."

"Well, let me think." Maru put a sarcastic hand to her chin and looked up at him. "You're always a little bit of a jerk. You make people mad. You don't care about anyone but yourself. You never even think about anyone else. That's a pretty good start."

"That's not true. I think about other people all the time." Saito looked startled. "Why do you think I don't care? I wouldn't be sacrificing my whole life if I didn't, Maru. You should know that by now."

"People don't like you because you don't like them, Saito." Maru finally succeeded in squeezing past him and out the door. Once on the porch, she looked back at him, gray eyes smoldering. "And I don't care what you do. I'll follow your orders because you're my leader, but there's no way I'll ever be friends with you." She turned away and hurried down the sidewalk.

"What is his problem?" she whispered to herself in exasperation. Suddenly she froze. "I forgot the earbuds." Hesitantly, she looked back at Rin's apartment. Saito was just coming out the door, shutting and locking it carefully behind him. He looked up and down the street, located Maru, and started walking toward her.

Maru rapidly considered her options. She couldn't run away. She couldn't ignore him. She couldn't keep walking. What on earth should she do?

She was on the verge of giving in to her first impulse, which was to run, but it was too late. Saito was calling to her.

"Wait, Maru!"

She stiffened defensively.

"I'm sorry." He stopped in front of her and bowed. "I apologize for my behavior earlier, Maru. I sincerely wanted to change myself."

Maru did not reply.

"Here are Rin's earbuds. You can take them to him if you want. I'm guess-ing that's what he asked you for." He straightened himself up and handed them to her.

"Thanks," she said briefly.

He nodded. "Maru, I have more questions for you. I know you don't like being around me, but will you please make an exception just this once and have dinner with me tonight?"

"In the cafeteria?"

"Of course."

Maru sighed inaudibly. "That's fine."

Saito smiled, and for once it was almost sincere. "Thank you." Immediately he turned away and almost ran down the sidewalk in the opposite direction.

Maru murmured to herself. "What does he want from me? Does he really think I have any answers?"

*****　　*****　　*****

"Sorry to interrupt." The white curtain was whisked open, and a doctor with a clipboard and stethoscope entered the room. "I need to check up on your friend. If you could come back in about ten minutes, I should be finished."

Naito, Kita, and Maru stood up. "Sure thing," said Naito cheerfully. "Can't wait to know what's wrong with him today. Have fun getting poked, Rin!"

The doctor closed the curtain and the door behind them, leaving them alone in the quiet, cool hallway. "I'm glad he's okay," said Naito, leaning back against the wall with a contented sigh. "Two days ago, when they brought him back unconscious, I thought he was done for."

"We all did," said Kita. "Right before our first mission, too! The timing couldn't have been worse."

"Is he really okay?" asked Maru. "He's had two surgeries already."

"Of course, he isn't recovered yet," replied Kita. "He'll probably need a few more surgeries. The bullet went right through the lower part of his lung, you know. Worst possible place. But nobody has said anything about discharging him, so we can assume he'll go back to his usual duties as soon as he's recovered. Don't worry too much, Maru. Although . . ." She giggled. "It's kind of cute, actually."

"Stop already." Maru looked away.

"What's wrong with you?" asked Naito. "Seriously, why are you so worried? Rin will be fine."

"Since when have you been a medical doctor?" said Maru gloomily, without looking at him. "Have you ever been shot in the chest before?"

"Listen, Maru." Kita put a hand on her shoulder. "If Rin had wanted to die, he would never have woken up. He didn't die because he has something to live for, and as long as that's true, he'll be fine."

"That was extremely philosophical," said Naito. "I have something even better. I overheard his doctors talking, and they said he's lucky to be alive, but as long as he doesn't start bleeding again, he should make a full recovery."

"All we can do is hope, I guess." Maru slid down the wall and seated herself on the floor.

"That's disgusting," said Kita. "Do you know how much blood we clean off these floors? Stand up. You're all germy now!"

"I don't care." Maru did not move. "I'll just shower later."

"Ugh! Nobody ever takes my advice anymore!" complained Kita.

"Hey, Maru, if you're really so worried about Rin, why don't we eavesdrop on his checkup? That way we can hear everything the doctor says," suggested Naito.

"Good idea!" laughed Kita, clapping her hands together. "And that will get Maru off the floor, too. Let's go!"

Maru stood up reluctantly. "All right."

Naito softly opened the door and crept inside, remaining hidden behind the curtain. He put a finger to his lips and motioned for Kita and Maru to follow him.

"I certainly can't make this decision for you," the doctor was saying. "I can tell you all the risks, but in the end, I don't know anything for sure."

There were a few soft clicks as Rin replied.

"On the other hand, you might never have any problems," continued the doctor. "There's no way to know—"

Rin's clicks interrupted him.

"Are you sure?" The doctor sighed. "If that's what you really want, I'll do it. Anyway, I promise you won't lose certifications, and we'll have you out of here in two weeks."

"What was that?" whispered Naito. "He's out of here in two weeks, but . . . ?"

Kita slapped him, and he was abruptly silent. "Get out in the hallway!" she hissed. "The doctor's coming!"

Maru dimly sensed Naito and Kita slide past her. She heard their stifled whispers, but their words meant nothing to her. She felt a pull on her arm, but in her position, she was as firm as stone. Nothing could have moved her.

The doctor came out from behind the curtain, saw her, and sighed. "What are you doing here?" he asked. She did not reply.

Gently he seized her shoulders and shook her. "Who are you?"

She blinked. "I'm Rin's teammate, Maru."

"Did you hear what I said?"

"I heard you say something about risks and that he would be out of the hospital in two weeks."

"That's it?" The doctor's eyes were serious. "Swear to me that's all you heard."

"I swear."

"Good." He released her shoulders. "You can talk to him if you want."

Maru nodded. "Okay. Thanks."

The doctor started toward the door, then paused and looked back. "Don't worry about your friend. He won't lose any of his certifications." The doctor smiled. "He's still an assassin first, and a human after."

*****　　*****　　*****

"What exactly was I thinking?" Maru asked herself irritably. "Why did I agree to meet Saito tonight?"

She would much rather have avoided the cafeteria altogether and spent her evening eating cookies on Kita's sofa. But it was too late to back down now. She gave one last twitch to her braid and started out the door, slamming it irritably.

"Sorry," said a voice behind her. She jumped and looked back.

"You're just standing there in the doorway?" She could barely make out a shadowy silhouette. "Saito? Is that you? Are you trying to scare me half to death?"

"No," he replied, coming out into the light. "I was just waiting for you. I can't meet you in the cafeteria after all. I have an unexpected meeting, and I wanted to let you know."

"Thoughtful," murmured Maru, hoping she had not shown him how startled she had been. "No problem."

Saito nodded. "I really didn't mean to scare you."

"No problem," she repeated nervously. "I think . . . if you can't meet, I'll stay here for now."

"All right. See you tomorrow." He bowed politely and started down the steps.

Maru drew a deep breath and tried to calm her racing heart. "Scary," she murmured, reopening the door and collapsing on the sofa. "Okay. I need to watch some scary movies. Twice in one day!"

CHAPTER 12

"What are we going to do about SAS training?" Kita asked through a mouthful of egg. "Maru probably shouldn't go by herself."

Naito shook his head. "Don't volunteer me, please. I thought the videos we had to watch were bad, but apparently the assassination ones are worse. A lot worse."

"Thanks for the support," mumbled Maru.

"It has nothing to do with you," said Kita firmly. "I'm sorry, but that's the truth. Neither Naito nor I would be able to help you if we went. I think we should ask Saito to cancel the training until Rin is better."

"She could ask somebody from another team," suggested Naito, but Kita shook her head.

"That would be overexposure to traumatic materials," she said calmly, shaking salt onto her plate. "We can't ask anyone who's already been in SAS training to add any more time. Either we get Saito's permission for exemption, or Maru goes alone."

"I won't go alone," said Maru sullenly.

"Well, Kita, should we ask Saito?"

"The question," mused Kita, tapping her fork on her lips, "is whether we should ask him ourselves, send Maru, or draft a formal report."

"Report is out. We don't have enough time. Maru's SAS is scheduled for this evening."

"Evening?" Kita dropped her fork. "Are you serious? SAS training at night? Right before curfew?"

Naito looked at his watch. "Nine o'clock."

"PM?" Kita was still disbelieving.

"That's what the schedule says."

"Oh, Maru, you're in for it now." Kita sighed and dropped her head. "SAS training alone, at night. Heaven help you."

"You're right, we've got to do something," said Naito. "We can do it, right, Kita? Surely Saito will see how crazy this is."

"You're both ridiculous." Maru stood up abruptly. "Do you really think Saito would listen to you? And more importantly, do you really think I care?"

Naito and Kita stared at her silently.

"At least Rin doesn't have to see it." Maru turned abruptly away and hurried toward the tray station. Her eyes were filling with tears, and she could not let Naito and Kita see them.

"I'm an idiot," she whispered savagely, pinching her arm. "I can do this. Saito won't grant an exemption. There's no way."

Nevertheless, she hesitated, looking back toward the cafeteria. Rin's usual table was vacant, and she looked away immediately. Her eyes switched automatically to Saito's table in the corner, half hidden with healthy palm trees. She could just see him sitting perfectly still, staring out the window and completely ignoring the plate in front of him.

"He doesn't look busy," she said half aloud. "I could ask him now."

She shook herself, then glanced reluctantly back at him.

"I have to ask."

Slowly she put her tray on the belt and walked toward Saito, gathering her courage *en route*. She could not stop thinking about what had happened the last time she asked him for a favor, and she prayed desperately to no one that history would not repeat itself.

Saito looked up as she approached. "Maru!"

"I . . . I have a favor to ask you," she began, but he cut her off immediately.

"Kita and Naito already spoke to me about it. You'll get no exemption this time either, Maru. You knew what you signed up for when you joined Rigel, and if you weren't prepared for this, then you should never have come. You're committed now, and I won't take responsibility for letting you back down."

"That's all you have to say?" asked Maru mechanically. She had expected rejection, but it still cut deeply.

"What do you mean?"

"I don't know." Maru turned away.

"Stop," said Saito quietly. "Listen to me."

 She froze.

"Do you think you're alone? Do you think you're suffering more than anyone else ever did? Is this really all about you, Maru?" Saito laughed bitterly. "Believe me, little girl, you haven't seen anything yet. Don't complain."

She squeezed her eyes shut in mental agony. Saito was right—it was all about her. She was being selfish. She should be glad that Rin was sick and missing training. And yet she was crying, complaining, begging for mercy she already knew she could never receive.

It was unfair. Life was unfair. She was unfair.

With her back to Saito, she let a few cautious tears fall from her eyes and trickle slowly down her cheeks. As long as no one saw her, she could cry.

She felt something warm brush her cheek. Saito stood behind her and gently put his hands over her eyes, covering them and darkening her vision. She tried to pull away, but he did not let go.

"Stop trying to be something you're not," he said, finally removing his hands and letting them slide down her cheeks and neck to her shoulders. He turned her gently around, and she dropped her eyes, nervous and ashamed of her tears. "You're weak, so don't try to be strong all the time. I promise it will break you. You're not alone, so don't try to shut everyone else out. Ask for help when you need it. Ask me." His grip on her shoulders grew tighter and tighter, squeezing, bruising, hurting Maru until she almost screamed.

"Let go of me, Saito," she whispered. "Leave me alone!" The pain in her shoulders crystallized her emotions into something she could recognize and process, and she shook herself free from his grip and stepped back. When she looked up at him, her tears were dry, and her eyes were angry. "Why should I ask you for help? You don't have all the answers either. And if you really think I'm so weak, why don't you grant me an SAS exemption, so you don't have to watch me break? Or is that what you want? Are you really the kind of person who takes pleasure in watching other people in pain? Are you really—" She paused in astonishment.

With one quick, giant step, Saito wrapped his arms around her and drew her into a tight hug. She was shorter than him, and her face was buried in his shoulder. She felt him rest his head on hers and stood momentarily paralyzed with surprise. Then she realized that she couldn't breathe and tried to pull herself away. But Saito held her tightly.

She gasped for breath and stammered, "Saito! Saito! Please let go! I can't breathe!"

At last, after what seemed like a century to Maru, he let her go and stepped back. There was no apology in his eyes as he looked down at her, only quiet pride and his usual bitter smile. "I don't think I'm the person you believe I am," he said, picking up his tray and pausing beside her. She looked up into his intense blue eyes and shuddered. "I don't think you believe I'm really that person either." Without another word he left her.

Maru sat down shakily in the nearest chair. "What was that?" she whispered, squeezing her shoulder where Saito had pressed it. "Why did he do that? What's wrong with him?" She lifted her hands to eye level and watched them shake, then clenched them tightly. "He can hug me, but he can't grant me an SAS exemption. He can be kind to me, but cruel to Rin. He can touch my face, but—" She paused. "Touch my face?" She put a hand to her cheek and patted it slightly, as if she expected Saito's hands to still be there.

"Why did he do that?"

*****   *****   *****

"On your way to SAS?" asked Kita that night, popping a pill into her mouth and swallowing it without water.

"Yup," Maru replied briefly. She shook her own pill bottle and peered inside. "I'm almost out."

"The pharmacy can refill those for you," said Kita. "So you like them after all? They help?"

"Sort of." Maru crossed her fingers behind her back. "I want to increase the dosage."

"That's probably okay." Kita shot her an uncharacteristically suspicious glance across the room. "But why?"

"I think it would be better that way," said Maru evasively as she put her coat on.

"Why?" Kita was unusually persistent.

"Because the pills help a little bit, but I think I need more."

"More help? Or more pills?"

"Just shut up, would you?" cried Maru. "I don't want any more advice from anyone!"

"Something happened to you," said Kita, approaching her. Maru flinched, remembering Saito. "You talked to Saito, didn't you? What did he say?"

"I'm—I'm going to be late!" Maru reached for the door handle, but Kita slipped between her and it. "You've still got twenty minutes. There's no point in being early, so give up already and tell me. What happened to you?"

"Nothing!" insisted Maru, trying to push her aside. "Nothing, I swear!"

"You're lying." Kita crossed her arms. "I can tell. I see something I don't like here."

"What? You see me? And you don't like me?" Maru smiled and laughed hysterically. "Nobody does! Why would they? I'm an assassin like Rin. I kill for a living. I make people's lives a living torment, and I don't even know why. That's who I am." She took a deep breath and focused her vision. "So you don't have to like me. You should hate me. Now let me go."

"I saw Saito put his hands over your eyes, and I saw him kiss the top of your head," said Kita softly. "Now is there anything else you want to tell me?"

"Nothing else happened."

"But you don't understand why, do you?"

"No. I don't care."

"Yes, you do. You wouldn't be human if you didn't care." Kita put a thoughtless hand on Maru's shoulder, squeezing it tightly where Saito had bruised it only a few hours before. "Maru, you—"

Maru hit her hand roughly away. "Don't touch me!"

There was a long pause.

"So he did hurt you." Kita stood on her tiptoes and gently pulled Maru's shirt off her shoulder. "Look at these bruises."

"I don't want to look at them. I don't want to think about people, or what happened or why. I don't want to care."

"You can't help caring." Kita poked the bruise, and Maru flinched. "I'm sorry. When you get back from SAS, I'll have something warm to put on it."

"It's cold for bruises," said Maru shortly. "Now please get out of my way. You know everything you want, right?"

"Yes, I do, but you don't." Kita did not move. "You still don't know why Saito did that to you."

"I don't care."

"You need to know."

"No, I don't. I don't care."

"Did you go see Rin today?"

Maru was rather surprised at the sudden change of subject. "No. Why?"

"Why didn't you go?"

"I'm sure he's tired of seeing me."

"Actually, I went to visit him this afternoon, and he told me that he missed you and wished you'd come more often. He also said that he thought you must be tired of seeing him, especially because he can't talk to you. What do you think about that?"

Maru was silent.

"You don't think, do you? Or at least, you pretend that you don't. Well, you'll have to pick someday. I don't think Saito will hurt you, so you don't have to worry about that. All right, you can go." Kita stepped aside.

Maru looked at her for a moment, fighting off an unnaturally violent instinct to slap her. She controlled herself after a struggle and went outside without another word.

"There are too many questions," she whispered savagely, walking rapidly down the sidewalk. "Kita is right. I want to know, but I don't want to take the time to find out. And I think I might want to forget once I do know."

Beyond heading in the general direction of the SAS building, she was paying little attention to where she was going. Twice she tripped over cracks in the old concrete, but she caught herself with her hands and ignored the blood dripping from them. The wind was cold, cutting through her open coat and chilling her skin. She put her hands in her pocket and left smears of red on the black canvas. Bowing her head, she plowed into the wind, blessing the pain it caused her because it helped distract her mind. She walked quickly, trying to leave everything else behind her. There was a mission, a task to be done, and as soon as it was over, she could be free again.

"Why does Kita care?" she asked herself aloud, looking up just in time to catch a vague glimpse of a wild, shadowy figure standing right in front of her.

"What—!" She cut herself off and jumped back. "Who are you?"

The figure approached her, and she took a few more steps back. "Don't recognize me? Good. Then this won't hurt you too much." The figure laughed horribly.

"What do you think you're doing?" Maru's thoughts were still clear. "Who are you? Tell me, please."

She stopped moving, and the figure came very close. She could feel his breath on her face as he said, "Yuri. Do you know me now?"

She thought for a moment, and then Ayano's face came suddenly to mind. Her teammate—the one who had finally snapped under pressure—Yuri. "I remember you."

He brought his face closer to hers, and she turned away in disgust. "Say whatever you want, and then leave me alone. I'm going to be late for training."

"It's nothing personal." She felt rather than saw his hand inch slowly to her waist. He wrapped his arm around her, and she struck him in the face. He let go and stepped back.

"You little—!" he hissed.

"You're crazy," said Maru quietly. "Wait until your senses come back to you and then maybe try to make up for your mistakes. But don't do anything you'll regret."

"Regret?" His eyes glittered in the moonlight, and with a sudden swift movement he pulled a knife from somewhere in his clothing and held it up to his face. "I won't regret this, believe me. I'll be happy the rest of my life if I can just take revenge on the people who made me like this." He laughed again, horribly, demonically, every sense dead in horrible pain.

"You're not going to kill me." Maru tried to catch his knife wrist, but he jerked it away with more terrific laughter. "I'll kill you first."

"Don't lie. You're unarmed." The light danced around the shining blade, and Maru's eyes could not focus on it. She felt suddenly afraid.

"This won't hurt," continued Yuri. He stepped back, bared his forearm, and quickly sliced the knife across it, leaving a trail of blood dripping and staining the ground. He held up his bloody hand to Maru's face and looked at her through his red fingers. "Ready?"

"You demon!" she cried, shrinking back. "Get away from me!" As she backed away from him, her hand felt desperately inside her coat. She had trained for this. She knew what to do. She had only one choice, and as horrible as it was, it was sheer necessity. Self-defense. Her hand found what she searched for and gripped it firmly.

"Now!" shrieked the madman, lunging toward her.

Everything seemed to slow down after that. Maru's hand emerged from her coat in a smooth, fluid motion. She felt the knife slash her arm, but somehow her mind did not register the pain. Her arm did not drop. She pressed the trigger, and her aim, as always, was perfect. One shot to the head. Two. The ground was swimming in blood. Maru did not fire again. Somehow the man managed to stand there for a moment, still looking at her with a pair of horribly lifeless eyes. Then she stepped out of the way and let him fall face first to the ground.

Her hands did not shake as she put her gun back into its place. She almost wished they did. Murder was not supposed to be this easy. But as she looked at the blood and the lifeless body that had once been a man, a child, an innocent baby even, she felt nothing except disgust and hatred. The man deserved to die.

She glanced down at her arm. Her coat had been slashed, and now she could feel a very slight pain where his knife had cut her so deeply. Her sleeve was soaked, and she put her hand over the wound to stop the bleeding. The warm blood flowing over her arm and around her fingers somehow comforted her. She shivered, and suddenly realized that she liked the pain. It was warm, life-giving, reviving. It gave her the ability to feel again, and she blessed it. Then she jerked her hand away and looked at it. It was covered with blood, dripping onto the ground.

Slowly, almost involuntarily, she reached down and picked up Yuri's knife. Had she made a discovery? She had to know for sure. She held the knife over her other arm, staring at it for a moment, then with a smooth, quick movement, brushed the blade over her wrist.

There it was again, that sensation of life and vitality. Motivation. A reason to feel. She closed her eyes and smiled, living momentarily in a dream world where pain was the only thing that added value to life. Then she snapped her eyes open. She realized what she had done, screamed in horror, and dropped the knife.

"Well done," said a voice behind her. She whipped around.

Saito stood with his hands in his pockets, nodding. "I didn't get here in time to help you, but I see you didn't need my help. You handled the situation perfectly."

He knelt beside the body and felt the wrist for a pulse. "He's dead. Excellent. Well, I'll have someone come and clean up. Get to SAS training."

Maru stared at him uncomprehendingly.

"Are you hurt?" he asked, looking at the bloody knife and then at her.

She nodded.

Saito smiled bitterly. "Did he cut you, or did you cut yourself?"

She did not answer, but he seemed to already know. "Don't rely on pain to keep you awake. You'll only end up hurting yourself more. Go to the infirmary and get patched up. I suppose it's all right if you skip SAS for tonight."

It was so easy.

Maru walked blindly through the wetness toward the hospital. There was something she wanted there, something more than bandages. Something healing and reviving. More even than pain. She put a thoughtful finger to the wound on her left arm. It was not very deep and had already stopped bleeding. It was not enough to keep her awake. She needed more. She needed to feel. She needed a friend, and the only person she could think of was Rin.

She hurried in through the hospital doors, looked up and down the hallway, and turned right toward the bedrooms. Rin would be asleep. She should not wake him, but the temptation was too strong. She found his door and opened it shyly, peering inside. There was a strange glow inside the room. She pushed the curtain back and saw that Rin was listening to his music. He was looking right at her, smiling, begging her with his eyes to come closer.

He glanced down at her coat and saw the tears and blood. In a split second he struggled out of the bed, knelt on the floor in front of her and examined her hands.

"I got in a fight," said Maru vaguely, trying to reconstruct the event in her mind. "Somebody attacked me with a knife. I shot him. He cut me."

Rin's eyes widened and he stood up, still holding her hands in his.

"It's fine."

Rin shook his head violently and pointed to the chair in the corner of the room. Maru sat down mechanically, and he went to the trolley by his bed and fumbled in the drawers. A moment later he was back with a warm, wet cloth, some gauze and tape, and antibacterial cream. He held his hands out to her expressively, asking her permission. She nodded wearily and closed her eyes.

Gently, very gently, he rolled up her coat sleeves and bared her forearms. The warm cloth felt soft on her skin as he cleaned away the blood, pressed gauze to her cuts, and held it tightly until the bleeding finally stopped. He taped it into place, patted it thoughtfully, then returned to the trolley and found another cloth. Wetting it with cold water from the sink, he brought it back to her and held it to her forehead, catching all the drips before they touched her shoulders.

Maru opened her eyes and looked down at him. He was smiling up at her, his eyes flitting from her eyes to her arms and somehow taking in every aspect of her exhausted form. She could not see his bright smile and beautiful blue eyes without some response, so she smiled back and closed her eyes again, relaxing in the safety of his presence. He removed the cloth from her forehead and brushed her hair back from her face. His touch seemed to relax her, and in a few moments, she drifted asleep.

*****   *****   *****

"Let us commend Maru for her stopping the attacker single-handedly, showing great courage, and becoming a role model we should all admire!"

There was a long and rather artificial applause. Maru stood silently on the stage, her hair blowing freely around her face, the cuts on her arm from the previous night throbbing painfully. These people were being tricked. She was not a role model. She was a murderer, an assassin, somebody worthy of death herself. She had killed, now she knew that her own death had to be violent. It was atonement. She could never have peace again as long as she lived, and these people were being told to follow her.

Now, as she stood looking at herself in the mirror, she did not see her own face. It was as if the mirror had suddenly become magical, because instead of her own she saw Yuri's face, shadowed and dim in the darkness. She saw fear and death and pain, and there was nothing she could do to change the image. She felt half-asleep, as if she were dreaming.

"You did a great job, Maru!" Naito had said after the ceremony. "I'm amazed you could take him down like that! You must have been scared."

"I wasn't," she had replied mechanically.

It was true.

Slowly she raised her hand up to her face. Her fist was clenched around the handle of her knife, four inches long, sharp and glittering brightly in the white fluorescent light. There was something she wanted to prove, and now was the perfect time. Now that she was half-asleep, she could wake herself up. First, she had to overcome her fear of the steel, and then she could be herself again.

She ran her finger along the dull edge of the blade. It felt silky to her touch. She rolled up her sleeve and looked at her left forearm, still bandaged from the day before. She ripped it off and threw the bloody bandage in the trash can. Then she took a deep breath and deliberately ran the blade along her wrist.

There it was again—that sharp, painful jerk that brought her suddenly awake and alive again. Pain was her friend. Pain could do something all the medications and friends in the world could not—it could bring her back suddenly to life. She smiled bitterly. At last she had found something she could rely on.

She cleaned the blood off her knife blade and folded it up. Somebody knocked on the door and tried to pull it open.

"Let me in!" complained Kita shrilly. "What are you doing in there? You're taking forever! Are you okay?"

There was a long pause while Maru looked at herself in the mirror, admiring her own brokenness.

"Yes," she replied at last. "Yes, Kita, I'm fine."

CHAPTER 13

"Congratulations," said Saito briefly. "You're in. Both of you."

Rin shook his head uncomprehendingly, leaning against the wall and breathing heavily. Maru glanced anxiously at him, then back at Saito.

"You both have jobs at CAUS. You should look more excited." Saito pushed a folder overflowing with papers into Maru's hands. "You'll need to sign and date these and give them back to me tonight. I've got your apartments ready to go, plus a bank account for each of you which you can draw on as you please. You start working the day after tomorrow. Rin, you'd better be ready."

He nodded and straightened himself up, still panting slightly.

"You'll move out of your rooms and into your new places tonight, so go start getting packed. You have the rest of the day off, but don't think of it as a break." Saito turned away.

Maru immediately ran after him. "Rin just got out of the hospital," she hissed into his ear, "and you want him to start work the day after tomorrow? He applied for a manual labor position, didn't he? What do you expect from him?"

"Everything, including his life," replied Saito coldly. "Don't interfere." He turned and stalked away down the long white hall.

Rin pushed his blue screen in front of her and typed, "Don't worry about it."

"I am worried about it!" insisted Maru. "You're not well enough to be doing anything! Saito should know that!"

Rin started typing, then paused and gazed thoughtfully at her. He looked down at her hands and touched them hesitantly. Finally, he reached for her forearm and started rolling up her sleeve.

"Stop it!" Maru shrank back. "Don't touch me!"

Rin took an apologetic step backward and typed, "I'm sorry. I just wanted to make sure your cuts are okay."

"It's been a week." Maru managed a shaky laugh. "They're fine, don't worry."

"May I please see them?" Rin paused. "I want to make sure."

"They're fine, I swear," said Maru, pulling her sleeves down to her fingers and holding them tightly. "Don't even look at me."

"Did you draw on yourself or what?" he typed with a puzzled smile.

"No!"

Rin bowed apologetically. He made a sign with his hand against his chest, holding up two fingers with his palm facing away from her. "This means, 'I'll see you later,'" he typed.

Maru copied the sign and turned away abruptly. She walked halfway down the hall before daring to mutter to herself, "Why now of all times? Why does he care about my arms?" She shivered and clenched her fists. "I can't let him see what I've done there."

She heard footsteps behind her and turned just in time to see Rin flying after her, dragging his holographic screen with him. He was moving so fast that it could not quite keep up and appeared as a long blue streak reaching down the hallway behind him. He paused in front of her, completely out of breath, then straightened up and put the screen between them.

He typed, "Are you hurting yourself?"

"What?" Maru was genuinely astonished.

Instead of answering, he flipped his screen out of the way and knelt on the floor in front of her. Gently, but irresistibly, he rolled up her sleeves and exposed her white forearms, both crossed and scarred with their half-healed red lines.

He looked at them for a moment, sank to the floor, and touched his forehead to the ground.

"Rin! What are you doing?" cried Maru, jerking her hands protectively to her chest. "What are you apologizing for? What is going on?"

Slowly he looked up, and she could read the pain in his eyes as he gazed sorrowfully at her self-inflicted wounds. He sat back on his knees and touched her arms, running his fingers thoughtfully over the bumps and scratches.

Then he stood up, brought the screen back between them, and typed very slowly. "I'm sorry. I'm so sorry, Maru. This is all my fault, I know. I wasn't there for you when you needed me."

"How is any of this your fault?" Maru asked irritably. "I'm the one who cut myself. I'm the one who's so messed up that I actually like the pain. It's me. It's all on me. This has nothing to do with you."

Rin's hands hovered over his keyboard. "Then why did you come to my room the night you got hurt?"

Maru's eyes widened and she stepped back. "I don't know," she muttered. "I wanted to wake up."

"Wake up?"

She nodded, and her thoughts became clearer. "I came to you because I felt like I was half asleep."

"And that's why you cut yourself?"

"Yes." She dropped her eyes to the floor.

"I'll wake you up every day. I promise." Rin's typing sped up. "I don't want you to hurt yourself. I don't want to see you live with pain like this. Please let me try to do this for you instead of cutting your beautiful arms. Please let me!"

Maru could feel the blood rushing to her face, and she turned away. "Okay," she said quietly. "But I won't promise to stop. If you can't help, it's okay. I'll just keep doing what I have been."

She felt a hand on her head and glanced back at Rin. He was patting her head, laughing silently, head tilted precariously to one side. Even through his smile she could see the despair in his eyes. Just for now, he had chosen to hide it.

"We don't know each other very well," he typed. "Maybe we should ask each other some questions."

Maru stared at him. "Well . . . okay then."

"I'll start." Rin thought for a moment. "Actually, let's go outside. Will you go for a walk with me?"

Maru nodded.

He smiled again. "Let's go to the gardens."

Maru followed a few steps behind him all the way, looking sometimes at his broad, strong back and sometimes at her own scarred arms. She suddenly realized her own weakness in submitting to this pain like it was the only drug that could improve her life. But Rin was strong. He had survived all on his own, with no friends and a river of innocent blood on his hands. She was incapable of doing anything herself. She *was* weak, just like Saito had said.

"Rin," she asked suddenly, stopping in the middle of the sidewalk, "do you hate me?"

He started as if she had electrocuted him, then turned to her with a worried look on his face. In a moment he had placed his screen between them and typed, "Why?!"

"I feel like everybody should hate me," she said thoughtfully. "But I'm being really overdramatic. I have nothing to complain about."

"I don't understand why you'd think that," he wrote. "It's so far from the truth. It's my fault for making you believe that I hate you. I don't, I swear. Please tell me how I can make you believe that."

"Really, you don't? Why not?"

Rin looked mildly confused. "Why would I?"

"You don't understand." Maru looked down at her hands. "I was happy when I killed Yuri—not because I was proud of myself, but because I wanted to see him die. He taught me that pain could bring me back awake."

"I thought the same thing the first time I killed a man."

"The first time you . . . ?"

Rin's fingers flew over the keyboard. "I was only fifteen. I was in a bad part of town and the man attacked me with no warning. I broke his neck and killed him in a second. And part of me was scared, but most of me was happy that something so evil was killed and crushed and gone forever." He sighed. "I think it's natural to want to see evil destroyed."

"But he wasn't always that way." Maru buried her head in her hands. "I haven't talked to Ayano since it happened. Yuri was her teammate, and I don't know what to say to her. I'm afraid she'll see the blood on my hands and think I'm a horrible person."

"It was time for him to die," wrote Rin. "He had done everything he was meant to in life. His mission was finished."

"What did he do?" asked Maru bitterly. "He died knowing that he was a traitor to everything he ever believed in. He died knowing that life was a lie. How can that be the end of his mission when the only thing he left behind was pain?"

"He left you stronger than you were before."

Maru blinked. "Stronger? I'm stronger?"

Rin smiled. "You didn't know?"

She shook her head.

"Your past makes you into who you are today," wrote Rin. "That doesn't mean that you should live there, but it does mean that without that experience, you wouldn't be talking to me right now. I wouldn't be able to help you like this. And I—" He paused and shrugged, half-smiling. "I wouldn't have been able to tell that story."

"Rin, how did you become an assassin?"

He thought for a moment. "Let's sit down and I'll tell you."

"Oh!" Maru bowed her head. "I'm sorry. I didn't mean to keep you standing like this. I'm so sorry."

"No problem," he typed. "It feels nice, actually."

He pointed to the closest bench, positioned his screen in front of Maru, and sat down beside her. "Where should I start?"

"At the very beginning, if you don't mind," said Maru. "I'd really like to hear your whole story."

Rin nodded. "All right."

Maru sat back against the bench and waited.

"I grew up mostly without my parents," he began. "I had four younger siblings—three sisters and one younger brother, and one brother who was older than me by a year. He should have been at home, but he never was, so I had to take care of my younger siblings. I had to protect them when my father came home drunk or my mother came home with another man. It was everything I could do not to run away and leave them in misery, but I wanted those children to be happy. I don't know why. Seeing them smile when I came home from school and work always made me want to keep going.

"My friends told me that I would feel better if I used drugs, but I refused because I knew that would make me into my father. And I never hated anyone more than him. Besides, I wouldn't be able to take care of my siblings if I used drugs and was half unconscious all the time. So, I tried to find an alternative. I tried books, movies, music, but none of it satisfied me.

"Then one day I met a girl from my school. Her name was Taylor, and she was the most popular girl in the whole school. Boys followed her everywhere, asking for her number, begging her to go on dates with them. She always refused. But one day she walked up to my desk and handed me a slip of paper with a shy wink. It had her number on it.

"At first, I didn't know what I should do, but my younger sisters all told me I needed to call her. So I did, and we talked for a long time. The next day, when I saw her at school, I realized just how pretty she was. It was no wonder everybody liked her. Physically, she was almost perfect. I was proud of myself for being liked by her, but it never occurred to me what might happen next.

"A few weeks in, she asked me if I wanted to be her boyfriend. I never stopped to think about how I really felt. I only knew that as long as I was with her, I was liked by everybody. And looking at her was enough to distract me at least temporarily. So I said yes, and then she told me what she wanted to do."

Rin paused and stared at the ground, tapping his finger nervously on his leg.

"She spent that night at my house. As soon as she left the next day, I felt so happy. I had finally found something that could take my mind off my horrible life, something that could distract me. So I wanted to see her again. She came the next night, and again the next. I started being nervous, because somehow, I realized that I was giving away something which barely belonged to me. But I couldn't stop myself. I wish I had tried harder. Now I regret everything I did with her." Rin buried his head in his hands.

Maru patted his shoulder, and he looked up.

"I told myself that it was fine. I'd be with her forever anyway, because she was so beautiful, and I had convinced myself that I really loved her. Then, two weeks later I found that she had been with somebody else the whole time. I had given her everything and received only heartbreak in return. But I never once blamed her. I felt so guilty for what I had done, and I swore I'd never tell anyone about it. I also swore I'd never fall in love with anyone again, because if I did, I had nothing to give them. I had made my choice and destroyed myself in the process."

"You didn't destroy yourself," said Maru quietly. "You gave away everything you had, so now all you have to do is find somebody who loves you as a person and not for what you can give them."

Rin stopped and looked at her, his bright blue eyes half hidden behind his thick black hair. "Who?"

"Who?" Maru was confused. "It could be anybody. You're . . . you're probably popular with girls anyway."

Rin shook his head with a half-smile and continued his story.

"After she left me, things started happening quickly. First, my mom left the family. After that, my dad started coming home drunk more but then he started hurting my sisters and little brother. He never dared to touch me because he knew I had already killed somebody, even if in self-defense, and that I could do it again. Honestly, I wanted to. But then he did it for me—he was found dead from an overdose one day. I was only seventeen, and my siblings were all younger than me, so we were sent to an orphanage. While I was there, I was scouted by Rigel, put through a series of physical tests, and brought here for further training."

"That's it?" asked Maru.

Rin nodded.

"It's just—over? You haven't seen your siblings since?"

Rin did not answer at first. Finally, he shook his head.

"Do you remember what they look like? Their names? Anything?"

He shook his head again.

"Rin, I'm so sorry." It was the only thing Maru could think of to say.

He smiled at her, but there was a hint of uncertainty in his face. Then he typed, "Tell me something. Maru, do you hate me?"

"What?" She started. "No, of course not! None of this was your fault if that's what you mean!"

"More than half of it was," Rin replied. "Think of Taylor."

"Well, that was a bad decision, but you said yourself that you can't let your past rule your life now," insisted Maru. "You said you gave up everything for her. You can't get it back, but you can make up for it."

"How?"

"By . . ." Maru struggled for words. "You could just tell the other person and see if they'll accept you for who you are, not for what you can give them. Like I just said."

Rin nodded vaguely, staring off into the distance. Finally, he smiled, dismissed his holographic screen, and leaned back against the bench.

"What do you hope for, Rin?" asked Maru. "What do you wish for that you don't have? What do you want to make of your life before you die?"

Rin's screen reappeared before her. "All I want is to know why I'm here. Right now, I have no reason to live, except—" He cut himself off abruptly.

"Except?"

He shook his head apologetically and did not continue.

"No reason to live," repeated Maru. "Well then, why didn't you die in the hospital?"

"I didn't say I had no reason. I said there was one reason." He paused. "It's enough. More than enough. I *want* to live."

"Wait, Rin." Maru stood dramatically in front of him and put both hands on his shoulders. "Did you just say that you want to live?"

He looked surprised for a moment, then nodded.

"Can I get a recording of that?"

He burst into silent laughter and nodded. Maru solemnly took a picture of his screen and sat back down beside him. "This coming from someone who tried to commit suicide five times."

He shrugged and nodded.

"Don't shrug! You tried to kill yourself!"

"What else could I have done?" he typed.

"I don't know! You could have at least tried to find a reason for living!"

"I've been doing that for a long time," he wrote. "I never get anywhere. The closest I've come is that there must be something outside our universe. Something that determines good and evil. Otherwise I wouldn't be feeling this way."

"Like what?" asked Maru.

"Like God, right?"

"I guess so." Maru did not like talking about abstractions.

"I know what you're thinking," typed Rin. "You're thinking that God must be some indefinite, changeable idea invented to make people feel better. That's what I think, too. But I also think He exists somewhere. He has to, otherwise humanity evolved to this point just to end in total despair. We might as well destroy ourselves now."

Maru shrugged. "Maybe."

"Don't be so pessimistic," he wrote, smiling. "Look how far that got me."

"Would you tell me something?" asked Maru suddenly.

He nodded.

"Why didn't you kill yourself? I know you wanted to."

Rin was perfectly still for a long time. Finally, he wrote, "I always told you that it was because of my own weakness. In a sense, it was. It was because I didn't know what would happen next."

"You believe that death is the end, right?" asked Maru, twisting her hair around her fingers. "So we just vanish?"

"What does that mean?"

"I don't know," admitted Maru. "If I did, I probably would have killed myself a long time ago. But if you're right and God exists, that means we have a reason to go on living."

"Which is?"

"To help other people. You said God sets the standard for right and wrong. We all know that helping people is right. Therefore, we're doing the right thing by living."

"But why should we do the right thing? What does that mean?"

Maru could not answer him.

"It would all make sense if God is anything like us," wrote Rin. "I don't mean to say that He's broken like us, because that wouldn't help things at all.

I'm talking about a God who cares about people and wants what's best for them. That would mean that doing the right thing is following God's plan, which brings good to humanity in the end. Does that make sense?"

"I think so," said Maru. "But why would God care about us?"

Rin shrugged.

"Surely you've got something better than that." Maru laughed.

"Not really," wrote Rin. "After all, every word I've said so far is hypothetical. What if God doesn't exist?"

"I don't really know. I never thought about it at all until I came here." Maru sighed and shifted to a more comfortable position. "Why does life have to be so messed up?"

"Maybe God could answer that question, too. But I have no idea how."

"That's the problem. If God really cared about us, He'd make Himself obvious."

"True."

There was a long pause, during which Maru struggled to think of the words to express what she wanted to say.

"What if we started looking?" she asked at last.

"What do you mean?"

"Well, a lot of people believe in God, right? So, what if we start asking them about it?"

Rin shook his head. "Rigel doesn't allow religion," he typed.

"Why not?"

"They've had too many recruits who got religion and then left, carrying away classified information with them."

"Oh, I see." Maru thought for a moment. "Well, we don't have to say anything to anyone. Just do a little bit of research." She laughed ruefully. "Finding the answer to all this is far more important than anything else right now, anyways, I think."

"You're right." Rin nodded as he typed. "I'll look into it with you if you want."

"Sounds good."

Rin smiled quizzically at her for a moment, then wrote, "So we can agree that we don't hate each other?"

"What?" Maru remembered. "Oh, about that." She shook her head, embarrassed. "No, I don't hate you."

"I don't hate you either. In fact, I think you're a wonderful person and I owe you a lot," he wrote back. "I want to help you, too. From now on I'm going to wake you up every morning. I'll try to make you laugh or something, but please tell me how I can make you stop hurting yourself."

"Okay, but you don't have to worry about it. Seriously, I will be fine." Maru doubted the truth of her own words, but she could not contradict herself. "There's nothing especially wrong with me. I'm just a little depressed right now."

"Taking your medicines?"

"Of course. But I wish I didn't have to."

"So do I."

"You don't take them, do you?" asked Maru curiously. "Why?"

"Partly because my father abused drugs when I was little," he typed cautiously. "Besides, I tried twice to kill myself with them. I was sick for a while, but otherwise they had no effect. Now the nurses are afraid to give them to me."

"I see." Maru could think of nothing else to say.

"That's all I can tell you," he wrote. "What about you, Maru? Why did you come here?"

"I met all the requirements," she said automatically. "I had good grades, I was physically strong, and I was interested in politics. And when I was younger, I was so scared of the Kalideyes that I only wanted to destroy them. I guess I was afraid of being a coward. That's why I came."

"I see. I'm sorry. I'm wasting all your time." Rin stood up.

"No, it's just fine," said Maru. "I'm glad we can talk like this. It's nice to have a friend."

Rin nodded slowly and smiled. "Can I walk you back to your room?" he wrote.

"Sure, thanks."

Rin paused. "On second thought," he wrote, "you might get in trouble with Saito if he sees us walking together."

"I couldn't care less," said Maru. "Unless it bothers you."

He shook his head and closed his screen, then held out his hand to help her up.

"Thanks." Maru stood up by herself. "It's okay. I'm already too lazy."

Rin chuckled silently to himself and started down the sidewalk.

Maru trotted behind him, trying to keep up without having to run. *Why does he care about walking me back to my room?* She shook herself. *Maybe because I got into trouble last time I tried to walk somewhere. That's it.*

Rin turned around suddenly. His lips mouthed something incomprehensible, and he pointed over his shoulder. Maru followed the line of his hand with her gaze.

"Oh," she said with disgust. "Saito."

Rin waved and disappeared abruptly into the bushes.

Maru was torn between laughing hysterically and running away. The two canceled each other, and she stood petrified in the middle of the sidewalk.

"Were you by yourself this whole time?" asked Saito curiously, approaching.

"Umm . . . yes," lied Maru uncomfortably.

"I see. From across the street, it looked like somebody else was with you." Saito's voice was quietly sarcastic. "There must be a squirrel in the bushes. They're rustling."

Maru could picture Rin shaking with silent laughter. "Could be," she replied idiotically, trying to look nonchalant.

"Don't forget that you need to be packed by the end of the day." Saito passed her without ever meeting her eyes.

"Yes sir," she said automatically.

"Sir?" Saito stopped. "Don't call me that, Maru. Just call me Saito."

"I'm sorry. It just came out, *Saito*." Maru stifled another sudden and almost incontrollable urge to laugh.

Saito continued without another word.

A few seconds later Rin emerged from the bushes, trembling in every limb with silent merriment. He looked up and down the sidewalk dramatically, hand shading his eyes which were already half-hidden by his hair, then looked at Maru and smiled cheerfully.

"Why does Saito always pop up out of nowhere?" she asked.

Rin looked amused and produced his screen. "You don't know?"

"Obviously I don't."

The screen disappeared and Rin turned away, a sly look in his bright blue eyes.

"You're not going to tell me, Rin?" Maru seized his shoulder.

Rin shivered and covered his ears with his hands.

"I'm sorry!" Maru held her hands up and backed away. "I'm so sorry, Rin! I completely forgot! Please forgive me."

He slowly dropped his hands and turned back to her. He was smiling, but his skin was pale and sweaty, and his eyes were half closed in pain.

Maru bowed desperately. "Are you okay?"

Rin gently straightened her up and nodded. Bending his wrist in front of his chest and holding up two fingers, he waved his hand in front of her, turned away, and ran in the opposite direction.

"Where are you—?" Maru did not finish the sentence. Rin was already too far out of earshot.

"What was that little thing he did with his hand?" She mimicked it, then remembered. "'See you later.' But why did he run away?"

"Poof!"

Maru started and nearly fell off the curb. "What? Who—?"

"It's meeee!" cried a familiarly shrill voice. Kita appeared from behind the bushes, fingers childishly spread apart in a peace sign over her right eye. "Do I look cute?"

"What?" Maru was too annoyed to answer.

"You really messed up there," observed the tactless Naito.

Maru glared at him. "Are you Kita's shadow? You never leave her alone."

"Well, it's 'cos she's my girlfriend," he clarified with a wide smile.

"No, I'm not!" Kita began, but Maru interrupted her.

"Stop the act and leave me alone, please."

There was a moment of silence, during which the only interruption was the gentle rustling of the leaves.

"I'll never get used to hearing you say that," sighed Kita at last. "I know we annoy you, but couldn't you at least pretend that we don't?"

"I'm sick of pretending," said Maru aloud, regretting her harsh words as she said them.

"Well then, start with yourself," said Kita. "Stop pretending that you don't care about Rin. Because it's obvious to everybody that you do."

"I never said I didn't," said Maru. "But I also never asked you for advice, so stay out of this." Burying her hands deeply in her pockets, she turned away.

"Wait!" Kita ran after her and pulled on her sleeve. "When you look at your hands, what do you see?"

Maru pulled them out of her pockets in surprise and glanced at the backs. "Nothing."

Kita gently reversed them. "Now what?" she asked softly.

Maru winced and squeezed her fists shut. "Blood," she whispered.

"Don't try to pretend that killing Yuri was easy for you. If it had been, you wouldn't be human anymore. I know you too well to think that." Kita's hands travelled up Maru's wrists, and she jerked them away. "Sorry."

"Don't be."

Kita sighed. "I'll leave you alone now."

"Thanks."

Maru watched expressionlessly as her friend trailed sadly away. Naito held out his arms to her, and Kita flew into them, crying bitterly like a little child.

CHAPTER 14

Maru stood in front of the mirror and fought with herself.

Blood. Pain. Death. The images burned relentlessly into her mind. Even Rin had run from them, covering his ears in a desperate attempt to silence the painful sounds he could not escape. She could not run. She was too weak.

"He promised he'd help me," she whispered to herself. Her fist tightened around the handle of the knife she held. Ironically it was pink and childishly blunt, borrowed from Kita's inefficient kitchen utensils. She ran her finger along the edge of the blade. A small drip of blood appeared on her fingertip, but she did not feel the pain.

"I choose not to rely on you, Rin," she said firmly, looking her reflection straight in the eyes. "I choose to rely on something I can control. I can control pain. Therefore, I'm not going to stop." She closed her eyes and whisked the blade of the knife across her wrist.

PART II

CHAPTER 1

"So empty," sighed Maru, placing her lonely bag on the floor beside her leg and surveying her new apartment.

There was not a stick of furniture anywhere in the rooms. Besides a bar-height countertop, the smooth expanse of open-concept was unbroken by any obstacle. Maru wondered dimly whether it would echo, and where she was going to sleep that night. On the floor, apparently. She sighed and opened her bag, rummaged inside, and produced a blanket.

"I need everything," she observed, looking inside. "I don't even have any normal clothes. All I have is—" she thought for a moment—"underwear, two books, a blanket, a credit card, and my watch."

She took the credit card from her pocket and looked at it. "Unlimited credit," she said doubtfully. "That's what Saito said."

With one more glance around the room, she made her decision. Abandoning her bag in the middle of the floor, she turned and ran back out the door, down three flights of stairs, and into the street.

"Where to go?" she asked herself. "I need everything. Literally, everything."

She stood undecided for a moment, waves of people passing her on every side.

She turned around, started walking, and ran slap into Rin.

"Ouch," she said, rubbing her head and looking dazedly up at him. "Rin? What are you doing here?"

He produced his screen and wrote, "I thought you'd want help."

"Is your apartment furnished already?"

He nodded.

"Why'd I get stuck with the hard work?" She laughed. "Well, thanks. I could use some advice. Right now, I mostly need a bed and some clothes."

Rin chuckled. "I don't know about clothes, but I can help you find a mattress. Follow me."

He seized her hand and pulled her behind him through the crowd. She was happy to stay in his shadow and avoid bumping into people, but Rin walked much faster than she did. She barely managed to keep up, almost running down the sidewalk.

Finally, after what seemed like hours, Rin stopped in front of a store, and he triumphantly pointed up to the sign, which was brief and to the point. *Mattresses.*

"Thanks, Rin!" cried Maru, catching her breath. "I would never have found this place."

Rin tapped his wrist.

"What does that mean?"

He chuckled silently and held up the wrist which usually wore his watch.

"I could have looked it up . . . ?" Maru sighed. "I left it back . . . where we lived before, because I didn't think I'd be able to use it."

Rin nodded slowly. Then he suddenly turned around and disappeared into the crowd, without any explanation of where he was going.

"Okay," said Maru to herself, looking doubtfully between him and the mattress store. "Well, I guess he's not coming back. Time to go inside then."

She opened the door and let herself in, looking hesitantly at the rows and rows of white, soft mattresses. Where to start? There seemed to be almost infinite choices.

"Can I help you?" asked a friendly clerk, coming up behind Maru and startling her.

"Oh! Sorry. Sure, that would be great." Her eyes shifted from him back to the mattresses.

"Do you like soft or hard?" he asked, crossing his arms in an obvious attempt to look professional.

"I don't know." Maru could not remember the last time she had any say what kind of mattress she slept on.

"Well, here's a soft one. Most people like it." The clerk made a fantastic gesture with his right hand as if he were showing off his own creation. "Try that first."

Maru dropped heavily onto the bed and snuggled into the soft padding. "I like it. I want this one."

The clerk looked surprised. "But we have hundreds of others . . . "

"It's okay. I want this one."

He sighed. "Okay, well . . . what size do you want?"

"I don't really care. Can't you just give me this one?"

"No, that's our display model." The clerk looked annoyed. "It's a full. You can go to the counter over there and order the exact same one." He hurried away and hid himself in the back room.

"That counter over there," repeated Maru vaguely, getting up reluctantly and walking toward it. "After Kita's sofa, this feels like heaven."

She ordered the mattress, stumbling over technical terms such as bed rails and box springs. When everything had been arranged, she paid with the credit card Saito had set up, sadly wishing that she had this much money in her real bank account.

"Are you going to deliver?" she asked as an afterthought.

"No, that's an extra charge," replied the clerk with a wide smile.

"Swindlers," muttered Maru, and she paid.

"I wonder where Rin went?" she asked herself irritably, talking loudly so that she could hear her own voice over the city noise. "And I have no way of contacting him, either. I'd better go buy myself a phone."

She looked right and left and across the street, wondering how to find the closest cell phone store. "I should have brought a map."

She saw somebody running toward her through the crowd and stepped back out of his way, but he stopped in front of her and smiled. It was Rin.

"Where'd you go?" she asked.

He handed her a silver shopping bag.

She rummaged inside and pulled out a small white box. "Rin? Is this a phone?"

He nodded and made a few quick motions with his hands, then stopped in embarrassment and looked at her.

She opened the box. "It really is. Rin, you didn't have to do this."

He laughed silently.

"Does it already have service, too?"

He nodded.

"Thank you so much! Now I won't get lost." She turned it on. "Oh, and can I have your number?"

He nodded, took the phone from her, and entered it in the contacts list.

"Thanks!" She put it back in the box and into the bag. "Ooh, you got a case, too?" She held it up and looked at it. "A kitten? That's adorable." Suddenly she started laughing. "You are so unpredictable, Rin. A kitten phone case? Really?"

He smiled slowly, his eyes never leaving Maru's face.

"I need a few more things for my apartment," said Maru. "You've been really helpful so far. Can you tell me where to find dishes?"

He nodded and held out his hand. Maru looked at him, confused. He held it up to his ear.

"Oh, you want to type something on the phone." She removed it from its box, snapped it into the kitten case, and handed it to him.

His thumbs flew rapidly over the screen.

"Want to get coffee first? Then I'll show you where you can buy everything you need," she read aloud. "Oh, sure. How do you know your way around so well?"

He smiled mysteriously, saluted, and started walking to the left.

"Wait up!" cried Maru, running after him. "What's that supposed to mean?"

Rin did not answer.

"It's hard to talk to you without your screen," complained Maru aloud. "Don't you have a notebook?"

The bag she was holding vibrated violently, and she pulled her phone and out looked at it. "Rin? How did you get my number?"

Another message appeared. "I paid for the contract, so I picked your number."

"What is it?"

Rin replied with a mischievously smirking emoji.

"What? Rin, what have you done?" Maru scrolled hastily to her settings and sighed. "Really? Of all the numbers you could possibly have chosen, you picked all sixes?"

"I had to pay extra for it, too," he wrote back.

"Why would you waste money on something like that?" Maru hurried to catch up with him.

"If it's Saito's money, I don't care," he replied, glancing back at her with a smile.

"You and Saito . . . " Maru paused. "What's the deal?"

"What do you mean?"

"Are you good friends?"

He shook his head.

"But you seem to know each other so well."

He nodded slowly and wrote, "I did tell you that we grew up together, right?"

"Oh. I'm sorry. I had forgotten."

"That's really all there is to the story. But you're right, we don't always get along well. We never really did."

"Do you want to?"

For a while Rin did not answer. Then he typed, "Sure."

"You could have picked something more vague," grumbled Maru. "Like 'maybe' or 'I guess.'"

He shrugged humorously. "It's up to Saito, not me. I did my best already."

"Is he younger or older than you?"

"Older by a year."

"How do you know that?"

Rin stopped in the middle of the sidewalk. "Why do you want to know?"

Maru looked up at him and blushed. "I'm sorry!"

His expression softened, and he looked back at his phone. "But seriously, why do you want to know?"

"I'm really not sure." Maru cracked her knuckles compulsively. "I was just curious. There's something here I can't quite explain, but I'm being ridiculously nosy. I'm sorry. I'll stop."

"No, it's fine," he wrote. As an afterthought he added, "I have nothing to hide."

"I didn't think that," explained Maru. He started walking again, and she hurried after him. "Really."

"Ik," he wrote back very briefly.

"Umm . . . Rin . . ." Maru was almost separated from him by a sudden rush of tourists. "Rin!" she cried. "Are you mad at me?"

A few pedestrians stopped to look back and forth between Maru and Rin, whispering suggestively or making small *tch* sounds if they were alone. Maru's already red face grew redder, and she ducked her head in embarrassment.

"What's wrong with me?" she mumbled, wondering what on earth she should do next.

When she looked up, Rin was standing in front of her. He put one hand on her head and patted it playfully, smiling the whole time. Maru stared into his eyes and wondered. He did not look happy.

"If you're mad, please tell me how I can fix it," she said desperately.

A tiny open space had cleared around them in the surrounding crowd, and all the nearby pedestrians were either watching eagerly or pretending to be entirely nonchalant. All of them were happy for any interesting moment to brighten their mundane daily lives.

Rin pulled her into a tight hug and sighed. Maru thought she could hear a quiet, rough voice say, "I'm not mad," but it must have been the voices of the people nearby.

He stepped back and shook his head, smiling.

"Thanks. I'm sorry if I did anything," said Maru, looking uncomfortably at the people around them. "Let's get away from here."

*****   *****   *****

Rin returned to the table with two paper cups of coffee in his hands. "Thanks," said Maru, taking the smaller one and immediately putting it down.

"You okay?" wrote Rin.

"Hmmmm."

There was a long pause.

"I disagree," said Rin, leaning back in his chair and smiling. His thumbs moved rapidly over the phone keyboard, but he did not take his eyes off her. "Tonight to cty ge in modus?"

Maru burst out laughing in spite of herself. "Do you have any idea what you just wrote?" she asked. "Tonight to . . . city be in . . . fashion? What?"

Rin smiled. "I'm the worst at typing without looking! But seriously, Maru, are you okay?"

"Yeah." She looked away.

"No."

"Yes, I am!"

"No."

"I swear I'm fine!"

"Then let me see your wrists."

Maru winced.

"I thought so."

There was another long pause.

Rin stood up, walked around the table to her chair, and knelt on the ground beside her. "I'm sorry," he mouthed.

"Get up, you idiot," she said harshly. "It's not your fault. It's mine."

Rin did not move, but a message appeared on Maru's phone. "Your arms are so beautiful. Why are you hurting them like this?"

She did not answer.

"I want you to be happy, not in pain all the time."

"Pain makes me happy," she replied sullenly.

"That's not true and you know it."

"Shut up!"

He looked up at her, and his lips twitched desperately as if he were trying his best to say something. Finally, he gave up and looked back at his phone. "I wish I could tell you."

"Tell me what? That I'm hateful and selfish and a horrible person? You can tell me that if you want. I don't care what you think." Maru still did not look at him.

"Tell you that you're beautiful and strong and that I've never met anyone like you."

"Liar."

"It's all true," wrote Rin. "I don't know how you can't see it but trust me. Everyone else does."

"Liar."

"I'm sorry I'm not explaining it very well." Rin sighed. "I wish I could say this to you in a voice you could hear."

"I can read what you're writing."

"Then believe me. Until I met you, I never cared enough to talk to anyone."

Maru read and re-read that last message. "Why?" she asked at last.

"I don't know exactly. I just wanted to."

"That doesn't make any sense."

"Yes, it does." He sighed and added, "Trust me. If I could explain, I would. I really want to."

"Why can't you? I'm listening."

He only shook his head.

"You're too mysterious, Rin." Maru tapped her finger nervously on the side of her paper cup. "But I'm sorry for being so rude. None of this is your fault, and for some reason it makes me mad when you don't believe that."

"Mad?"

"More like sad," Maru corrected herself. "Hurt. Depressed. Guilty. Something like that. Is there a word for all three of those together?"

"Despair? Depression?" he wrote, standing up and returning to his seat across from her. "I don't want to make you feel that way. I'll stop blaming myself if it helps you."

"I don't believe you."

He reached a hand across the table and gently squeezed hers. "I swear I'll stop if you'll stop hurting yourself."

Maru shook her head.

"Please."

She shook her head again, eyes filling involuntarily with tears. She blinked them away in disgust, but somehow, they would not stop.

"I don't think I've ever asked you for anything before. Please, just this one thing. It would make me happy," he wrote.

"Why do you care?"

"I don't know yet, but that doesn't matter."

"Stop asking me for this," sighed Maru. "I can't stop now. Give up already?"

His fingers traveled up her wrist and to her forearm. She felt them run over her scars, new cuts, and half-healed scratches. His gentle touch seemed to warm and heal them almost immediately. The pain faded away, and for once she did not regret it.

A moment later he withdrew his hand and wrote quickly, "I'm sorry."

"So am I," said Maru without looking at him. "I've made everything miserable for you. I've made you worry about me for heaven knows what reason, and I'm so sorry. If I can make it up to you, please tell me how."

"You don't need to," he wrote. "It's my pleasure. Really."

"You're not being serious." Maru stood up. "Do you mind if we go now?"

He nodded and put some money on the table.

"I can pay," began Maru, but he shook his head emphatically and smiled.

"Okay, thanks." She sighed again. "I owe you a lot."

"Nothing," he typed quickly, then put his phone in his pocket and held the gate open for her.

CHAPTER 2

Maru's phone vibrated next to her ear, waking her sharply from a deep sleep. Reluctantly she rolled over and picked it up, holding it sleepily near her face.

"GOOD MORNING!" it said with superabundant capitals and several heart emojis. "Can you believe how nice it is to have a phone?"

"How'd you get my number?" Maru wrote back sleepily. "Is this Kita?"

A few seconds later came the reply. "Yup!" said the writer cheerfully. "Sure is! Rin gave it to me."

"You saw him last night?" Maru sat up and sighed.

"Later in the evening. He told us that you two went to coffee together and that he helped you find some things for your house. I have a question about that!"

"Sure," said Maru reluctantly.

"Was it a daaaate?"

Maru slammed her phone irritably into her pillow. "Stupid Kita," she muttered to herself. "Why would she think that Rin would want to go on a date with somebody like me? That would never happen."

Another message popped up. "So? Was it?"

"No!!" Maru wrote back firmly.

"You protest too much!" Kita wrote back, but Maru ignored the message and got out of bed, leaving her phone behind.

"Not thinking about that," she insisted stubbornly to herself. "Not thinking about Rin. Only thinking about the mission." She surveyed herself in the mirror, trying unsuccessfully to smooth her rumpled hair. "I look ridiculous," she said mildly. "Absolutely ridiculous."

Slowly, sleepily, she pulled on the clothes Rin had helped her find the day before. They flattered her strong, feminine figure and made her gray eyes stand out beautifully, but she did not notice. Reluctantly she brushed her hair and put it in a neat bun, fastened a pair of silver earrings, and sighed.

"Somehow I don't feel like going to work today," she told herself conversationally as she poured a bowl of cereal. "I wonder if I'll see Rin?"

She ate her cereal slowly, reading the news on her phone as she did so. "Another Kalideyes killing?" she murmured. "Maybe I'm doing the right thing after all. A child this time, too. Why was he such an important target, I wonder?"

A vivid image from SAS training surfaced suddenly in her mind, and she winced. "I'll never let myself believe that I'm good again," she said with a rueful laugh. Then she shook herself. "Why am I lying to myself when I'm all alone?"

She put her bowl in the sink and rinsed it out thoroughly, taking her time and slowly rubbing the porcelain with her fingers. It felt soft and silky, a little like the blade of her knife.

A knock on the door jerked Maru out of her thoughts, and the bowl dropped to the sink with a clatter. "Postman?" She opened it and found herself looking up at Rin, who immediately marched past her inside.

"Why do you keep showing up lately?" she hissed. "Who do you think you are—?"

She heard a rustle behind her and turned around. Rin was standing by the counter, gesturing triumphantly to a vase of cheerful yellow flowers that had not been there before.

Maru blinked. "What?"

He sniffed suggestively, and she smelled the flowers. "Beautiful," she said, "but why, Rin?"

Her phone vibrated. "I thought they'd make you happy," he had written.

"Sure, but why did you get—?" Maru stopped suddenly.

Rin smiled. "I got them for you because I thought they'd make you happy. Is that so hard to understand?"

"Kind of," she looked alternately between him and the beautiful flowers. "It really is nice of you, Rin. Thank you."

He nodded, smiled again, and tapped his wrist.

"Is it time to go already?" Maru was so used to communicating with him that she did not pause to think about what he meant. "I'm ready if you are."

He held the door open for her, and she locked it behind them.

"I always forget to do that," she said aloud. "I'm going to forget a lot of things. This life is very different already."

"Mm," agreed Rin.

Maru stopped dramatically. "Rin, did you just say something?"

He shook his head and looked away, embarrassed.

"No, seriously. I think you just said something." Maru laughed. "If you can do that, you can say anything you want!"

Her phone vibrated. "Do you really think I can't speak?"

"What? What does that mean?"

He turned away.

"Wait, Rin." Maru twitched his sleeve. "I want to know what you meant by that."

He sighed and pulled out his phone. "There's a psychological reason why I don't talk. I'm confident I am physically capable of it, although I haven't done it in years."

"Please try," insisted Maru. "If it's because you're nervous, you don't have to be. I just want to hear your voice."

Rin opened his mouth obediently, held it for a moment, then closed it with a sigh. "I can't," he wrote. "It sounds stupid, but I really can't."

"Why not? Is there any way I can help you?"

"Why do you want to hear it?"

Maru was rather confused. "I don't really know. I guess I'm just curious. I think it would be nice."

"Don't worry about it." Rin returned his phone to his pocket and started down the stairs.

"You really aren't going to try anymore?" asked Maru, following him. "You must not really want to do it, then. I know you could."

He shook his head silently.

"Okay then."

They continued in silence to the bottom of the stairs, where Rin paused for a moment and reluctantly pulled out his phone. "Don't you think that loud noise hurts?"

Maru was surprised. "I guess so, if they're really loud."

"A baby screaming?"

"Annoying, but not painful."

"A gunshot?"

"Maybe a little."

"A man's voice yelling in your ear all day?"

"I don't know. What are you getting at, Rin?"

"That's why I don't talk. I hate loud noises, so I don't want to make them myself."

"That . . . " Maru searched for the right words. "That is ridiculous. And it's not the reason you never say anything. If you're really that paranoid, you could just whisper. Besides, you don't seem to mind our sniper rifles."

"That's different," was all he typed.

"They're loud," she said.

"But not in the same way," he replied, typing quickly. "I don't know if it has to do with frequency or what, but they're all right. It's voices I hate most of all."

"Why?"

Rin chuckled silently. "You never give up," he wrote. "You don't really want to know. Besides, it will only sound like I'm complaining, which I'm not. I wouldn't be where I am now without his influence, so in a way I'm actually grateful."

"Whose?"

Rin paused for a very long time, and Maru was afraid he was going to put his phone away without answering. Finally, reluctantly, he wrote, "My father."

Maru jerked his phone away from him. "You're grateful to him? For leaving you all alone when you most needed him? For making you take care of his children? For sending you to an orphanage, where you got scouted? You're grateful? How much of an idiot are you?" Her voice lowered suddenly on the last sentence, and she dropped her eyes, ashamed of her outburst. "I'm really sorry, Rin," she added softly. "I shouldn't have said that."

He nodded silently.

"Here's your phone back." Maru handed it to him. "We're going to be late for work. Why don't you get a taxi? I'll just walk."

"I'll go with you," he wrote, taking his phone back. "I'd like to walk, too."

"I'll try to be a little nicer," sighed Maru. "I really am sorry, Rin. I still don't know how to keep my mouth shut. Everything I say is always so bitter, but somehow I can't stop myself from saying it."

"Better to say it than not. Don't silence yourself," he wrote briefly. Then he looked sideways at her and smiled. "Besides, I'm honored that you want to say it to me. I wish I could reply."

"You are replying," said Maru, looking at her phone. "This counts as talking, Rin. I shouldn't have pressured you to use your voice. It makes me happy that you talk to—" She cut herself off abruptly, half wondering what was going to come out of her mouth next. "Anyway, thanks for getting these phones yesterday. Now we can talk more often."

"So you do like it?"

Maru read and re-read the message. "What does that mean?"

"You enjoy talking to me?"

She nodded. "'Course." Then suddenly she blushed and looked away. "I'm sorry if I come across as rude or anything. I mean, I know I do, but—"

A gentle touch to her shoulder stopped her mid-sentence. Her phone started vibrating, and she looked at it. "I am always happiest when I'm talking to you."

She looked uncomprehendingly back and forth between his sparkling blue eyes and his last message. "What?" she said at last, with a shaky laugh. "How is that possible?"

"Don't ask me," replied Rin. He smiled and added, "Who wouldn't enjoy talking to you? I know I'm not the only one."

"Kita and Naito? Oh, I know they're tired of me. They just need somebody to vent to even more than I do."

"Not them. Ayano, and—"

"And?"

"Too lazy to delete that last 'and'," replied Rin, without looking at her.

"And whom? I don't have any other friends."

"Saito."

"You think he likes talking to me?" Maru laughed despite herself. "Seriously? What Saito are you talking about?"

"The one we all know and love," wrote Rin with a rueful grimace. "I wish he didn't."

"Didn't what? Why are you so hard to get information out of? Come on, what are you thinking about?"

Rin shook his head. "Nothing."

"Nothing?"

"You."

"You're thinking about me?" Maru was puzzled.

He nodded.

"Okay . . ."

She did not know what else to say, and Rin put his phone thoughtfully back in his pocket. Burying his hands deeply in his pockets, he tucked his chin into his coat collar and focused his gaze gloomily on the ground.

"Are you mad at me?" Maru poked his arm.

He shook his head without looking at her.

"Is there anything you want to tell me?"

He stopped abruptly and looked at her, his eyes desperately sad, his tall figure still drooped. Maru stared straight into his eyes for a single moment, then took a few involuntary steps away from him.

"Rin?" she whispered. "What's wrong? What is it?" Her hands were ice cold, and she squeezed them together in an unsuccessful attempt to warm them. She cursed herself for her strange actions, but somehow, she could not help it.

Suddenly he smiled, and although it was obviously artificial, it made Maru less nervous.

"We're going to be late," she reminded him, and he nodded. They continued together down the sidewalk, neither saying another word until they reached their building.

*****   *****   *****

"Why?" mumbled Maru to herself as she followed her guide through the maze of cubicles. "Why am I here?"

She had long ago tuned out the guide's incessant stream of chatter and questions she had no time to answer. Her eyes took in every bit of the rather gloomy scene: cubicles everywhere in regular geometric patterns, walls and floors and ceiling equally colorless, people expressionless and tired. She shuddered.

"What should I start with?" Maru asked, unintentionally interrupting her guide. Anything was welcome if it would take her mind off this dark place.

"Sure!" babbled the guide. "If you'll just look over here at this machine, which you'll be using a lot, you'll observe that we keep these wipes nearby so you can clean it as soon as you're finished. The boss didn't want to, but apparently, it's a law now. Personally, I like them a lot, because I think it helps keep the office germ-free. We take great pride in cleanliness here—we don't want our employees missing days because they're sick. Hard work is a core value of this company, and you can't work hard if you have a cold. So please be sure to use these wipes . . . "

Her mind wandered as he prattled on and on, barely pausing for breath. She closed her eyes and tried to think, but her mental processes were interrupted by a recurring image. Rin. Why was he foremost in her thoughts? She snapped her eyes open and blinked rapidly, praying desperately that her cheeks were not red. Why should she be blushing?

The thought only made her more miserable, and the guide paused his flow to say, "Are you hot?"

"N-no!" she stammered. "You were saying?"

"Oh, about the library." He smiled comfortably and continued.

Maru followed him absently around the room, completely lost in her own thoughts. Rin. Why Rin? She hurt him, but he wasn't angry. In fact, he was doing his best to help her. That was it. She thought of him so often because he was kind to her. It was a way of satisfying her own selfish needs. She blamed herself bitterly, wishing she could go back in time and learn to know Rin without his artificial smile.

"Get out of my head!" she cried.

At once every eye in the office was turned to her, and the guide stopped in astonishment. "What did you say?"

"I-I'm sorry," she muttered, looking desperately at around all the wide eyes. "Did I say that out loud?" She put a hand to her head and laughed hollowly. "I was just thinking about—about—"

One of the ladies closest to her put a sly finger to the side of her nose and nodded. The other women laughed, winked, and returned to the desks. The men looked confused for a few moments longer, took the hint, and went back to their work. Obviously, they were still curious.

"Were you listening to me at all?" asked the guide suspiciously, his smile becoming suddenly plastered.

"Oh, yes. Keep going, please," said Maru in relief. "I'm listening."

She followed him around the building for another two hours, yawning occasionally, blinking to keep herself awake, and desperately fighting with her own thoughts. The fingers of her right hand would occasionally creep to her left forearm, running with shivery delight over her cuts and remembering how Rin's warm touch had felt against them. She did not hear another word of what her guide said, nor did she know where anything was, but at least she was happy in her own indefinite way.

"That's the end," concluded her guide at last. Maru was relieved. "Any questions?"

Maru did not have enough information to ask questions without looking ridiculous and revealing her ignorance, so she merely said, "No, thanks. Back to my cubicle now?"

He nodded. "And don't forget, you can always come talk to me. It's wonderful that you also like chemistry," he added randomly. Maru realized that she must have somehow subconsciously participated in the conversation. "I've been an amateur ever since grade school. I do love explosions, especially red ones. That's my favorite color. See you later!" He waved with a cheerful smile and left Maru alone in the hallway.

"Sorry about him," said a voice behind her. She turned around abruptly, and to her astonishment, found herself face-to-face with Naito. "He took me for a tour yesterday afternoon, so I know how it goes. My name is Naito, by the way. I am new here, too." He held out his hand amiably with a sly wink.

"Maru," she said briefly, shaking his hand and looking him up and down in confusion. "Where . . . where do you work?"

"You mean where's my office?" He stuck his tongue half out. "You don't actually care, do you? But I'll show you anyway. I think it's on the floor above yours, actually." He seized her hand and pulled her toward the elevator. "By the way, what were you talking about earlier when you said, 'Get out of my head?' Don't tell me there's somebody you like. I'll never get over it."

"Get away from me!" hissed Maru as the elevator doors closed behind them. "What are you doing, you idiot? What's this stupid little act?"

"Aww, don't be so harsh," he complained good-naturedly. "I just wanted to have a little fun."

"Am I just imagining it, or are you trying to hit on me?"

He shook his head. "I'm just teasing, I swear. I wouldn't want to fight Rin over you anyway. I'd get myself killed."

"What did you say?!" Maru was enraged. "Take it back! Take it back or I'll kill you myself!"

"Whoa, okay!" He pried her strong fingers off his collar and shook himself. Immediately as he did so, the elevator doors opened, and two curious employees looked inside. "'Scuse us," he said coolly, and walked past them. Maru did not get off.

"Are you getting off?" asked the two employees. "This is the top floor."

"Oh, no," Maru said acidly. "I'm going down. For some reason it made me go up first."

"I see," said one of them. The rest of the ride was silent.

"Is it really that obvious?" Maru asked herself, trailing through the cubicles in vain search of her own. "Why can't everybody and everything just stop reminding me of Rin?"

She sat down at one of the desks and picked up a nearby pen, twining it through her fingers. "Why—"

"Sorry," said a voice. "That's my desk."

Maru jumped up in embarrassment. "Sorry, sorry," she said, bowing rapidly. "I'm new here, and I don't know what's going on yet."

"Oh, it's okay." The man gestured to the next cubicle. "I know they were preparing this one for a newcomer. That's probably yours."

"Thanks." Maru hurried around the corner and sat down in the chair, resting her head on her hands so that she was not visible from the opposite side. "Why do I always have to be such an idiot?" she mourned.

Her phone vibrated, and she pulled it out of her pocket. "Good luck!!" from an unknown number.

"Who are you?" she wrote back irritably. There was no reply.

I guess I should get started. She leaned back in her chair and looked around. *What am I even supposed to be doing?*

A head peeked over the partition. It was the man from the next cubicle over. "You're a secretary, right? In charge of scheduling?"

"I think so."

He laughed. "You're not sure? Well, that's okay. You'll figure things out soon enough. These need to be entered into the computer." He reached over and plopped a giant stack of papers on the desk in front of her. Maru snapped to attention. "Each one has a name, date, and event. They need to be added to the company calendar, which you can find under Programs, then More Programs, then Extras, then Add-ons."

"Programs, More Programs, Extras, Add-ons," muttered Maru to herself, turning on the computer and scrolling through the menus. "Got it. Do I just hit this plus button?"

"Yup." He nodded, still looking over her shoulder. "You've got this down already. Did you work with computers often before coming here?" Before she could reply, he added, "Oh, I forgot. You've probably been doing this forever. Everybody uses computers, I guess."

"Not me," said Maru before thinking. Then she hurriedly corrected herself. "I mean, I did. You're right, everybody does. But I didn't use it for work very much."

"What did you do before you came here?"

Maru froze. "What did I do before I came here?" she echoed with an uneasy laugh. "I mostly just did school . . . a few internships . . . that's it."

"What did you major in?"

The truthful answer would have been national security and politics, with a minor in specialized economics, but that was not what she had written on her resume. "Business," she lied fluently.

"Oh, nice. Me too," said the man. "Hey, if you need anything, just let me know. I'm free after work, too, if you want to get coffee."

"Thanks," said Maru. "I might take you up on that. If you could fill me in on what's going on here, that would be great." To herself Maru added in a whisper, "Business casual. What does that mean?"

"Sure. There are some great coffee shops near here. How long have you lived in the city?"

"About forty-eight hours," replied Maru with a sigh. "I like it so far."

"It's great, especially when you know all the best places. I like spending the weekends just walking around and looking for bookstores, coffee shops, stuff like that."

"Maybe I'll try that sometime," said Maru absently, wondering privately if Rin would go with her.

"I always recommend it," he said. "My name's Kousuke, by the way."

"I'm Maru," she said, standing up and shaking the hand he offered over the partition. "Nice to meet you."

"Likewise," Kousuke said politely. "May I ask what brought you here?"

"You mean, why I want to work here at CAUS?"

"Right."

Maru cleared her throat. "I always like being a part of new enterprises. If there's something that can captivate all of mankind, it is scientific experiments properly handled and brought before the public eye. I'd like to show the world what science has to offer and becoming a participant in such a dangerous but beautiful scheme has always been my dream." To herself again she added sarcastically, "Never say in ten words what you can say in a hundred."

"Wow, you express yourself very well." Kousuke looked admiring. "But if you like science so much, why don't you work in that division? I'm sure they need secretaries over there, too."

Maru shook her head grandly. "It's because I don't have enough scientific training. My degree was in business, so I'm best suited for keeping things in line—over here." Her high vocabulary failed her at the last moment, and she was forced to resort to prepositions.

"Oh, okay. Well, that's really cool. I'd have to say that the main reason why I work here is so that I can afford to live in the city." He laughed nervously. "The weekends are my favorite days, because I'm free to do whatever I want and indulge my hobbies."

"What are those?"

He blushed like a girl. "I love graphic novels," he confided in a half whisper. Maru winced. "Ever since I was little, I've loved them."

"I see," she replied uncertainly. "I . . . I have friends who like them, too."

"But you don't?" Kousuke sighed. "I don't understand how it's possible not to like them."

"I do," Maru reassured him. "I do, but it's not a hobby."

"Oh." He looked cheerful again. "Well, I guess I can understand that. Collecting them is my favorite thing to do. I think I have—" He paused and thought. "—seven hundred volumes now."

Maru blinked. "Seven hundred . . . ?"

"Every genre you could possible imagine." His eyes glowed. "I love them all."

Maru involuntarily inched backward. "Really?"

"Yup." He stopped himself. "Sorry. I get a little carried away."

"Oh, no problem."

"So what do you like to do?"

"Umm . . . " Maru had to think. "I don't usually have very much free time . . . but I like reading and watching movies, I guess. I read graphic novels too—sometimes."

"Oh, nice." Maru could tell that Kousuke was doing his best not to say anything else about the subject. "Well, I'll let you get back to work. It was nice meeting you. What time are you finished?"

Maru looked at her phone. "Five, I think."

"Okay, me, too. Still want to go for coffee, then?"

"Sure. Thanks."

"No problem. I'll come get you then, I guess."

"Sounds good." Maru waved politely as his head disappeared behind the partition.

"I think I sound businesslike," she observed in a whisper as soon as she was alone. "It's a cross between casual and formal . . . casual and formal . . . casual and . . . " Her phone vibrated and her mumbling died away. The message was from Kita.

"I thought you might want Ayano's number!!!!!!!!!" it said, with a superabundance of emojis and exclamation points. "So you can talk to her!! She hasn't left yet but she has a phone, I guess. Idk how but who cares! How's work going??"

Maru copied the number and added it to her contacts before replying briefly, "It's fine."

"Did Naito flirt with you?"

Maru clenched her teeth. "Stop with this."

"Well?? Did he???!!"

"Yes."

"Oooh!! He told me he was going to, but I thought he'd at least wait until I could see, too." Maru could picture the disappointed expression on Kita's face, and she closed her eyes to try shutting out the image. "We're going to have a talk later!!"

Maru did not feel obligated to reply, so with a sigh she silenced her phone and turned to the computer. Spreading the hand-written schedules on her desk, she looked mournfully between them and the digital calendar.

"So boring," she murmured with a sigh. "Right about now—" she glanced at her watch—"I would be doing PT or something with Ri—" She stopped.

Her phone screen lit up. "You were going to say Rin, weren't you?"

"Kita!! Are you listening, you little sneak?!" Maru hit the send button with an angry tap.

"Don't hit your phone so hard," came the sweet reply. "Yes indeed I am."

"Through my phone? I'm turning it off!" Maru suited action to words and slammed the unfortunate device into a drawer.

A few seconds later the whole desk vibrated, and Maru froze. The vibration did not stop after several tense seconds, and she tore the drawer open and glared wide-eyed at her phone. "That won't help you!" said Kita triumphantly. "Naito can control your phone, you know!"

"These people are crazy," muttered Maru. The vibrations finally stopped, and she put the phone back in the drawer.

"Calendars. Schedules. Work. You're a big girl now, not a teenager texting in school," she told herself disdainfully. "Here we go. I'm not going to get distracted again."

CHAPTER 3

"Miss Maru."

No response.

"Miss Maru?"

Maru blinked out of a computer haze and looked up at the ceiling. "Hello?"

"It's Kousuke."

She spun around in her chair and focused her eyes on his face. "Oh, sorry."

"Headache?"

"I think so. I don't know." She put a hand experimentally on her forehead. "Yup, I have a headache."

"Still up for that coffee?" he asked, leaning against the edge of the partition. "I spent half the afternoon thinking of places to go."

"Did you really?" Maru stood up and stretched. "Of course, I am."

"Great. Want to ride with me?"

"Sure. I walked here this morning."

"Oh, so you live close by."

"Not too far. It's about a ten-minute walk."

"Would you prefer to walk or drive, then?"

Maru did not like the idea of getting in a stranger's car. "Let's walk." She stared deep into his eyes. They were brown, cheerful, and humanly expressive. He did not look like a Kalideyes, but he might be one of the half-humans. She shivered. If that was the case, then he was one of Rigel's assassination targets.

"I'm sorry," she said, recovering herself and plastering on a very artificial smile. "I'm ready if you are."

"Sure," he said. "Are you okay? We can stop by a convenience store and find you some headache medicine if you want."

"No, I think I'm okay. It should go away." Maru put a thoughtful hand to her neck. "Actually, everything hurts right now."

"Well, it's your first day of straight office work. You'll get used to it."

"I hope so. I hope it doesn't take too long."

"By the way," added Kousuke, "can I get your phone number? We might need to talk if you have any questions about what to do, or something like that."

"Sure." Maru racked her brains. "I'm sorry, I just got a new number this morning. Let me get my phone out and see what it was."

"No problem." Kousuke already had his out of his pocket.

Maru opened her drawer, pulled out her phone, and turned it back on. Immediately it started vibrating with messages from Kita: "Where are you? What are you doing? How's it going? Aren't you going to come visit later? I miss seeing you all day! What's going on now? Why aren't you answering?"

Maru sighed and scrolled past them.

"Here's my number," she said. "It's . . . oh, it's all sixes."

"What?"

"Every digit in my number is a six."

He laughed. "Did you have to pay extra for that?"

"Yes . . . yes I did. Or rather, the person who bought the phone did. It was a friend of mine." Maru suddenly realized that she was being too specific.

"Probably to be funny, I guess?" suggested Kousuke. "Well, that's easy to remember. I'll send you a quick message, so you have my number, too."

"Thanks." Maru put her phone in her pocket.

"Got everything? Need me to carry anything?"

"No, thanks," said Maru. "I've got it."

"All right then. The coffee shop I'm thinking of is just down the street. I know it's a little late, but . . . " He paused and looked back at her. "We could get dinner instead, if you want."

"I'm up for anything," said Maru, secretly wishing she could go imme-diately home and to bed. "My friend helped me find everything I needed for my kitchen yesterday, so I can always make dinner later if you'd rather do coffee."

"It's up to you."

"Let's do coffee, then." Maru picked the shortest path home.

"Sounds good."

In silence they headed toward the elevator. Maru's head throbbed pain-fully, and she found herself gently rubbing her forehead with the tips of her fingers.

"Are you sure you're okay?" asked Kousuke worriedly. "You're pretty pale."

"My head really does hurt," she said ruefully. "Sorry. I'll be fine."

"Do you mind if I change the plan a little?" Kousuke pressed the eleva-tor call button. "Let's stop by the closest convenience store and find some medicine. I know exactly where it is, and it's on the way to a nice restaurant. I'll buy you dinner, and then you can go home and get some good sleep. Does that sound all right?"

"You don't have to," protested Maru feebly, but Kousuke overruled her.

"It would be my pleasure. Besides, I'm sure you have plenty of questions we can talk about while we're eating dinner. I don't want you to feel sick the whole time, though, because that would be miserable, so let's get your medicine first."

"Okay . . . " Maru felt vaguely uncomfortable but could not quite define why. "Dinner?"

"If you're okay with that."

"Sure, that sounds great."

The elevator doors opened, and Rin stepped out. He stopped abruptly in front of Maru and Kousuke.

"Rin . . . ? What are you doing here?" asked Maru.

He looked blank for a moment, then smiled slowly and shook his head.

"Umm . . . Kousuke, this is Rin," said Maru. "Rin, this is Kousuke. He works beside me."

Rin nodded silently and held out his hand.

"Nice to meet you," said Kousuke politely.

Rin nodded again.

"Do you need anything?" asked Maru.

Rin's confused expression changed suddenly to a bright smile, and he shook his head, gesturing energetically toward the rows of cubicles.

"You're looking for something?"

He sighed and nodded.

"Okay. I'll see you in the morning, then." Maru realized suddenly that she would much rather spend the evening with Rin, but she had already committed to Kousuke. "Good night."

Rin smiled, waved, then turned and started toward the cubicles.

Kousuke called the elevator again. "A friend?"

"From school."

"Oh, nice." He held his arm across the door as Maru entered the elevator. "He's very quiet."

"I've never heard him say a single word," said Maru. "It's an open question whether or not he can actually speak. When he wants to say something, he usually writes it down."

"Interesting. Any reason for such prolonged silence?"

"I don't know exactly," answered Maru truthfully. "I guess I should warn you about something. Don't ever touch him on the shoulder."

"Hmm? Why not?"

"Again, I'm not sure exactly why that's a problem for him. But it makes him extremely . . . nervous."

"I see. That's good to know, especially if I'm going to be seeing him often." The elevator ground to a stop and the door opened. "Funny that he works here, too. Are you together?"

"Are we what?" Maru's cheeks reddened. "What?"

"Oh, you're not a couple?" Kousuke laughed boyishly. "Sorry. That was a weird question, but I always like knowing where people stand."

"Oh. Okay." Maru did not understand. "No, no, no, it's nothing like that."

"Good to know. I would have felt bad if I was taking his girlfriend out like this."

"Out?" The word escaped Maru's lips before she could stop it, and, blushing furiously, she could think of no way to correct her mistake.

"Never mind." Kousuke looked away. "I'm just being ridiculous, as usual. That's what I get for reading so many romance novels."

"Maybe." That was the best reply Maru could think of.

"Headache medicine!" announced Kousuke. "That's what we'll get first. Want to walk or take my car?"

"Well, I guess you are probably going home from here," said Maru. "You're parked in the garage, right? I can walk to the convenience store while you go get your car, and we can meet at the restaurant. Just tell me how to get there."

"Are you sure? I'm happy to drive if you'll wait a minute for me to get back."

"It's okay," said Maru firmly. "This will save some time, and you don't have to worry about me. Do I just walk right?"

"Left," corrected Kousuke. "You can't miss the big store. Once you stop there, just keep going left and you'll get to the restaurant. It has a big brown awning, and it's called _L'Aile ou la Cuisse._"

"That sounds fancy," commented Maru. "Is it French?"

"Yes. I think it has something to do with a chicken," replied Kousuke. "I'll meet you there, then. You sure you're okay to walk?"

"Of course." Maru nodded.

"Okay. See you there!"

Maru watched him enter the stairs to the garage, then sighed and looked irresolutely at the elevator. "I really wanted to talk to Rin," she muttered to herself. "I have a few minutes, I guess." On an impulse she ran to the elevator and pushed the button. The doors opened immediately, and she pressed the button for her floor.

"Why am I doing this?" she asked herself conversationally, leaning against the back of the elevator. "I'm wasting Kousuke's time." By the time the elevator had climbed to her floor, she was already regretting her decision. But she did not change her mind. As soon as the doors opened, she hurried into the cubicle farm, wishing vainly that she was taller so she could see over the partitions.

"Rin?"

He was standing in front of the window, perfectly still, hands clasped behind his back. Not a muscle moved as Maru approached, and she fought off an urge to tap him on the shoulder and shout his name.

"Rin?"

He looked back at her in surprise. His expression clearly asked, "What are you doing here?"

"I wanted to talk to you," explained Maru. "I'm supposed to be meeting Kousuke somewhere for dinner, but I didn't want to leave without . . . seeing you, I guess."

Rin shook his head and produced his phone. "Don't make Kousuke wait."

"Okay." She looked at him closely. "I'm sorry, I can't quite tell what you mean from your text. Are you saying that because you want to be nice, or do you really not want to talk to me?"

He shook his head violently and wrote, "Of course I want to talk. But you can't make people wait like this, especially when a guy asks you to dinner."

"What are you, a relationship counselor?" Maru regretted the words the moment they were out of her mouth, and she started to protest. "No! It's not like that! You just said something weird that made me think about it! This is not a date or anything!"

Rin chuckled and typed, "It's okay. Go see him."

"No, it's not okay! You should know that this is not a date! We're just going to talk about work stuff, so don't . . . don't . . . " Maru could not finish her own sentence, and her words died away into confused mumbling.

"It's rude to make somebody wait like this. We can talk tomorrow, so go on."

Maru's eyes sparkled with irritation. "Fine. I'll go."

"No!" wrote Rin in reply, but Maru did not even look at her phone.

She was halfway to the elevator when she felt a gentle tap on her arm, but she shook Rin's hand off and continued.

Right as she reached the elevator and was about to press the button, a firm hand gripped her shoulder and stopped her. Rin pushed his phone into her face, and she had no choice but to read the message. "You know I didn't mean to hurt you. I'm so sorry if I did."

"Okay," she said, turning away.

He typed a little more and held it up to her.

"I'm glad you stopped to say it wasn't a date. The truth is, I came up here to look for you because I wanted to know if you'd go to dinner with me tonight. There's something I really want to tell you about."

Maru blinked. "Dinner with you . . . ?"

"Could we make it tomorrow night?" he wrote.

Maru nodded dazedly. "Sure . . . "

Rin smiled. "Thanks. Can I pick you up? As of this morning, I have a car."

Maru nodded again. "Sure . . . but hold on. How did you get a car when I don't even have furniture?"

Rin hesitated. "I'm still not quite recovered. I can't walk to work from my apartment."

"Oh." Maru was surprised. "I thought you were supposed to be well enough to go on this mission. Are you sure you're okay?"

He nodded and smiled. "I can't wait for tonight. Really."

"Me . . . neither." Maru's hands were cold. "I have to go now, Rin. You were right—I am being rude. I'm sorry. I wish I could stay."

He shook his head. "It's okay. Have fun tonight."

"Thanks." Maru darted into the elevator and frantically pushed the close button without pausing to see if Rin also wanted to descend.

"Dinner," she said aloud. Then, even louder: "Dinner! What does that mean?"

"It means nothing," she announced as the elevator doors opened. "Nothing, nothing, nothing, nothing, nothing. The more I tell myself that, the better. Nothing, nothing, nothing . . . "

She walked outside onto the sidewalk, a breath of cool air bringing her back to herself. "It's just time to spend with friends and co-workers and talk. That's it. Nothing more." She did not notice that she was almost running down the sidewalk.

Passing the convenience store without a second thought, she was still muttering to herself. "Dinner, nothing. Dinner, nothing. Am I a rude person? Those computers are so slow . . . nothing."

"Where are you going?" asked an amused voice. She stopped abruptly. "This is the restaurant I was telling you about. Are you ready for dinner?"

"Oh!" She winced. "Sorry, Kousuke. I . . . got lost."

"No problem. I thought you might miss it, which is why I waited out here for you. Did you have any trouble finding the convenience store?"

"None at all," Maru lied. She had not even seen it.

"Excellent. I have my usual table reserved inside, so just follow me."

"Fancy," murmured Maru as they entered and paused for a moment under a graceful crystal chandelier. Their waiter led them down a soft padded carpet to a table in the far corner. Maru slid into the comfortable seat and looked around in amazement. She was so used to the sterile cafeterias of Rigel that she could barely believe such luxury.

"I'll be right with you," said the waiter with the faintest trace of a European accent.

Maru opened her menu. "What do you usually like?"

"Caviar," said Kousuke. "It's one of my favorites. The escargot is excellent, too."

"What's that?"

"Snails in butter and garlic."

Maru hid her face behind her menu, hiding her laughter. There was no way she was eating either fish eggs or snails tonight. Her eyes traveled up and down the main courses and settled on a relatively safe choice: a "croque monsieur," which was apparently a sandwich with cheese and egg.

"I think I'm in the mood for something a bit less fancy. I'll try the *crokwa* . . . *croc* . . . this." She pointed to it.

"*Croque monsieur*," said Kousuke easily. "I come here often, so I know how to pronounce all their dishes. That's an excellent choice. The egg blends perfectly with the cheese, and the result . . . " He kissed his fingertips.

"I'm going to guess," said Maru humorously, "that food is another one of your hobbies."

He nodded. "I always enjoy good food when I can get it."

The waiter returned, and they placed their orders.

"So," said Kousuke, settling back in his chair, "how was your first day of work?"

"Just fine," said Maru. "Entering the schedules took a long time, but it's all finished now."

"Did you book the tickets yet?"

"The what?"

He laughed. "You have to buy tickets for the people who are travelling," he explained, taking a sip from his drink. "I'll show you how tomorrow. It's easy."

"Oh. Thanks."

He nodded and looked her up and down. "You know, I'm glad you agreed to come here with me tonight. I don't get to do things like this with others very often, especially not with people like you."

Maru did not know how to interpret his words. "Thanks for inviting me," she said uncertainly. "I'm glad . . . I'm also glad we came."

"Really? I thought you'd rather be with your friend from work," said Kousuke with a slight smile. "I thought for a minute you were going to leave me there."

"Oh . . . no." Maru was suddenly tongue-tied. "I wouldn't . . . I mean, I do need to talk to him, but we can do that anytime."

"I hope I didn't make things awkward."

"No, no, of course not." Maru wished they would get back to the innocent subject of tickets and schedules.

"Sorry." Kousuke raised his wineglass in the air and looked at it against the light. "I like learning about the people I work with. But tell me, please, if my questions offend you. I do know how to stop my mouth from running."

"I wish I did," said Maru ruefully.

"But you don't seem like the talkative kind to me."

"Not usually, but sometimes it just happens." Maru laughed. "I've made so many people hate me because I can't shut up. It's becoming a problem."

"How so?" Kousuke unfolded his napkin. "Do you talk too much, or ask too many hard questions?"

"Both. I ask hard questions, give advice where it isn't needed or wanted or helpful, and then try to cover it up. I end by making myself look like an idiot."

"I don't think you could possibly do that," said Kousuke thoughtfully. "But we all say things we shouldn't sometimes. Can you give me an example? Maybe I can help."

"Well . . . " She hesitated. "Remember how I explained that Rin never talks, and nobody knows whether or not he actually can? This morning I tried to make him say something out loud. I teased him about it and acted silly. I think that hurt him, and I wish I hadn't said anything about it."

"Oh, I get it." Kousuke winked. "You don't want to make him feel bad."

"Of course not," agreed Maru. "I don't want to make him feel bad. Why would I? But the thing is, I keep making the same mistake over and over again. I ask him all the same questions and of course I hurt him every time. He says he doesn't hate me, but I don't see how that could be. Our relationship is . . . " Maru laughed nervously. "It's weird."

"I think you look pretty good together," said Kousuke sweetly. "Like it or not."

Maru was not amused. "You have no idea what he's really like."

"But you do?"

Maru did not reply.

"I'm sorry. That was a little harsh," he said. "But what I really meant is, I don't think you know him quite as well as you think you do. Obviously, your questions don't hurt him like you just said, because he still wants to spend time with you. Also, obviously, he was coming to our floor to look for you. I think he just wanted to leave us alone. Far be it from me to get in the way of something like that." Kousuke held both hands up in the air and shook his head. "It would take a braver man than me. There's something funny about— what did you say his name was?"

"Rin."

"Rin . . . let me think. The name means 'quiet one' or something like that, doesn't it? Maybe 'serious' is a better translation. Dedicated. Reserved. I can think of synonyms all day, but the point I'm trying to make is, that name really suits him. There's something in his face I can't quite explain."

"Sadness," said Maru. "I've heard his childhood story. It's horrible."

"Oh? And was he able to talk as a child?"

"I think so. Why?"

Kousuke put his elbows on the table. "Well, I'm just wondering if childhood trauma caused his inability to speak. You said he also freaks out when people touch him on the shoulder, which makes me think of PTSD. I should know. I was abused as a child." He laughed ruefully. "But that's aside from the point. I bet your friend has PTSD."

"Really?"

"Does he have any other triggers?"

Maru thought. "Loud noises," she said. "Especially guns and country music, of all things. And he hates it when anybody touches him and says his name at the same time."

"Hmm . . . everything is somehow related to noise. Could it be that his house was noisy when he was little? His mother and father argued?"

"He didn't say anything about that. In fact, he said his father was gone most of the time, and he never mentioned his mother."

Kousuke snapped his fingers. "Perhaps it's because of his father."

"What?"

"Maybe his father abused him. That would explain all the triggers, especially if his father listened to country music. Maybe he would yell Rin's name while beating him, or maybe his voice was loud. That would explain both why Rin never talks and why he hates being touched."

"True. But about the guns . . . ?" Maru's voice trailed off as she said the words.

"Did you think of something?"

"No . . . no . . . it's nothing." Maru realized suddenly that she was talking too much and shut her mouth abruptly to avoid saying anything she would regret.

"Oh, okay. Well, I think we're on to something. It's too bad he has such a sad story, but at least now we have a mystery to solve."

Maru was annoyed. "Rin isn't a mystery. He just likes being confusing sometimes. It's his way."

"I know, I know. Like I said, I didn't mean to make either of you mad. Forgive me." Kousuke put his hands together and bowed.

"Here comes the food." Maru changed the subject abruptly. "You might not want to put your face in it."

Kousuke sat up. "It's beautiful," he said cheerfully. "As always, the food is sure to be excellent. Do you need anything else to drink, Miss Maru?"

"No, thanks."

They ate silently, never meeting each other's eyes. Maru did not notice how the food tasted. Her thoughts were elsewhere, outside the restaurant, visualizing what Rin must have been like as a child. She could not picture him letting himself be abused and hurt by his father, but he would certainly do anything for his siblings. Maybe Kousuke was right. Still, he had no business prying into Rin's affairs. Even Maru had never dared to ask for details about his father.

"Are you still there?" Kousuke waved his fork in front of her. "Miss Maru?"

"Sorry!" she said, snapping back to reality. "I was just thinking."

"I know. Me, too." He pushed his plate back and put his napkin on it. "Are you almost ready to go? I know you said you were tired, and I also know—" he winked "—that you didn't stop at the convenience store for medicine."

"What . . . ?"

"It's okay, but I'm sure you want to get home." Somehow, while Maru had not been paying attention, Kousuke had paid the bill and finished his dinner. "No hurry, of course. I could spend hours here with you."

Maru's eyes widened. "Actually . . . I'm ready."

"I've paid, so we can go."

"Thank you," said Maru, standing up and walking outside. "We didn't get to talk much about work, but I still enjoyed this."

"Me, too." Kousuke's smile disappeared. "Do you want to do this again sometime?"

Maru nodded. "Sure. I have to learn all the unwritten customs about work, right?"

Kousuke's laugh was hollow. "Ri-ight," he said. "Let's go. Want me to drive you home?"

"No, that's okay," said Maru. "To be honest, I could use some time to clear my head. I'd like to walk."

"All right, then. Let me know if you change your mind." He waved and closed his eyes with indefatigable good humor. "See you tomorrow!"

Maru waved back and smiled brightly. As soon as Kousuke was out of sight, she sighed bitterly, and the facade dropped.

"What now?" she asked herself. "I'm sorry, Rin. I shouldn't have told him about you."

CHAPTER 4

Maru was awakened before the sun was up by a message from Kita. "Gooooood morning!!!" it began. "Thought you might want this. Text this number and see who it is!!!"

"Who is it?" she replied sleepily.

"Text them and see! Hehe and thank me later!! Naito and I are going on a date today after work!!!!!!!!!!"

"Hmm. So they're dating after all. Wonder where they're going. Actually . . . I wonder where Rin and I are going."

She examined herself in the mirror. "Not that it matters. It's not a date anyway, right?" Her forearms were red and scratched, and the cuts that she refused to let heal throbbed painfully. Maru rubbed her fingers absently across them. "I wonder if I have any cute clothes with long sleeves. If Rin doesn't want to meet right away, I could go look for something."

"What time do you want to meet today, and where?" she wrote to Rin.

His reply came quickly. "Dinner and a walk?"

"Sure."

"Then would you prefer to meet me at work or at your apartment?"

Maru did not want to be teased by Kousuke. "At my apartment. Can we meet at six?"

"Sounds great," Rin replied. "I'm looking forward to this. There's something I really want to talk to you about. I think I might have found the answer to our questions."

"What? What questions?"

"The rest is a surprise!" he replied with a wink emoji.

"Okay," Maru replied briefly. Inside she was deeply curious.

Her phone vibrated again. "I'm sorry I can't walk with you to work today," Rin wrote. "I'm already at work, so I have to go. See you this evening."

"Cool," replied Maru. To herself she added, "I guess I should be getting ready, too."

She clicked back to Kita's enigmatic messages and copied the number she had sent. "Who is this?" she typed and said aloud, carefully enunciating every syllable. "I got your number from a friend, but she wouldn't say whose it is."

The reply came a moment later. "Is this Maru? This is Ayano's phone number, but I'm Kala, her roommate. She's in SAS training."

Maru flinched. "Sorry," she replied. "Yes, this is Maru. Don't let me interrupt anything."

"Yk how much wed like to get out of it," came the ungrammatical reply.

"Yup."

"I'll tell her you texted when she gets out."

"Thanks. I might not be able to reply right away since I'll be at work."

"Np."

Maru turned her phone off and put it on her bed. "Work is going to take forever today," she muttered. "Let's see . . . Ayano, shopping, Kousuke. What am I going to say to him? Deny everything. Shopping . . . I can do that over lunch. Nobody will ask where I went, since nobody knows who I am. Then I can come back here after work and get ready." Her thoughts were disorganized. "I can make this work."

She dressed herself, flipped her hair quickly into a messy ponytail, and surveyed herself in the mirror. "I miss the days when I dressed down for work," she observed.

Her walk to work was much shorter than the day before, and she did not waste time. Once arrived, she ascended the elevator and made her way through the cubicles to her personal six square feet. There was a pile of papers on her desk that had not been there the day before.

"Good morning!" said a voice. Kousuke's head appeared over the partition. "I left some things there for you. I wrote some directions about how to book the tickets and hotel rooms, plus information on travel reimbursements. Everything you'll need should be right there."

"Thanks," said Maru without enthusiasm. "I'll get to it, then."

"You don't have to finish it all today," said Kousuke. "That would be asking way too much. Just prioritize based on the closest travel dates."

"Sure thing." Maru sat down and put her phone in the drawer.

*****   *****   *****

The lunch hour arrived at last, after what felt like many hundreds of hours to Maru. She looked up from her computer and focused her eyes on the window, hoping that the suspicious throbbing she felt behind them would not turn into a headache later. Automatically she reached for her phone, and, holding it far from her face, looked through her messages.

"Nice to hear from you!" Ayano had written. "How's the new job? How's life in general? Are you dating Rin yet?"

Maru poked Ayano's icon. "Weirdo," she said aloud, then wrote, "Of course not! Don't say weird things like that. The new job is fine, but boring. I'm having headaches, too."

"Oh, too bad," replied Ayano a few seconds later. "I might get cut off here, because I'm supposed to be in training, but I want to talk to you. If I get in trouble, there's nobody to save me. But I thought Kita said you and Rin were going to dinner tonight?"

I'll kill her! She clicked to Kita's messages and wrote in all capital letters, "ARE YOU SPYING ON ME?"

"Of course!! Hehe!!!! It's fun to!!" came the reply.

Maru growled and returned to Ayano's thread. "I didn't tell her that."

"Sorry. Sounded like fun to me. Gtg—I'm going to get caught. Have fun tonight!!"

"Yeah, right." Maru turned her phone off. "Take that, Kita. I'm going out now."

"Leaving already?" asked Kousuke.

"I have to run some errands," said Maru. "I'll be back after lunch."

"Sounds good." He turned back to his sandwich. "See you then!"

***** ***** *****

Maru put on her new clothes and surveyed herself nervously in the mirror. She was dressed simply in a dark, flowy shirt with the necessary long sleeves that covered her scars. It fit comfortably but tightly and flattered her. She had arranged her hair in a bun on top of her head, and, for the first time in several years, did her own makeup. When she looked in the mirror, she saw nothing but flaws. Her eyes were too sad, her lips refused to smile, her skin was too pale.

She turned away. "This is how I look," she said. "It doesn't matter anyway. I'm ready."

Nervous and feeling anything but ready, Maru went outside and stood on the porch to wait. A few wisps of her hair blew around her face in the evening breeze, and she brushed them impatiently aside. Rin was not there yet, so she leaned against the cold brick and pulled out her phone. It vibrated immediately.

"Have fun!!!" Maru did not even need to see who the sender was to recognize Kita's exuberant style. "DAAAATE!"

"That's a little creepy," replied Maru frigidly.

"I know, but I'm so excited!!"

"Why did you tell Ayano?"

"Because I knew she'd be excited, too. Come on, don't drill holes in our favorite ship. Call me crazy, but this is fun to watch!"

"Promise you won't text me until tomorrow morning."

"Morning?!! I'd better keep an eye on you the whole evening! I'll text you every five minutes!!"

"No!" replied Maru. "Don't."

"I will!!"

"No."

"I will!! Starting now!! I'll text Rin, too!!"

"Okay then. I'll leave our phones here." Maru looked up. "I see Rin coming. Goodbye."

"Hey! Don't leave me behind! Seriously, Maru. I'm sorry I made you mad. Don't leave your phone."

Maru ran up to Rin. "Can you give me your phone?"

He handed it to her, a confused look on his face.

"Kita said she'd text us both every five minutes unless we left them behind, so I was just going to put them in my room."

Rin chuckled silently and nodded.

Maru fled up the stairs, dropped the phones on her bed, and took one last look at her reflection in the mirror before rejoining with Rin.

He had produced a notebook and pen from his pocket, and when he saw her coming, turned his message to face her. "Thanks for coming tonight. I've been really excited about this."

"Me, too," said Maru. "Thanks for inviting me. What are we doing first, dinner or walk?"

Rin paused to write in his notebook. "How about dinner?"

"Sounds good." Maru nodded. "Where are we going?"

"To my car, if that's okay," wrote Rin. "The restaurant I want to take you to is a few blocks from here."

"Are you sure? You don't have to drive me."

"Why wouldn't I want to?" He showed her his note and smiled. "The only thing that would make it better is if I could talk to you. But we can pass notes at the restaurant. Meanwhile, how was your day?" He closed the notebook and put it back in his pocket.

"It was fine," said Maru. "There isn't much to say about it. I filed paperwork most of the day, bought airline tickets, arranged travel reimbursements. Life in the real world is boring if it's always like this."

Rin held the car door open for her, and she slipped inside. Everything was incredibly clean, and the car smelled new. She slid her seat back, and Rin closed the door.

"You work in the shipping department, don't you?" she said as he got in the opposite side. "So you do a lot of manual labor?"

He nodded.

"I wish I could do that. I don't think I'm made to sit at a desk all day. Plus . . . " She laughed ruefully. "There's Kousuke. He means well, but he always wants to talk to me or give me more papers or tell me how to do things."

Rin glanced at her, interrogation in his eyes.

"The guy you met last night by the elevator. He sits in the cubicle next to me. This morning, when I showed up for work, he had hand-written ten pages of instructions. Then he wouldn't stop sticking his head over the partition and asking me how I was doing, whether I wanted any coffee, or where I was planning to go for lunch."

Rin shook his head sympathetically.

"He's nice, though. And I know he's just trying to help. Rin, am I talking too much?"

He smiled and shook his head again.

"I really want to hear how your day went. You'll have to tell me at dinner."

At that moment, the car slid smoothly into a parking spot, and Rin put it in park and turned it off. Before Maru could move, he was out of his seat and holding her door open, face invisible in the shadow of a streetlight.

"Thanks," she said, uncomfortably aware that she was avoiding his eyes. "Where . . . where are we going?"

He pointed down the sidewalk toward a brown awning.

"Nice," said Maru.

Rin took out his notebook and wrote, "Is this okay?"

"Oh, it's great!" said Maru, stumbling over her words and talking at almost incomprehensible speed. "Great!"

Rin's expression was unreadable as he returned the notebook to his pocket, but Maru thought he looked nervous.

"Are you okay?" she asked on an impulse, wondering what her own answer to that question would be. She felt suddenly shy.

He nodded thoughtfully.

"Welcome," said the waiter. "A table for two?"

Rin produced his notebook and held it up to her.

"Reservations? All right . . . this way."

She picked up two menus from the basket and led them to a booth by the front window. "Does this work?"

Rin nodded and she put the menus down. "Someone will be right with you."

Maru slid into the booth and looked out the window as an excuse to avoid looking at Rin. "It's so pretty outside tonight," she babbled. "I used to love looking at the stars when we were still . . . still . . . and now I don't get the chance because we live in the city and it's too bright all the time. We've only been here a few days, but I can't get used to—" She paused as Rin pushed his notebook under her nose.

"Are you nervous?"

She took a deep breath, laughed painfully, and nodded.

He took the notebook back and scribbled a few more lines. "You don't have to be. If I'm making you nervous, just tell me."

"You're not—" Maru paused. "Okay. You are making me nervous."

"Why?"

"So direct." She sighed. "Well . . . I don't know, to be honest."

"You aren't afraid of saying most things. What's going on? Is everything okay?"

"I guess that's it," said Maru, still looking out the window. "Everything is okay, and I'm not used to it. I wonder if I have the right to think it's okay after what I've seen. And done. I killed Yuri, you know."

"In self-defense."

"Does that make any difference?"

"I wish it did," he wrote quickly.

"Right." She put her head on her hand. "Isn't there something you wanted to talk to me about?"

"Two things, actually," he wrote. "Something I want to talk to you about but can't, and something you have to know about. But I'd rather wait until later if that's okay."

She read the note. "You can't? Why not?"

He shook his head mysteriously and smiled.

"What's wrong with you now?" she asked.

"I don't think you'd want me to tell you anyway."

"Who cares? You'll know how I feel about it once you tell me."

He flinched and did not reply.

"I'm sorry, Rin. I didn't mean to be . . . like that."

"It's okay," he wrote. "I have a question for you. Why did you come here tonight?"

"Because . . . " Maru paused in thought. "Well, because you invited me and I thought it would be fun."

Rin nodded.

"I have a question for you, too," said Maru. "Why did you ask me to come?"

"Because of what I wanted to tell you. But I think it's better that we just talk like this," he wrote.

"Okay."

They were interrupted by the waitress, who took their drink and dinner orders in a high-pitched, artificial voice. Maru's fingers were twining in and out under the table in nervousness the whole time. Having dinner with Rin was different than training with him. She wondered what he wanted to ask.

"Do you enjoy having dinner like this?" asked Rin, looking down at his paper as soon as the waitress left.

"Yes, it's a really nice way to . . . unwind from work," answered Maru. "But Rin, if there's something you need to tell me, please stop hesitating. I won't get mad, I promise."

He shook his head. "Now's not the time."

"Okay." Maru gave up. "I guess I should change the subject, or we're going to be talking about this the whole dinner."

"Right." He paused. "Here's a weird question. How do you feel about Saito?"

"Saito? Our team leader, Saito?"

Rin nodded.

"He's . . . well, to be honest, I haven't quite decided about that yet. Sometimes I feel like he just goes off into his own head and forgets what he's doing, and then I'm afraid of him. He's so unpredictable that I never feel safe around him, yet somehow, he can motivate people to do almost anything he wants. But what exactly do you mean, how do I feel about him? Did I answer your question?"

"Do you like being around him?"

Maru shook her head slowly. "I hate to say this, but no. I don't like it at all. I don't think he was made to socialize."

Rin chuckled silently. "Most people think that."

"What do you think of him?"

Rin paused for a long time with his pen hovering over his notebook. Maru noticed that his hand was shaking ever so slightly.

"I respect him," he wrote at last. "But I can't say I like him either. Not as a friend." There was an even longer pause before he wrote the last word.

"Didn't you say he was your cousin?" asked Maru curiously.

Rin nodded. "And Kita said that was a lie."

"Such an obvious one that she couldn't help pointing it out," laughed Maru. "How direct of her. But was it a lie?"

He nodded.

"Is Saito related to you?"

He nodded again.

"Can you tell me how?"

Seconds ticked by, lengthening to a minute. Maru regretted asking, but curiosity was devouring her as she sat and patiently waited for Rin to write the word—

"Brother."

"What?" Maru's eyes widened. "Saito is your . . . brother? Are you serious?"

He nodded.

"Older or younger?"

"Older by a year."

"And now he's your team leader . . . ? Always . . . Rin . . . how on earth do you put up with him?"

"I don't know." He chuckled in spite of himself. "He pulls rank and as a person I don't like him, but he's my brother. And I can tell that he's always fighting with himself."

"About what?"

"Everything. He hasn't had a moment of peace since he was born."

"Oh." Maru paused. "Sometimes I can see that, but he hides it so well."

"It's a mask, just like the ones you and I wear."

"Oh," said Maru again.

He smiled. "I wish I could be more honest with you."

"About what?"

"Two things. Just two. Everything else you know about me is true."

"So there's something I know about you that isn't true?"

"No, it's just something you don't know at all."

"When are you going to just tell me?" Maru looked at him slyly. "Come on! I'll get Kita to stop leaving books outside your room if you tell me."

He laughed silently and put a thoughtful hand to the right side of his chest. For a moment his eyes closed, as if he was thinking deeply about something. Then they snapped open and his serious look faded.

"It's nothing really."

"It's something! I don't want to make you uncomfortable, but you've got me curious. Can't you give me a hint?"

"No."

Maru sighed. "I'll stop asking, then."

The waitress made a timely appearance with their food, chatting the whole time and relieving the rather tense atmosphere. Maru blessed her internally, hiding her face in her napkin.

"Sorry," wrote Rin. "I've made things worse."

"Worse? No, it's just fine. I was curious, and I asked too many questions. You know me. I always do this."

"No, really, it's my fault," wrote Rin apologetically. "Let's talk about something else for now. I have plenty to tell you about later."

"Okay," said Maru, and searched her brain desperately for something to say.

"How's work going so far?" asked Rin.

Maru did not remind him that he had already asked; she was happy to have anything to talk about. "It's going fine," she said. "How about you?"

"Fine," he wrote briefly.

They ate in silence for a few minutes.

"Have you talked to Kita and Naito?" Rin tapped his pen on the paper and looked across the table at Maru.

"This morning," said Maru, her eyes dropping in embarrassment as she remembered exactly what Kita had said. "Yup . . . this morning."

"How are they?"

"Fine, I think."

"Dating yet?"

"I think so," laughed Maru ruefully. "I hope it's true. Maybe they'll get off my case."

"What's your case? Somebody you like?"

Maru could feel the heat in her cheeks. "No . . . no . . . no."

Rin smiled lopsidedly. "Really?"

Maru shifted uncomfortably in her seat.

"Are you finished eating?" The notebook appeared suddenly by her plate.

"Oh." Maru had forgotten about eating. "Yes . . . I think so."

"No hurry," wrote Rin with a genuine smile. "I'll wait."

Maru shook her head. "No, I'm done."

"Good. There's something I'm really excited to tell you about."

"I'm really curious." Maru managed her own small, shy smile.

"Do you mind if we go to the park?"

"That sounds great."

"I can't . . . " There was a pause while Rin tapped his pen anxiously. "I can't walk very far tonight. Sorry about that. We might have to sit down."

"That's just fine," said Maru. "Maybe we can sit by the lake, if you're okay with that."

"Perfect. It's beautiful there."

"Okay. I'll have them split the check."

Rin shook his head. "I'll pay."

"No good. I can talk and you can't, so I'm going to have her split the check!"

Rin smiled. "I already paid."

Maru blinked. "What?"

"Don't worry about it," he wrote. "Too long to explain."

"Oh, okay." Maru was puzzled. "Well, are you ready?"

He nodded and picked up his long black coat from the seat beside him. Maru could not help noticing that he looked particularly handsome. Irritated with herself for her weakness, she slid out of the booth and slid past him toward the door.

The sound of Rin's footsteps behind her stopped abruptly, and she looked around. Rin was standing by the counter, smiling beautifully. She choked and started coughing.

"I lied. I hadn't paid," Maru read aloud. "But I have now." She glared accusingly at Rin. "Seriously? You'd stoop that low?"

His eyes twinkled with amusement as he held the door open for her.

"Are you okay?" she asked, stopping him suddenly. "Something—something—I don't know exactly what it is. You seem really excited, I guess."

Rin looked thoughtfully up at the sky and nodded, pulling out his notepad. "I think tonight is going to be a wonderful night," he wrote. "For both of us."

CHAPTER 5

"So what did you want to talk to me about?" asked Maru, leaning against the railing and looking out at the lake. The wind blew her hair gently around her face. She looked up at Rin curiously.

He looked deep into her eyes, and Maru wondered if he was going to reply. For a long, tense moment they stared at each other, each wondering privately what the other was thinking.

Rin was the first to drop his gaze. Fumbling in his pocket, he removed his notebook and started writing. "Do you have some time?"

Maru glanced at her watch. "It's only eight. I have all the time you need."

He nodded. "Then let's talk about other things first. I want to enjoy the time I have with you."

"Okay," said Maru hesitantly. "What do you want to talk about?"

"I don't know," he wrote, smiling ruefully. "I just want to talk. You have no idea how much I wish I could use my voice right now."

"What did your voice sound like?" asked Maru curiously.

Rin thought for a moment. "People told me it was deep and a little rough," he wrote at last. "And very quiet. I was always quiet."

"Did you ever yell?"

"No."

"Did you ever listen to loud music?"

"No."

"Why don't you like country music?"

Rin sighed. "Did Kita tell you about that?"

"I think I asked her about it once," said Maru evasively.

"I hate it because that's what my father listened to all the time." Rin paused. "He would beat my siblings and make the music louder and louder. He wanted them to scream so loudly that he could hear them over it."

"Did you ever scream?" asked Maru softly.

"No. I knew that it would make him beat me more if I stayed silent. Then he would be too tired to hurt my little sisters." Rin's hand moved thoughtfully to the right side of his chest. "I still have scars on my neck and back from that."

"I'm so sorry." Maru did not know what to say.

"I don't regret it," he said. "My experiences made me who I am now. The only thing I regret is how I responded."

"Responded? What do you mean?"

Rin smiled. "I should tell you," he wrote. "You've probably guessed already."

"Tell me what?"

"I hate loud music because my father played it all the time. I hate gunshots because I heard them almost every day. Snipers are different. I'm not sensitive to them anymore. But most of all, I hate loud voices, because my father yelled, and my sisters screamed in pain." His hand shook as he wrote. "So, I swore I wouldn't be like him. I started being quiet, and one day I found that I didn't want to speak to anyone. That went on for five years, until I met you. You were the first person I really wanted to talk to. Then I wished I could learn to speak again, but I think it's too late now."

"It can't be too late," protested Maru. "You could get therapy. You could learn to speak again, if you've forgotten how."

He shook his head. "I don't think I've forgotten. It's just so unnatural. To be very honest, Maru, I'm too afraid to try." He looked out across the lake and focused his eyes on the distant trees before turning back to his notepad. "I'm sorry this is hard to read. It's getting dark. Maru, that's the first time I've used your name like that."

She nodded. "I like it, but it makes more for you to write."

"That doesn't matter. If you like it, I'll keep doing it." He looked shyly at her. "Would you tell me something?"

"Sure, anything you want."

"What's your real name?"

Maru hesitated. "I wasn't . . . they told me not to . . . "

"I won't tell anyone, and I'll tell you my name if you want. But it's okay if you'd rather not."

"No," she said thoughtfully. "I trust you." She tried to disguise the inexplicable excitement she felt by lowering her voice and making her face expressionless. "My real name is Tanaka Makise."

Rin smiled. "That's a pretty name," he wrote. "Isn't there somebody who got re-named Makise?"

Maru nodded. "Yes, I was a little startled at first. It seemed odd that somebody else could have my name. But how in the world do you even remember that?"

He immediately looked away. "I saw the expression on your face when the name was called," he wrote. "I thought that might have been you."

"You were looking at me?" Maru blushed and blessed the darkness for hiding her face. "Why?"

Rin did not move at all for a long time.

"I'm sorry for asking." Maru was speaking very quickly and nervously. "I shouldn't have. I was looking at you, too. I looked around at everybody. The ceremony was so interesting, and I had no idea who would be my teammates. Then it was you—Rin!"

He had suddenly sunk to his knees, arms crossed over his chest, breathing heavily. The notebook he had been holding slipped over the rail into the water, but Maru did not notice that.

"Rin! Why are you bowing? Why are you—?" Maru knelt beside him. "Rin? Are you all right? Answer me!"

He did not look up at her, and his eyes were hidden under his thick black hair. She put her hands to his face and tilted it gently up to her. "What's wrong?"

His eyes were squeezed tightly shut in pain and he made no attempt to reply. His breathing became more and more difficult until he was almost choking, and Maru could only watch in horror as he struggled for air. Suddenly, with a deep sigh, he stopped breathing altogether and fell forward against her shoulder.

She quickly lowered him to the ground, where he lay on his back, eyes still closed, chest motionless. A thin stream of blood trickled from the corner of his mouth and stained the pavement.

"Wake up!" she pleaded desperately. Her hands felt for her pockets, but there was no phone there. The sidewalk was empty in both directions, and there was nobody to call for help. Tears of frustration and fear came to her eyes as she put her hand over Rin's mouth to feel for breath. "Please wake up!"

His eyes flickered open and Maru sighed in deep relief. "Did you hurt yourself?" she asked, almost conversationally. If Rin was awake, he was unstoppable. Nothing could hurt him now. "You really scared me there. Should we go ho—"

"I love you," said a deep, rough, beautiful masculine voice very close to her ear. "I'm sorry I didn't tell you before. I love you, Makise."

"Rin?" she whispered; eyes wide.

His hands felt for hers and squeezed something metal into them. It was his car keys. "Go back to my apartment," he said quietly. "Drawer on the right. I left a letter for you."

"You're not going anywhere," she insisted. "I'll get you back to your car and we'll get to the hospital. I'm not going to let anything happen to you. Not now." Her eyes filled with tears again, and she stood up abruptly. "I can't carry you, but somehow we'll get there."

"Don't," he said, closing his eyes again. "I knew this would happen if—"

"I'm not giving up!" cried Maru hoarsely. "Don't you either!"

She looked up and down the sidewalk again. Still nobody. But there was a small booth under a streetlight which might be a pay phone. She glanced back at Rin. He coughed weakly, and the trickle of blood became a stream. She had to do something, and there was not much time left for her to try.

"I'm going," she decided aloud. "I'm going to the pay phone. It's only a hundred yards away. Rin, wait for me, please."

His eyes opened and met hers, and he managed to smile. "I'm glad I told you," he whispered. "It was the last thing I wanted you to know. I'm sorry, Makise. Please do your best to forget about me."

"I won't," she insisted, kneeling beside him. "I'm not going to forget you, because you're going to be all right. Just wait for me."

He took a deep breath and said nothing.

"I love you, too," said Maru as she stood up. "Don't forget that. I love you, too. I need you, Rin! Please, please, please don't give up!" Her vision was blurred with tears as she turned and ran toward the pay phone booth.

It seemed ages before she got there. In those few seconds, during which Maru ran faster than she ever had before, she learned many things she had never really known before. She learned about fear, about friendship, and finally about love. Now she knew how she really felt about Rin. She knew now that it was almost too late.

Her fingers touched the cold metal door and tore it open. Desperation lent her speed, and she dialed the emergency number with shaking hands.

"Help," she said pitifully. "I'm at Soren Park. My friend has collapsed. He's bleeding—internally, I think. There's blood coming from his mouth. Please hurry."

The operator assured her in a dull, toneless voice that help was on the way, and Maru put the phone back in its rest. Her sweat was cold, her muscles were weak, her hands shook uncontrollably. But she knew she had to get back to Rin as quickly as possible. She steadied herself as best she could, opened the door, and started running back down the sidewalk.

"Rin," she panted as she got closer. "I called for help. The doctors are coming to save you. You're going to be fine. They're—Rin—"

She slowed and fell to her knees beside him. "Please answer me," she begged, squeezing his strong, pale hands between her own small ones. "Not yet. Just a few more minutes. Please . . . " His hands were icy cold.

Slowly her gaze travelled from them up to his face. It was pale, stained in places with blood, but somehow it was still beautiful. His eyes were closed, and his pale lips were smiling ever so slightly. His soft black hair ruffled around his face in the evening breeze, and he looked as innocent as a sleeping child. Maru could not bear to look at him. His peace tore at her heart, and she buried her face in her hands and cried bitterly.

A few minutes later—what seemed like ages to Maru—the medics arrived. Maru withdrew to the railing and looked out over the lake, already knowing there was nothing they could do. Gently, quietly, they informed her that Rin was dead. She barely heard them. Her life had been almost perfect less than a half hour before, and now she was living in a dream. A nightmare.

She did not turn away from the lake until the medics had gone, taking Rin's body with them. She could not bear to look at his face again. But she knew that she could never forget how he had looked. Peaceful. Quiet. Happy—not superficially, but happy in a deep, eternal sense. She had never seen that expression on his face when he was alive. Death had, after all, been a release for him.

Slowly she looked back. There were still a few spots of blood on the pavement, and when she closed her eyes, she could see Rin lying there. She could hear his voice ringing in her head, feel his cold hands in hers. She almost felt she could touch him if she reached far enough. And yet there was still a barrier she could never cross. Rin had found peace. For her, there was only despair, and nothing she did could change how she felt. The emptiness in her heart would never go away. Bitterly she cursed ever having met Rin, Naito, Kita. All the happy memories she had with them could never make up for pain like this.

"Where did you go?" she asked aloud, reaching her hand tentatively out into space. "Rin? I need you here. Why did you have to leave me?" She paused. "If you knew this was going to happen, why didn't you tell me?"

She wanted to let herself go, to scream and cry and vent her fury on something. But she did not know whom to blame. Nobody had caused Rin's death. It was just something that was meant to be, something planned since the beginning of time. Who had planned it, and why? Maru did not know, and there was nobody she could ask.

Slowly she knelt on the pavement and traced little circles around the blood spots with her finger. The stain could be washed out of the pavement, and everybody else could forget what had happened, but this night would be written indelibly on her heart forever. She closed her eyes and heard Rin's voice clearly in her head: "I love you. I'm sorry I didn't tell you before. I love you, Makise."

"I love you, too," she whispered. "I'm sorry I didn't tell you before. I should have. I love you, too—"

He'd never had the chance to tell her his name.

"Please step aside, Miss."

Maru looked up, confused, into the face of a police officer.

"Do you know what happened here?" he asked. "Are you a relative of the deceased?"

She shook her head.

"Then please wait here for a moment. We'll take a statement, and then you can go. You're not in trouble." He offered her a hand and helped her to her feet. "Can you briefly explain what happened from your point of view?"

Maru opened her mouth to say something. The whole scene flashed before her eyes, and she couldn't force herself to speak. Her gaze dropped to the ground.

"All right," said the officer gently. "We'll contact you if we need any further information. Can you tell me your phone number?"

Maru took a deep breath to clear her head. "Sure," she said, startled by how scratchy her voice sounded. She repeated her number to the officer, and he recorded it on his notepad.

"Thanks," he said. "All right, Miss, you can go."

Maru turned away and looked dazedly around. Rin was gone. The medics were gone. The officers were talking with each other in low voices and ignoring her. A whole part of her life was over.

Slowly, painfully, she started walking back to Rin's car. The keys had been in her pocket, unthought of, since he handed them to her. Now, she knew that she had to find her phone and tell someone. Ask someone for help. Beg and pray for mercy from this torment.

It took her nearly a half hour to get back to his car because she walked so slowly. She passed nobody on the way, and she was thankful that she did not have to hide her face. She did not know whether she wanted to be alone or with someone who could help—if there was such a person. She had never felt more isolated in her life. Her hands shook uncontrollably, and the more she tried to get control over herself, the worse she felt.

She paused next to the road. Bright, blurry cars flew past her, all oblivious to her life. She was insignificant to them. They probably would not notice even if she walked out into the middle of them. That was one way to end her life and perhaps find the same peace that Rin had. Her eyes were dry as she looked out into the traffic and contemplated her own death. Would it hurt? No, it would be instant. Would she regret it? No, that was impossible. She took a step forward, a step closer to death.

Then she remembered something.

"Drawer on the right. I left a letter for you."

His voice was loud in her ears, and she jerked herself back from the road. She could not die yet. She had to know what Rin wanted to tell her.

She ran back to the parking lot and unlocked Rin's car, then paused before she started it. Where was she going? Rin had never told her where his apartment was. She looked uncertainly around the car for any clues, but there were none. It was empty of unnecessary clutter.

"Kita would know," she muttered, getting out and slamming the door behind her. "Kita knows everything."

She had two options: run back to the pay phone or drive back to her apartment and use her own phone. Which would be faster? She hesitated for a moment, then got back in the car. Running to the pay phone would drain her energy too much.

The drive to her apartment seemed longer than ever before. She took the first parking spot in her lot, jumped out of the car, and took the steps to her floor two at a time. Her hands shook as she tried to fit her key into the lock. She paused, squeezed them tightly together, and tried again. The door opened. She rushed inside without bothering to close it and seized her phone off the counter.

What is Kita's number?

A few moments later it came to her, and she dialed it.

"Heyooo!" cried an inappropriately cheerful voice on the other end of the line. "How's your daaaate? It is a date, right? You're going out with him, right? Rin didn't try anything funny, did he?"

"No time," said Maru abruptly. "Where is Rin's apartment?"

"What? Why d' you wanna know that?"

"No time. Where is it?"

"Mmm . . . " Kita thought for a moment, and slowly recited his address. "But how are you going to find it if you don't have GPS?"

"I know where that road is. Thanks."

"Hey! I want to know what's going—" Maru slipped the phone into her pocket, slammed her apartment door behind her, and locked it quickly.

"No time, no time," she muttered. The run back to Rin's car seemed even longer this time. She slid into the driver's seat and started the ignition, her hands still shaking, then switched quickly into gear. The car shot backwards, and within seconds Maru was on the main road.

Everybody seemed to be getting in her way, pulling out in front of her, lingering too long at red lights, or slowing to a leisurely pace when Maru could not pass. She cursed bitterly and honked the horn, wondering at the same time why she was in such a hurry.

About twenty minutes later, after innumerable starts and stops, Maru pulled up in front of Rin's apartment and took the closest parking space. The steps to the second floor were steep, but she took them two at a time. Then she paused. Rin's door was locked, but it appeared she had no key. *Why had he given her only his car key?*

After staring at the door for a moment, she sighed deeply. "I can't stop now," she said, picking up the neighbor's iron doorstop. "I might as well break in."

Tentatively at first, then with more force, she hit the window with the doorstop. After a few attempts, it shattered, and she crawled in carefully across the broken glass.

"Desk," she muttered to herself. "Drawer on the right."

She found it quickly and opened it. Inside was a neatly folded stack of papers from Rin's notebook, written in tiny print on both sides. Maru picked it up and turned it over. Her name was written on the outside.

Quietly, willing herself not to cry, she sat down on Rin's sofa and unfolded them. The letter was lengthy. She curled her legs up under her and began to read, tears falling from her eyes to the crinkled paper.

CHAPTER 6

Dear Maru,

If you're reading this, then something must have happened to me. You probably know already that I expected it. It's not very hard to explain how I knew. Remember when I was in the hospital after being shot on the special mission? The doctors told me that my wound might reopen. If it did, my lungs would fill with blood and I would suffocate. They gave me the choice between retiring and never doing anything strenuous for the rest of my life or continuing work and hoping for the best. I chose the latter, and here we are. I'm sorry, Maru. For your sake, I hope we never became close. But I don't know how long I can hold out.

I hope I never tell you this, and I hope you don't already know. In fact, I'd rather not tell you now, but I can't die without saying it. It's my own fault. I love you, Maru.

You know the story of my past and how guilty I am, and that's why I'm trying my hardest not to let you find out. But if I die, and if you read this, then you should know. I hope it doesn't hurt you too much. I promise that everything I ever felt for you was pure and genuine and so incredibly, beautifully painful. You're the first person I've felt this way about. You're beautiful, kind, strong, graceful. I can't tell you enough about how special you are to me, or how much pain it causes me to think that you'll only know this after I'm dead. I wish there could have been more between us, but for your sake there can't be. That's okay as long as you know that I love you and only you. Please don't forget that, no matter what happens to me.

I hope I found the courage to tell you before I died, but if not, I should explain something very important. It hurts to say this. I've done everything I could my whole life to avoid coming to this conclusion. But it's inevitable now. I've done my research and made my decision, and I hope I can help you. It's about those questions we ask ourselves every day—why am I alive? Why am I here? What is the meaning of life and death? I think I've finally found the answer to all of them. Please stay with me while I explain. It won't be easy.

The first question I have to answer is, why am I here? What purpose does my life have? I thought about this for a long time. Evolution means that humanity came here by chance and that our lives have no real meaning. Thank God that's wrong. And I mean that literally, because I've changed my mind about everything. I think evolution is a lie—a lie that has cost so many people their lives. It almost killed me, because it forced me to believe that I am meaningless. If we were created, Maru, doesn't that mean that there is a plan for us? A reason to exist?

You're probably very confused right now, and I can't blame you for that. But please keep reading. Haven't you ever felt that your life was empty? I know you have. We all have. But it doesn't have to be that way if there is a reason for life and a Creator who made you specially for that reason. I tried too hard to figure out who He was. I read every book I could get my hands on, but none made sense until somebody gave me a little black one. It's in my desk if you want to have it. Christians call it the Bible, and they say that it was written by God through the hands of man. I think that's true, because I read it and I found the answers to all my questions. I believe in God now, Maru. That's why I'm not afraid to die. I know what will happen to me.

So, in order . . .

1. Why am I alive?

I'm here because God made me to be here. To be honest, I've always thought that evolution was improbable, but I had to believe it because I had no other choice. Now I don't. The universe exists because God made it, and you and I exist because God made us. That's a beautiful, simple answer, isn't it? I almost wish I could take credit for it.

2. Why am I here?

This question was hard for me to answer. Why do I have to suffer so much to make other people happy? It doesn't make sense. Why would I want to do that? But the answer is actually simple. It's my way of honoring God.

I don't know how much you know about Christians, but they believe that God is perfect, and humans are sinners. Because sin is the opposite of God, we can't be in His presence, no matter how hard we try to be perfect. To make up for that, He sent His Son to die like a human. Think about that, Maru. He lived in heaven and saw only perfection and love and beauty and light. But He gave it up to suffer something worse than either you or I have ever experienced. Agonizing death and exposure to the worst of humanity. He died to atone for our sins. He traded His perfection for our imperfection so that we could become perfect in God's eyes. That means you're perfect, Maru. (I already knew that!) It also means that no matter how guilty you feel, all you have to do is believe in God, believe that He sent His Son, and ask for forgiveness. It's simple. And then you can serve the greatest leader ever—the One who created this entire universe and made the stars and made you and me. It's an honor I don't deserve, Maru. I thought I would have to spend the rest of my life hiding from my guilt and shame, but it's amazing the freedom I've found.

3. What is the meaning of life and death?

Humans are on earth to do God's will. This makes sense, doesn't it? After all, we were created by Him. So while we are alive, we are trying to know Him better and do what He wants us to do. And when we die, we can finally go back to being in His presence, even though we don't deserve it.

The evidence for this God is overwhelming, Maru. Even the simple fact that there's always a hole in your heart that's waiting for something to fill it is enough. You and I already know that nothing on Earth can do that, but I've asked for help and forgiveness and I swear to you on everything we value that it's true. I make mistakes. I'm always going to, but now I'm forgiven, and I don't have to carry the shame with me everywhere I go. You'll say it's psychological, but no mental trick could have done this for me. I tried to kill myself so many times, even though I was getting the best mental help the doctors could offer. I'm so happy I failed, because if I hadn't, I would never have known all this. Nor would I have known you, Maru.

Think about it. When you're hurting and crying, ask for help. Test God and see if His promises are real. Please do it for me, Maru. I want to die knowing that you're safe and loved and happy. I only want what's best for you, and I want you to feel the relief I've found.

There's one more thing I think you should know. I never told you anything about what happened on that special mission, and I think it might be important now. I'm not sure about everything, but there's strong evidence that I don't think you should ignore. I'm sorry. I might be too late already.

A few months ago, I caught Saito, my brother, secretly talking to a CAUS worker. I heard him talking about classified Rigel information, and later I asked him about it. He said the CAUS worker was really an undercover Rigel agent undercover, but he had no proof of that and he refused to give me the agent's name. I was so angry, Maru. I thought he had betrayed everything I worked so hard for. I started writing up papers accusing him of treason, but he forced me to reconsider. After all, he was my brother, I loved him despite everything, and I had no solid proof. So I dropped the charges. But I was never convinced that he was innocent.

Only he and I knew exactly what plans had been made for my mission. I can't think of any possible way the attackers could have known who I was unless he told them. I hate to think that Saito tried to kill me, and that's why I never said anything about it. But I can't keep it to myself any longer, because I'm afraid of what he might do to you and Kita and Naito. He's not above betraying you to death or worse. Maru, if you're reading this and I'm dead, that means I can't protect you anymore. I tried blackmailing him, saying I knew he was a traitor and if he tried anything, I would report him. That won't work now. You must find Kita and Naito and get back to Rigel. Report Saito. Tell the authorities that I died because of him. I can't promise they'll listen, but it's worth trying. And above all, never trust him.

That's everything I wanted to tell you. I'm so, so sorry that I couldn't say any of this with my voice. I was too much of a coward to change that, but I should have tried harder. I should have let you see who I really was, but I was too afraid of what you would think of me. I'm sorry. I can't apologize enough. I hope you forgive me, and even if you don't, I really just want to tell you.

Please, whatever you do, think about what I wrote in this letter. Ask for help and you'll receive it.

I love you, Maru.

Ishida Rin

P.S. In case you didn't know, Ishida Rin is real my name. I hope you told me yours before anything happened. I always really wanted to know.

CHAPTER 7

Maru folded his letter and put it in her pocket. She was trying not to feel anything; if she did, her emotions would overwhelm her, and she would not be able to kill herself. So, very calmly, she walked over to his desk and picked up the Bible. Thoughtfully, she flipped the pages, looking at each one without seeing what it said. Then she put it back on the desk.

"So you died believing a lie," she said coldly. "That's what made you look so happy. That's the only way anyone could be happy."

With one last glance around, she shut the front door behind her, shoved her hands into her pockets, and walked down the stairs to the street.

A very deeply buried part of her hoped that Kita would be there to stop her. Somewhere down inside, she wanted to live and find the meaning of life and happiness. But by far the larger part of her was intent on dying. She had mentally prepared herself to the point where there was no going back. Death was inevitable. It was something she looked forward to.

Down the steps, down the sidewalk, down the street. She had to pick a place where there was plenty of traffic, because she didn't want the driver to see her and be able to stop in time. She would never have the courage for a second attempt. So she kept walking, head down, eyes dry, mind blank.

A few minutes later she stood at a busy four-way intersection. She paused on the curb, waiting for the little walk sign to turn red. The cars would start moving. Taking one long, last look to the right and left, she drank in the beauty of the life around her. None of it changed her mind in the least. These people were happy. All the better for them. She could not take part in it.

The sign changed to red, and everything seemed to happen in slow motion. The first car sped up and flew by. Maru stepped out into the road and stood very still. She could not look at the car coming toward her with dreadful slowness. She closed her eyes. Something bright illuminated her vision, but she did not look at it. She stayed in her position. A moment later she heard some loud, unrecognizable noise. For a moment she wanted to run, wanted to change her mind and stay alive. But it was too late. And then there was darkness.

*****   *****   *****

Beep.

Monotonous.

Regular.

Blinding white light.

Maru's eyes fluttered open. So this was what happened after one died—whiteness everywhere, inability to focus on anything, soft, muffled voices all around. She thought she saw faces above her, but they were covered by something white. There were some regular beeps in the background. An incongruous thought flitted across her mind: is death really made of machines? Then suddenly her vision focused, and she could hear again.

"She's waking up," a voice said. "Oxygen mask, now! We don't want to lose her again."

Lose me? What's going on?

Something was pushed over her face. Maru fought the sense of suffocation and tried to force herself to take deep, even breaths. After all, she was already dead, and there was nowhere else to go.

The life-giving oxygen cleared her mind still more, and her muscles relaxed. She heard a voice say clearly, "I think we've won, folks. Congratulations."

"Where am I?" she asked, fighting the thing over her nose and mouth. "Who are you?"

"You're in Kei Hospital," said the voice. It was masculine and friendly and deep. "What on earth made you think it was a good idea to walk out into the middle of the road? There's plenty to live for, you know. You're too young to die like that." The man patted her shoulder. "But don't think about any of that right now. Focus on getting well."

"What happened?"

The doctor shrugged. "You were hit by a car," he said. "The driver called the emergency number."

"No." Maru was puzzled. "What happened before that?"

He shook his head and handed her a folded stack of papers. "This was in your pocket."

The handwriting brought everything back to Maru, and she tried to bury her face in the pillow. The oxygen mask slipped off her face and she gasped for breath.

"I read the letter."

Her eyes snapped to his.

"A lot of pretty words. I think you had a good friend in Ishida Rin, whoever he was. I've seen too much death to believe what he said, though." He smiled. "Now you rest."

Maru clenched the papers tightly in her fist and closed her eyes.

The doctor picked up a syringe and held it over the line in her arm. "By the way, I don't know anything about your friend. However, I do know one or two things about the organization he worked for. I'm guessing you work there, too. Don't let anyone else see that letter. You don't want people to know." He pushed the needle into her IV, and Maru's eyes grew heavy.

***** ***** *****

Several hours later, she awoke to find the room empty. The mechanical beeps were still audible, but they sounded much further away. The oxygen mask was off her face and lying on the table beside her.

"The letter," were her first words. She glanced down at her hand. It was still there, crumpled and torn at one corner.

She brought the papers above her head so that she could read them. "Ishida Rin," she repeated thoughtfully. "I like that name." Her eyes filled with tears and she pressed the papers to her chest. "I'm sorry I couldn't come with you. I tried, Rin. I promise."

"Awake yet?" The doctor's cheerful voice echoed in the small room. "I thought so. You're a pretty strong girl, Tanaka Makise."

Maru started. "Tanaka Makise . . . ?" she asked faintly.

"I put two and two together," said the doctor. "It wasn't difficult. Somebody named Rin said before he died—"

"Hold on! What do you mean?' The paramedics told me he was dead."

The doctor shrugged flippantly. "I wasn't there. But you were, apparently, so my guess was right."

Maru nodded, her eyes filling with tears. "Why didn't they tell me he was still alive?"

"Oh, don't cry." He patted her on the shoulder. "The only thing he said before he died was the name 'Tanaka Makise.' I figured that had to be you." He eyed her. "However, that name doesn't match any of the documents we found on you. Your license calls you Shiota Maru."

"That's my name," said Maru, turning away from the doctor to hide her tears. "Tanaka Makise was a friend of Rin's."

"So," said the doctor slowly. "I see."

"I'm not Tanaka Makise."

"Documents never lie." The doctor held up Maru's license and looked at it closely. "I worked in forensics before I became an emergency doctor, and I know a forged license when I see one."

"It's not forged." The surprise in Maru's voice was not entirely fake. She had compared her fake license with a real one and could tell absolutely no difference. "Besides, you already know everything about me."

"Who was Ishida Rin to you?" asked the doctor, sitting on the edge of the bed. "I'm curious. How did you get to know him?"

Maru was silent for a moment. "We met at work," she said after a while.

"I see. What kind of work?"

"We both worked for C—" Maru stopped herself. "You already know the answer."

"Yes, yes." The doctor stood up. "I just wanted to make sure. Well, Tanaka Makise, you're doing extremely well. You didn't even break any bones—just suffered a severe concussion. I think you're ready to leave."

"I told you, my name is Maru."

"Don't worry about the details," said the doctor briskly. "You're leaving, and there's nothing I can do about it."

"What?" Maru put her hands to her head. "Can't I stay another day? I don't feel very well. And I don't have anywhere to go."

"That's wrong." The doctor motioned graciously to the door. "Actually, you do have somewhere to go. These gentlemen will be taking you right where you need to be."

Two men in black suits entered the room and looked down at Maru. "Tanaka Makise?"

"I told you, that's not me," insisted Maru nervously. "Who are you?"

One of the men went to the other side of the bed and seized her arm. "Get up. You're coming with us."

"And you're just going to let this happen?" cried Maru, looking at the doctor. "Who are these people? Where are they taking me?"

"They are the federal police," replied the doctor. He waved a syringe at her. "Apparently you're more dangerous than I thought. By the way, if you're wondering how Ishida Rin died—" He winked.

"How did he die?" screamed Maru, trying to wriggle free. Her head was throbbing, and she could not think straight. "Tell me!"

"He was shot by one of our agents," said the man on her left. "We thought we'd finished him off, but apparently we were wrong. Luckily nature did our work for us."

"You killed Rin? You shot him? Why? What did he do? You—you—let me go!"

"We're not letting you go," said the other. "I'm glad you didn't kill yourself before we came along. We can make it ten times more painful." He snickered.

"Don't say anything like that," cautioned the doctor. "You're safe with me, but you never know who else may be listening."

Maru clenched Rin's letter tightly. "I'll go with you," she said at last. "I can see that I don't have any choice."

"Good idea," chirped the doctor. "Hold onto that letter, too. I'm sure Kaede will want to read it."

"Kaede . . . ?"

"Prepare for some fun," said the doctor cheerfully. "Adieu! It was excellent talking to you. You're welcome for saving your life."

"I didn't want to be saved," cried Maru. "I wish you'd let me die."

"Well, I didn't," said the doctor. "You'll thank me someday."

"No, she won't," said the man to her right. "Let's go."

They pulled Maru out of the bed and set her on her feet. Her legs shook and her head swam. She staggered dizzily into the doctor, who laughed and helped her balance.

"By the way," he said as they were about to leave, "do you recognize me?" He looked her keenly in the eyes.

Maru glanced at him coldly. "No, I do not."

"I have plenty of funny habits," he said with a wink. "I say 'oh' a lot, for example, and 'by the way.' I'm also very naturally outgoing. And I work for the federal police, but you've seen me somewhere else."

Maru tried vainly to place his face. It seemed familiar, but she couldn't remember who it belonged to. "I don't know you."

"Oh, come on," he said. "It's not every day that I get to go on a date with a pretty girl like you. That's not something I would forget easily. I'm rather sad you don't remember me."

Maru blinked twice and focused her eyes on his face. "K-Kousuke," she stammered at last. "Is that really you?"

"Sort of!" he replied, laughing. "But my name isn't Kousuke. It's Haruko." He bowed.

"Knock off the silliness, you psycho," said one of the men roughly. He shook Maru's arm. "We're leaving."

Haruko waved cheerfully. "See you later!" The door closed before he finished his sentence.

The hospital staff cleared out of the way as Maru and the two men approached. She was taken outside, handcuffed, and forced into the back of a long black car. The men took Rin's letter from her, and she was too proud to protest. After all, there was nothing she could do. She had no idea who they were or where they were taking her.

This would be the moment., She stared out the window. *If I'm ever going to believe what Rin said, I should ask for help now.* But she did not.

After about a half hour of driving, the car pulled to a stop in front of a prison. Maru shivered. The whole place looked cold and unfriendly and lonely. She wished she had fought harder to escape, but where could she run? If she stayed with Kita or Naito, she would only bring them trouble. If she went back to Rigel, she could very well risk exposing their entire operation. No, there was nothing she could have done better. Maru hated feeling trapped, and she had never felt it so strongly in her life.

The men looked at each other. "Solitary," said one, and the other nodded in reply.

They unlocked the back doors and helped Maru out, holding tightly to her arms as they did so. There was no possible chance for her to escape as they led her through the fence, past a row of ugly flat buildings, and into the back door of the flattest and ugliest of them all.

Maru stuck her elbows out and stopped at the door. "Stop," she said. "Where are you taking me?"

"Get in," said one of the men roughly, shoving her inside. She fell to her knees but stood up again immediately as they jerked her arms.

"Why?" she asked bitterly. "Why? Why? Why me?"

"You're a traitor," said one of them. "A murderer, assassin, killer. How many lives have you taken?"

"One," mumbled Maru. The question felt as if it came directly from her conscience.

"One," snorted the man. "I see. So, you're a virtuous little girl who likes to confess. Don't worry, we'll get a lot more answers out of you before the end of the week. Possibly before the end of the day."

"Shut up," said the other shortly.

"Why are you going to the end of the hallway?" the other asked conversationally. "Any of these rooms is fine."

"True. In here then."

They bundled Maru through a side door into an empty, dark, windowless closet. She had barely time to look around her and see that there was no furniture or anything else in the closet before the door shut with a click. All light was instantly extinguished. Maru had never been in a room so dark in her entire life.

"Hello?" she whispered tentatively.

She reached forward with her arms and hit a wall. Taking two steps in the opposite direction, she hit another wall. She could feel both sides of the room simultaneously when she reached with both arms. Therefore, it must have been about three and a half feet square, completely dark, completely empty.

Maru reached her arms up the wall, hoping vainly that there would be a door or a source of light. Her fingers barely touched a switch. She flipped it desperately, and the tiny space was suddenly illuminated by an unbearably white light. It endured for a few moments only, then vanished again into blackness.

She flipped it again, and this time, nothing happened.

"God," she murmured, sliding down the wall and burying her face in her hands. "I want out of here. I need out of here." She felt tears forming in her eyes, and since there was no one to see them, let them slide softly down her cheek. "Why didn't You let me die when I tried to kill myself?"

She repeated the last sentence to herself over and over, raising her voice with every repetition. "Why didn't You let me die?" she cried at last, burying her face in her hands. "I didn't ask for anything special. Everybody dies. Why can't I pick when I want it to happen? It's Your fault! Your fault that I'm here! If You even exist, I'm only here because You planned for this to happen! From the beginning of time, You knew. You could have made life happy for me. You could have saved me, but You condemned me to hell. I'll never serve a leader who betrays His people like that."

She sighed and cried a little more, letting her long legs extend up the wall and stretching them as best she could.

"At least I should thank God that Rin isn't here," she said, letting her head rest against the wall behind her and staring up into complete darkness. She raised her hand in front of her face; it was completely hidden in darkness. "This would have killed him. I think he would have died like this with absolutely nothing left inside. Maybe I can will myself to die like that. Is it possible to will yourself to die?" Maru did not know how to find out, and something deep inside her was too scared to try.

"Exactly what would happen to me?" she wondered. "Would everything be just like this? Darkness?" She shivered. "I can't die if that's what it means." Her hands travelled up her arms, hugging herself, and she could feel the scars of her wounds on her left forearm. The touch gave her an idea. "Pain," she muttered. "It can wake me up from this dream. This has to be a dream. I'm hallucinating." She raised her forearm to the level of her face and tried to see it. "I don't need a knife to cut myself." Slowly she leaned forward and bit her arm until the blood flowed.

She was rather surprised how much it hurt. It was not the sharp, quick pain of her knife; it was dull and only got worse as she lowered her arm to her side. She could feel drops of blood running slowly down the side of her mouth, and suddenly she was horrified. What had she done? Why in heaven's name had she bitten herself? What kind of monster was she turning into? She wished she could escape from herself. Life was a trap that held her down. She could not die, and she could not change. There was no chance for her. No escape.

Suddenly a crack of light streamed in, almost blinding Maru. It disappeared as quickly as it had come, and someone was in the room with her.

"Who are you?" she asked, trying to keep her voice steady. She could feel the person's shoes touching her legs, and she shrank into the corner.

"It's me, Kousuke," said a quiet voice. "I thought I'd come see you."

"Haruko," she said coldly.

"Kousuke," he corrected. "I'm sorry, Maru. I had no choice. I didn't want to report you, but I had to. After all, I work for these people, and I can't show favoritism."

Maru did not reply.

"Anyway, I'm afraid you're in for it now," he said quietly. "They're going to torture you."

"Why?"

He sighed audibly. "Because they know you work for Rigel," he said. "Because they know that Rigel is an anti-government organization. They're a bunch of assassins, in other words. What they don't know is exactly why you do it, and that's what they want to figure out. They'll do whatever they need to for answers."

"No," said Maru simply. She did not believe him.

"Maru—"

"Do you want to help me, Haruko?" she asked.

There was a long silence.

"I do," he said at last. "I betrayed you. I feel like a wretch, Makise. That is your name, isn't it?"

She nodded, but of course he could not see her. "Bring me some painkillers," she said drily. "Lots of them."

"Why do you want—?" He stopped abruptly. "No, no, no! I'm not going to let you kill yourself like that, Makise. You deserve better. That's why I'm here."

"What are you, a hopeless romantic? What do you think you can do? Can you get me out of here?"

"No," he said frankly. "I got you in, but I can't get you out. I'm sorry. The damage is already done."

Maru slid further down the wall. "Then what can you do?"

He shifted. "I could bring you Ishida Rin's Bible."

Maru snapped to attention. "How did you know about that?"

"I was watching both of you," he said. Slowly he added, "I guess you really could say that Rin's death was my fault. Did it never occur to you to wonder how I knew everything I told you about him? It's because I shadowed him on his first mission. I didn't pull the trigger, but I might as well have. I got all the credit, too."

"You really are a wretch," remarked Maru.

"That hurts, coming from you."

"But it's true."

"Do you want the book or not?"

She did not want to say yes, but something deep inside her seemed to take control of her voice. "I want it."

"I'll bring you a light, too," he said. "But don't get caught using it, or they'll probably be able to figure out how you got it. I'll be back, Makise. Can you stay in the dark like this for one more day?"

"A whole day? In the dark? With nothing to do?"

"Count," he suggested. "Start at some high number and subtract sixes. Or sevens. Or whatever."

"You idiot."

"I'm doing the best I can," he snarled, suddenly angry. "Do you want me to kill you now?" Maru felt something cold touch her throat and wondered dimly how he had known exactly where she was.

"Yes," she said, and closed her eyes.

The cold thing shook, then vanished into the darkness. "I can't," said Kousuke's stifled voice. "I wish I could, Makise. Do you want me to leave you the knife?"

Maru hesitated.

"Can you really bring me Rin's Bible?" she asked at last.

"Yes."

"Leave me the knife. Promise you'll be back tomorrow, whenever that is."

"I promise," he said immediately. Maru felt a wooden handle slipped into her hand. "There's the knife. But please give me a chance to get you out, Maru. I'll try my hardest. Don't do anything you can't undo."

"You're one to talk," she scoffed. "You got me in here, and now you want to get me out? Why?"

"Because you're you," said Kousuke simply. "I can't explain it any better than that. I think you would have done the same thing for Ishida."

"Rin," she corrected automatically.

"Ishida," he repeated. "I don't deserve to call him by his familiar name."

"I didn't either," said Maru dreamily. "I wish he was here. I'm glad he's dead."

"What?" said Kousuke.

"Never mind," said Maru. She could not wake her mind up fully. It was as if she were operating from inside a deep, inescapable haze. "He suffered enough. At least it's all over for him."

"Don't think that way."

"What would you prefer?" asked Maru sarcastically. "Would you like me to get up and dance?"

Haruko did not answer.

"Bring me a light," begged Maru, subsiding. "Please just bring me a light. And Rin's Bible. I guess you probably know where he lives."

"I'll be back tomorrow without fail. In a few minutes, they're probably going to come get you and ask questions. Answer them, Makise. It'll be much easier for both of us if you just answer." He paused. "And I'm Kousuke, not Haruko."

"I won't," she said mechanically. Kousuke let himself out, and the brief crack of light appeared again. Maru snatched at it with her hands as if she expected to capture it and hold it with her, but it disappeared without trace the instant Kousuke shut the door.

"Stay with me," she murmured. "Don't leave me in here alone!"

CHAPTER 8

It seemed like hours to Maru before the door finally opened again. The extreme monotony of the room, its darkness and small size, all contributed to the torment. Maru was half asleep when it opened. The light almost blinded her.

"Come with me." The voice was familiar.

"Haruko—?"

"Not Haruko. Kaede," he said roughly. "And come on." He pulled her up by her arm, and she was so surprised that she never tried to resist.

"How many personalities do you have?" was all she said as he pulled her out the door. Her mind was too numb to think of anything else.

"That's none of your business. Come with me." he said shortly.

Multiple personalities . . . ? I think I read about that. It must be some kind of mental condition. I wonder if he has—

"Dissociative—" Maru was hit violently across the mouth. She staggered back and fell against the wall, but Kaede pulled her roughly to her feet.

"I told you to shut up."

She did not open her mouth again as he dragged her down the hallway.

"Get in." He opened a door to their right and pushed her inside another side room.

This one was larger—about eight feet square, with a table in the middle. The lights were still blindingly white, and Maru blinked several times before her vision finally adjusted. In one corner was a loud stereo radio, and besides that and the table, it was empty.

"Wait here," commanded Haruko, retiring and locking the door behind him.

Maru sat down on the table. This was certainly an improvement on her previous imprisonment. Her fingers tapped nervously on the table as she wondered where she was and what was happening to her.

The door opened partway. "Matsui, federal police," said a voice from behind it. Then its owner appeared. He was a small, wrinkled man, half bent over, with a face as sharp as a weasel's. Maru instinctively shrank away from him.

"No need," he said briefly. "Lay on the table."

Maru stared at him blankly.

"Lay on the table."

"No. I won't." Maru stood up and backed against the wall. "Who are you? What are you going to do to me?" She could hear her fast heartbeat in her ears.

The man whistled. The high-pitched sound echoed around the room, and Maru covered her ears.

Two newcomers entered and seized her already bruised arms. They turned her around and pushed her down against the table, so that she lay on her stomach, and the first man slowly tied her down until she could not move at all.

"What are you doing to me?" she demanded nervously. "Are you really Federal police? Why am I here in the first place?"

"Because you're a traitor," replied Matsui simply. He nodded to the other two men. "You can go now."

They left and closed the door tightly behind them.

"Now," said Matsui. "Tell me, is your name Tanaka Makise?"

Maru shook her head insistently. "No! I've told you already that my name is Maru."

He nodded. "You're lying, of course. Your heart rate is elevated. Do you work for Rigel?"

"Rigel? What is that? You know already that I work for CAUS. How many times do I have to tell you? Let me go already!" She struggled against the ropes, but they did not give at all.

He nodded again. "You're lying again I'll have to be a bit more extreme." He turned to the stereo and turned it on, then adjusted the volume until it was almost unbearably loud.

"Stop!" begged Maru, desperately wanting to cover her ears. She could not get her hands free. "Stop! Please, just stop!"

"I don't like to hear the noise you make," he explained, yelling over the horrible music.

Maru screamed when something touched her back. She had no idea what it was. The feeling was so dull that it was unrecognizable, but it was there, and it refused to go away, no matter how hard she struggled against the straps that held her firmly against the table. She bit her lips until they bled, and finally, when she thought she could not stand it anymore, it vanished, and she relaxed limply.

"That was step one," she heard dimly over the haze around her. "Are you willing to talk yet?"

Maru realized with horror that what had just happened would happen again unless she told everything she knew. There was no escape.

"No!" she whispered and tensed every muscle defensively.

*****   *****   *****

Whether the torture lasted for a few minutes or a few hours, Maru was never able to tell, nor did she remember being taken back to her original closet. She only knew that when she woke up, she was there, her legs tucked under her and her shirt torn to rags in the back. She tried to move, but somehow her muscles refused to respond. She was stiff, and every small movement hurt.

"I can't be alive if this is what life means," she muttered, looking toward the ceiling. Of course, there was no escape there either.

Thirsty and in a desperate attempt, she felt around the space, searching for a bottle or anything damp. Her hand closed around something plastic and cylindrical, and she tore it open and put it to her mouth. Water.

"Thank you, God," she murmured to nobody in particular as the liquid coursed down her burning throat. "Thank you, God."

The water was not pure. She felt suddenly sick and dizzy, and realized dreamily that she had been drugged. She laughed at herself for not anticipating it. If only the drug would kill her, the torment would be over. Her head dropped loosely to her chest, and she gave into its effects and fell into a deep sleep.

"Sorry," she mumbled with a yawn, right before she lost consciousness.

*****   *****   *****

When she woke up, the room felt somehow even smaller than it had before. She put a tentative hand to the side. It hit something warm and soft.

"You're awake," said a masculine voice. "Glad to see that."

Maru blinked ineffectively. "Haruko? Kaede? Who are you?"

"Kousuke."

"What was that about?" asked Maru. "What happened? Did I fall asleep?" She tried to stretch. Both her arms hit the wall, and she yelped in pain.

"No, not unless you count being drugged as falling asleep," he said. "I can tell you that everything we wanted to know, we dragged out of you. That's going to hurt tomorrow."

Maru put both hands to her head. "It hurts now," she said thickly. "I have a terrible headache. And I hurt all over."

"It'll only get worse," he said absently. Then suddenly he burst out, "Why didn't you just say all that?"

"Say what?" Maru leaned back against the wall and shut her eyes.

"About Rigel."

She was dimly puzzled. "What? What did I say about Rigel?"

"The Kalideyes . . . the modified humans . . . why didn't someone just tell us?"

"Tell you what? What are you talking about?" Maru blinked sleepily. "Who are the Kalideyes? What is this Rigel thing?"

"Properly," said Haruko, "Rigel is the name of a bright blue star. It's also the name of an organization which recruits only people with blue eyes, because that way they know for sure that the aforementioned recruits haven't been modified."

Maru rubbed her eyes and looked in his direction. "You sound like you're in a good mood for once. Is that because something good actually happened?"

"Probably," he said. "First let's get you out of this closet. You have only yourself to blame for this whole mess."

"What are you—?" The door swung open, and Maru's eyes snapped shut. "It's too bright out there! Shut the door!"

"What, you want to stay in there forever?" he said. Maru felt a gentle hand slide over her eyes. "Look through my fingers. Open your eyes slowly. You'll be able to see again in a minute."

Maru followed his advice. The white light was nearly blinding, but it was beautiful at the same time. Maru felt as if she was seeing it for the first time. It filled her senses and almost made her drunk with its beauty.

"Wake up." The hand over her face withdrew slowly. "Can you see now?"

She nodded.

"Good. Well, follow me. I'll do my best to explain, but there are plenty of things to do. If only somebody had told us sooner! You call yourself a secret organization of pros, but you're actually all idiots in disguise."

"That's a bit harsh," said Maru, rubbing her eyes. "Do you have any headache medicine?"

"Sure." He felt around in his pockets and found a pill bottle, but he paused before handing it to her. "I shouldn't have said that. You're right, it was way too harsh. I'm sorry."

Maru did not reply.

"I hope you know I'm really sorry," he said.

"I hope you know how hard it is to believe that." She snatched the bottle from his hand. "You could be trying to poison me again for all I know."

"I'm not," he assured her. "I swear I'm not."

"It's not like I have a choice other than to believe you." Maru studied the label. "What's this?"

"Don't ask. Trust me, it will work. It's specifically formulated to help people who have been—" he waved his finger in the air "—*treated* like you were."

She glanced at him quickly. "Why do you sound like a completely different person all of a sudden?"

He sighed. "If I knew, I'd fix myself."

Maru swallowed one pill without water. "Fine. What exactly happened to me?"

"Don't ask questions about that, either. What I have to explain—and it's going to take forever—is what happened *because* of you."

"What did I do? What's going on? Why lock me up if you're just going to let me out a few hours later in worse condition than when I came in? And who are you anyway?" She took a step back. "You sounded completely different two minutes ago when you came to get me."

"Why are you in such a hurry?" he mimicked, raising his voice to match Maru's. "Come into my office and I'll explain. I'm the only one left here. Everybody else is busy."

He held open a side door to Maru. She entered warily, looking around carefully at the sparse furniture and seating herself as far into the corner as possible.

"Oh, don't worry," said Haruko. He dropped into a chair behind the desk.

Maru sighed bitterly. "Not that it matters, but do you really have different personalities, or is this just an excuse for betraying me again?"

"I have several of them, actually." Kousuke or Haruko, Maru was not sure which, waved a finger in the air. "Well, the thing is, you're actually on our side."

"I have no idea what you mean. I don't even know who you are." Her eyes darted around the room, plotting possible escape points. She had an uneasy feeling that something was not right.

Haruko put his fingers together thoughtfully. "It's very hard to explain. The thing is, all this time, the Federal Police believed that Rigel was an extra-governmental organization intent on terrorizing and murdering the population. We knew it had something to do with the modified humans, but we had no idea exactly what. Now, from what you said when you were drugged and tortured, we know why you're doing it."

"That is more than I know myself," said Maru truthfully. "Look . . . is this a trick? It simply has to be, because I don't know anything about an organization called Rigel. But beside that, how can you say you are on my side when you admit to drugging and torturing me? I don't think the police are allowed to do that in the first place. And there is no reason for me to be a special criminal."

"Not a trick," smiled Haruko. "Trust me, Maru. This is no joke. I'm the only one left here because my coworkers went to Rigel to investigate. They're hoping for a kind of alliance or partnership."

"Oh." That was all Maru could think of to say. "So you know about the Kalideyes . . . ?"

Haruko nodded eagerly and leaned across the table toward Maru. "Of course. You told us all about them. Modified humans who have died and whose bodies are now being used to harbor artificial intelligence which can be remotely controlled. Oh, yes. Believe me, I know."

"And you know why we're trying to kill the modified humans?" Maru was still skeptical.

"Yes, but I don't understand everything yet. I wasn't there when you were questioned, so I'm getting only second-hand information. Please explain again." He leaned his head on his hands. "I'm curious."

"Sure, you are," Maru muttered to herself. Aloud she added, "What's wrong with second-hand information? You really think I'm going to tell you all that stuff again? Besides, you just said that you knew all about it."

Haruko sighed and looked away. "The more information you tell me, the more I can help Rigel."

"I'm still not convinced that you want to help us at all," said Maru doubtfully.

"Well, I can get the information from the guards' report, and you can tell me if I'm wrong," said Haruko. "Any problems with that?"

"I guess not." Maru tried to ignore the throbbing pain in her head.

"All right." Haruko reached into his desk drawer and produced a clipboard. "You were asked why Rigel wants to destroy the Kalideyes. Your answer: 'It's because we don't want their bodies to be converted into Kalideyes when they die. The government is insisting that they be preserved because we don't know how to make them anymore. So we have to kill them before the government can find them, and—'"

"That's fine," interrupted Maru, looking away. Had she really been that direct?

"Excellent," said Haruko. "But who in the world is making these Kalideyes? Also—" he tapped his fingers on the desk "—can you explain the bizarre name?"

"The name is because neither Kalideyes nor modified humans can have blue eyes," sighed Maru, still without looking at him. "It's because scientists couldn't artificially replicate the genetic material of blue eyes. And we don't know exactly who is making the Kalideyes."

"But you have a guess, I think."

"CAUS." She was in too deep to go back now.

"Central Agency of United Scientists," purred Haruko. "You know they're sponsored by the government, right?"

Maru blinked. "What?"

"How could you believe idiotic lies like I told you just now?" he asked, standing up and yawning. "You're very gullible. I'll have you know something." He put his hands on her shoulders and looked straight into her eyes, a faint look of amusement on his face. She leaned as far back in her chair as she could, terrified by the expression in his eyes. He did not let go. "I know all about Rigel. I know all about the Scientists, and since you're never getting out of here alive, I might as well tell you now. CAUS made the first modified humans. We use their forms after death. And then we began to kill them and make what remained into the world's most powerful robots, which could be controlled remotely, and which looked exactly like real humans. The only difference, as you know, is that they cannot have naturally blue eyes. Unfortunate, but true. And frightening to somebody like you, with those gray eyes. They're genetically blue, right?"

"How did you know?" gasped Maru, her skin crawling. "How did you know?"

He drew away from her and stood in front of the door, continuing without answering her question. "I'm sure you can guess that the Kalideyes are used for discreet missions like assassinations. Sometimes you hear horror stories on the news about how somebody went crazy and became a serial killer. Of course, some of those criminals really were just ordinary psychopaths who deserved death anyway. But most of them were our Kalideyes. We used them to kill anyone who was close to the truth. We used them to kill criminals. We used them to destroy evil. We used them to—"

"Then you're the only evil ones left in the world," blurted Maru. She stood up and leaned heavily on the desk. Her head ached horribly, but she ignored it. If these were going to be her last words, she had to make them count. "I don't know what you did to me or those people, and I don't care. All I know is that we were right, and you're all murderers. I know the truth, and I'm going to take it where it belongs."

"I'll kill you," said Haruko lazily, leaning against the door.

Maru was enraged by his self-confidence. "You won't have a chance," she said, smiling to hide her emotions. "I know this version of you. You'll ask for mercy, but you'll get the same treatment you gave Rin—the pain of knowing that you're sure to die in misery."

"You can't get out," said Haruko. "I lied when I said everybody was gone. They're all still here, and you can't escape."

"You didn't lie," said Maru. "I know, because I was looking as we walked down the hallway. Besides, at this point, I don't care if I die. In fact, I'm ready to die now, so please kill me, Haruko." She spread her arms open and looked at him defiantly. "Kill me!"

He hesitated.

"Why are you so scared?" mocked Maru. "Kill me, Haruko! Where's all your self-confidence gone? Just hurry up and do it!"

Irresolutely he pulled a gun from his pocket and held it up.

With one quick movement she stepped toward him. The gun went off, but Maru anticipated it and ducked. She plucked it out of his shaking hand and laughed.

"So much for all your big words," she mocked. "You're at your weakest when you're switching. Who are you now? I don't know, and I don't care. All I know is that all this pain and misery is your fault, and I want to watch you die." Pressing the gun to Haruko's forehead, she fired before he had a chance to reply. He twitched sharply and slid to the floor.

After the echoes had died away—which seemed to Maru to take forever—she opened the door cautiously and looked outside. Nobody was visible in the hallway. She marched coolly out, leaving the office door swinging open behind her.

Maru was feeling deliriously and insanely happy. Adventure. Love. Hate. All the most violent emotions were tangled up in her mind, and it left her reeling. But she was not insane. She was only exhausted, and still suffering the most horrible physical pain. She was limping, dragging her right foot behind her. Somehow the fact never occurred to her until she accidentally put her full weight on it. With a yelp of pain, she sat down suddenly on the floor.

"What?" she asked herself irritably, tugging her shoe off and ignoring the involuntary tears running from her eyes.

Her sock was caked in dried blood, which she examined before tossing it aside. "They must have done something to me," she muttered. "It's better now to know. I can take care of it once I get out of here."

Without bothering to replace her shoe, she continued limping down the hallway toward the exit.

Surprisingly, nobody met her along the way. She let herself out the door and into the street, and there was still nobody. No guards, no pedestrians. She had no idea where she was, and her foot was in so much pain that she could barely walk. Reluctantly she sat down on the curb.

"No phone," she murmured. "No food, no money—nothing. How am I going to get back to Rigel? And where on earth am I?"

She waited for nearly an hour, dozing occasionally and waking herself up when she fell backwards against the wall. Her emotions and thoughts were completely blank, like a pure white light. When she slept, she did not dream.

At last a car drove by, and she forced herself to stand up. Wearily she walked out into the road and held out her arm. The car slowed.

"What do you want?" asked the driver, who looked as if he were still in high school.

"A ride," said Maru.

He surveyed her up and down with obvious alarm in his eyes. "You look a little scary," was his final conclusion.

"I don't care what you think of me," said Maru sullenly, opening the door and seating herself in his passenger seat. "Take me wherever you're going."

"To school. Is that real?" He pointed to her gun.

Maru looked at it as if she were seeing it for the first time. "No," she said. "It's just a prop."

"Okay." He was obviously relieved, and Maru could not believe that some-one so naive could possibly exist and continue to exist throughout high school. "My school is downtown."

"Then take me there," she said. "I'm going to sleep. Wake me up whenever you want to throw me out."

"Will do," he said, pressing the accelerator. The car leapt into motion, and Maru's head bounced against the seat. "Sorry. I get nervous sometimes and—"

"Just as long as it doesn't make you run your mouth," said Maru, shutting her eyes.

He did not say anything for the next twenty minutes, and Maru quickly fell into a deep, refreshing sleep.

CHAPTER 9

"Wake up," said a hazy voice. "Waaaaake up."

Maru started. "Haruko?" she asked in a shaky voice.

"What? No! It's the girlfriend of the idiot who picked you up off the street and drove you here."

Maru blinked and looked out her open window. "Girlfriend . . . ?"

"You're at school now," said the girl, tossing her thick black hair. "And you're obviously too old for that. I don't know what you thought you were doing, but you'd better get out of here. Now, before I report you to security or beat you up myself."

"Somebody's direct," said Maru, rather amused. "Little girl."

"Little girl notwithstanding, I don't take big talk from people like you. So get out."

"Who's taking it now?" asked Maru, obediently opening her door and stepping out into the adjacent parking space. "Have fun with your boyfriend. And—" she paused. "Tell him to find another way to school."

"What?" The girl put both hands on her hips and stared at Maru.

"Tell him not to drive past the place where he found me ever again if he wants to stay alive." Maru turned away, put her hands in her tattered pockets, and strolled slowly down the street away from the school. She could see herself in her head, and suddenly she started. She had absolutely nothing left to lose. Half-consciously she put her head in her hands and laughed hysterically, tears running through her fingers.

"Where am I going to go now?" she muttered through her sobs. "Food . . . water . . . where am I going to find it?" Her head throbbed.

The horizon seemed to tilt, and she felt her feet slipping. Half-consciously she put her arms out in front of her, but it was the wrong direction to break her fall. Before she knew what was happening, she found herself stretched dizzily on the hot pavement.

"Hey, wait," said a voice behind her. "Are you okay?" Maru's eyes closed sleepily, and the voice faded away into a dull roar.

Something wet hit her face, and Maru blinked, suddenly conscious again. That same girl was pouring water over her face, eyes wide with concern. "What happened? Are you thirsty? Hungry? What's wrong with you? Do you need to go to the hospital?"

Maru laughed weakly. "I haven't eaten for two days. And I forgot the last time I drank anything. Don't try to help me."

The girl fumbled in her pocket and produced a battered granola bar. "Eat this," she commanded, holding it over Maru's nose. "And you can have my water. I haven't drunk from it yet."

Maru tried to sit up, but the dizziness overwhelmed her, and she was forced to lay back down. "Small bites," said the girl, unwrapping the granola bar. "I'll help you."

She poured a little of the water into Maru's mouth and broke the granola bar into tiny pieces, which Maru chewed as best she could. Then Maru lay very still for a few minutes, closing her eyes against the bright sun overhead. Her head slowly ceased to throb, and she managed to sit up. Slowly her thoughts cleared, and the ache all over her body condensed into a very bitter, horribly painful heartache. She couldn't quite tell if it was guilt or sadness or pain or all three, but it hit her as hard as bricks. She gasped for breath.

Yuki patted her on the back. "Feeling better?"

Maru nodded, choking down her emotions. "Thanks. You're a lifesaver." Her voice was surprisingly steady.

"By the way," said the girl, almost shyly, "about earlier. I didn't mean to imply anything. Well, I did, but I've changed my mind now. I think what I said was unjustified, and I'm sorry." She bowed slightly.

"It's fine," said Maru flatly. "I deserved it, if that's what you want to know."

"I didn't ask," said the girl, straightening. "My name's Yuki."

"Nice to meet you," said Maru. "I've forgotten who I am. You can call me—" she hesitated. "You can call me Makise."

Yuki eyed her suspiciously. "Is that actually your name? Or are you some super-secret assassin with fifty-two different identities? Who just goes around saying they've forgotten who they are?"

Maru laughed. It refreshed her for a moment, and then the ache came back. "You have no idea how close you are to the truth," she said. "But Makise is my real name. Tanaka Makise, if you really want to know."

"So, you are an assassin," mused Yuki. "That's cool. I'd like to do something adventurous like that one day. I've always dreamed of—"

"Yuki." Maru stood up shakily, leaning on Yuki's shoulder. "Don't say that. You don't know what you're wishing for."

"Is it really that bad?"

Maru nodded.

"Can you tell me about it?"

Maru hesitated. Finally, her desire to tell someone outweighed the need for caution, and she sighed. "Will you get in trouble for skipping school?"

Yuki nodded. "But I don't care."

"All right, then. Let's just sit out here and talk. I don't think I can stand up like this for very long anyway. Do you know anywhere quiet?"

"Sure. Everywhere is quiet when the others are in class. We can just sit here, if you want."

"Not particularly. I don't want to get reported to security."

Yuki laughed. "Oh, I was just bluffing," she said. "There's no security here. Come with me."

She led Maru around the corner of the school building. There was a dilap-idated wooden bench along the wall, and Yuki sat herself carefully on the end.

"No offense," she said, "but you're covered in all sorts of nasty stuff. Stay on your side."

Maru looked at her hands. "Blood, mostly," she said drily. "I hate it. I hate myself. I shouldn't even be talking to you, but to be honest, it's a relief to say this to someone. Maybe you can help me make sense of it."

"I'm a high schooler," said Yuki sarcastically. "And you think I've seen more than you? Basically, you just confessed to being an actual assassin. That's no joke."

"No," agreed Maru. "But as an outsider, you might be able to help me make some sense of what's going on. Sometimes I feel like everything is in my head, but I can't—I can't get rid of this."

"Okay."

"I guess I'll start from the beginning." Maru leaned back and looked up at the sky. "I'm not going to tell you who I work for or what we do. But I was on a team of five people—Kita the psychologist, Naito the computer scientist, Rin the assassin, myself, and our leader named Saito. We were working downtown."

"Working?" interrupted Yuki.

"Investigating," corrected Maru. "That's all I can tell you. Rin and I were working together, and Kita and Naito were somewhere else. We—"

"And Saito?"

"Stayed at headquarters."

"Why?"

"Because—" Maru paused. "I don't know, actually."

"You'd better figure it out," said Yuki. "What kind of assassin are you if you don't even know what your team leader is doing?"

"Leave that for now," said Maru irritably. "Anyway, about three weeks ago, Rin was on a special mission, which was originally assigned to me. I backed out, and Rin went instead. I don't know exactly what happened, but he ended up in the hospital for a long time. He always said he wasn't in pain, but I knew better, so I went to see him every day. I can't believe he never . . . told . . . me." Maru's voice shook. "Yesterday—at least I think it was yesterday—he and I were talking. We were out in the park, and there was nobody else nearby. We—"

"Was it a date?"

"Do you want to hear the story or no?"

"Sorry, sorry. Go on."

"He collapsed because of complications from his original injury," continued Maru. "I ran down the street to call an ambulance, because we both left our phones in my room. And when I came back, he was dead." Maru's eyes were perfectly dry, and she was almost surprised at herself. "Probably it was stupid of me, but I tried to walk out in front of a car that night. Unfortunately, it stopped in time, and I was hospitalized for a minor concussion. The staff recognized me, and I was . . . " Her voice trailed off as she wondered how to explain such misery and horror to a high school girl. How would she explain it to herself? Was all this pain in her head? Was it real?

"You were what?" Yuki interrupted. Her compassionate eyes encouraged Maru to continue the story. "Makise, what happened?"

"Tortured," said Maru briefly. "They drugged me and did . . . other things. I know what they did, but all I really remember is that it was the worst pain I've ever felt."

"Did you talk?" Yuki's eyes were glowing.

"No," said Maru firmly. "No, I did not. But . . . " Her façade crumbled. "They drugged me, and I told them everything I know."

"So let me guess." Yuki crossed her arms judicially. "You blame yourself for Rin's death."

Maru blinked away the tears that were forming in her burning eyes. "How did you know?"

"It's pretty obvious," said Yuki. "You were supposed to take his mission, but you didn't, so he went instead. Because of that mission, Rin was killed. Not to mention the fact that you tried to kill yourself right after."

"Right. You're right. That's how I feel about it—like I killed Rin. I did kill him."

"Did you ever actually kill anyone? Rin doesn't count."

Maru nodded.

"Once?"

Maru shook her head.

"Twice?"

She nodded.

"Three times?"

She shook her head. "No."

"Not that it matters," said Yuki. "Get it together, girl. You're not much of an assassin right now if you're going to feel this way about the people you've killed."

"What do you expect me to do?" sighed Maru. "It's not those people. They deserved to die. But I killed my best friend. Which . . . " Her voice trailed off. "I didn't know it was possible to feel like this."

"You didn't kill him. And it's stupid for you to think that you did," insisted Yuki. "Rin's death was an accident, and you couldn't have prevented it no matter how hard you tried. In fact, if you must blame someone, blame him for not telling you that he might collapse. Maybe if you had known in advance, you could have done something about it. Secondly, did you learn anything about the people who tortured you?"

Maru nodded. "Plenty, I guess. But does it matter?"

"So get yourself back to whomever you work for and tell them!" cried Yuki, jumping up. "What are you waiting for? You're looking for motivation to live–you've got it right under your nose. I have my own car. I'll take you."

"No, no, no!" cried Maru, coming suddenly out of her head. "I can't get you involved with me. I'm a murderer. Why do you even trust me?"

"Why do you trust me?" asked Yuki. "My intuition about people is never wrong. I've had plenty of chances to test it, so now I'm going to take it for granted that I'm right and help you as much as I can."

"Thanks, but no thanks," said Maru firmly. "I'm not going to kill you, too. What about your boyfriend, anyway? He's going to think I kidnapped and murdered you."

"That was a lie," said Yuki. "I'm not anyone's girlfriend. I made that up because I wanted to protect him. He's such a wimp."

"You're a strong girl," said Maru. She gazed into Yuki's bright blue eyes. "And your eyes . . . they're blue . . . "

"I knew it!" cried Yuki triumphantly, clapping her hands. "Rigel! You work for Rigel!"

"Well for heaven's sake, shout it across the parking lot," said Maru drily. "I said I was suicidal, but I can think of better ways to die. How on earth did you know that, anyway?"

"Sorry," said Yuki. "But you idiot! Why didn't you tell me earlier? My brother works there."

"Name? I probably don't know him."

"He has the same first name as one of the people on your team. Ishida Rin."

"Ishida Rin. That name sounds fami—" Maru's mouth dropped open. "What—!"

Yuki jumped up. "Did you know my brother? Was he really on your team?"

"I knew him," Maru said absently. The knot of guilt became even tighter.

"Oh, maybe you can take me to see him!" said Yuki cheerfully. "If you know him well, I mean. He doesn't talk much. The last time I heard him say anything was before my dad died and we went to the orphanage. He didn't even say goodbye, and I wanted to thank him for taking care of me for so many years."

"You can't," said Maru shortly. Her breath became fast and short.

"Why not?"

"Didn't you hear me say that my friend's name was Rin?" She seized Yuki's shoulders and shook them. "Did you hear me say that?"

"Yes . . . ?" Yuki's eyes widened. "My brother Rin? Ishida Rin?"

Maru nodded violently.

Yuki was silent.

"I'm sorry, okay? Do you hate me yet? Please say you do." Maru let go and dropped to her knees. "I'm so sorry."

"No, I'm sorry," said Yuki, her eyes softening and filling with tears. Maru felt them drip on her bowed head. "I never told him."

"He knows," said Maru, rubbing her own eyes. "He told me his story, and I could tell that he was happy with his choices. Who knows . . . maybe he's watching us now. And if he is, then he's happy with who you are, Yuki. But me? He has to hate me. I even hate me."

"Maybe," she said doubtfully, sniffling. "It's okay. I haven't seen him for three years, so why am I crying? Stop blaming yourself and get up."

"Cry," advised Maru, standing and turning away. "I wish I had."

"So can you please tell me?" asked Yuki, tapping her arm. "Was he happy?"

"Rin tried to kill himself five times. He never spoke a word to anyone until right before he died. But in the end, I think he was happy." She sighed. "I can't explain it. I don't know why. But he discovered something important to him, and it made him happy."

"What were his last words?" Yuki sniffled, and Maru could tell she was trying her best to hide it.

"'Please do your best to forget about me,'" said Maru after a long pause.

Yuki clenched her fists. "I won't," she said. "I won't ever forget him and what he did for us. And I'm going to make up for not being a better sister by helping you."

"There's one more thing you should know," said Maru. "My team leader, Saito, is Rin's older brother."

"Saito . . . ?" Yuki paused, and her voice dropped. "I barely remember how he looks, because I almost never saw him. But that wasn't my oldest brother's name."

"We were all assigned new names when we first came to Rigel," replied Maru. "Rin told me how they were related."

"Okay." Yuki started to bite her finger, then drew it reluctantly away from her mouth. "Well, that's all the more reason for me to come with you. I want to help, so what can I do? Don't try to say no. I'm doing this for Rin, not you. Or Saito."

Maru nodded numbly. "I understand," she said. "But I'm probably going to be killed. If you're with me, you'll die, too. Are you sure you want—?"

Yuki nodded. "Please! Take me with you!"

"Okay then," said Maru, wishing she could refuse. "I won't tell you no. Tell the nurse that you're sick with the stomach flu or something, and then get in your car and take me to Rigel. I'll tell you where to go."

Yuki nodded and took off running toward the front entrance.

Maru stood up slowly, wincing in pain. Her pocket crunched, and she froze. Her hand almost involuntarily reached in and produced Rin's letter, crumpled, faded, torn, but still completely legible.

She unfolded the letter and skimmed the first page. "Why me? Why? Who am I to you? You'd want her to read it, wouldn't you? I love you, Rin. And I'm so, so sorry I couldn't save you."

"What are you talking about?" Maru looked up. Yuki stood in front of her, arms crossed, eyes dry and sparkling. "Let's go."

"I'll drive," said Maru.

"My car's the black Jeep in the corner."

Maru chuckled. "Nice ride. I'm going to have fun driving this."

"If you wreck it, I'll kill you myself," said Yuki, sliding into the passenger seat.

Maru started the ignition and smiled at the strong roar of the engine. "Read this," she said shortly, handing Rin's letter to Yuki. "Don't say anything until you've finished it. And stop putting on that artificial face. I know you can't be feeling like that."

"Same goes for you." Yuki unfolded the letter.

"I'm serious," said Maru, but Yuki did not reply.

They drove for a few minutes in silence. Then Yuki said, in a very subdued voice, "I'm done."

"Then give it back," said Maru, holding out her right hand.

Yuki crumpled the papers and put them in her hand. "You shouldn't have let me read that. It was too personal."

"What, did it embarrass you?"

"No." Yuki sighed. "How do I explain this? I never really got to know my brother. He was always busy and working so that we'd have food, or studying so that he could get a job, or distracting my dad so he wouldn't beat us. I feel guilty for not being sadder, I guess. I don't know. But because of this letter—" she looked abruptly out the opposite window "—I guess I know him now."

"Then I'm glad you read it."

"Did you love him, too?"

"Yes." Maru's voice fell to a strained whisper. "Yes, of course I did."

"Did you tell him?"

"Right before he died." She kept her eyes fixed on the road.

"Then I know he died happy," said Yuki. "His only regret must have been that you two couldn't be together longer."

"And that he didn't get to see you," said Maru bitterly. "And that he tried to kill himself so many times. And so many other things."

"Rin was happy when he wrote this letter," insisted Yuki. "I know that for sure. And that's all I need to know."

"What do you think about the middle part?" asked Maru, changing the subject abruptly.

"That stuff about God?"

"Right."

"I think he believed it," said Yuki. "And . . . what he says about it is pretty compelling."

"Are humans really just animals?" asked Maru. "Because that's what we are if we have no purpose in life."

"Is there anything other than God that can give that purpose, though?"

"I've looked, believe me," said Maru. "I can tell you that there isn't."

"Well, then, I think we're both pretty certain that we aren't animals," said Yuki. "We think and feel and cry, and we all know that animals don't do that. Don't you think that makes us a little more—I don't know, important? Not to mention the fact that we're sitting here having this discussion. Animals can't do that either. So, I don't think saying that humans are just animals is a valid answer."

"That's easy for you to say."

"Why should it be hard?"

"Why should God be a personal God?" retorted Maru.

"Well, an impersonal God couldn't give meaning to anything."

"So, you really believe in a God?" asked Maru incredulously.

"Yup."

"Did you . . . before you read that letter?"

"Nope."

"You change your opinions too quickly." Maru sighed.

"Why shouldn't I change my opinion when there's plenty of evidence?" asked Yuki. "Rin was suicidal long before you knew him. I think the only reason he continued to live was because he wanted to keep us safe. If he found something that could change him so much, why shouldn't I believe that it's real? If you don't like that example, then I could just say that the historical evidence for Jesus' life and death is overwhelming. Did you know that almost all scholars, atheist and Christian, believe that Jesus existed? The Bible isn't the only book that talks about him. My teacher said that there are more than forty different documents from way back then that talk about His life and what He did. I know because I had to write a report about it."

"That doesn't make Him God, Yuki."

"No, but that's because you're looking at all the evidence separately. Put it together, and you've got a very, very good case."

"Do you really think that?" asked Maru wistfully. "I wish it was true."

"I'm telling you that it is true," said Yuki. "But what do I do now that I believe?"

"I think Rin said to ask for help."

"Okay." Yuki looked around doubtfully. "Umm . . . God? Jesus? You up there? We could use a little help. And some proof that You're real." Suddenly she began to laugh. "Oh, we're so stupid! We missed it!"

"Missed what?"

"The sign!"

"What sign?"

"Don't you think it's a little odd that you met me?"

"Well, yes. It was an interesting coincidence—"

"Don't give me that," snapped Yuki. "There are millions and millions of people here, and you happened to meet me. Rin's little sister. I think that's pretty good proof."

"Or it could be a coincidence."

"I'm surprised God hasn't given up trying to convert you yet," said Yuki, snuggling into her seat. "You're so obstinate."

"Sorry," said Maru. "I've seen a little too much to think there can really be a God."

"That's your fault, not His," said Yuki. "Humanity has free will, so it's our fault and not God's that this world is messed up."

"Whatever," said Maru. "Let's talk about this later."

"You said yourself that you think you're going to get killed," persisted Yuki. "So shouldn't we talk about it before that happens?"

"So I can go to heaven? Is that it? Yuki, it's too late for that. Look at what I am. I murdered a man this morning. I didn't have to. I could have tied him up, knocked him unconscious. I killed him because I wanted to. It made me happy. This blood on my hands—" she took them off the steering wheel for a moment "—isn't mine. It's his. I killed him for fun." Maru did not look directly at Yuki, but she could sense her shiver at the last words.

"What good is a God who can't forgive?" Yuki said after a pause. "I had a neighbor who was really nice to us—when she wasn't drunk. She read the Bible to me and my siblings sometimes. It seems like there's a verse about this somewhere."

 Maru did not reply.

"Here it is," Yuki chirped. "I looked it up on my phone to make sure it's right. 'For all have sinned, and fall short of the glory of God.'"

"There's some news for you."

"But there's another one." Yuki squinted at the phone. "Believe in the Lord Jesus Christ, and you will be saved."

"It doesn't say 'forgiven'," said Maru.

"How about this!" said Yuki triumphantly. "'For God so loved the world that He gave His one and only Son, that whoever believes in Him shall not perish, but have eternal life.'"

"Still no forgiveness."

"How can you possibly be this dense?" cried Yuki. "Don't you get it? God is perfect. If you were perfect, you wouldn't want sinners around—you'd want to punish them. You'd need to punish them, because that would be justice. But instead of punishing us, God let His Son die. Which means we can be with God. That's true forgiveness."

"Whatever," said Maru. "Could we please stop talking about this for a few minutes? I need some time to think about what I'm going to tell Saito."

"You brought it up," Yuki reminded her. "But that's okay. I'll be quiet. I guess I'd better think about what I'm going to say to him, too."

"Thanks," said Maru shortly.

She gripped the steering wheel tightly and tapped her left foot lightly on the floor. "Saito," she murmured. "Why did it have to be you?"

"Who? What?"

"Saito," said Maru absently.

"What about him?"

"He is hard to talk to," she explained shortly. "I have never once had a normal conversation with him. Every time we start talking, something weird happens."

"Like what?" asked Yuki curiously.

"He just . . . he . . . " Maru hesitated, suddenly feeling unreasonably ashamed. "Nothing."

"What's wrong with him? Did he ever do anything to you?"

"Yes . . . no."

"Is that supposed to mean something?"

"I guess," said Maru vaguely. "It's really nothing. He's just very quiet, and he gets off subject easily."

"Off subject?" Yuki nodded wisely. "I could have guessed that."

"I thought you said you never saw him."

"I didn't."

"So how do you know?"

"I don't know. I guessed."

"I'm not kidding, Yuki. What are you not telling me?"

"Why do you care?"

"Don't be that way."

"I can't really explain it. Besides, you said you wanted me to be quiet."

"This time it was you, not me, who started the conversation," said Maru irritably. "It doesn't matter. We're here."

"This just looks like an ordinary office building. Kind of boring," observed Yuki, looking around.

"Well, all these buildings belong to Rigel," said Maru. "You didn't see it, but we passed security on the way in."

"If they don't know my car, then how did they know to let us pass?"

"I flashed the lights in the code pattern."

"Wow, cool!" Yuki was suddenly enthusiastic. "So it's like a real spy agency."

"Not really."

"No, seriously," Yuki said, hanging out the window and looking all around with renewed interest. "You have the coolest job in the world!"

"Did you forget everything I said about the people I've killed?" Maru parked the car and turned off the ignition. "In fact, since you seem so curious about everything, I shot another Rigel member on the sidewalk."

"You did . . . ?" Yuki's smile faded

"To be fair, he tried to kill me first," said Maru calmly, opening her door. "I don't think about it anymore. Come with me."

Yuki hastily jumped out into the adjacent parking space. "Where are we going?"

"What time is it?"

Yuki looked at her phone. "Almost noon."

"Then we're going to the cafeteria. Saito should be there." Maru paused. "What's his real name, by the way?"

"What's the point of having a fake name if I tell you that?" Yuki winked. "Saito is a much better name, anyway."

"You're more secretive than I am," said Maru. "I still can't believe that I picked up a high school girl off the street. I basically kidnapped you. What am I doing?"

"Let's both be glad you didn't do anything worse," said Yuki.

"Direct as always."

Yuki nodded. "Of course. I wouldn't say anything if I didn't mean it."

Maru looked at her. "I don't think you mean half of what you say right now. It's just filler."

"What?"

"Filler—meaningless content to take up space. You're not thinking about what you're saying, are you?"

"No," she admitted, lifting a nervous finger to her mouth. "I'm really not. I'm thinking about Rin, and how cool you are, and all the stuff we talked about on the way here. To be perfectly honest, since you already think I'm so direct, I'm also a little scared. Mostly about Saito. I haven't seen him in years, and to be honest, I'm scared of him. I don't remember it very well—" Yuki squeezed her eyes shut "—but I think he used to hit us when we were little. My siblings and me."

"Saito hit you?" Maru's eyes widened in surprise. "Really?"

"Doesn't that sound like him?"

"It's not impossible, I guess. But he doesn't seem like the kind of person who would waste energy on something like that, even if he wanted to."

"Waste energy?" Yuki shook her head. "You obviously don't understand."

"Well, you don't understand what it's like to murder someone. So let's agree to misunderstand and get this job done."

Yuki tapped her finger nervously against her lip before replying. "Okay, okay. I'm coming with you."

"Yuki. Are you sure you want to do this? Once Saito sees you, there's no going back."

She nodded. "Of course, I'm sure."

"Okay then." Maru held the door open for her. "Let's see if you can recognize him."

Yuki stopped in the middle of the doorway and looked around the room. "It's so white," she said dazedly. "And . . . I don't see anybody I know."

"Try the back left corner," said Maru, who could not see past Yuki.

There was a long pause.

"I forgot how much I hated you," said Yuki at last.

"Don't try to remember now. Come on." Maru pushed her forward.

"On second thought I want to go back—"

"Come on!" Maru seized her hand and pulled her toward Saito's habitual corner.

He was sitting at the table reading something on his watch screen. Slightly to his left was a cup of coffee, and in front of him was an untouched dinner roll on a napkin.

"Shui!" cried Yuki shrilly.

Saito twitched and looked around. "Shui . . . ?" he repeated. Then he saw Yuki, and his expression became almost panicked. "What are you doing here? How did you find me?"

Yuki marched up to him. "I have so many questions for you," she began, breathing heavily. "Why didn't you come back? Why did you leave us all alone? Why did you let Rin die?" Her voice rose to a scream. "Why . . . Why . . . why?"

"Shhh," said Maru hastily. "Yuki, you and Saito can discuss this later. Please be quiet for now."

Yuki retired reluctantly.

Saito froze. "Rin is dead?"

"Yes," said Maru shortly. "It was a complication of his injury from a few weeks ago."

"Suddenly . . . ?" His face was bloodless.

"Very."

He sat down at the table, still with his back to Maru.

"That wasn't all you came here to tell me."

Maru was annoyed. "That's it?" she asked bitterly. "You're not going to acknowledge that your brother is dead?"

"Did Yuki tell you that, too?"

"No. Rin told me himself."

"I see. Go on."

"Don't you have anything else to say? Your sister has questions for you. I have questions for you. Our whole team is looking to you for help. Doesn't that mean anything to you?" asked Maru hotly.

"Why should it matter?" he asked, raising the coffee cup to his lips with a shaking hand. "There's nothing I could have done to prevent any of this. Tell me what you came here for and then leave. Both of you. I don't want Yuki here."

""At least let me finish," said Maru, struggling to control her temper.

"Then get to the point."

Maru swallowed her anger and began, "The government is working on the side of CAUS. I was held prisoner by federal police and interrogated for about twenty-four hours after Rin died."

"The federal police," interrupted Saito, "were here a few hours ago. They want to work with us to shut down CAUS."

"What?" Maru was confused. "But Haruko said—"

"They told us about him also," said Saito, turning away again and sipping from his coffee. "A crazy psychopath with split personalities. They left him there with you because they hoped you'd kill him."

"I did," said Maru.

"Well done. Well, I don't guess there's anything else you need to tell me."

"That's it?" she asked in angry surprise. "Nothing else?"

"If the federal police get involved, CAUS will be shut down in a matter of days."

"I know, but how do the police know we're telling the truth?" She bit her lip.

"It had something to do with Haruko," said Saito. "Apparently he was the head of the federal police. He used his agency to protect CAUS, and probably he was being paid substantial bribes. His split personalities got the better of him eventually. Today they said he was stark raving mad. Besides, we have plenty of scientific data about how the Kalideyes are being used. Nobody could reasonably doubt."

"So he was telling the truth?" Maru clenched her fists. "I killed him when he was telling the truth."

"It doesn't matter as long as he's dead," said Saito. "Now both of you can leave. Get Yuki away from this mess."

"I want to talk to you before you kick us out," interrupted Yuki from behind Maru. "Don't you have time for that?"

"No," said Saito. "I don't want you to come here anymore. I am sorry you aren't happy to see me, but I did the best I could for you. I would appreciate a little gratitude. Now Maru, please take her with you and find her a safe place to stay."

Maru wondered if Yuki was going to cry.

"Okay," she said quietly. Without another word to Maru or Saito, she turned and walked to the door.

"Why aren't you taking this seriously?" Maru asked coldly.

Saito sighed. "I am taking it very seriously, but I'm not sure what to do. I need somebody to be on my side for once."

"You have me and Kita and Naito. We're your team. We're on your side. I'll tell Kita and Naito to come back." Maru turned away.

"Rigel will be disbanded," said Saito, his voice sounding oddly distant. "They don't need to come back here."

"Rigel will be . . . ?" Maru stopped. She had not thought that far ahead. "They're just going to shut us down?"

"If the Kalideyes cease to exist, there won't be any reason for us to exist either."

"So we just . . . disappear?" Maru turned back to face him. He was looking at the floor.

"I don't know yet." He looked up. "Forgive me for what I said earlier. I acted unprofessionally, so I apologize. But now you see why I'm on edge. It's partly my responsibility to make sure everyone is safe and taken care of after Rigel is disbanded."

"Can you please focus on the problem at hand?" said Maru. "Talk to Yuki. Come to Rin's memorial service. I saw it listed for ten o'clock tomorrow on the declassified board. There's time to figure the rest out."

"I will," he said. "I promise I will. But when will I see you again?"

"Me? I don't know," said Maru noncommittally.

He paused. "All right."

"Now I need to go find Yuki a place to stay since nobody else will." Maru regretted her sarcasm as soon as it left her mouth, and she tried to soften it. "Contact me if anything comes up."

"Thanks, Makise."

"That's Maru," she corrected as she turned away. "Rigel's not done for yet."

CHAPTER 10

"I'm so sorry I talked like that in front of you and everyone," said Yuki without looking at Maru. "I'm an idiot. I should have kept my mouth shut."

"I don't think you said anything that isn't true," said Maru. "What now?"

"You tell me."

"Are you hungry?"

Yuki shook her head.

"Well, let's go to my dorm. You can spend the night there if you want." Maru paused. "On second thought. I keep forgetting you're a high schooler—which is a compliment, by the way. But I guess you have to go home."

"No, I don't," said Yuki. "I live in the school dorms. They'll never miss me, because they don't take roll. If I don't show up to class tomorrow, they'll think I'm still sick."

"Okay," said Maru. "You sure?"

"Mhm."

"Well, let's drive to the dorms then," said Maru. "It's only about a five minute drive." She climbed into the driver's side of the Jeep. "Yuki, can I ask you a question?"

"Sure."

"How in the world did you get this beautiful car if you don't even have to drive to school?"

Yuki's face lit up with pride. "I won it," she explained. "There was a national writing competition last year, and I won the first prize out of eight thousand entries."

"Eight thousand—? Wow, Yuki! That's amazing!"

"I love writing," said Yuki enthusiastically. "It always makes me feel like I'm living in another world without actually having to experience the pain and problems the characters do. I've always wanted to write a novel that will really move people, but the stuff I've written so far is mostly dry historical fiction. I've never really had a good story to tell."

"Well, you have one now," said Maru.

"Could I really write about this? I thought you'd tell me to keep everything a deathly secret."

"If Rigel disbands, it will be all over the news anyway," said Maru. "So you can write about it. Just don't send the manuscript anywhere until I tell you it's okay."

"Thanks!" cried Yuki. "You have no idea how much better that just made my day."

"It would be so easy for Saito to do something." Maru sighed absently. "Why doesn't he get to see this side of you? I just met you, after all. You're so open."

"Well, so did he," said Yuki, suddenly losing her smile. "I'm a completely different person since I saw him last, and I think he knows it."

"You called him Shui, right?"

"Ishida Shui."

"I see."

"I bet he changed his name, though."

"Maybe. In any case, he got a new one when he came here. We all get new names once per year or when we switch missions."

"Isn't it hard to remember?"

"You get used to it, I think. Rin had at least five different names."

"That's kind of cool," said Yuki. "I still can't get over the fact that there's a real-life spy in my car. What better day could I ask for? Plus, I get to write about it, which makes everything even better."

Maru looked down at her bloodstained, scarred arms. "You aren't scared of me?"

"Why?"

"Just look at me."

"It's not that bad compared to what I've seen," said Yuki. "Did you tell Shui that you killed somebody this morning? Haru-something?"

"Yes."

"It doesn't look like anything happened to you."

"Don't say that," said Maru. She parked the car and leaned on the steering wheel. "It's nice to be callous to everything, I guess, but it makes me feel less than human. And guilty for having no feelings at all about something that should have torn me apart."

"You cried when my brother died, didn't you?"

"To be honest, I don't remember," said Maru. "The only thing I know for sure I'll never forget is how Rin's voice sounded. It was too beautiful. It reminded me of something, but I can't quite remember what."

"When I was little," said Yuki, "I used to be really shy and scared of people because of what happened at home. The last thing I remember Rin saying to me was, 'Don't silence yourself. Be whoever you want to be, and people will love you for who you are.'"

"'Don't silence yourself,'" repeated Maru. "I've heard that before."

"Really? Did he say it to you, too?"

"Yes, but I don't remember what we were talking about when he said it."

Yuki jumped out and shut the door hard. "Can you give my keys back?"

Maru handed them to her. "Are you sure you're okay to stay with me?"

"Sure, why not?" Yuki looked her up and down.

"You can take Kita's room. I usually sleep on the sofa."

As they walked inside, Yuki said, "Wow. Who decorated this?" She ran her hand over the crystals on the chandelier.

"Not me. It's a long story, actually."

"I see."

Maru opened the bathroom door. "I'm going to shower. Tell me if anybody tries to get in."

"Tries to get in . . . ?"

"Your brother or a girl named Ayano are the most likely visitors. Don't let anyone in until I'm out of the shower, unless you feel like having a private conversation with Saito-Shui."

"Saito-Shui," repeated Yuki. "That's actually not a bad name. But I don't want to talk to him, so I won't let anyone in."

"Thanks." Maru found all the pieces to a spare training uniform scattered across the living room furniture and gathered them into a messy ball. "I'll try not to take very long."

"No hurry." Yuki was looking at the bookshelf. "Was it you or Kita who collected all these books?"

"Kita. You can read them if you'd like."

Yuki backed away. "Reading graphic novels would completely ruin my image."

Maru laughed in spite of herself. "Well, if it helps at all, I read them. So did Rin, apparently."

"Of course, he'd read all the really violent ones."

"I guess so. I never actually saw him doing it." Maru waved from behind the bathroom door.

"Hey, wait!" Yuki called after her. "Can I have some cookies?"

"Eat whatever you want. Just make sure it hasn't gone bad, because I don't think anyone's been here for a while." She paused. "Yuki, how are you this strong?"

"I'm not." Yuki was not facing her, but Maru could hear her voice change. "I'm not."

"Then stop trying to pretend." Maru gently wrapped an arm around her in a hug. "That's not helping. Just stop."

Yuki nodded silently, and Maru went back into the bathroom.

Her eyes turned immediately to her own bedraggled reflection in the mirror. She was truly a human disaster, with her hair sticking straight up in some places and beaten down in others, her clothes torn to rags, and blood-stains like polka dots every few inches. There was a long cut across her face. Maru had no idea how it had gotten there.

"It's better than I thought," she said irresolutely, patting the top of her head. "No wonder Yuki threatened to call security on me."

Her bloodstained knife, the one she had used to cut her wrists, was still sitting next to the sink where she had left it. She picked it up now and ran her finger thoughtfully along the sharp edge of the blade. It did not cut, but Maru would hardly have cared if it had. It brought back more memories than she had bargained for, and for the first time in days, her emotions overwhelmed her, and she fell to her knees.

"At least I can still feel," she gasped, covering her ears with both hands. "It hurts too much. I can't stand this."

Who's going to fix this? Who's going to fix me? If there is a God, does He care enough to help me change?

*****   *****   *****

"Why does everybody want to do my hair?" complained Maru. "I never do anything with it myself."

"That's exactly why," said Yuki. "It's because you're so gorgeous that it's a shame to let it go to waste. Hand me that brush."

"It's just not important to me, if that makes sense," said Maru with a sigh. "Oh, well. I don't mind if you do it."

"Then hand me that brush. Not that one—the one on the left."

"They look the same to me," said Maru, examining them closely, one in each hand.

"They're not." Yuki jerked it away. "You're just making this process slower."

"Like I said, I really don't mind," said Maru.

"Good."

There was a long pause.

"You're pretty good at brushing without making it hurt."

"It's just because I'm doing it correctly. Anybody could do the same if they really wanted to."

There was another pause.

"Yuki, tell me a little about yourself," said Maru. "We just met today, and I feel like there's a lot more that I should know. What do you want to do for a living?"

"I'm already doing it. I write."

"Have you published anything?"

"Two full-length novels," she explained, carefully parting Maru's hair. "One was about this war in Africa, and the other was about Siberia."

"Oh, so they were historical fiction?"

"Yup," replied Yuki. "I had to do a lot of research, but it was fun. It's funny—I really don't like studying history, but I really do love reading and writing historical fiction."

"Well, that sounds more interesting than reading it out of a giant textbook," said Maru.

"Definitely," agreed Yuki. "Did you go to college, Makise?"

"Yes."

"How long ago did you graduate?"

"Just last year, actually."

"And did you always know what you wanted to do?"

"Pretty much," admitted Maru. "My father worked for Rigel."

"Neat!" cried Yuki. "Well, I'd love to work here, too."

"You won't have the chance," said Maru gloomily. "Rigel will be disbanded as soon as CAUS is out of the picture."

"Really?" Yuki sighed. "I wanted to do something interesting for once."

"There'll still be plenty of things you can do if this kind of job appeals to you," said Maru. "But make sure you see both sides of the picture, Yuki. This job is horrible. To be honest, I often wish I hadn't come."

"That's not right," said Yuki. "Your past experiences shape you into the person you are today, right? So without them, you wouldn't be you. You wouldn't be you, Makise."

"I'd be a much better, cleaner version of myself. You know, it was just this morning that I—" She stopped. "You don't need to hear about that."

"Forget the 'she's-in-high-school stuff' and get to the point. It's not like you're going to scar me for life any more than I already have been." Yuki laughed drily.

"Fair enough," said Maru. "Well, here you go then—a full confession. When I killed Haruko this morning, I did it because I was angry, not because he deserved to die. I could have escaped without doing it, but I did it, and now I don't feel any remorse about it. It might as well not have happened. In fact, I barely even remember doing it."

"Do you remember what his face looked like?"

Maru shook her head regretfully. "I was so furious that I didn't even notice."

"Did he deserve to live?"

"I don't think so, but who am I to make that choice? It is not like I am going to be right every time. Besides, he had split personalities, so I never really knew who he was at any given time. He might have been an angel for all I know." Maru could not bear to look at her own reflection in the mirror. She could not force her face to be any sadder. "I should regret it . . . but I don't."

"And you really don't think that you wishing you could regret doing it really is you regretting it?"

"What was that crazy convoluted sentence?"

"You regret not regretting it," persisted Yuki patiently. "And you don't think that's really you regretting it?"

"I don't know. That confused me more than it helped."

"Well, sorry," replied Yuki, applying a choking whiff of Kita's hairspray. "Take yourself a little less seriously, Makise. It's almost over. Three of your four teammates are alive and doing well. They're here to support you. And so am I."

"That's nice of you," said Maru. "But something isn't right, and I don't know what it is."

"Are you sorry you killed those two people?"

Maru shook her head. "The first one was self-defense. I'm sorry for killing both of them. And I'm really, really sorry that I actually enjoyed doing it. All that blood on my clothes earlier—"

"Wasn't yours," finished Yuki. "I know that."

"But what can I do? Unless I do what you're doing and decide to believe in a God, nobody can ever forgive me. It's not like I can just apologize to Haruko."

"I wish things were that easy," said Yuki. "There are a lot of things I'd still like to tell Rin. But I can't, and I think we both have to accept that. Besides, what's wrong with believing in God?"

"Nothing and everything," said Maru equivocally.

"That makes no sense and you know it."

"Well, God doesn't make sense either, so why worry about it?"

"I don't get your logic," said Yuki. "Would you please look at yourself in the mirror? You already look like a model."

Maru did not see anything beautiful about the reflection that stared back at her with worried, exhausted eyes. "Can you hurry up a little bit? I really want to get some sleep."

"Sleep!" cried Yuki. "Right after I finish? That's never going to work! You'd better at least go to dinner."

"You had fun doing it, right? So, who cares if anyone sees me?"

"I do," said Yuki firmly. "Although . . . on second thought . . . Makise, what happened to your neck?"

"How should I know?"

"It's bleeding," said Yuki. "Ugh. You have some really bad cuts running straight down your neck and down your back. What on earth did those people do to you?"

"You don't want to know," said Maru. "Are there any bandages in here?"

"I'll look around," said Yuki, investigating the cabinets and closets. "You sit right there and don't move."

Maru waited patiently through the chorus of drops, bumps, and bangs while Yuki searched.

Suddenly all the noise stopped, and Yuki said, "You don't think I'm like Saito-Shui, do you?"

"What? Why would I think that?"

"You told him that he was wrong for not being able to feel anything," said Yuki in a very subdued voice. "But I don't feel anything about Rin. I barely even cried."

Maru turned around to see Yuki sitting on her knees in the middle of about fifty scattered tissue boxes. "I really am sad," she said, looking up eagerly. "I really am, I swear. And there's so much I wish I could have done. But I don't feel anything really deeply. I guess I never expected to see him again anyway, and I accepted that a long time ago."

"You're nothing like your brother," Maru assured her. "What would you have done if I brought you back here to see Rin?"

"Cried because I was so happy," said Yuki. "It sounds really dramatic, but it's true."

"Then I don't need to explain to you why you're different than your brother."

"Okay." Yuki looked around at all the boxes. "I guess I'd better clean this up."

"I'll help," said Maru. "I didn't know Kita got colds this often. Or maybe it was seasonal allergies."

Maru paused and looked at the girl. "Yuki, you know you're not your brother, right?"

"I'm not convinced." Yuki sighed, poking a box. "After all, we are family, so that means we should be at least a little bit similar."

"Not at all. I'm nothing like either of my parents. I wish I were, though. I admired them."

"And what happened to them?"

"They died before I graduated from college."

"Sorry. I shouldn't have asked."

"No, it's okay." Maru placed a carefully balanced stack of tissue boxes on the top closet shelf. "I like talking about them, because they really were such amazing people."

"Well, that's not the case with Saito. I wish he wasn't related to me, or that he'd left before I was born. Anything."

"Don't underestimate him," said Maru. "I said some harsh things about him earlier, but I was focusing on his negative qualities to make my point. He is a good leader, I think. And he has a very strong character."

"In what way exactly?"

"It's hard to explain," said Maru. "I think in reality he feels bad about what he did, but he doesn't want to let his feelings distract him from what he has to do now."

"That makes him weak, not strong." Yuki stood up. "Let's not talk about that right now. Can I finish your makeup, or do you really want to go to sleep?"

"If you don't mind, can you do it in the morning?"

"Sure, that's no problem." She put the brushes into a pink basket and slid it under the counter. "Say, can I really borrow one of those graphic novels? I haven't read any since I was little. Anything to distract me. I'm never going to sleep."

"Go ahead," invited Maru. "And raid the kitchen since we aren't going to dinner."

"Oh, I did that while you were in the shower. There were some really good cookies and a small bar of Belgian chocolate."

"Kita always kept the weirdest things." Maru collapsed on the sofa. "Good night, Yuki."

"It's only five o'clock."

"Whatever," yawned Maru.

"Can I leave this place and walk around a little?"

Maru sat bolt upright. "No, Yuki! Don't!"

"Okay. Relax, please."

"The people here are dangerous. So don't go anywhere without me, please."

"Oh, fine." Yuki picked up a stack of books from the shelf. "I was too young to read these the last time I had any graphic novels. I guess I'll start here."

"Blood, guts, and gore. A fine choice."

"Not for you. Anyway, good night, Makise." Yuki sighed. "I'm happy to be here, believe it or not."

"I still think I shouldn't have brought you." Maru curled up under a blanket and closed her eyes.

"Too late for that."

CHAPTER 11

"Breeeeaaaaaakfast," said a low, rather creepy voice in Maru's ear. "Are you hungry? Get up. You've slept for about sixteen hours, which is ridiculous for somebody your age. You're supposed to be responsible and all that adult stuff, so why are you still lying in bed like it's your day off? Get up!"

"Sixteen . . . ?" Maru blinked. "Where am I? Who are you?"

"You know who I am. I'm the person who got up early to make you eggs."

"The eggs in the fridge are expired."

"So I went out and got new ones. With your money, by the way. Sorry."

"Oh? You went out? Even though I told you not to?"

"You're not exactly the boss of me," observed Yuki cheerfully. "Here, you can even have breakfast in bed."

Maru picked up the fork and glared at Yuki.

"So you want me to start calling you Chief Makise now? Is that it? Besides, you're not that much older than me."

"Proper etiquette requires you to refer to your elders respectfully, even if it's less than a year age difference," said Maru. "By the way, did you see Saito-Shui while you were out?"

Yuki nodded silently.

"Did you talk?"

"I guess you could say that," she said hesitantly. "We passed each other on the sidewalk. Shui said hello and continued on his way."

Maru twitched. "What time is it?"

"Almost nine-thirty."

"Rin's funeral is at ten." Maru threw off her blanket and almost upset her eggs. "I have to be there."

"You've got time. It's here at Rigel, isn't it?"

"The memorial gardens are about five minutes' walk," said Maru from the closet. "But I don't want to be late."

"You won't," said Yuki. "I ironed your dress uniform." This is your dress uniform, isn't it? I found it and ironed it for you this morning."

Maru blinked. "How'd you know . . . ?"

"It's obviously the fanciest thing you own." Yuki put it on a chair.

"Aren't you going to spend any time on yourself, Yuki? It doesn't matter if my uniform is a little wrinkly."

Yuki shook her head. "Who cares about me?"

"I do," said Maru firmly. "You already have too much on your mind. I don't want to make things worse."

"This helps distract me," said Yuki with a shrug. "Let's get over to the memorial gardens. Do you think Saito-Shui will be there?"

"He'd better be," said Maru. "I won't forgive him if he's not."

*****   *****   *****

The memorial gardens were quiet and peaceful. It was a little field edged with small bushes and pretty flowers, lined up and down with pale white, unmarked crosses. Nobody could be buried in the Rigel memorial gardens, but each member who had died in or out of service was commemorated anonymously with their own cross. Its simplistic beauty never failed to overawe Maru into respectful silence. One day her own cross would be there, and, surrounded by the sense of peace and quietness, Maru half wished it would come sooner rather than later.

"Doesn't it make you want to die?" said Yuki aloud.

"I wish it didn't," said Maru.

Yuki shrugged. "I wonder how the people feel about it."

"The people?"

"The people those crosses are here for. I bet Shui spends a lot of time here."

"Saito? Why do you think that?"

"Because he always liked quiet, lonely places. I guess they helped him think or something. I can picture him standing here thinking about his schedule or reading some huge, dry book that nobody else would pick up."

"Do you wish you had a closer relationship with him?"

"Of course. Not that it matters. I'm fine by myself." Yuki straightened. "But it would be nice. I don't think I could do it unless one of us changed, though."

"Am I interrupting anything?" said a voice from behind them.

Maru spun around. "Ayano!" she cried. "What are you doing here?"

"I heard about Rin's death. I'm so sorry, Maru. I wish there was something I could do to help you."

"So do I," said Maru. "These past few days have been the worst ever. But are you okay? Have you stayed here this whole time?"

Ayano nodded. "Nothing happened. Everything's been quiet."

"I really envy you," began Maru, but Yuki interrupted with a cough. "Sorry, sorry. Ayano, this is my friend Yuki. We met yesterday. She's Rin's little sister."

"Two assassins in two days!" crowed Yuki. "I feel blessed beyond compare."

Ayano laughed ruefully. "Do you think we should let her go to SAS training?"

"No!" cried Maru.

"What's SAS?" asked Yuki.

"What time is it?" asked Maru abruptly. "Saito's supposed to be coming."

Ayano looked at her watch. "Nine fifty-seven."

"He's going to be late."

"If he comes at all," muttered Yuki.

"Oh, surely your team leader will come to Rin's service," said Ayano cheerfully. "He can't possibly be that careless."

"Yes, he could," said Maru gloomily. "I made him promise to come, though."

"He won't flake on *you*," said Ayano. "But you're right, he is going to be late. I don't see him anywhere."

They waited in silence for a few minutes, the grass rustling softly around their ankles and making the only perceptible noise.

"Shui," sighed Yuki at last. "You promised."

"We'll start without him," said Maru ruthlessly. "I knew he wouldn't come. Ayano, where do they keep the crosses?"

"They make a new one for every service."

Maru went to the nearest bush, pulled out her knife, and cut off two branches. "Ayano, go find a nail and hammer," she ordered. "We'll put these together and make our own."

Ayano silently went back toward the parking lot, while Maru carefully peeled the branches and cut a notch in one for the other to fit across it. Then she cut each end to a point and scratched a messy 'R.I.' at the base of one stick.

Ayano came back with the nail and hammer, and Maru fastened the two pieces of wood together. The resulting cross was radically different from the clean, neat white crosses already lined up, but it was beautiful in its own rugged way. Maru hammered it into the ground in an empty space at the end of one of the rows.

"Does anyone have anything poetic to say?" she asked, crossing her arms and stepping back.

There was a long pause.

"I'm going to tell you now," said Yuki, her voice barely audible, "how much I appreciate everything you did for me and my siblings. We didn't deserve to have somebody like you as our older brother. I'm just happy that you were happy before you died. I wish it had been me instead of you. I wish you were still here."

Maru felt a tear slipping down her cheek. Subconsciously she traced its slow path, wishing all the time that she could keep it in.

"I know how you felt about Maru," said Ayano softly. "I hope you had a chance to tell her."

Maru nodded silently.

"I know that made him happy."

"Thank you," said Yuki, wrapping her arms around Maru in a bear hug. "Seriously. Without you Rin would have been lost."

Another tear made a slow path down Maru's face. "I'm sorry I couldn't do more," she choked. "I should have saved him."

"You couldn't have done anything better," protested Yuki. "You were there when he needed you, and I know you made life so much brighter for him. Thank you, thank you, thank you so much. I know he would have said the same thing if he was here."

The little group became silent again.

"Now we have to focus on the living," said Maru at last. "Kita. Naito. We need them back here. And I need to know if the police have arrested the CAUS scientists yet."

"I'll find that out," said Ayano. "You take care of your teammates. Yuki, do you need a ride back to your house?"

She shook her head resolutely. "I want to stay here and help you."

"Are you sure that's a good idea?" said Maru. "I can't get you out of trouble once you're in it."

"I'm sure," said Yuki. "I'm never going to get a chance like this again. You're only young once, and I want to see this through."

"Good," said Maru. "Ayano, tell me if you see Saito around. I want to murder him."

"Please don't," replied Ayano. "But don't worry, I'll definitely tell you."

"Yuki, I'll need to borrow your Jeep."

"Sure thing."

"Do you mind staying here while I talk to Kita and Naito?" asked Maru hesitantly. "I have to tell them everything—about Rin, and—"

"Can I stick with you, Ayano?" asked Yuki. "Would I bother you?"

"Of course not," said Ayano. "I'll lend you a spare uniform, and nobody will ever notice that we have a new recruit. You can even come to training if you want, but it's going to be pretty hard."

"Ayano," said Maru, "whatever else you do, please find Saito."

"I promise I'll find him if he's findable."

"Thanks."

Yuki saluted. "Onward, Colonel Makise! Or Maru, or whatever your name is. Everybody calls you something different."

"Whichever you prefer," said Maru. "My real name is Makise."

"Well, you are always going to be Makise to me, because that is how you introduced yourself. So . . . onward, Colonel Makise! Do not wreck my Jeep, or I will make you eat expired eggs for breakfast tomorrow."

"I'll be back here before night, most likely, but if I'm not, you both have free run of my dorm. Yuki, the code is six-seven-five-nine." Maru waved. "Wish me luck!"

"You need more than luck!" Ayano yelled after her, but Maru paid no attention.

She was rapidly becoming a fatalist: whatever happened, happened, and there was nothing she could do about it.

"How can I possibly break any of this news to Kita and Naito?" she murmured thoughtfully to herself, starting Yuki's Jeep. "We have all given up so much for this. What is life going to be like once it all goes away? Are they going to erase our memories?"

She laughed at herself for that last thought. Was it even possible to really erase memories?

*****   *****   *****

All the rehearsing in the world did Maru absolutely no good when she was standing in front of Kita's door, awkwardly twisting her fingers and wishing she was a thousand miles away.

"Ma-RUUUUU!" cried Kita, throwing open the door. "You're alive and safe and well and I was so scared! You'd better have a good explanation for why you haven't talked to me in daaaaays!"

"I've told this story so many times already," Maru said automatically. "I'm starting to believe it never happened."

"Hurry up and get inside," said Kita, pushing her across the threshold. "Naito's here, too. We've been trying to figure out how to get in touch with you and Rin for days now! Why'd you let us be stressed all this time when you were fine?"

"I wasn't—"

Kita cut her off. "Just say it! Where were you?" she cried shrilly, flinging her arms around Maru and squeezing her tightly. "You said something weird about wanting Rin's address, and then you just disappeared for days and days and days. I left you so many messages, but you never called me back. Where's your phone, Maru? Didn't you know we would worry?"

"We were afraid something happened to you or Rin," said Naito, appearing suddenly around the corner. "Not to be a parent or anything, but you have to keep in touch with your teammates. We're supposed to worry about you." He sighed. "I'm glad you're okay."

Maru pulled herself away from Kita's frantic hug. "I'm not okay."

"What? What are you talking about?"

"Rin is dead," Maru blurted, with absolutely no preparation whatsoever. "The federal police arrested me and kept me prisoner for two days, trying to figure out Rigel's relationship with CAUS. Now they're working together. And I met this girl named Yuki, and—"

"Stop, stop!" cried Naito. "Rin? What happened to Rin?"

"His lungs collapsed," said Kita, burying her face in the sofa pillows. "I knew this would happen. I should never have let him go."

"You knew?" Maru stared at her. "You knew this whole time that something like this might happen? Is that . . . is that what the doctor meant when he said that Rin might have complications?"

Kita nodded. "The doctors told me that if he got hurt again, he wouldn't have time to get to the hospital—he would just suffocate." She sniffled. "I didn't want to worry you, so I didn't tell you that."

"So we could have done something?"

"No. It was bound to happen sooner or later. The only question was whether Rin would kill himself faster by choosing to remain an active Rigel member, or whether he would try to conserve his life by taking a less demanding job. That's the choice he made."

"Rin lived for three weeks knowing that he was going to die . . . ?" Maru sighed. "He didn't let it show at all."

"That's the kind of person he was." Naito sat down heavily in a kitchen chair. "So what now? What was all the rest of the story you were telling?"

"Okay. The head of the federal police was a man by the name of Haruko," Maru began. "He was secretly working on behalf of CAUS. Because of him, I was arrested and interrogated for about two days—I think—before I finally escaped by killing Haruko. When I returned to Rigel, I found out that our leaders had shown some of our scientific reports to the federal police who had come to investigate. Apparently, they had proved to them that the Kalideyes are real, and that they are being used to terrorize the population into submission."

"If CAUS and Haruko had succeeded," Kita interrupted, "they could have set up their own military state."

"That's not going to happen now," said Maru. "The federal police are on our side, and now that Haruko is dead, they can defeat CAUS. In fact, they're going to do it today."

"I think you're missing the point," said Naito. "CAUS couldn't have gotten away with making the Kalideyes without some support."

"From Haruko," said Maru, puzzled.

"From the federal police," agreed Naito. "But you really think that's all the help they needed?"

"Are you saying that the government was also on their side?" asked Kita. "That's impossible, or the federal police wouldn't be helping us now."

"The federal police, contrary to popular belief," said Naito wisely, "aren't part of the government. They're independently contracted, which means they can act on their own."

"You really think the government . . . ?" Maru stood up and paced nervously in front of the window. "That's impossible. Somebody would have thought of that sooner."

"It's not impossible," said Kita. "Naito actually has a point. It's possible. But I agree with you that it's very unlikely."

"Well, shouldn't we have this conversation with Saito?" asked Naito, drumming his fingers on the table.

"Which reminds me," said Maru. "He promised to be at Rin's memorial service this morning, but he never showed up. Where on earth could he be?"

"Who knows." Kita sighed. "He's always missing when he's most wanted. Well, we'll have to go look for him. Can Naito and I get a ride back to Rigel?"

"Sure," said Maru. "I'm borrowing Yuki's Jeep."

"Who's Yuki?"

"That's a long story," said Maru, opening the door. "Come with me and I'll tell you on the way back."

CHAPTER 12

"Home!" cried Kita, looking around. "I love being here. I'll be sad when we all have to leave. I have so many good memories—"

"Now's not the time for nostalgia," observed Naito. "We have to find our team leader, MIA as usual."

"I asked Ayano to look for him," said Maru. "Does anyone have her phone number?"

"I do," chirped Kita. "Here, Maru. You talk to her."

The phone rang a few times. "Hello?" asked Ayano's scratchy voice. "Kita?"

"This is Maru. Kita and Naito are with me. Did you find Saito?"

"Not a trace of him. The police are concerned, too. They say if he's not back by tomorrow, we need to go look for him in the city."

"Why?"

"Maru, you'd better put me on speaker. Kita and Naito need to hear this, too."

Maru obediently clicked the speaker on and waited.

"Apparently Rin had evidence that Saito might be a traitor," said Ayano slowly. "Yuki told me about it. She said Rin wrote you a letter right before he died, explaining that he hesitated to accuse Saito even though he had plenty of evidence. Is that true?"

"Yes." Maru's mouth was dry.

"Well, this is an awfully odd time for him to go missing. CAUS doesn't know that Haruko was killed, but if they did, they'd know we were coming after them. They'd be prepared. And we think Saito might have gone to give them that information."

"Rin didn't mention any specific proof in the letter."

"Can you tell me exactly what he said?"

Maru felt in her pocket. The letter was there, exactly where she had put it that morning. She had not looked at it since then.

"Hold on," she said, unfolding it and focusing her eyes on the wrinkled pages. "He says . . . he says: 'There's one more thing I think you should know. I never told you anything about what happened on that special mission, and I think it might be important now. I'm not sure about everything, but there's strong evidence that I don't think you should ignore. I'm sorry. I might be too late already.

"'A few months ago, I caught Saito, my brother, secretly talking to a CAUS worker. I heard him talking about classified Rigel information, and later I asked him about it. He said the CAUS worker was really a Rigel agent in disguise, but he had no proof of that and he refused to give me the agent's name. I was so angry, Maru. I thought he had betrayed everything I worked so hard for. I started writing up papers accusing him of treason, but he forced me to reconsider. After all, he was my brother, I loved him despite everything, and I had no solid proof. So I dropped the charges. But I was never convinced that he was innocent.

"'Only he and I knew exactly what plans had been made for my mission. I can't think of any possible way the attackers could have known who I was unless he told them. I hate to think that Saito tried to kill me, and that's why I never said anything about it. But I can't keep it to myself any longer, because I'm afraid of what he might do to you and Kita and Naito. He's not above betraying you to death or worse. Maru, if you're reading this and I'm dead, that means I can't protect you anymore. I tried blackmailing him, saying I knew he was a traitor and if he tried anything, I would report him. That won't work now. You have to find Kita and Naito and get back to Rigel. Report Saito. Tell the authorities that I died because of him. I can't promise they'll listen, but it's worth trying. And above all, never trust him.'"

"That's it?" asked Ayano.

"That's it."

"That's more than enough. I'll need you to repeat that to the police. Can you come here?"

"Where's here?"

"The mess hall."

"We're on our way."

"I'll bring Yuki. See you there." The phone clicked, and Maru handed it back to Kita.

*****   *****   *****

"This alone is almost proof," said the officer, looking intently at Maru. "Are you prepared to swear that Ishida wrote this letter?"

"Of course."

"And are there any witnesses to Ishida's character?"

Maru, Kita, Naito, and Yuki all raised their hands solemnly.

"We'll start looking for Ishida Shui, code name Saito, as soon as possible."

"Question," said Kita. "What will happen if you find him?"

"We'll execute him, of course. If we find him guilty."

"Rigel has charge of the trial, right?"

"It's unofficial, but I guess that'd be fine. After all, we haven't officially joined with you yet. Anything you want to do is okay for now—we'll look the other way."

"So we get to decide the punishment?" demanded Kita.

"If you want," replied the officer. "Again, we won't stop you. But if you're going to execute him, you need to do it today before Rigel officially becomes a government organization. Otherwise you'll get in trouble, of course."

"Are we needed for anything?" asked Naito before Kita could continue

"No, you can go." The officer turned away.

"Then, Kita, will you go for a walk with me?" asked Naito. "I think you need a break from this."

Kita nodded silently.

"Ayano, Yuki," said Maru. "Let's see if we can find something fun to do. Something to take our minds off all this. Do you want to go swimming?"

Yuki looked a little more cheerful. "Where?"

"Sure, I guess we can." Ayano chuckled. "You have the weirdest ideas. The lake is muddy, but I guess that's not a problem."

"I'm in," agreed Yuki. "But I didn't bring any extra clothes."

"You're about Kita's size. You can use hers."

Yuki skipped off toward the dormitories, followed reluctantly by Maru.

"Why are you so cheerful all the time?" Maru asked Yuki.

"Because of the same person Rin must have talked to before he wrote you that letter."

Maru hesitated. "God?"

"Right."

"We're not going there right now," said Maru firmly, unlocking the door. "I've heard enough about that."

"Please? Won't you just give it a chance?"

"Why should I?"

"What kind of evidence do you want? I did my research before I bought into all this stuff, you know. Now I'm convinced it's right."

"Let's start with scientific evidence, then," agreed Maru reluctantly. "You can tell me while we're changing."

"Okay," said Yuki. "How did the universe come into existence?"

"It always existed."

"Then how come the universe is expanding? Doesn't that mean it started expanding from a point?"

"What was that point?"

"The beginning," exclaimed Yuki. "The universe is expanding. We know this for sure through direct observation. We also know how fast it's expanding; therefore we can trace it all back to a single point."

"Well . . . " Maru could not think of an argument. "What if it just started expanding recently?" she asked weakly.

Yuki shook her head as she browsed through Kita's clothes. "No good. When we look out into space, we see stars that are far away. Their light takes a long time to get to us, so we see them the way they were a long time ago. And they're moving away from us."

"I'm not a scientist. How about circumstantial evidence?"

"Oh, please," sighed Yuki. "You're the biggest single piece of circumstantial evidence anyone could ever ask for."

"What?" asked Maru irritably.

"You're always asking about God," said Yuki wisely. "It's not just because you wish He existed. It's because you know He does, and you want a reason to believe it."

Maru froze abruptly. "What?"

"Don't you ever feel that your life would be pointless without something or someone to give it meaning?"

"Always," said Maru. "Everything I do is pointless if everyone is going to die anyway."

"Unless you're on this planet for a reason. Evolution doesn't give you a reason to live. We might as well commit mass suicide right now."

"True . . . " agreed Maru hesitantly. She paused to think before slipping on her white uniform shirt. "I don't know why I can't believe this, Yuki. In fact, I should really phrase it another way. I think you're right. I think there is a God. I just don't know why it should be this God you and Rin are talking about, or why He should take a personal interest in me."

"That's easy," said Yuki. "It's because He created us. If you make your own world, you'd want to make sure everything worked out right, wouldn't you? God feels the same way about us."

"But how can God fix me?"

"All you have to do is believe that the sacrifice He made when He sent His Son to die on the cross was enough to pay for our sins."

"That's way too easy."

"Right? I thought so, too."

"Can you please answer my question?" Maru quickly buttoned up her shirt. She did not want Yuki to see the scars on her arms.

"What was the question? Of course it's easy. God wanted to make it as easy as possible."

"Why?"

"I told you that God loves us, and I told you why. Now figure out the rest yourself. Maybe try asking God." Yuki skipped off toward the door.

"Wait up!" Maru trotted after her. "Okay. How?"

"How do you talk to God? Well . . . like I said . . . all you have to do is tell Him that you believe He sent His Son to die for you. Then start acting like it."

Maru leaned uncomfortably against the door. "Umm . . . God?" she began, then closed her eyes instinctively. "This feels a little bit like an audition. Why am I talking to a God who made the entire universe and all the billions of people who live here? And what about the aliens, if there are any . . . ?" She laughed uneasily. "Well, Yuki tells me You care about me. In any case, I believe You sent Your Son to die, and I believe You exist. I don't know if I believe You care about me personally, so if You do, please show me. I need something to change." She took a deep breath. "I swear this right now. If You don't change something within ten days, I will kill myself."

"No!" cried Yuki, but Maru ignored her.

"I'm out of options," concluded Maru, opening her eyes.

"I'm not sure . . . I'm not sure . . . " Yuki followed her outside. "I don't think that was quite right."

"I guess we'll find out."

"But what do you expect from God?"

"I expect to not feel empty and purposeless anymore," said Maru briefly. "I expect not to hate myself. I expect to find something in life that's worth being here for."

"God can give you all those things, but you're not supposed to make bargains with Him like that."

"I need proof," repeated Maru. "This is the only way I can think of to get it."

"Well, there is some verse about 'testing everything', but I think you might have it out of context."

"What do you think changed for you?" asked Maru curiously.

Yuki shrugged. "I stopped worrying, because it didn't seem necessary. And I think it helped me get past my hatred."

"That's deep," said Maru.

"That's all you have to say?" Yuki looked disapproving. "Well, something will change for you. I know it."

"If it does, my story will sound even crazier than yours." Maru pointed. "Let's think about something else for now. There's the lake."

"Yippee!" cried Yuki, darting forward and leaving Maru behind.

"Brooding?" said a voice behind her.

Maru started. "Ayano!"

"Sorry. I thought you must know I was standing right here. I've been following you for the past minute and a half." She paused. "By the way, I asked the sergeant about Saito. Nobody's found him yet, but there's a squadron on its way to CAUS now."

"Specifically to look for Saito?"

"Yes, that's how the sergeant made it sound."

"Do you really think he would betray us like this?"

"You knew him better than I did," said Ayano.

"I saw Rin's letter. And my first instinct was to believe him."

"First instincts are right more than half the time," said Ayano. "I'm sorry, Maru. Believe me, I know how you feel. Remember Yuri."

"I'd rather not remember him," said Maru. "It's a bit depressing."

"Speaking of which, you seem a bit more down than usual. Thinking too much? Run low on your medications?"

"No, I just have a lot to think about. I've decided to give believing in God a serious try."

"You did *what*?"

"I said, I've decided to believe in God. I'm serious."

"That's hard to believe," said Ayano, "considering that you're the best atheist I know. Not to mention the fact that there is no God."

"I hope there is," said Maru. Then she laughed weakly. "It's weird. I prayed that something would change within the next ten days."

"And if it doesn't?"

"Then I said I would kill myself."

"Not that again," sighed Ayano. "If you do it, then I will too."

"No!" Maru was startled. "This is purely a personal decision, Ayano."

"I've been through the same things you have, Maru. I have as much of a right to end my life as you."

"But I don't want you to do it. Please, Ayano. Promise you won't do it just because of me. You always seem happy. Isn't there anything you want to live for?"

"Now you're trying to talk me out of it? Such hypocrisy. Don't even go there."

"Look at Yuki." Maru pointed toward the lake, where Yuki was diving, splashing, and laughing loudly enough for them to hear. "She believes in this God. I really think she might have something, and if she does, I want it."

"Why? Isn't she always like this?"

Maru shook her head. "Yesterday I had to tell her that her brother was dead. Not to mention her relationship with Saito—"

"Which is?"

"He's her brother."

"What?" Ayano's face was a humorous mixture of confusion and disbelief.

"So you can imagine what these last two days have been like for her. And her father abused her as a child. I've heard the stories. It's horrible. And yet here she is, laughing like a four-year-old in a park. How do you think she manages it?"

"No idea. But it's impressive. I wish I could have something like that."

"But if there is a God, and that's why Yuki is so happy, then count me in. I don't know what I'm believing, but something with that much power over a person must be real somehow."

"Not just her imagination?"

"Do you think imagination would be enough to cover up everything you and I feel?"

"No."

"I guess the same goes for Yuki, then." Ayano sat down on the grass. "Well, this has been an interesting conversation. The first one I've had for a while."

"Speaking of which, what's been going on with you?" Maru sat down beside her.

"Nothing much. My whole team has been in therapy for the past three weeks. Therapy is basically the same thing as prison, and about as effective. It doesn't change what happened. The truth is, I think I'm better qualified to handle this mess on my own."

"Mess?"

"Oh, please. Don't tell me you don't think this place is a mess."

"Well, that's nothing new. Why therapy?"

Ayano looked sarcastically amused. "It's so we don't all go berserk like Yuri did."

"Really? They think you'll catch his craziness or something?"

"That's a weird way of putting it, but I guess you could say that."

"When do you get out of therapy?"

"Soon, this imaginary God of yours willing." Ayano laughed. "But it sounds like there won't be a mission for a long time, if ever."

"Hey!" Yuki waved at them. "Aren't you going to swim? You both have suits, don't you?"

"Sorry," Ayano called back. "We're on our way."

Yuki trudged across the muddy bank and approached them, her hair dripping softly into the grass. "You look super serious. The water feels nice, you know. Why don't you stop acting like adults for a few minutes? I really don't think you're that much older than I am anyway. Let's swim."

"It doesn't have anything to do with age," sighed Maru.

"Right," laughed Ayano, jumping to her feet. "You're a million years older than both of us, Maru. I'll come with you, Yuki. Are you sure the water isn't cold?"

"Absolutely!"

Maru watched them run, laughing and making wet footprints in the muddy bank. They really were children. Ayano she knew was only acting, but Yuki really had something.

She lay back in the grass and closed her eyes against the bright light. Where were Kita and Naito? Where was their team leader? And for that matter, where was Rin? Could he see her right now? And if so, was he still pitying her misery and nearly killing himself to make her happy?

She sat up suddenly, her right hand instinctively squeezing her left wrist. For once, she had all the pain she could ask for. She did not need to use a knife–her mental agony was overwhelming her and keeping her awake far more efficiently than mere physical pain.

"I only have to take this for ten more days," she reminded herself half-aloud, settling back into the grass. "I think I can hold out that long."

Far away, she thought she heard a faint voice screaming her name. Maru squeezed her eyes shut and ignored it, but it would not go away. "Maru! MARU!" It was getting louder and closer. Irritably she rolled to her side and blinked lazily. "Kita—?"

"They found Saito." Kita's delicate form shook with her heavy, rapid breathing, and she gasped for air before continuing, "They found him at CAUS."

"So he was a traitor after all." The news was so expected that Maru barely felt any emotion, and she was rather surprised.

Kita shook her head. "He wants you to come."

"Me? Why?"

"I don't know, but he's promised to tell everything if they'll only bring you to the interrogation room."

Maru glanced irresolutely at Ayano and Yuki, who had not seen Kita approach and were having a splash fight.

"The interrogation rooms, you said?"

"Number five."

"Tell Ayano and Yuki where I've gone. Don't let them follow me, and don't you follow me either. I promise I'll tell you everything once I'm back."

Kita nodded. "Are you sure you don't need anything?"

"I'm sure." Maru struggled to her feet and began walking slowly toward the buildings.

Her thoughts were mixed, and she could not quite sort them out. Above all the others was a nagging curiosity about why Saito could possibly want to see her. Why not the rest of the team? Why did he refuse to confess until she was present? She shook her head in disgust. A traitor like him did not deserve anything from her, and in that moment, she made up her mind to hate him.

"And what do you deserve?" It was Rin's voice.

Maru froze and looked around nervously. Of course, there was no one anywhere near her. She looked back at the lake. Kita had joined in the fun, and she could see all three of her friends. They were far out of earshot. But that voice . . . she would be prepared to swear that she really heard it.

"I didn't say I deserve anything," she remarked aloud, stuffing her hands into her pockets and continuing. "I only said that Saito deserves to be hated."

"And you?" it replied.

"I deserve to die," she said simply.

Suddenly as she said the words, she realized what they truly meant. Physical death was not the only thing she deserved. That could be painless and beautiful and even happy. It was punishment—real punishment. Not only would it claim her life, it would slowly consume her whole being until she could no longer remember who she was.

"So how do I avoid that?" she asked the voice conversationally.

It did not reply.

"What am I doing? Talking to voices in my head?" Maru shook herself.

She paused in front of the building and looked around before swinging the door open wide and walking inside.

"Maru," said a familiar voice. Surrounding the speaker were three guards all armed with black rifles, and they looked at Maru as if she had just descended from space. She took an involuntary step back.

"S-Saito," she stammered.

"I sent Kita to ask you to come."

"Why?"

He still did not look at her. "Because I thought you deserved to hear this."

"You want me to know who you really are?" Maru snickered, and with a sudden return of confidence she walked up to him and stared up at his shadowed face. "Are you sure about that? You killed your own brother."

He twitched. "I did not."

"You're responsible for his death," hissed Maru. "No matter how you look at it, no matter how many excuses you make, that's still the truth. Face it, Shui. You're a worse murderer than he was."

"I have faced it," he replied calmly. "Every night. And since you told me—"

"There'll be plenty of time for conversations like these in the courtroom. It's not safe to stand here," grumbled one of the guards.

"I'm coming with you," said Maru, stepping out of their way.

Nobody replied to her, and she trailed after them. Saito—or Shui, as she now called him in her mind—walked straight and tall, head erect, soft black hair just brushing his straight shoulders. He really did look like a leader, and Maru found herself wishing bitterly that things could have been different. But no external appearance could change the man's evil.

"Are you really going to confess?" she murmured, turning her head to the ground. "You're really going to say you betrayed us?"

"Would you rather I stayed quiet?"

Maru stopped abruptly. Shui was looking at her.

"Would that make you any happier?"

She could not think of a reply.

"I know it sounds selfish," he said slowly, almost shyly. "It's my fault."

"Do you regret anything?"

He nodded. "What do you want me to do?"

"I don't care what you do now," she said sullenly, still without looking at him. "I can't believe you killed your own brother."

"I didn't," he protested. "I swear I didn't."

"Then explain how he ended up dead!" cried Maru, her self-restraint suddenly snapping. "You selfish jerk! You really think you can blame this on everyone else?"

"I didn't know what was going to happen." Shui put a hand over his face. "I swear I didn't know. I told the people not to hurt him. I don't know what went wrong."

"You sent him there," said Maru, breathing heavily. "You sent him there without knowing how things would turn out. And then you didn't look one shred of sorry when I told you how it ended."

"I am sorry. I swear I'm sorry." He dropped to his knees and bowed his head to the floor. "I'm sorry, Maru. I hurt you most of all, and the only thing I wanted was to make you happy. I'm sorry. I'm so, so sorry."

"Nothing you say will make it right now." She crossed her arms and looked down at him contemptuously. "So get up off the floor. Apologizing isn't helping anyone."

"I still have to say it." He stood up slowly and looked at Maru with a bitter, sorrowful expression on his usually bland face. It was an almost heartbreakingly pathetic gaze, begging her silently for something. She did not care enough to know what it was.

"Keep going," she muttered, and the group started on its way again.

A few doors down the hallway, they stopped and turned into a little side room. One of the guards held the door open, while the other two pulled Shui into the center of the room. There was a small metal chair, and that was the only thing in the room.

"The interrogation will take place through the glass," one of the guards told Maru. "The next door down."

She nodded.

"You don't look so well," he commented.

"Would you?" she snapped back.

He shook his head mutely.

CHAPTER 13

Maru settled back in her seat. She could see past the three professional interrogators into Shui's lonely room. He was sitting very still, head bowed, hands tied around the back of the chair. Maru could almost find it in her heart to pity the sadly humbled figure, once tall and proud, now weak and bitterly shamed. But it was all his fault, as she reminded herself over and over.

"Saito!" said one of the interrogators sternly.

He started and looked up. "Yes?" he said after a brief pause.

"Your original name was Ishida Shui, correct?"

"Yes."

"You are twenty-four years old?"

"Yes."

Maru blinked in surprise. His deep, painful blue eyes looked much older.

"You know what the charges against you are?"

"Yes."

"You swear to answer everything truthfully?"

Shui did not answer for a moment. Finally, he said, "As long as Makise is in the room with you, then yes. I swear to answer truthfully."

"Do not call her by her proper name," warned the other interrogator. "Let's begin. Were you involved with CAUS?"

"I was."

"Did you know they were working directly against Rigel?"

"Yes."

"You knew this when you were working for them?"

"Yes."

"To which agency did you originally—"

"These questions are pointless," said Shui brusquely. "Let me tell you the story, and then you can ask whatever you want."

The interrogators had a whispered conversation, then nodded. "Go ahead, whenever you're ready."

"I was recruited by CAUS four years ago," said Shui shortly. "They told me that they wanted to use these Kalideyes machines to make the world a safer, better place by killing the criminals and putting the fear of God into everyone else. Idiot that I was, I believed everything they said. The first thing they asked me was to seek employment with Rigel and explained that I would need blue eyes. My eyes—" he blinked "—are naturally green. The CAUS scientists provided me with the genetic material needed to make them blue, which is how I was able to pass Rigel's test. It was their fun little experiment, and, even though the drugs made me sick, I did everything they asked without question. I believed in them.

"Rigel was in need of recruits, and they were happy to hire me. CAUS had taught me to hate everything you stand for, and even now I don't think they were completely wrong. They said you were murderers, that you are using the Kalideyes as an excuse to kill, that you wanted to take over the world. Well, both sides were wrong. But at the time I thought that one of the conflicting voices held truth, and I followed the one I knew best.

"I was surprised when my brother Rin showed up to training. I had no idea he had been recruited, and because I didn't want him to ever know what I was doing, I tried to have him removed. I tried my hardest to hate him. We hadn't seen each other for four years, so I expected it would be easy. But I couldn't do it. When he was put in my group, I pushed him away as hard as I could, and he kept coming back. He kept trusting me.

"Of course, he found out eventually. We shared more with each other than anyone would have thought, and it was inevitable. For some reason he didn't betray me, although he didn't promise to keep my secret. I hate to think it was because he cared about me." Shui paused and sighed bitterly. "I'd rather think it was because he was afraid, but I know that isn't true. Rin treated me the way I never dared to treat him."

"Stick to the point," interrupted one of the interrogators harshly.

Shui nodded. "Although Rin knew, he didn't report me, and I continued working for CAUS. Slowly I was beginning to doubt the lies they had told me, but what could I compare it to? I planned assassinations that I was ashamed to think about. I watched people die. I watched their minds twist and break under the pressure, and it was my fault. I was a double agent working for the worst parts of both sides. I couldn't break away from both, and I didn't want to commit to one. So I did my best work for both.

"Rin's mission was a challenge for me. I sent a message to CAUS, telling them to capture but not kill him. I thought I had enough influence to make sure he was safe, but it nearly killed me to find out how wrong I was. Seeing him in that hospital bed was one of the worst moments of my life. His eyes looked the accusation his lips would never speak, and it hurt more than I wanted to admit.

"I thought about killing myself, but that was an easy way out of the mess I had made for myself. I knew I had to choose between CAUS and Rigel, but I put the decision off as long as I could. After all, I had friends at CAUS, too. It wasn't a simple choice between right and wrong—it was a desperate struggle between two horrible evils."

There was a long silence.

"Continue," prompted one of the interrogators.

"I had absolutely no intention of killing Rin, or Naito, or Kita, or you, Maru. I failed to make the right decision, and I deserve any punishment you think is just. That's my confession, and if you want any more information, I'll give it to you. I have nothing to lose."

"You realize," said Maru, "that what you've already said is plenty to get you capital punishment."

He nodded.

"Just as long as you know that every bit of this is your fault."

"Please be quiet, Miss Maru," said the interrogators in eerie unison. Then one of them continued, "Ishida Shui, we will report this to your superiors as soon as possible. The decision is up to them, but I'm fairly sure we all know what the punishment will be."

"Please," said Shui, bowing his head in exhaustion. "I'm ready. I have been for a long time."

The interrogators had another hurried consultation, then got up and left the room without further instructions to either Maru or Shui.

A long silence followed, during which Maru struggled to contain herself. There was so much she wanted to say, so much blame she wanted Shui to carry. She hated him, deep inside, but she could not bring herself to admit it.

"You're a harsh judge, Makise. Can I call you that?"

She crossed her arms defensively. "No."

"Maru, then. I'm sorry."

"You think I'm a harsh judge? Why should I care what you think?"

"I don't suppose you should," agreed Shui humbly. "But don't you think I've been broken enough? I'm not asking you to help me. I'm ready to die, and I think we can both agree that I deserve it. I'm only begging you to forgive me. Please, Maru. You couldn't possibly know how much this matters to me."

"You should have thought of that sooner."

"I did. I spent hundreds of nights thinking about it. But I wasn't as strong as my brother. All my life I've made the wrong selfish decision, and I'm beginning to think I can't help it."

"Oh, you can," said Maru sarcastically. "Just like I can't help coming in and blowing your head off with my rifle."

"You're welcome to if that would help at all. In fact, please do."

Maru was caught off guard by his deference.

"What can I do to show you how sorry I am?"

"If there was anything, I would have already made you do it," said Maru. "But since there isn't, you'd better just go to prison and spend the last few days of your life thinking about how miserable you've made mine. Not to mention Rin's."

He moaned and leaned forward, pulling against the ropes that held him tightly to the chair. "Stop, Maru! If I think about it anymore, I'll go crazy."

"I've never seen you lose yourself like this," said Maru coldly, standing up. "Get it together. Nobody cares anymore."

"You can't possibly believe that," he panted, chin resting loosely against his chest. "You can't. There has to be something else."

"I don't think there is."

"How can you live with yourself, thinking like that?" said Shui desperately. He raised his head and looked at Maru with blank eyes. "Do you hate me?"

"Yes."

"Did you love Rin?"

It cost Maru a struggle, but finally she answered. "Yes."

He dropped his head again. "Then I'll stop apologizing. I understand now. There really isn't any possible way you could forgive me."

"SHUIIIIIIII!!" cried a voice. "Where are you? Shui!!"

"Yuki!" cried Maru.

Yuki's face was pressed to the glass window. "You didn't do it," she cried, tears streaming down her face. "You didn't do it. Tell them you didn't do it!"

"That would be a lie," he said quietly, turning away from her as best he could with his hands tied behind him.

Yuki hit her fists against the glass. "No!" She looked up at her brother. "I don't want you to die like this!"

"Like how?"

"You can't lose everything you worked so hard for now!" she insisted. "Maru, please let me in!"

Maru hesitated, then complied. Yuki darted into the room and threw her arms around her brother.

"Yuki . . . " Saito whispered. "I abandoned you."

"Yes, you did, but without that I wouldn't have become the person I am today. Just because you make a mistake doesn't mean that everything will turn out badly. Yes, there are consequences. I know—" she choked. "I know they're going to kill you, but you don't have to carry this guilt to your grave. Please, Shui!"

"I'm listening," he said. Slowly he put his arms around Yuki. "I've missed you. And I'm sorry. I shouldn't have left you. I shouldn't have let our brother die. It's my fault, and I'm so sorry."

"Stop saying that," said Yuki. She sat down on his knees. "I forgive you."

A lonely tear trickled down Shui's cheek, and he closed his eyes.

"But I can only forgive you for what you did to me," she whispered, pulling away from him. "You have to ask somebody else to forgive the rest of it."

"I tried," he said. "I tried. Maru—"

"Not Makise," corrected Yuki, shaking her head. "God."

"God?"

"You need more than human forgiveness, Shui. It's not just you. We all do. So why don't you apologize to God first?"

"I think," said Maru in a strangled voice, "that she might be right. And you're not the only one who needs to ask for forgiveness."

"What are you talking about?" Shui looked at her, and his red eyes pierced straight through her heart.

"Hating you," she murmured softly. "I had the right to do it, but it hurts me even more than it hurts you. I have to let it go if I expect anyone to ever forgive me. The depression . . . the pain . . . the hatred . . . holding onto this can't be helping."

"God can forgive . . . ?" Shui shook his head. "I'm glad that works for you. It's a beautiful thought, really. But I can't just believe it now."

"Maru and I do," said Yuki. "Why isn't that enough? Can't you believe that we've thought about it long and hard and gone over all the evidence hundreds of times? You don't have time to do what we did, so can't you just take our word for it?"

"I don't deserve to believe it," he said, pulling Yuki into his chest again and stroking her long black hair. "I don't deserve for either of you to forgive me, either. I just want to sleep."

"You mean you want to die?" Yuki sniffled.

"I want to die," he admitted, dropping his head and squeezing her tightly. "But not now that I've found you again, I could almost live for you. I wish I had the chance to try."

"And if you don't get that chance, what are you going to do?" asked Maru. She approached slowly and sat down a few feet away from Shui's chair.

"Are you sure this isn't just an emotional response? You've both been through a lot."

"Well—" began Maru, but Yuki interrupted her.

"You stay with someone you love forever, and that's not just an emotional response."

"This really isn't for me." Very gently he pushed Yuki away and brushed her hair away from her eyes. "But I appreciate the thought. Yuki, you need to leave now."

"Why?"

"The interrogators will be back in a few minutes. I don't want you to be here for that."

"Please let me stay, Shui. I haven't gotten to talk with you at all, and—"

"Leave now."

Yuki stood up slowly and backed away. "Okay."

"What are you two doing in there?" The interrogators had returned and were seated on the opposite side of the glass. "You two need to leave the room, now. You're not supposed to be in there."

Maru grabbed Yuki's hand and opened the door. "Yes, sir," she answered, then added, "Say goodbye now. You can stay outside, but you can't talk anymore."

Yuki looked back at Saito. He smiled.

"Thanks for coming to see me," he said. "I needed it. Thank you."

Yuki's eyes filled with tears as she left the room, followed by Maru.

"Stand next to the glass. Don't go where we can't see you," said the interrogator closest to Maru. Then he continued, "Well, Ishida Shui, the decision was made quickly, as we all expected."

He nodded.

"Strictly speaking, since Rigel is not a government organization, we have absolutely no right to put you to death. However, I have the commander's promise that he will look the other way in your case. Therefore—" he looked down at his paper "—you are sentenced to capital punishment."

Maru put an arm around Yuki's trembling shoulders.

"We'll be back in a few minutes with all the proper materials," said the interrogator shortly. "Get that little girl out of here. She's not old enough for this." Maru thought she could detect a hint of pity in his voice as he looked abruptly away.

"Please let me stay," begged Yuki. "I promise I'll be fine. Please let me stay."

"Take her out," he repeated, looking at Maru.

"Yes, sir." She turned to Yuki. "If they say you have to leave, you have to leave. And I think they're right." She pushed Yuki out into the hallway and followed shutting the door to the interrogation room behind them.

"At least don't walk with me," sighed Yuki, rubbing her wet eyes. "Let me have some time alone."

Maru hesitated. "Well, okay. I guess that's fine."

"I'm not going to get myself killed. Thanks for staying with him, Maru. I understand what you're doing, but I wish you wouldn't make me leave."

Maru let go of her shoulder and took a few steps back. "It's for the best."

"How do you know that?" Before Maru had a chance to answer, Yuki took off running down the hallway, never once looking back.

Two of the three interrogators followed her slowly down the hallway, while the third stopped beside Maru. "Are you cleared to stay?"

Maru showed him her clearance card on her watch display.

"Are you sure you feel safe?"

She nodded.

"I'll wait out here in the hallway then. We can't have him escape." He leaned against the wall and looked away.

Maru turned slowly back to the interrogation room, her feet dragging the floor reluctantly. Her emotions were in so much turmoil that she could not sort out how she really felt. She only knew that seeing the sorrow and regret in his face again would shake her and hurt her more than she felt she could stand. It had nearly broken her heart once, and she was not quite sure why. Where had all her bitterness and anger gone? Why had it been replaced with such deep, implacable pity?

He was still sitting quietly in his chair, hands on his knees, looking absently into the interrogation room.

"You don't really believe in a God, do you?" he asked without looking at her.

"I do."

"Why?"

"It's—" Maru was suddenly embarrassed. "Well, Yuki gave me all the evidence I needed. Besides that, I prayed this morning that God would show me something within ten days that could change my mind about who He is. And He did."

"What was it?"

"I feel like I can breathe again," said Maru slowly. "The hatred and the pain and bitterness were heavier than I ever thought. Giving them up has freed me more than I could ever have imagined it would. This change is all the evidence I need."

"I wonder what that feels like," said Shui regretfully. "It's too late for me to find out now."

"Why do you think that?"

"Aren't you supposed to serve God?" asked Shui. "I can't accept Him right before I die. That wouldn't be fair."

"Think about it this way," said Maru. "What could you possibly do that would help God?"

"I . . ." Shui paused. "I don't know."

"Let's face it. You're not powerful enough to create this whole universe out of nothing, so there's not really anything God needs you to do."

"Then why does He care about me at all?"

"Because He made you." Maru smiled. "He made you."

"I still feel like I should have earned something."

"You couldn't possibly. This has to be a free gift, otherwise it's completely meaningless. You of all people should know that it's impossible to be perfect."

"I do." He smiled wryly. "I still think it's too late."

"It will be too late once you're dead," said Maru desperately. "Think, Shui! Why doesn't this make sense to you? What questions do you have?"

"It seems so far out of reach . . ."

"It's not," said Maru. "I can tell you that it's not. This changed your brother, Shui. You know how many times he tried to kill himself. In the end he wasn't afraid to die, but he wasn't afraid to live either."

"I wish I could have lived like that." Shui sighed. "There was so much more I wanted to do, so many things I wanted to say."

"Like what?"

He did not answer.

"This is the most important decision you'll ever make, Shui. It's more important than deciding whether or not to stay loyal to CAUS. It's more important than deciding whether or not to assassinate a target. It's eternal."

They were interrupted by the door to Shui's room swinging quietly open. One of the interrogators stood there, a small box in his left hand.

"Are you ready?" he asked.

Shui nodded.

"I'll try to make this as quick as possible." He knelt down beside Shui and opened his box. Two syringes laid within.

"Why use a paralyzer?" asked Shui. "I don't need the extra time, and I promise I'm not going to run away."

The man hesitated. "It'll hurt."

"Does that matter?"

"Are you sure?"

Shui nodded. "How long does this take?"

"A few minutes at the most."

He nodded. "Go ahead, then. Skip the paralyzer and kill me now."

The interrogator filled a syringe with clear liquid from a bottle and held it up. "Are you sure?" His voice shook slightly.

"This is your first time, isn't it?" asked Shui. "I'm sorry it had to be me. I'm sorry you have to do it at all."

"It's my job," said the man firmly. "Hold out your arm."

Shui looked at Maru. "Are you sure God can forgive me?"

She nodded. "I'm absolutely sure."

"Okay. Then I believe you."

Maru sighed with relief. "You accept that God exists? That His Son died for your sins? That you really are forgiven?"

"Yes. I believe Christ died for me." Without another word, he bared his right forearm and presented it to the interrogator, who gently pushed in the needle.

Shui closed his eyes. "One more time, Makise, I'm sorry," he said, his words slurring. "And thank you for being—the only—light left in my life." He slid off his chair and landed in a heap on the floor. "I can't . . .breathe . . . "

"It's almost over," Maru assured him, tears collecting and running slowly down her face and onto the glass in front of her. "Almost."

"Tell Yuki . . . that I . . . "

"What is it?" Maru brushed her tears away and leaned close to his face. "Shui? Tell her what?"

He did not reply.

"I'll take care of her," said Maru, crying softly into her sleeve. "I wish there was more I could do."

The interrogator's hands were shaking as he replaced the syringe and bottle in his box. It shut with a loud click which echoed around the silent room. "I'm so sorry," he said desperately, touching his forehead to the floor in front of Maru. "I've never seen anyone look so sad."

"It's okay," she said, quickly collecting herself as best she could. "I'm sorry for crying. That must have made your job ten times worse."

"Did I do the right thing?" the interrogator asked, looking between Shui's prostrate, huddled form and Maru's tearful face. "Did I?"

"He had to die," said Maru. "Somehow or another. And I'm pretty sure he was ready."

"How can anyone ever be ready to die?" he muttered, standing up and tucking the box under his arm.

Maru smiled through her tears. "I've almost figured that out." Without another word she turned and ran out into the hallway.

"Yuki!" she cried, pausing right outside the building. "Where are you? Yuki?"

"Here," said a muffled, tearful voice. Maru looked to her left and found Yuki huddled on the far end of a bench.

"Your brother is dead," she said quietly, sitting down beside her.

Yuki nodded and sniffled.

"But I think he found what we've all been looking for, right before he died," Maru added.

Yuki nodded again.

"So can you tell me?" asked Maru, putting an arm around Yuki's shoulders.

"Tell you what?" Yuki did not look at her.

"Tell me how to find it, too."

"It's not like all your problems are going away," sighed Yuki, hugging her knees to her chest. "It's not like you're going to be happy, or that there won't be times when you still want to die."

"I know that," agreed Maru, "but if God is real, and if He's personal like you say, then He must have some kind of plan for my life. I need that assurance, Yuki. I think I could go through anything or do anything or lose anything if I only knew why I was doing it. Not to mention that if He really wants me to follow His plan, He'll help me, right?"

"'Course," replied Yuki. "He'll help you if you ask."

"And you said He forgives mistakes, right?"

Yuki's mouth twisted in an almost invisible sarcastic smile. "Mistakes?"

"Sins, bad things, whatever you want to call them. All the stuff I've done wrong, whether I knew it at the time or not. I need direction for my life and forgiveness for my sins." Maru tapped her finger nervously on her leg. "Can God really give me all of that?"

"That and more." Yuki wiped her tears away with a childish clenched fist and looked at Maru. "If you ask, and if you believe that God sent His Son to die for you."

"Jesus, right?" said Maru uncertainly.

"Yup. Because you made mistakes, somebody had to take the punishment, because God is completely just. But He's also merciful, and so to show His mercy, He sent His Son to take the punishment for you. That's forgiveness."

"And will I . . . I don't know, *feel* forgiven?"

Yuki nodded firmly. "Trust me, you will."

"Okay then. Do I just . . . tell God that I believe it all, or what happens now?"

"It's called praying," said Yuki. "And yes, all you have to do is talk. Say what you're thinking, kind of like when you threatened to kill yourself if God didn't come through for you."

"Well, He did." Maru laughed uneasily. "That probably sounded stupid."

"Nothing you say to God sounds stupid to Him," said Yuki. "Besides, He obviously listened, because here you are."

"Your brother showed me that I need to forgive," said Maru. "I did that, and it helped so much already. But this is about God forgiving me."

"Right."

"Okay, so . . . " Maru closed her eyes. "Here I am after a lot of hard work, God. I don't know how I got here. All I know is that you had something to do with it. I believe that you sent your Son to die for me, like Yuki said. I really think you've been trying to get me to find you this whole time, and that meeting Yuki was the last step in your plan for me to figure out who you are. Yuki says you're always with me, and looking back, I think that's true. I don't understand why you let Rin die, but maybe that was also part of the plan. I need what you've promised, God. I need your forgiveness, because I've made a lot of mistakes. I need your plan, because I've wasted a lot of time. And to be honest, I still really need somebody to listen to me and pull me out of this horrible depression. I can't do this by myself. I can't be self-sufficient anymore, so please show me how to rely on you instead." Maru opened her eyes and looked shyly at Yuki. "What now?"

Yuki smiled and hopped off the bench. "You did it!" she announced. "How does it feel?"

Maru thought. "Like I don't have to worry anymore."

Yuki held a wise finger in the air. "You're right. It's not that you won't worry—it's that you don't have to. I'm happy for you, Maru."

"It's like—" Maru searched for words. "It's like I dropped something heavy. I don't feel . . . I honestly don't feel guilty anymore." She looked at her hands, rather confused. "My hands aren't bloody anymore."

"That's because guilt is real, and if guilt is real, so is forgiveness."

"Well, what do I do now?" Maru looked up quickly. "I don't want to lose this."

"Start living!"

"What?"

"Live like you just found out the greatest thing ever. Tell everybody about it. Show everybody that it's real. And don't forget to ask God when you need help."

"Ask—?"

"Read the Bible or sit down and talk like you were just now." Yuki smiled. "It's almost too easy."

"But don't I have to—I don't know—change or something?"

"That happens as a result of coming to know God," said Yuki. "You don't have to change before you know Him, and you don't have to magically become a saint."

"Good." Maru looked comically relieved.

"But don't stop talking to Him," cautioned Yuki. "You said you wanted advice, right?"

"Of course."

"So just keep asking." Yuki smiled. "I thought this was going to be the worst day ever, and it still kind of is. But I'm happy for you. I really am."

Maru stood up and hugged her. "Thank you, Yuki. I have no idea what I would have done without you and Rin.

"Oh, you're welcome," she said. "It goes both ways. I have no idea what I would have done without you and Rin either."

"Can we talk about this a little more?" said Maru. "I don't think I understand everything yet."

"Neither do I," said Yuki, sitting back on the bench. "But we can talk as long as you want."

"I'm also trying to avoid telling Kita and Naito about Saito," admitted Maru, sighing deeply. "I'll set my timer for thirty minutes. We can talk, and then I'll make myself tell them."

"I'm rooting for you," said Yuki unenthusiastically. "Let's talk then. One half hour. You talk first, and I'll answer all your questions. Then you have to let me cry."

"I don't even know where to start," said Maru. "So tell me, Yuki. What should I know about God?"

CHAPTER 14

"So Saito really was a traitor." Naito cursed bitterly.

"That's not helping now." Kita hid her head in his shoulder. "I don't understand."

Maru did not say anything.

"Where's Yuki?" asked Kita after a long pause. "Did she see—?"

"Shui—Saito, I mean—made her leave," said Maru. "I don't know where she went."

"She was with Ayano earlier." Kita sighed. "I envy how happy she is. I guess she didn't know him very well anyway."

"That's not why," said Maru shortly.

"Did Shui . . . say anything special to you before he died?" asked Kita.

"We talked a lot." Maru leaned back against the pillows and looked out the window. "It's like I told the interrogator earlier. He was ready to die."

"I guess there wasn't much left in life," began Naito, but Kita interrupted him. "How can you say he was ready to die? He had so much to live for. Any idiot could tell that from looking at—looking at—never mind. But why do you think he was ready to die?"

"Because he finally found peace," said Maru. "He asked the interrogator to skip the paralyzing drug, so he ended up suffocating to death."

"What kind of peace is that? An illusion?"

"No," said Maru. "It's the same peace that made Rin happy before he died. Curious yet?"

Kita and Naito both nodded.

"It's a long story," began Maru, curling up into a tight ball. "And it's really thanks to Yuki that I can even tell it. Are you ready to stay here for a while and listen?"

"Sure," said Naito, and Kita agreed.

Maru took a deep breath. "For the third time in one day, here goes."

CHAPTER 15

"It's still standing." Kita pointed to the little makeshift cross, which was wildly out of place in the neat rows of smooth, white crosses.

"I didn't know I was strong enough to get it so deeply in the ground." Makise poked it, and it wobbled. "Well, it doesn't matter if this thing stays here forever. It's not like any of us will forget."

"Right." Kita squeezed Naito's hand. "You know, I thought it would be fun to do something ceremonial now that we're here."

"So did I," said Naito. "But you first."

"No, you first!"

"I won't say a thing until you spring your surprise." He smiled. "Seriously, Kita, come on!"

"Well," she said, stepping back and bowing. "This is the one year anniversary of Rigel's demise. Not a bad thing, I would say."

"Depends on how you look at it." Makise crossed her arms. "We could never have defeated CAUS if the federal police hadn't helped us."

"Correction," said Naito. "We could never have defeated CAUS if you hadn't killed that crazy psychopath guy."

"Haruko," mumbled Kita.

"I guess that was his name." Makise sighed. "I still don't like thinking about that. To be honest, I don't understand why any of this had to happen."

"Haruko was looking out for himself," said Kita. "He helped CAUS run their KASU program because they bribed him and promised him that he

359

would have a leading role in whatever new government they decided to set up. We told the federal police that CAUS was responsible for controlling the Kalideyes, and they told us that Haruko was responsible for keeping that a secret. Voila. It was so simple after all, if only we had started by working together."

"Somebody messed up big time," said Naito. "We should have been in communication with the federal police long before any of that happened."

"We were," said Kita, "but you know we didn't have enough proof that the Kalideyes were evil, nor that CAUS was responsible."

"It all seemed pretty legit to me when I signed up," said Makise.

"Well, yes, but we had to convince the entire government to get a move on it." Kita laughed light-heartedly. "That, as you can imagine, isn't exactly the easiest thing ever. They didn't want to believe us—they wanted to believe in the new technology that was supposed to let people live forever. Too bad for them that God didn't let that happen."

"I don't care," said Naito firmly. "It's all over now. All the CAUS workers were arrested and put in prison for life or executed. And the secret to making the modified bodies is completely lost."

"And what if somebody finds it again?" suggested Makise morbidly.

"Pessimistic today," grinned Naito. "Why worry about it? If somebody finds it again, we'll all know what to do this time. Things will never be like this again."

"You're both so boring," complained Kita. "Who cares about the government? 'CAUS did this, CAUS did that.' You know there's one more thing we have to celebrate, right? It has been exactly one year since Naito and I last took those poisonous ADPA's."

"Anti-Depressant-Personality-Adjustment," said Makise rapidly. "Is that what you're talking about?"

Kita nodded. "Not to mention, those scars on your forearms have all healed."

Makise rubbed them absently. "I guess so. I'm much happier now. Sometimes I really can't believe I did that to myself—it's like a bad dream."

"You've changed," said Kita carefully. "Do you think Naito and I have changed, Makise?"

She looked at them critically.

"It's got nothing to do with appearance, silly." Kita spun in a circle. "I already know how cute I am."

"Your humor is more—I don't know, *real*," said Makise thoughtfully. "You were just acting like an idiot before—no offense—but now when you laugh it's cute and pretty and from your heart. Yes, you've both changed."

"Offense taken," said Kita gravely. "Well, who cares what you think? Thanks to you, Naito and I are both happy now. Although Ayano still needs some work."

"I'm doing my best," said Makise. "We're going to talk about it over coffee on Saturday."

"Why couldn't she be here today?" asked Naito.

"She's at rehearsal with Yuki."

"Oh, so they do everything together now?" Kita laughed. "I knew it would be good for them to live together. I bet Yuki is nagging her even more than you."

"Probably," agreed Makise. "I know they're both happy, though. Ayano takes good care of her."

"But do tell," interrupted Naito. "What was your surprise going to be?"

"Oh!" Kita jumped up and down like an excited child. "I think we should all say our real names!"

Naito blinked. "I'm so used to calling Makise by her code name that I almost forgot about it."

"And you still call me Kita, too," she reminded him.

"Because you act like a kitten," he said playfully, pulling her hair. "Kita-kitten!"

Maru watched in silent amusement.

Kita yelped and pulled away. "Not fair!" she protested. "It's fine if you want to keep calling me Kita. I like that name. But that was going to be my surprise, so now you have to tell me yours."

He suddenly blushed red. "Well—"

"Come on, we're all so curious," said Makise, who had been Naito's confidante for the past three months.

"Well—" he began again, looking shyly at Kita. "Umm . . . "

"Go on," encouraged Makise.

He dropped to his shaking knees. "Kita, I love you. Will you marry me?" he asked in one desperate breath.

There were a few seconds of complete silence, during which Kita's eyes became progressively wider and wider. "Of course!" she gasped at last. "Of course, of course, of course! Eeeeek!"

"Really?" Naito looked shocked. "Are you serious? Maru—I mean, Makise —said you'd say yes, but I thought—"

"You idiot!" Kita wrapped her arms around him and squeezed tightly. "I've just been waiting and waiting!"

"Me, too," he agreed. "Kita . . . I love you."

"I love you, too! Oh, silly, how did you ever think I'd say no?"

"I don't know . . . it just seemed . . . so impossible . . . "

"When? Where?" Kita still did not let go of him. "Soon, please!"

"In a church, don't you think? As soon as possible!"

"Of course! Someplace special to both of us." Kita giggled.

Naito suddenly pushed her away. "Kita," he asked, cheeks cherry red with embarrassment, "can I kiss you?"

For answer she pressed her lips gently to his.

"Now is the time," observed Makise to nobody in particular, "that I should maybe sneak off."

She turned her back on the two blissfully happy lovers and stalked slowly through the rows of crosses. There was one in particular she was looking for. A little over a year ago, she had cut a deep mark into the center so that she would never forget exactly which one it was.

She still remembered. It stood at the opposite end of the memorial garden, stiff and sterile except for the blemishing mark. Makise pulled a few weeds from around the base and threw them aside.

"The truth," she murmured to herself. "You found the truth, so it's all right. You and Rin both."

She lay back on the grass, closing her eyes to shield them from the bright afternoon sun.

"It must be so much easier," she said aloud, half-laughing, "to die like you both did rather than go on living without the person who matters most to you."

The grass brushed gently around her cheeks, and a little breeze tickled her skin. The warm sun lulled her into a half-asleep state, and her muscles relaxed slowly into peaceful rest.

"To go on . . . without the person who matters most to you," she whispered to herself, curling up into a tight ball. "Rin . . . I miss you. And Shui . . . I can't help missing you, too. It's hard to live like this when everybody else is so perfectly happy. Why did you both have to die and leave me behind?"

Suddenly she sat up, smiling and laughing blissfully in the soft, warm light.

"It's because I have work left to do," she cried aloud. "I'll do it. I'll finish everything. I'm here for a reason, and I'm not going to let anything beat me."

She put her hands together and bowed her head reverently.

"Thank you, God," she began, "thank you for getting me this far. Thank you for giving me a reason to live. Thank you for sacrificing Yourself so I could escape despair. And most of all, thank you for always being there when I'm stuck. I didn't know it at the time, but You never once let me go too far.

And You gave me Rin to support me the whole way. Please help me to finish whatever it is You created me for. I promise I'll try my hardest."

She opened her eyes and brushed her fingers thoughtfully through the grass.

"Also," she added quickly, closing her eyes again, "thank you for never letting me feel alone, even without Rin."

She stood up and held her arms out, eyes still closed.

"And one day, I know we'll all be together again." Her hair blew softly around her face, and she sighed, letting her arms drop slowly to her sides. Happy laughter drifted over from the front of the garden, and she looked back. Naito was chasing Kita playfully through the trees.

Makise smiled. "Thank you, God, for that."

EPILOGUE

I'm feeling unusually nostalgic today. It's a weird mix of happy and sad, good memories and bad. I really can't help thinking back to my time in Rigel, even though I never had a moment of mental peace like this while I was there.

It's kind of like the first time I got my eyes fixed. The difference between how I saw before, and my new vision was so dramatic that I felt like things had always been this way—like it was perfectly normal for me to suddenly see everything. I couldn't imagine going back to how things were before. My depression is exactly the same way. The change between depression and peace was so sudden that I barely noticed, and it feels like I've always been this content. But when I think back to how things were before—when I wanted to kill myself, when I cut my own wrists, when I thought the world would be better off without me—I realize just how much things have changed.

Before, I used to feel like a failure because my life wasn't perfect. I tried to fix it, but things only got worse, reminding me of how weak I really am. Kita used to write the phrase 'self-sufficiency' in her journal over and over, trying to be something she never could. I know how she felt, because I tried the same thing.

Admitting that I couldn't do it was hard. I want to be self-sufficient. I want to take care of my own life. I want to be fine on my own. But at some point, I had to face that trying to do everything by myself simply wasn't working.

I tried learning to rely on Rin, and it took me a long time to really open up to him. My relationship with him was like a little piece of what I have now, making my life not quite happy, but at least bearable. When he died, I lost all of that. When he died, I realized that I couldn't be self-sufficient. I couldn't even rely on other people. That's why I walked out in front of a car, hoping to end it all and stop being forced to struggle for something impossible. At the time I didn't know—actually, didn't believe—that there was another way.

Realizing that my life is not my own has changed my opinion on several things. First of all, I don't care what happens to me—not because I want to die, but because I know that when I die, I will have accomplished everything I was created to do. Knowing that somebody created me with a specific purpose in mind affects everything. Life is no longer circular or pointless or worthless, and I can get out of the hellishly repetitive loops I was stuck in before. I don't have to worry about making my life perfect, because perfection doesn't matter. Somebody else can do that for me.

The final discovery I made was a little surprising. It's actually thanks to Shui that I'm able to write this part at all, and I can't thank him enough, even though I was never able to say it while he was alive. I didn't realize it at the time but holding onto the pain that other people caused me was just like carrying around a bunch of extra garbage. I thought I had let everything go, saying something along the lines of, "Who cares? I don't. Why worry about it?" But that wasn't enough. When I was forgiven by God, He let everything go. Absolutely everything. He erased all my guilt, and that was something I hadn't done for the people in my life. I had to spend an hour saying their names out loud, exactly how they had hurt me, and that I really, truly forgive them. It was hard, and that was one of those moments when I had to ask God for help. It would never have occurred to me to do that on my own. But I did it, and now I don't have to spend my mind thinking about and trying to self-heal the scars they left. I'm completely free of all that, and I honestly think I needed that kind of forgiveness more than they did.

There are still days when I'm sad, and remembering Rin is the hardest. I wish he had lived, because there are so many things I want to share with him.

I want him to see the person I've become. I hope it would make him happy to know that it's all because of the letter he left me—that's really what I want to tell him. It seems like I think about him every day.

It's okay. One day I'll get to see him again, so I just have to wait patiently.

In the meantime, there's plenty to do. I want everybody to know this peace. I want everybody to defeat the voice that always tries to isolate. It told me that I had to be alone, that I didn't matter, that my life was worthless, that I had nothing to accomplish, that the world would be better off without me. It was a lie. It was all lies and I almost lost my life because of it. No more. I've heard the only true voice, and I want everyone else to hear it. I want to live and share that story.

The last thing I want to say is, please remember you're not alone. Remember that you're loved. Remember that no matter how often you're told to die, your life has a purpose designed by God Himself. And it's always worth living for.

Despair is a lie, and you are made in God's image.

-Makise

For more information about
Lauren Smyth
&
Made for Mercy
please visit:

www.laurensmythbooks.com
@lsmythbooks

For more information about
AMBASSADOR INTERNATIONAL
please visit:

www.ambassador-international.com
@AmbassadorIntl
www.facebook.com/AmbassadorIntl

If you enjoyed this book, please consider leaving us a review on
Amazon, Goodreads, or our website.

Stories
- of the -
NIGHT

LAUREN SMYTH

Alisen, a teenage girl, is routinely awakened by the same terrifying dream. The nightmare gets more detailed and longer every night, but the terror remains the same. She tries to dismiss it as something she ate, or maybe a book she read, but then she meets Kale.

Kale is having the same nightmares.

Believing there must be a deeper meaning, Alisen and Kale delve into politics and biblical prophecy. Together, they discover that everything in their dreams has a counterpart in real life, which leads them to believe that something terrible is coming. Is there any way to avoid this catastrophe and save thousands of lives? Or will their worst dreams come true? They must choose whether to turn to God or to each other to save them from the very end of the world.

Stories of the Night combines political intrigue, biblical prophecy, and military adventure into a suspenseful story that leaves the reader with the choice of where to place their ultimate hope.